THE END DRAWS NEAR . . .

"Know, Gagnrad, that in the land far to the south where once Borr raided, a new power grows. It rises on the ashes of the Dark Empire and promises to rival it in evil. Its leader is one called Surt, the Black One."

Gagnrad drew a sharp breath. He knew that name! Voden nodded. "Yes. It's the same. The cutthroat wizard that raided with my father, whom Borr left behind on the Vigrid plain to die of his wounds. He survived by bargaining for life with the foulest of powers, and now he's determined to carry out the curse he flung at my father's back."

"But surely, now that Borr is dead . . ."

Voden laughed silently, his eyes glowing strangely. "Surt's hatred goes beyond Borr. It goes to all of his blood, all of his race. He will have his vengeance—no matter the cost . . ."

Twilight of The Gods

Book III:

Three Trumps Sounding

DENNIS SCHMIDT

ACE BOOKS, NEW YORK

This book is an Ace
original edition, and has never
been previously published.

TWILIGHT OF THE GODS BOOK III:
THREE TRUMPS SOUNDING

An Ace Book / published by arrangement with
the author

PRINTING HISTORY
Ace edition / January 1988

ISBN: 0-441-83287-3

Ace Books are published by The Berkley Publishing Group,
200 Madison Avenue, New York, NY 10016.
The name "ACE" and the "A" logo
are trademarks belonging to Charter Communications, Inc.

PRINTED IN THE UNITED STATES OF AMERICA

10 9 8 7 6 5 4 3 2 1

This book is dedicated to
Odin.

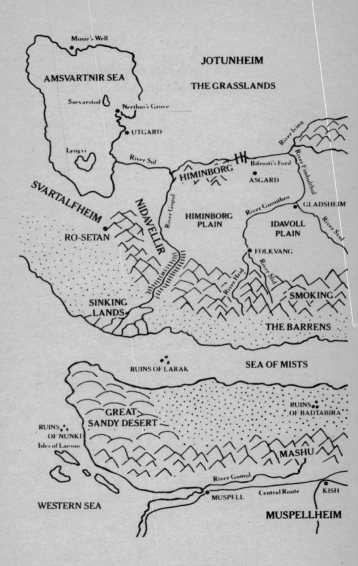

VODEN

I

HE stood on the top of the barrow and looked northward. Somewhere beneath the lush spring grass his grandfather lay, looking in the same direction, on guard against the Jotun. Slowly he turned to the east. The sun was beginning to rise, the diffused light of the early morning sky swiftly condensing in a point on the horizon. His mother, also in the barrow, faced that direction, eternally gazing toward far-off Prin, the small country high on the eastern slopes of the Kunlun Mountains from which she had come so many years ago.

Finally, almost as if against his will, he turned southward. There in the foreground lay the city of Asgard. Beyond the city the Himinborg Plain rolled off southward to the horizon. Eventually it ran up against the forests of Vanaheim and disappeared beneath the towering trees. To the west he could make out the looming upthrust of the Himinborg itself.

His eyes drifted down from distant vistas to the patch of still-raw earth at his feet. The grasses would soon establish themselves over the spot. For now the black soil was exposed where they had opened the barrow to place his father. Borr's dead eyes gazed southward so he could keep watch on the Vanir.

He brought his gaze back to Asgard. Most of the houses destroyed by the Jotun had been rebuilt, though traces of the fires lit by the Sons of Ymir could still be seen. On a wet day the whole place smelled of ashes. The palisade around the city was mostly rebuilt, but there were weak spots and even breaches here and there. By midsummer it would be complete once more.

Three men stood slightly behind the watcher. One was a muscular giant with a shaggy mane of red hair and a bristling beard. His face was round and florid, his expression truculent. He carried a large hammer in his right hand.

The second was tall and slender with a long, narrow face of pale, almost translucent skin. It ended in a neat white beard. Fine white hair covered his head, which had only one ear. His expression was grave and thoughtful. He seemed agelessly old.

The final man stood shyly behind the other two. His legs were unusually long, and his body seemed short by comparison. He was all angles and awkwardness.

"I tell you it's a stupid idea," the giant rumbled. "You got away from them once. No sense in going back again. Can't trust the bastards, that's what I think."

Voden smiled slightly, turning to gaze fondly at Tror. "It's easy to understand why you hate them so, old friend, after what they did to your father and sister. Yet they did no less to my brother and father, and I don't hate them. Hate is too simple, too easy. The Jotun are more complex, more . . . more interesting than that. True, they've been the enemies of the Aesir ever since they first appeared out of the north and east." He sighed. "Buri fought them all his life. So did my father. For as long as I can remember they've raided south onto our plains every summer. And we've repaid the compliment by raiding north across the Iving. I killed my first man in one of those raids, Tror, when I was only thirteen. I have no great love for the Jotun."

"Then why go back? By Fornjot's icy balls, Voden, the last time you went they hung you on the damn tree in Nerthus's Grove. It's a miracle you survived. Who knows what they'll do this time? I tell you it's a trap, this damn invitation. Don't go. Besides, we need you here. There's still so much to be done. . . ." His voice ran down beneath the steady stare of Voden's right eye. But it was the left one, the one that was always closed, that finally made him drop his glance and shuffle nervously.

"I don't think it's a trap, Tror. Hrodvitnir himself has invited me. And the invitation was seconded by the White Bear, the leader of the Trul. They offer a truce."

"Truce!" the redheaded giant snorted angrily. "You could

sooner make a truce with a forest cat or a wolf than with the damn Jotun!"

Heimdall cleared his throat, and Voden turned his glance to the pale man. "What do you think, Heimdall?" he asked.

"Tror is correct that the Aesir cannot trust the Jotun in most things." Tror grunted agreement. "But this is a very special case. When you survived nine days and nine nights on the tree, the Trul realized you were one of them. They had to acknowledge that you have the Galdar-power, indeed that you may even have it more powerfully than most of them. I even think the White Bear has some understanding of what happened between you and the Bones of Audna. But they are not sure of you, are not precisely certain of what or how powerful you are. To be of the Trul but not of the Jotun is contradictory. To have the Galdar-power but never to have received training in it is also contradictory. And to have the runic lore, even to possess the Bones of Audna themselves, yet never to have sought them, is the greatest contradiction of all. These are things the Aesir have never been involved with.

"So I imagine the purpose of the invitation from the White Bear is to find out more about you. A powerful unknown makes them nervous.

"The reason for Hrodvitnir's invitation is similar. He seeks to become Warlord of the Horde. Should he achieve his goal, you will be his major enemy. The more he knows about you, the better. Now he can afford to be friendly because the immediate barriers to his rise to power are internal—other Jotun who covet the position or back those who do. A friendship with you, a mighty shaman and leader of the Aesir, would clearly enhance his prestige and improve his position among the clans.

"So there are good reasons for the invitation. Yet I would hesitate to say it is safe to go."

Voden smiled. "I never thought it would be. Even if I assume that Hrodvitnir and the White Bear are no threat, there isn't one of the Sons of Ymir who wouldn't like to slip a knife between my ribs and get credit for killing the son of Borr. No, my friends, I have no illusions as to the dangers of crossing Bifrosti's Ford and riding north to Utgard again.

"But I can also see the advantages. As much as the Trul and Hrodvitnir would like to know more about me, so would I like to know more about them. If Hrodvitnir does become

Warlord, it would be wise to know as much as possible about the man. If we have to fight him, I'd rather not fight blindly. And I feel I could learn as much from the Trul as they could learn from me. My training in the Galdar-power has been sadly fragmentary. Perhaps I am as powerful as the White Bear believes. Without training, much of my power is wasted. And I have a nagging feeling that I'll need every bit of strength I possess before long." He paused and gazed off toward the southern horizon. When he spoke again, his voice was somber and musing. "I sense my fate approaching. There are dark things moving. A time of trial comes, gathering speed and power as it rolls toward me. My mother gave me a hint of it long ago. I must be ready."

He straightened up. "So. I've decided. I'm going."

"Then I go too," Tror said in a tone that allowed no argument.

"And I," Heimdall added with finality.

The leader of the Aesir turned to the long-legged man who had remained silent throughout the conversation. "And you, Honir, my old friend, are you determined to come too? We've already shared the dangers of one stay in a foreign land. Are you game for another?"

Honir turned red and his gaze dropped to the ground. Then he looked up and met the glance of Voden's single eye. He simply nodded and then looked away again.

Voden stretched out his two arms and placed a hand on each of Honir's shoulders. "Very well, then," he said to the three of them. "We leave tomorrow at first light. Gagnrad will be in charge until we return. I've already talked to him about it. There won't be any raiding, because of the truce Hrodvitnir has promised. And given the drubbing Borr gave them, I doubt the Vanir will pose any threat for the moment. The timing is perfect."

"Huh," Tror harrumphed, "perfect for walking into a trap, if you ask me." He raised his great battle hammer Mjollnir toward the north and shook it. "But there'll be some crushed Jotun heads if they try anything."

Jotun sentries spotted them as they were crossing the Iving. They hadn't ridden more than a few miles north from the river when they saw a band of some fifteen horsemen riding hard toward them. Heimdall turned to Voden and said, "It is

Hrodvitnir. That small friend of his is with him. I assume the others are also friends and retainers.''

Tror shook his head in wonder. "Wish I had eyes like that. Damn Fornjot's icy balls, all I can see are some specks on the horizon."

Voden's chuckle came from deep within the recesses of the hood he had taken to wearing since his return to Asaheim from Mirmir's Well. "Heimdall could describe every detail of their equipment as well. Are there any of the Trul with them?''

"No," Heimdall replied instantly. "Most of them bear devices of the Thursar clan, though there are a few from the Bergettins and the Rimthursar. Interesting. It would appear that Hrodvitnir is gathering allies from clans other than his own. I wonder why there is no one from the Risar?''

The Jotun approached at a gallop, yipping and calling out as they came. Voden noticed that Hrodvitnir wore his wolf's-head helmet and his flowing cape made from the pelt of a huge wolf. In his right hand the Jotun warrior carried a long stick which was curved at the tip. It was wrapped in brightly colored cloth, and feathers hung from the tip.

When the Jotun reached them, Hrodvitnir and the small warrior who rode by his side halted and the others split into two groups and surrounded the four from Asaheim. The horsemen rode around them in a circle, raising a loud cry. Finally the riders stopped and opened the circle on the side facing Hrodvitnir. The wolf-helmeted warrior howled ferociously and spurred his horse through the opening, heading directly for Voden. As he raced forward, he held the crooked stick out to the right. At the last moment, just before he crashed into the chief of the Aesir, he pulled his horse to its haunches in a sudden stop, reached out and touched Voden with the tip of the stick so that the feathers brushed his face. Then he jerked the horse's head around, spun it on its two hind feet, and raced back to the edge of the circle. When he reached it, all the riders gave a great cheer.

Hrodvitnir acknowledged their homage with a wolf howl and a shaking of the feathered stick. He spun his horse around again and rode slowly back toward the four Aesir, a wide grin on his face. Riding up to Voden, ignoring the other three, he leaned to the right and held out his hand. The Aesir held his own out, and the two clasped each other by the forearm.

"Welcome," Hrodvitnir said in a loud voice which carried to all in the circle. "Among the Sons of Ymir you have gained the names of Sidhott, because of the hood you wear, and Hangagud, because you hung on Nerthus's Tree for nine nights and nine days. But these are not clan names. Now I will give you a clan name, one that makes you brother of Hrodvitnir, so that all men may know that to raise their hand against you is to raise it against me and my entire clan. I name you Mjodvitnir since you have lived among the Vanir and tasted their golden liquor. Welcome, Mjodvitnir, son of the Great Wolf."

Hrodvitnir leaned slightly forward and said so softly that only Voden caught the words, "Glad you didn't blink or panic when I counted coup on you there. Don't know quite what would have happened if you had. These boys are a little wild and unpredictable at times."

Voden smiled slightly and nodded. "I'll keep that in mind. Anything else I should or shouldn't do?"

The Jotun warrior gave a lupine grin. "Just follow your instincts. They seem to be almost as good as those of a Jotun."

"Very well," Voden replied. Before anyone could move, he drew his ancient iron knife with his left hand. With a quick slash, he cut the back of his own forearm, then that of Hrodvitnir. A gasp rose from the Jotun as he let go of the startled warrior's arm and leapt to the ground. There he stuck the knife, crimsoned with both his own blood and that of Hrodvitnir, into the ground. He pulled it out and with his fingers pulled off the dirt that had mixed with the blood. This he formed into a tiny ball which he held cupped in his hands. He lifted it toward the sun and cried out, "Blood of Aesir, blood of Jotun, blood of the two sons of the Great Wolf, mixed with the flesh of Mother Nerthus. Accept this as an offering of faith, Father Gymir!" With that he opened his hands and a butterfly fluttered up into the sky. Every eye watched as it ascended higher and higher until it disappeared from sight.

Everyone turned to Voden and Hrodvitnir. The two men's eyes were locked on each other. Utter silence reigned for several heartbeats until the Jotun suddenly threw back his head and roared with laughter. "Very neat!" he cried. "The White Bear is right about you! Oh, that was even better than sitting still on your horse when I counted coup. Welcome indeed, Mjodvitnir!'' He looked at the tiny slash Voden had cut on the back of his forearm. It was still oozing a few drops of blood. He licked the blood and burst into laughter once again. Leaping from his horse, he clasped Voden warmly in his arms. "This will be even more interesting than I thought," he whispered. Releasing Voden, he called out to his men, "To Utgard!" With a roar, they all turned their horses toward the northwest and began to ride. Voden and Hrodvitnir mounted and rode in their midst.

At the very back of the group a small Jotun warrior rode alone, a strange smile playing about full, curved lips.

The arrival in Utgard was a noisy one. The plain immediately in front of the city of wagons was covered with men, women, and children beating on drums, shaking rattles, blowing on horns, and generally making a racket as the group surrounding the four Aesir approached. Occasionally one of the older boys would dash up to one of the Aesir, touch his horse or leg, and then run off again, whooping and leaping in joy.

As they rode through the crowd, Hrodvitnir waved to people he knew. Some smiled and waved back. Some frowned and ignored him. Voden watched carefully, wondering how much prestige the Jotun warrior was gaining from this event. The smiles he was receiving were probably from allies, the frowns from enemies. Voden tried to memorize both sets of faces.

He glanced over his shoulder at his companions. Tror was grim-faced, his brow set in a scowl, his mouth tight-lipped and truculent. Heimdall was taking in the whole scene carefully missing nothing, his face impassive and solemn. Honir, on the other hand, was grinning with shy pleasure. He had already established a game with the boys who ran up to count coup on him, touching them back before they could escape. Whenever he did it, everyone around him whooped with pleasure.

They finally found themselves confronted by a line of young women in white hide dresses, their shoulders covered with capes of the same color hide, intricately worked with designs made from the dyed quills of porcupines. They were barefoot and bare headed. The left half of each girl's face was painted black, the right white. Each held an ash branch, the

top turned downward, in the left hand, and a fan of five
eagle feathers pointing toward the sky in the other. They
danced back and forth with a slow, shuffling rhythm, chanting a soft song as they moved. Voden listened carefully and
could just make out the words. They were strangely accented
and had the flavor of the elder tongue.

> *"Ho, Nerthus, Mother, tree giver.*
> *Ho, Nerthus, Mother, grass giver.*
> *Ho, Gymir, Father, light bringer,*
> *Ho, Gymir, Father, rain bringer.*
> *Ho, listen to the Kwuda,*
> *Ho, listen to the going-out people.*
> *Ho, listen to the Tepda,*
> *Ho, listen to the coming-out people.*
> *Ho, we are the ones who took the udders,*
> *Ho, we are the ones who took the prize.*
> *Ho, we have the Adalbeahya,*
> *Ho, we have the Tai-me."*

Most of it made no sense at all to Voden, but he listened all
the same, trying to guess at meanings, memorizing it for later
review.

Hrodvitnir gestured to the party to halt and dismount. He
leapt lightly from his horse and knelt in front of the young
women. Voden and the others followed his example. The
dancers shuffled forward until they were able to reach out
with the ash branches and the feather fans and touch the
heads and shoulders of the kneeling men. They continued
chanting as they brushed the Aesir and their escort.

When the dancers stepped back, Voden looked up to meet
the eyes of the White Bear. Standing with the chief shaman of
the Jotun were the other members of the Trul, dressed in their
animal robes and masks. The White Bear held a figure in his
hands. Voden noted that everyone was averting their eyes
from the image. From beneath the protection of his hood he
gazed at it. It was about a foot high, carved from a strange,
black wood, and covered with long, flowing hair. The carved
features were those of an ancient woman with wide, staring
eyes, and full, twisted lips. The figure seemed to be looking
directly at him. He met its gaze for a moment, then felt a chill

run up his spine and dropped his glance. There was power in the thing, whatever it was.

The White Bear was chanting softly. Voden concentrated. The shaman's language was even more obscure and ancient than that of the young women. He would have sworn some of the words were like those in the original tongue! If so, the Jotun were as ancient as the Vanir! The White Bear sang:

> "Hai, yah, hai, yah,
> Gadombitsouhi, Old Woman Under the Ground.
> Hai, yah, hai, yah,
> Gadombitsouhi, Old Woman Under the Ground.
> Mother of Kingepnir,
> Sister of Nerthus,
> Aunt of bears,
> Cousin of owls,
> Hai, yah, hai, yah."

With a swift motion the White Bear made the image disappear beneath his voluminous fur robe. Voden was certain he was the only one who saw it go. The head shaman of the Trul held his empty hands wide and cried out in a strong voice, "Ho, Gadombitsouhi has gone back under the ground! She has given these visitors her protection! She has taken their spirits with her to her house beneath the ground!" The other Trul thundered their response. "Ho! Gadombitsouhi has willed it! Ho! Gadombitsouhi has willed it!"

The White Bear looked at the visitors and said, "Come. We have built the K'ado Lodge, for it is time to dance to Gymir. We will greet you there properly, beneath the Eye of the Father."

Voden, Tror, Heimdall, Honir, Hrodvitnir, and the Trul moved as a group through Utgard, the city of wagons. For the first time Voden noted that the wagons were arranged in a series of concentric circles, radiating out from some central point, toward which he guessed they were now heading.

In a few minutes his surmise was proven correct. They came to the last circle of wagons. In the middle of the circle was a large open area and in the middle of the open area, a circular building, approximately sixty feet in diameter. It was made of painted cow skin stretched over a framework of branches. The wall of the building was about eight feet high.

A roof rose from the edges toward the center. It was made of cedar and cottonwood branches, and only partially covered the building. Voden estimated that there was an opening in the top about twenty feet across. Through the open space a thirty-foot pole, made from an ash tree, thrust up toward the sky. Near the top, facing toward the east, the head of a black bull was fixed. Voden could make out several small bundles tied to various branches.

They approached the building from the east. There, covered by the hide of a black bull, was an entrance. A flat stone lay on the ground before it in such a way that anyone entering had to stand on the stone. The White Bear held back the hide and gestured for them to enter.

As he stepped inside, Voden discovered that a group had already gathered there. About twenty in all, they were clearly the chief men of the Jotun. They sat in a half circle around a small fire, proud and haughty, gazing at the Aesir with cool, calculating eyes. Voden and the others sat where the head of the Trul indicated.

Once they were all seated, with the Aesir farthest to the east and nearest the door, an old man sitting directly across from Voden stood and held an object up toward the sky then down toward the earth, and finally toward the four directions of the universe. "Sacred above, sacred beneath, sacred all around," the old man chanted in a reedy voice. "This is Peta-owihankeshni, the fire without end. It burns in the sacred Chanunpa. It joins us all in one—earth, sky, trees, grasses, four legs, two legs, winged ones, we are all one family." With slow solemnity the old man reached into the fire, took a small branch from it, and held it to one end of the object. He sucked softly on the other end and Voden was surprised to see smoke come from the far end and then from the mouth of the old man. As he and everyone in the circle watched the smoke rise toward the sky, the old man said quietly, "This is the breath of Tunkashila, the living breath of the great Grandfather Mystery, rising to Gymir." Then the old man sat back down and passed the object to the man seated on his left.

As the object approached Voden from his right, man after man puffed on it and blew a little smoke from his mouth. At one point it became empty and had to be refilled. As it got closer, Heimdall, who was seated directly on his right, leaned in to him and whispered, "This is what is known in some parts of Yggdrasil as a 'pipe.' Suck in gently and hold the smoke in your mouth. It is a bit harsh when you are not used to it. They call that which is in the pipe chan-shasha in some places, kinnikinnick in others. Do not cough or you will lose face. Blow the smoke out gently, toward the sky.''

The pipe reached Heimdall and he demonstrated the technique to Voden. The Aesir chieftain could sense Honir and Tror to his left, leaning toward him, watching Heimdall. Voden took the pipe from Heimdall and looked at it. It was about two feet long, the bowl made from a reddish rock and the stem from some kind of wood. The stem was wrapped with thin strips of rawhide, and symbols resembling the runes decorated it. Twelve feathers from the tail of a spotted eagle dangled from the stem near where it was attached to the bowl. He placed it in his mouth, sucked gently, and filled his mouth with the smoke. Then, gazing skyward, he exhaled slowly, watching the smoke rise. There were grunts of approval from the Jotun in the circle. Calmly, he passed the pipe to Tror.

The red giant either hadn't heard what Heimdall had said or purposefully ignored it. He inhaled deeply. His breath caught in surprise as the smoke hit his lungs. He closed his mouth in dismay, trying to hold in the cough that welled up from his chest. His face turned red, the veins in his neck bulging with his efforts. But the smoke was too much for him, and he finally exploded, the smoke spewing forcefully from his mouth as he coughed mightily. He coughed several times, his eyes watering, his shoulders heaving. At first dead silence greeted his performance. Then someone chuckled, and soon the whole circle was laughing good-naturedly at Tror's plight.

Angrily, he passed the pipe to Honir, who smoked it perfectly. His many years in Folkvang among the Vanir had made him careful of such situations and adept at handling them.

As the pipe went from hand to hand, the smoke rose and curled upward toward the open area in the center of the lodge. Voden watched the swirling shapes that formed and dissolved as they ascended to Gymir. He allowed his mind to drift with them, to merge with them, to rise up and up into the sky. As the smoke spread, he let his consciousness spread with it to permeate the space around him. He explored every nook and cranny of the lodge, twined around the men seated in the circle, looked down on the building, up at the sun, out at the city of wagons. He felt a power in the lodge, and especially in the tall pole placed in its middle. There was a strange image hung on the pole, made of stone, wood, hide, feathers, and paint. It exuded even more power. Slowly he returned to his body, wondering at what he had seen and sensed. What was this building and why had it been built? An idea began to grow in his mind.

When the pipe had finally gone around the whole circle, the White Bear, who sat at the northern place, rose and spoke. "The Sons of Ymir welcome the Aesir and the White One to Jotunheim. You will be free to come and go among us as you will. From now until the snow falls you are one with us. No hand will be raised against you, no voice speak harshly to you. Nerthus will guard you. Gymir will guard you. Gadombitsouhi will guard you. You have smoked the holy Chanunpa with us and are our brothers. Is there anything you wish?"

Voden looked around. "What is this building?"

"This is the K'ado Lodge," the white bear replied. "There in the center is the can-wakan, the sacred tree. On it is the Tai-me. You see offerings and the head of the black bull. It is the time of the dance to honor Gymir. It is the time of the K'ado Dance."

"Who will dance this dance to Gymir?" Voden asked.

"Those who have pledged to do so. They will dance it four years in a row. It is no easy thing to do."

Voden paused and looked around the lodge again. Suddenly he threw back his hood so that all could see his face clearly. "I have hung on the tree in the grove of Nerthus," he said with calm intensity. "I would now dance to Gymir."

A chorus of surprised grunts came from the Jotun around the circle. The White Bear stood very still until the noise subsided. Both his eyes were fixed on Voden's single one. "This thing few men have done, to sacrifice both to Nerthus and to Gymir. It is a great thing. And a dangerous one." He paused as if considering.

"You have done it," Voden said, knowing that he was right.

The chief of the Trul nodded. "Yes. I have done this thing." He considered the Aesir for several moments, then nodded again, slowly, with determination. "Gymir will accept your pledge. It will be so. You must be purified, for the

K'ado begins in just a few days. Yes. You will dance to Gymir.''

Two of the Trul took him far out into the grasslands. They found a spot at the top of a slight rise, just above a small stream. With bowls made from ash wood, the Trul scooped out a slight depression in the ground. One of them took sixteen willow sticks about five feet long from a bundle they had brought with them. They pushed the sticks into the ground in a circle, tying opposite ones together to form the framework of a small dome. Then they covered the framework with hides from black bulls, one of the hides serving as a door flap.

The small hut finished, the Trul took several smooth stones from another bundle. Using some ash wood, they lit a fire and placed the rocks in it. When they were glowing redly, the Trul instructed Voden to remove his clothes and enter the hut. Then one of them, using deer antlers, carried several of the glowing rocks to the hut and placed them in the center, directly in front of Voden. The other Trul handed the Aesir a skin bag full of water. ''Squirt the water on the rocks,'' the Trul told him. ''Squirt four times, until the air is full of steam and you can see nothing but whiteness.'' The other Trul handed Voden a little bag filled with dried herbs. ''When the air is white, place these on the rocks. We will bring new rocks as these cool.''

Voden sat back as they closed the hide flap. He squirted water on the rocks. They hissed and snapped, wheezing and calling out to him. He called back, singing to them in their own language, murmuring in the original tongue.

He squirted again and the air became heavy with moisture. The rocks moaned, and he moaned in response. He squirted a third time. The air became thick. He squirted a fourth time and the air turned white. He dropped the herbs over the rocks, and a strange, sweet smell filled the hut.

He began to sweat profusely, the water cascading down from his body. Voden closed his eyes and felt the heat of the steam soak deep into him. It sank through his skin, into his flesh, down to his very bones. As it sank, it forced the water from him, old water, dirty, fouled water. The heat soaked in and flushed him out.

The whiteness pressed against his skin, against his face,

against his mind. He let himself drift with the heat, yielding to the solid pressure of it. It was purifying him, emptying him, renewing him.

The flap opened and one of the Trul added two glowing rocks to the pile in front of him. When the flap was closed again, he squirted more water on the rocks. They hissed in surprise and the air became opaque. He was floating in a cloud far from the earth, far from anything, permeated by heat, surrounded by a bone-deep glow. Wave on wave of warmth broke over him.

He was never sure exactly how much time he spent in the steam bath. It seemed like an eternal instant, a moment that seceded from time and lasted forever during the blink of an eye. When the Trul finally pulled back the door flap and told him to come out, he felt totally renewed, cleansed to his very marrow.

II

VODEN counted some forty Jotun gathered in a milling group in the open area in the center of the K'ado Lodge. All were dressed as he was, with soft moccasins on their feet and white cloth breechclouts wrapped around their loins. Most had painted designs on their bodies and faces. Several had eagle feathers braided into their hair.

Around the edges of the circular lodge, members of the Trul sat, beating softly on small drums or shaking gourd rattles. Four older women, their cheeks bearing the scars of deep slashes, dressed in black skin dresses and capes, stood in the center of the lodge by the pole that rose into the sky. The White Bear stood with them.

The leader of the Trul raised his hands to signal for silence and attention. Everyone fell mute and the drumming ceased. The White Bear looked around at the men and women who filled the K'ado Lodge and spoke softly. "Soon Gymir will raise his eye over the edge of the world and spy out our K'ado Lodge. Then we will begin to dance for him. We will dance for four days and four nights without stopping. We will not eat. We will not drink. We will seek a vision to give our lives meaning and direction. All here have pledged this time to Gymir for four years. Some are in their last year. Others are just beginning their dance." He gestured to the four women. "These are the widows of four fallen warriors. They have cut the pole and dragged it here. They will stand about the pole, one looking east, one west, one south, one north, to guard against the approach of evil spirits. They hold four of the ten Adalbeahya to protect all the dancers. This man"—he

17

pointed to an older Jotun, whose body was painted in red and yellow—"is the Keeper of the Tai-me which is the chief protector of this dance. He is of the Thursar, a member of the Ka-itsenko society. His Ka-itsenko name is Gui-k'ati, Wolf Lying Down. These four"—he indicated four men grouped near Wolf Lying Down, all of whose bodies were painted with intricate designs in several colors—"are his helpers. They know all the songs and dances and will lead you. None of these five will stop dancing for four days and nights. None of these five will stop singing for four days and nights. None of these five will eat or drink for four days and nights. They will give of themselves to guard and guide you.

"Know this is a time of danger. Your spirits will be close to the surface of your minds at all times. Perhaps they will decide to leave your bodies and wander around for a while. Evil spirits may be lurking about, waiting for them, hoping to grab them and take them away to the Alterjinga. Against this the Tai-me guards. Against this the four Adalbeahya guard. Against this the five guard."

A strange humming sound suddenly filled the air. Voden looked up to trace its source and realized it came from the head of the black bull fixed to the pole, facing east. The White Bear raised his hands again. "Gymir comes. The black bull has seen the edge of his mighty eye peeking over the horizon. You must now all come forward one by one and make your pledges of pain."

Instantly a Jotun stepped out of the group and approached the White Bear. He was a young man, about Voden's own age, with a scar that ran from just above his right eye diagonally downward to the bottom of his left cheek. He was painted in white and black patterns which resembled lightning strikes. "I pledge two skewers," he said boldly, holding up two narrow pieces of bone about six inches long, sharply pointed on both ends. The White Bear nodded approvingly and motioned to the red-and-yellow man. The latter stepped forward and took the bone skewers. He grasped one of them like a knife and jabbed it into the flesh of the young man's chest, pushing it under the skin until it came out again. About an inch and a half of it stuck out of the flesh on either side. He repeated the procedure with the other skewer. The blood flowed freely down the young man's chest. Everyone watched with great intensity. When the young man neither made a sound nor even flinched, a chorus of approving grunts came from the watchers.

Amazed, Voden watched as others came forward to have the same treatment done to them. As he stared, he felt someone approach him from behind. He turned slightly to see a slender Jotun, fully dressed, standing by his side. He recognized Hrodvitnir's companion. The Jotun smiled slightly and held out two bone skewers. "Thought you might want these," the slender warrior said with a malicious grin. For a moment Voden stared at the Jotun, but the other neither turned away nor showed any discomfort beneath his one-eyed gaze. The grin continued to play about the full lips, slightly mocking, as if daring the Aesir to respond.

Voden smiled a strange, secretive smile, reached out and took the skewers. He touched their tips with his thumb and discovered they were as sharp as needles. With a nod to the slender Jotun, he stepped forward toward the White Bear. "I pledge two skewers to Gymir," he said quietly.

Dead silence fell over everyone in the K'ado Lodge and every eye turned to gaze at the Aesir. He stood taller than the others, his single eye looking directly at the White Bear. The leader of the Trul took the two skewers from Voden and gazed at them. Then he looked beyond Voden to where the slender Jotun stood watching. "You do not belong here in the K'ado Lodge, Lao-Kee," he said with just the slightest edge of annoyance in his voice. "You are not dancing. Do not presume too much on your position. Go now."

The slender Jotun laughed lightly. "I had no intention of staying, O mighty bear of white. I merely brought something our Aesir friend had forgotten." Lao-Kee bowed mockingly to the assemblage. "I leave you to your four days of fun." With another grin and laugh, the slender Jotun left.

When Lao-Kee was gone, the White Bear slowly turned and handed the two skewers to the red-and-yellow man. The man took them hesitantly, as if not too sure what to do. He looked at the leader of the Trul, a question clear on his face. The White Bear nodded.

The pain was greater than the Aesir had expected, but not as bad as he had experienced many times in the past. His face remained impassive and his stance relaxed. When both skewers had been fixed into his chest, the red-and-yellow man stepped back and gazed at him. Approving grunts went up in a chorus from all the dancers and the others gathered in the lodge. Even the White Bear nodded as if pleased.

When all those who were pledging had done so, the four widows came forward with long leather thongs which they tied around the ends of the skewers. The other ends of the thongs were tied high up on the pole by one of the younger Trul, who climbed up as quickly as a squirrel. Each dancer had some fifteen feet of slack.

Now the Trul seated around the outside of the lodge began to beat their drums and shake their rattles again. The beat was slow and almost stately. The five leaders began to shuffle about in a dance, singing softly, joined by the widows and the other dancers in the choruses.

> *"Ho, Gymir, we dance to you.*
> *Ho, Father, we dance to you.*
> *You who brings us light,*
> *You who brings us rain,*
> *You who gives the bull his strength,*
> *You who gives the stud his strength,*
> *You who gives the warrior his strength,*
> *Gymir, we dance to you.*

As they danced, the men with the skewers through their chests pulled back to the ends of the thongs that held them to the pole. Voden followed their example and felt the pain shoot through his body. Every time they pulled back, the dancers would grunt a loud "Ho!" The blood flowed down their chests, staining their white breechclouts and dripping to the ground.

The song changed, but the dance went on and on. Voden kept up with the others, pulling back against his tether when they did, grunting when they grunted, moving forward again when they moved. Soon his mind was a blur of red pain, his whole body throbbing with anguish which radiated out from the torn and abused flesh of his chest until it filled every inch of his being. He lost track of the time.

As the sun rose and began to shine more directly into the K'ado Lodge, the heat grew. Before long sweat was pouring from Voden's body, the salt entering his wounds, making the pain even greater. He danced in a daze, allowing the rhythm of the chanting, the shuffle of the feet, the beating of the drums, the shaking of the rattles, to take over his mind. His breath began to move in and out with the thump of the drum. His heart beat in sympathy with the rhythm that surrounded and enveloped him.

At some point the pain began to dull and he rose beyond it. He leaned back against the thongs, letting them hold him up. Gymir stood above him, his glorious eye glaring down. Voden gazed up at it in wonder. The light entered him and filled him.

Two specks appeared in the light and came gliding down toward him. "Hugin!" he cried in greeting, recognizing them. "Munin!"

"Hai, little brother," Hugin croaked, "I bring you a thought!"

"Hai, little brother," Munin squawked, "I bring you a memory!"

Voden laughed with delight. "What thought do you bring, Hugin? Is it a happy one?"

The raven settled on his shoulder and looked down at the skewers stuck in his chest. "As happy as these. I will sing it to you in a voice as smooth and soft as that of doom.

> "Garm howls loud before Gnipa cave,
> fetters will burst, and wolf run free.
>
> Yggdrasil shakes and on high shiver
> the ancient limbs for the giant is loose.
>
> Fast move the sons of Ymir and fate
> sounds high in the call of the horn.
>
> Loud blows Heimdall, his horn aloft;
> In fear quake all who Hel-roads ride."

"Enough!" Voden cried, his face grim and shaken. "I would hear no more! Your thought beats against my mind and booms out horrible echos!"

Munin landed on his other shoulder and croaked. "Then hear the echos in the memory I bring you. I sing it in a voice you know well, one that whispers from the past.

> "An ax-age, a sword-age,
> shields will be shattered;

A wind-age, a wolf-age,
before the world is shattered!

The sun goes black,
Earth sinks from sight,
the heavens lack
their starry light!

Smoke billows high
by fire driven,
flames lick the sky
and heaven's riven!"

Voden began to shake, his teeth chattering loudly in his head. "Vestla," he moaned. "You speak in the voice of my dead mother! This is a bitter memory you bring me, Munin."

"Drink it to the lees, then, little brother, for though it be a memory, it is one of the future, not the past. Yet there is more!" The two ravens began to chant in harmony.

"From the south fares Surt
bearing bane of forests,
the sun of battle-gods
shines from his sword.

Tall crags are shattered
and great mountains sink;
the dead throng Hel-way
and fire leaps heaven-high."

"No more!" Voden shrieked. "I cannot bear to hear it!"

"Hear it?" Hugin croaked. "Nay, little brother, you will live it! It is your fate, and it approaches!" With a cry, the two ravens leapt into the air and disappeared into the blinding light of Gymir's eye.

A great darkness rose up and crashed down on Voden. He collapsed, slumping slowly to the ground.

Pain woke him. A tearing, throbbing anguish beat at his mind and drew it back to consciousness. He was lying on his side, the skewers still in his chest, the thongs taut. The Aesir, his head spinning, rose slowly to his feet. For a few moments he stood stupidly gazing about him. Then he felt the rhythm of the drums coursing through his veins and he began to shuffle to their beat. He was dimly aware of the other figures moving with him, dancing as if they were all one huge beast. The chant filled his mind, trying to push out all thought. Briefly he wondered what time it was. He looked up and saw the sun standing overhead. How much time had passed? How long had he been dancing? Minutes, hours, days? The throbbing of the drum and the pain in his chest overwhelmed his mind and he lost all ability to think.

Geri and Freki walked next to him. "We bring you tidings," they rumbled. He nodded grimly, knowing they were dark. "The fire bearer stirs. The mighty Serpent begins to move. The Tree is shaken to its roots. Nidhogg grows restive."

"What shall I do?"

"Bind the mighty wolf. Beware the hidden one, the deceiver, one whom none call Lodur. Get you a son and call him Vidar. Give him a sword and teach him to thrust."

"What shall I do?"

"Build a hall in Gladsheim and call it Valholl, with more than six hundred forty doors. Gather warriors about you and call them Einherjar. Feed them good meat from the boar and give them milk from the goat to drink. But you shall give your meat to us and drink only mead."

"What shall I do?"

"Finish the dance. Learn all you can. Bind the wolf. Beware the deceiver. We go." The wolves ran off through the walls of the K'ado Lodge.

Voden danced, leaning back against the thongs with all his remaining strength. He tugged and pulled. The pain seared his chest, rose up and seared his mind. He cried out in a loud voice, singing his power song.

> *"In days gone by I once was Ygg*
> *Ere Voden they did name me.*
>
> *And I was Har and Jafanhar*
> *And also hailed to Thridi.*
>
> *Bileyg I'll be and Vafudar*
> *Till falls the mighty Ash Tree.*

> *Then I'll be Ygg as once I was*
> *Ere Voden they did name me."*

He lunged backward and felt a rending pain, a tearing of flesh and muscle. The skewers ripped through his flesh and he fell back, hitting the ground with a crash. With a great cry, he plunged into darkness.

When he woke, he almost laughed aloud. Two worried faces peered down at him. One gazed at him with dark, almond-shaped eyes. Beneath the eyes was a snub nose. The mouth was solemn, but wrinkle lines at its edges told that it was always ready with a smile. Below the mouth was a wispy white beard. And how long the ears were!

The other face was slender, with fine features, black skin, and dark eyes sparkling with intelligence and humor.

As he gazed at the two faces, another one appeared behind and above them. The bristling red hair and beard were well known. "Huh," grunted the giant warrior. "About time you woke up."

"Kao-Shir, Anhur," Voden said quietly.

"None other," the man from the Sunrise Empire said with a quick smile. "My, Voden, I must say I always find you in the most unusual situations!"

Voden sat up and grasped their hands in greetings. "How did you find me here in Jotunheim?"

Anhur answered grumpily, "We just followed the trail of mayhem and destruction. It was a short trip, really. Only two thousand or so of his stories long!"

"I've met your friend Heimdall," Kao-shir said excitedly. "The things I'm learning from him are endless! Why—"

Anhur interrupted. "Endless nonsense! By Sekmut, can't you see the lad's still a bit unsteady? Give him a moment to gather his wits about him before you go running off!"

Kao-shir looked deep into Voden's open eye. "I think," he said quietly, "the lad very much has his wits about him. I also think he is a very different lad than the one we watched head north along the eastern shore of the Amsvartnir Sea. You found Mimir?"

Voden nodded solemnly. "And drank from the well."

"Ah," Kao-Shir replied laconically.

"Now he's chieftain of the Aesir," Tror said defensively.

"Although you'd never know it seeing him lying here in a damned Jotun wagon! Are you happy now, Voden? Can we go back to Asgard?"

Voden looked down at his chest. Two red scar lines showed where the skewers had ripped through the flesh. "More of your healing work, eh, Kao-Shir?" he asked.

"Mine and Heimdall's," the other man replied with a shrug. "He knows a lot, Voden. Why, only a few minutes ago we were discussing—"

"Would you like something to eat, Voden?" Anhur asked, fixing Kao-Shir with a withering glance. Without waiting for a reply, he reached behind and produced a bowl full of stew. The Aesir chieftain suddenly realized he was famished, and took the bowl from the Svartalfar with a grunt of thanks. Anhur beamed with pleasure as Voden ate.

Between mouthfuls, Voden questioned Kao-Shir and Anhur about their travels. They were in the middle of a long tale of their journey to Nidavellir, to search for the Dverg, when the canvas flap at the end of the wagon was suddenly pulled back, and the head of a huge wolf was thrust through the opening. There was a terrific snarl and a wild howl which sent them all scrambling for their weapons.

Before any of them could defend against the gigantic beast, another head appeared next to the wolf's. It was the sarcastically grinning countenance of Lao-Kee, Hrodvitnir's slender friend. "Hello, there," the Jotun said in a mocking tone. "Do you like my wolf robe? It seemed appropriate that I gift it to the mighty Aesir chieftain known in Jotunheim as Mjodvitnir, the Mead Wolf. Is he awake yet?"

Voden sat up and met Lao-Kee's grin with one of his own. "This is the third time you've brought me presents, Lao-Kee. First on the tree, then in the K'ado Lodge, now in my wagon. I understand the appropriateness of the first two. Why is this one so?"

"Because during the dance to Gymir you were visited by two great wolves, no?"

Voden looked intently at Lao-Kee. "Yes. But how could you know that? I'm the only one who can see them. . . ."

Lao-Kee smiled smugly. "How I know isn't important. The fact is, they came. With allies like that, the name Mjodvitnir is most appropriate and this wolf robe is precisely the correct gift from someone who wishes to be your friend."

Lao-Kee climbed into the wagon and held the robe out to Voden.

The Aesir looked at it carefully. The wolf had been huge. "Did you kill it yourself?" he asked.

The Jotun warrior nodded. "Yes. I ran it down on horseback and killed it with two arrows, one through the left eye, the other through the right ear. It is the largest wolf ever killed in Jotunheim. Hrodvitnir was very jealous."

Voden looked at the Jotun with an appraising glance. "Well, it appears the size of the warrior has little to do with the skill of the warrior. I would do well to take lessons from you on shooting from horseback."

"True," Lao-Kee replied airily. "I'm the best in Utgard. I'm even better with a knife. Though I will admit that someone with the reach on me can even up the odds a bit. However, I can still win by throwing my knife." With a swift, fluid movement, the Jotun pulled a knife from somewhere, twisted around and flung it across the wagon. With a solid thunk it stuck deep into one of the wooden hoops that held the canvas over the wagon. The hoop was round and no more than two inches in diameter. The knife had struck the hoop dead in the center.

Lao-Kee turned back to grin at Voden, to discover the Aesir's iron knife out and only inches away. The Jotun's eyebrows rose in surprise. "Very fast. The rest of your friends barely had time to touch their weapons. But look at my left hand, the one that didn't throw the knife."

Voden's eye moved to Lao-Kee's left hand. There was a knife in it, ready to throw. The Jotun chuckled at the look on Voden's face. "I'd never throw my only knife. And I have two more on me as well." Voden nodded, smiled broadly, and returned his knife to its scabbard.

Kao-Shir, who had been staring intently at Lao-Kee ever since the Jotun had appeared, spoke. "Lao-Kee is no Jotun name. What was your mother's name?"

The slender warrior turned dark eyes on the yellow-robed old man. "My mother, may she rest in Paradise, was named Lao-Feh."

"And your father was a Jotun?"

"Yes. Farbautnir, one of Bergelmir's brothers. Hrodvitnir is my half brother."

"Lao-Feh was from the Sunrise Empire, wasn't she?"

"From one of the northern provinces. The Jotun raided, and Farbautnir captured and raped her. I'm the result. She could never adapt to the Jotun way of life, and died when I was young. I've adapted quite well. It's an old story."

Kao-Shir nodded. "Yes, an old story. But to one who must live it, it's always new and harsh."

The Jotun shrugged. "I never knew the Sunrise Empire. I barely knew my mother. All I've ever really known is the life of following the herds and riding across the endless plains of Jotunheim. I'm happy."

Kao-Shir smiled. "We're alike, then. We've both left the Empire and neither of us regret it. I, because I know the Empire all too well, and you because you don't know it at all."

"Ha!" Anhur crowed delightedly. "So all your knowledge and all his ignorance come to the same thing in the end!"

"Yes," Kao-Shir said slowly, thoughtfully, "in this case, they do indeed. But I'm more like the skull in the story told by Chuang Tzu. He was on the way to Ch'u—"

"Stop!" cried the Svartalfar. "No more stories! Give my poor mind a rest. Every time you—"

Before he could say anything more, the flap at the end of the wagon opened again and the White Bear stuck his head through the opening. He nodded to everyone and spoke to Voden. "It appears you are up and about. I would like to speak with you, but the wagon is so crowded it might be best if you would come out rather than having me squeeze in. I assume you are able to walk?" Voden nodded. "Good. I'll give you a few moments to dress. Meet me in the K'ado Lodge." He disappeared with a nod.

"Am I invited too?" Lao-Kee called out. The Jotun warrior's eyes were twinkling with mischief. The only reply was a growled *"No!"* Lao-Kee laughed silently and winked at Voden. "I'll peek through a hole I found in the south side of the lodge. Only to keep watch over you, of course. After all, we're friends now, and what are friends for?" With a conspiratorial grin, the Jotun left.

As Voden pulled his shirt on, Tror grumbled. "Don't like the sound of it. Going all alone into that damn lodge again. Who knows what those damn Trul have up their sleeves?"

Voden looked at Heimdall. "Tror has a point. Any idea what the White Bear wants?"

"Some idea," Heimdall mused. "It seems the visions you had during the dance were very powerful. So powerful, indeed, that several others shared them. One of them went mad as a result. I rather suspect, therefore, that the Trul wish to examine you further to find out more about your power. You have hung on the tree, danced in the K'ado Lodge, and possess the Bones of Audna. That much they know. But they have never actually seen you actively use your Galdar-power. Yes, this could be some sort of test, Voden."

Voden looked thoughtful. "A test? A magical test, perhaps? Yes. That wouldn't surprise me at all." He pulled his hood up over his head and his face disappeared. "But haven't they guaranteed me safe conduct here in Jotunheim?"

"I doubt the test would be conducted here in Jotunheim," came Heimdall's reply.

"Ah," Voden responded. "Of course. It would be in the Alterjinga. The White Bear never mentioned safe conduct there. And Hrodvitnir couldn't guarantee it there either. Well," he continued as he stood, "this could be most interesting." With a slight wave to them all, he parted the flap and stepped out of the wagon.

III

VODEN stepped through the door of the K'ado Lodge to find ten Trul seated in a circle, waiting for him. The White Bear was at the part of the circle farthest from the door. He motioned Voden to a place directly opposite, nearest to the door.

For several moments everyone sat silently. Eventually the White Bear took a bowl from the ground in front of him and held it up to the sky, then down to the ground, and finally in each of the four directions. He passed it to his left. Each of the Trul took what looked like a greenish-brown seed pod from the bowl and stuck it in his mouth. When the bowl reached Voden, he followed their actions and placed the seed in his mouth. When the bowl again reached the White Bear, it was empty. Voden noticed that the Trul had begun to chew the seed slowly. He followed suit. The outer shell broke easily, and he bit down into the pulpy inside. It tasted bitter and harsh, but it made the saliva flow copiously in his mouth. He swallowed and felt a numbing warmth spread down his throat and into his stomach.

As they all slowly chewed and swallowed, the White Bear began to speak softly. "In the Long Ago Time the good spirits dwelt in the west and the evil ones in the east. Ymir created the Jotun and all the animals and placed us in the middle to live together in harmony. In that time we could speak with the animals and the birds and they could speak with us. We could even talk with the gods directly since they dwelt with us and walked among our wagons. To this day an image of the goddess resides in a wagon in the grove of

Nerthus. The spirit of the goddess enters that image when we call on her.

"We lived happily in that Long Ago Time until the bad spirits began to spread sickness and death over the earth. Some who lost their loved ones became angry and cursed the gods. This made the gods angry in turn, and they withdrew to a separate realm, the Alterjinga, leaving us behind in our misery. When the gods left us, we lost the ability to speak with the animals and the birds. We lost their wisdom. They fell mute. The Jotun were utterly alone in the world.

"Those who had cursed the gods realized their mistake and called on the gods to forgive them, to come back and dwell among the Jotun once again. They prayed for help against the sickness and death the evil spirits had spread across the earth. Day and night they cried out, pleading and begging.

"The gods heard their cries and decided to take pity on them. They would not return to earth to dwell amongst the Jotun, but they would send someone to help against the evil spirits. They would send a shaman filled with the Galdar-power to the Jotun. They turned to Vilmeid, the god of the Galdar-power, and gave him the task to carry out. He chose the eagle, filled him with the Galdar-power, and sent him to the earth.

"But the Jotun could no longer understand the language of the birds, and now that men and animals lived shut away from each other, they had no confidence in a mere bird. The eagle returned to the gods and told them what had happened. The gods conferred and reached a decision. They would send the eagle back with the ability to confer the power of the shaman on the first Jotun it met.

"The eagle returned and came upon a woman sleeping beneath an ash tree. The eagle had intercourse with her. Then, his job done, he returned to the Alterjinga.

"The woman began to swell with child. This was surprising to everyone because she was known as a woman of great virtue, and no man had ever lain with her. She grew and grew, greater in size than any woman had ever been. Then, ten months later, she gave birth to a gigantic son. He was called Asvithnir and he was the first shaman in the world, the first Jotun to have the Galdar-power. He helped the people, going into the Alterjinga to plead directly with the gods when the people fell sick. He went to the east and wrestled with the evil spirits, saving many souls from their grasp.

"Asvithnir gathered ten disciples around him and taught them to shamanize, taught them to develop the Galdar-power that lay within them. He showed each of them how to create one of the Adalbeahya, the Ten Grandmothers, the medicine bundles that contain the power of the Jotun.

"We are the Keepers of the Adalbeahya, the descendents of those first ten, the disciples of Asvithnir. We are all of the Trul, shamans of power and experience. We are of the Jotun, but we have the Galdar-power and serve dark and awful Vilmeid.

"What Asvithnir was for us, Dain was for the Alfar and Dvalin was for the Dverg. The Vanir have the Seidar-magic and serve Svarthofdi. They have no dealings with the mighty Vilmeid.

"Before this time no Aesir has ever had the Galdar-power. The shaggy men of the southern plains have always worshipped the bloody Fornjot, the most evil and destructive of gods." The leader of the Trul paused as grunts of agreement came from the other nine in the circle.

He fixed Voden with a bright-eyed stare. "But then you come along. Voden. Vafudar. Bileyg. Thridi. Jafanhar. And even, by your own words, raised in power song while in deep vision, Har, the highest, and Ygg, the dreadful, the terrible.

"You come along. You live among the Vanir. You have raven and wolf Hamingjur. You drink from Mimir's Well. You possess the Bones of Audna. You hang on the Tree for nine nights and days. You dance to Gymir.

"You have the Galdar-power."

A deep silence fell over the group. All ten of the Trul leaned slightly forward. Voden ignored the other nine and kept his eye focused on the White Bear. The leader of the Trul met his gaze and nodded slightly. "Yes. You have the Galdar-power. I can sense it in you. It surges powerfully. But it is erratic, undisciplined, untrained. You have done many things, but left some important ones undone."

The White Bear closed his eyes as if to concentrate. His voice became distant. "Once you were very sick. So sick you almost died. You did not know your own mind. Dreams lived on during the day and there was no longer any line between waking and sleeping. You passed through that sickness and now know the way to guide others.

"Once there was a teacher named Jalk who took you to the cloud realm. There the Hamingjur tempered your bones. Two were missing and two of your blood have died to replace them.

"Once you made a journey to the Great Tree itself. Father Bear taught you many things. The Mother of Animals whispered wisdom in your ears. And even the twisted thing yielded its secrets to you.

"You have traveled far, Vafudar. Your power is almost mature. It lies, coiled and waiting, at the base of your being, ready to leap forth. You must do one more thing to release it fully. One very dangerous thing. You must journey to Niflheim, the misty realm of the dead. This is the realm where Glitnis Gna and Erlik Kahn hold sway. Where Nidhogg gnaws on corpses. Where there is no light and no hope. Only when you have gone there, into Eljudnir itself, the hall of Glitnis Gna and Erlik Khan, and returned, can you fully serve Vilmeid.

"Vilmeid has revealed this to me. You must go. You must go."

So intent had he been on the words of the White Bear, that Voden had not noticed the other nine Trul had taken drums from somewhere and begun to beat softly on them. The seed was gone, chewed thoroughly and swallowed. He felt slightly dizzy. The sound of the drums carried his mind back to Jalk and his first important journey into the cloud realm. Jalk had recognized the raw Galdar-power in him and sought to give it direction. The old man had died in the attempt. Now he was somewhere in a nest on the Tree, waiting to be reborn.

The throbbing of the drums grew in intensity and began to invade his mind. The sound lifted him out of himself and carried him to a point over the center of the circle of Trul. He could look down and see them all. The White Bear was making strange motions with his hands over a point inside the circle just in front of him. To Voden's surprise, an opening appeared in the ground.

The White Bear looked up to where he hovered. The creature pointed down at the hole. "That is the way you must travel. Down into Niflheim. Vilmeid has so willed it. You must go."

A tremendous whirlpool of force pulled at Voden, and he

felt himself being sucked down toward the hole. He heard the White Bear call out in a far-off voice, "One must risk great loss to achieve great gain! One must make the leap to reach the other side! One must lose himself to find himself! Go now to Niflheim and complete your journey!"

With a cry, Voden plunged into the hole. Swiftly he was pulled downward, moving faster and faster as he sped through the darkness. Then he began to slow down, and a gray light diffused across the vast space he had entered. Gently he floated to a surface that resembled an endless gray desert.

In the far distance, barely visible through the dim light, he saw a towering hall which he realized must be Eljudnir, the abode of Glitnis Gna and Erlik Kahn. Even from this distance he could hear the sighing, moaning wail of hopelessness that rose from the hall to spread throughout Niflheim. The sound grated against his spirit and made him shiver with despair and horror. He took a deep breath to get hold of himself. Then he set out in the direction of the hall.

Before long he came to a huge chasm that stretched off endlessly to his right and left and lay directly across the path he had to follow to get to Eljudnir. He approached the edge of the chasm and peered into its depths. There, writhing and hissing, he saw the vast coils of Nidhogg. In addition to the Striker that Destroys, he could discern other serpents. Moin and Goin were there as well as Grabak, Grafvollund, Ofnir, Svafnir, and others too numerous to count. Between and beneath them were countless corpses, half gnawed and rotting. A stench rose from the abyss, and Voden drew back in disgust.

The Aesir set off to his right, searching for a way across the chasm. He walked for a long time without success. Finally, in the distance, he saw a stone tower built right at the lip of the abyss. He approached it and knocked loudly on the tower's wooden door.

The door opened a crack and two red eyes peered out of the dark that brooded within the tower. "Yessss?" a hissing voice asked. "Yessss? What do you want?"

"I seek a way to cross the chasm. I'm going to Eljudnir."

A hissing laugh met this statement. "A way across the chasm! So he can go to Eljudnir! Ha! Best he just come in and give us our dinner! Yessss!" A clawed hand reached out to grab him.

Voden swiftly drew his knife and slashed the hand. There was a screech and a hiss of anger and fear from within the tower, and the door began to close. Voden reached out and held it open with his left hand. "I seek a way across the chasm," he growled. "Tell me where it is or I'll cut more than the back of your hand!"

The creature in the dark tower whimpered. "Don't hurt us. We'll tell him. The only way across the abyss is right behind this tower. Yessss. Though it is worthless to him. He might as well step in and be our dinner, he might. Surely that's better than falling into the chasm and being gnawed by Nidhogg. Well, well, if he must try to cross the chasm, then he must. Such a pity. Such a juicy meal lost." The door slammed shut.

Voden turned away and went around behind the tower. There, stretching across the yawning gap, was a huge sword, edge upmost, its hilt firmly on the near edge of the chasm, its point far off on the opposite edge. In wonder, the Aesir bent over to test the blade. It was razor sharp. How long was it? he wondered. A hundred yards? Two hundred? It was hard to judge in the misty, dim half light that filled Niflheim.

How could he hope to cross such a bridge? He would have to move with incredible speed and perfect balance. There could be no misstep, no hesitation, no momentary wavering while he tried to gain his balance. Even the slightest pause and the blade would cut his feet and he would tumble into the depths. He glanced down and met the eyes of Nidhogg. The serpent hissed expectantly.

There was no choice. He brought his mind to a point of concentration, thinking only of his crossing, how perfect, how swift, how sure it must be. Then, without a second thought, he moved forward, out onto the blade of the sword.

A blur of smooth, sinuous motion, he flowed with incredible speed and unerring balance. His weight never settled long enough in one place to put enough pressure on the sword blade so that it might cut. In a moment he stood on the far side of the chasm. Without bothering to look back, he strode forward toward Eljudnir.

It wasn't long before he came to a new barrier. This was a wall, so high he could barely see the top. It stretched off in both directions as far as the eye could see. Voden approached it and examined its surface. It was like glass, and gave no possible purchase for hands or feet.

He stepped back and studied it. Suddenly a gate opened in the wall and revealed a long passageway that led to the other side. Voden was about to step forward and enter when the walls of the passageway began to move together and the gate came crashing shut. The Aesir stood and stared at the flat, empty wall. If he had stepped forward into the passageway, he would have been smashed to a pulp when it had slammed shut!

Then the gate and passageway opened again and again slammed shut. Considering, Voden stepped back and watched as the cycle was repeated several more times. He carefully estimated the length of the passageway and the amount of time it stayed open. He calculated that if he ran faster than he had ever run in his life, if he moved without the slightest hesitation as soon as the gate opened, he just might get through in time before it slammed shut: If his estimate was off even slightly, he was doomed. He watched a few more openings and closings, getting into the rhythm of the gate and the passageway.

As the gate began to open again, he launched himself like an arrow shot from a bow. His legs pumped faster and harder than they had ever moved. His arms pumped with them, helping to drive him forward. His lungs snatched huge chunks of air to fuel his exertions. He could feel his heart pounding and straining.

From the corner of his eye he saw a tiny movement as the walls of the passageway reached their farthest open point and began to move back together again. He still had a few yards to go. Could he make it? With a tremendous effort he leapt forward, throwing all his energy into a mighty jump that carried him to the end of the passageway just as the walls slammed shut. He fell to the ground in a heap, sobbing in air, his heart pounding so wildly it seemed about to burst, his body trembling from his efforts.

For several moments he was too weary to do more than just lay there and breathe. Finally, his heart beating more normally, he stood and began to walk once more. He passed through a low range of black hills. From the crest of the last of them, he beheld a river, and on its other side, Eljudnir. There was a bridge across the river. Standing next to the bridge was a tall figure dressed in black armor, obviously some sort of guard.

Slowly Voden approached. He was about twenty feet away when the figure in black armor called out, "Who is this who comes" Voden halted. The guard then called, "Who is this who has passed the grinding gate Nagrindr? Who has come through the dark hills of Nadafjoll? Who now approaches the Gjoll Bridge?" The voice was deep but soft and harmonious. Voden realized the figure in armor was a woman.

"I am Vegtam, son of Valtam," he answered, knowing better than to give any creature in Niflheim his true name. "Who are you?"

"I am Modgudr, the Maid who guards the bridge. Why do you come here, Vegtam?"

"I seek Eljudnir. I come to see Glitnis Gna and Erlik Kahn."

"Yet you are not one of the dead," came the reply.

"No. Vilmeid has sent me on this task."

"Ah," Modgudr responded, "then you may pass."

Voden nodded and, as Modgudr stepped back out of the way, moved to cross the Gjoll Bridge. When he passed the maiden, he glanced from the corner of his eye and found that in her place stood a tall pillar of black rock.

On the other side of the Gjoll Bridge, the way lay over a hill and down into a valley. The hall lay in plain sight on the other side of a large gate. Voden walked up to the gate and struck it three times with his fist. He waited several moments for a response. When none came, he struck the gate three more times, slamming his fist into it with even more strength. The sound of his knocking boomed loudly in his ears. Still there was no response. Summoning all his strength, he crashed his fist into the gate three more times, the thunder of his pounding making the very ground tremble. He might as well have been tapping like a butterfly for all the response his knocking brought.

Frustrated, he stepped back and estimated the height of the gate. Tall, but perhaps not too tall. He paced back some thirty yards and then turned and ran. At the last moment he leapt up into the air, soaring up and up as Hugin and Munin would soar in the sky. He cleared the top of the gate and landed in an unceremonious sprawl on the other side.

He picked himself up, dusted his clothes off, and gazed in wonder at Eljudnir. The hall was huge, more than three times the height and width and length of any hall in Asaheim. Its door was on the northern side. The roof and walls were made from a wicker work of serpents. Their fanged mouths gaped wide and poison dripped from them. The moaning sound Voden had heard from afar was now an air-shattering shrieking which went on and on and battered against the ears and soul with a mindless fury.

Voden walked through the door of Eljudnir. As he entered, thousands of faces turned toward him. Some were green and just beginning to swell. Others were black and putrid. Yet others had bone showing through where pieces of rotten flesh had fallen away. Here and there were skulls with only a few strips of dried flesh still clinging to them. Voden ignored them all and strode down the middle of the hall toward the High Seat.

As he approached it, he noticed that the bodies that crammed the benches on both sides of the hall were in a better and better state of preservation. The closer he got to the High Seat, the handsomer and richer they became, until those who stood around the High Seat itself looked like rich lords and ladies.

He stopped before the High Seat and gazed upward. Two figures were seated in it. One was a tall, gaunt man with a long face and dark black hair. His features vaguely reminded Voden of the Jotun. Next to him was a short, round woman, with skin so pale it was almost transparent. Her hair was white and lifeless. Voden had never seen anything like either of them before. He realized they could only be Glitnis Gna and Erlik Kahn, the lord and lady of Eljudnir, rulers of Niflheim.

Erlik Kahn's flat eyes gazed down at him. For several moments the lord of Niflheim simply stared, his mouth curled in a sneer of contempt. "What," he finally said, his voice a hollow snarl, "is this that creeps before us?"

"I am a wanderer come from afar," Voden answered. "My name is Vegtam and I am Valtam's son. Vilmeid sent me here to learn from you."

Erlik Kahn stroked his chin and fixed Voden with a considering gaze. "Vegtam, eh? You seem rather puny to be from Vilmeid. Would you like to test your skills against those here in my hall, little Vegtam?"

Voden looked around. The people surrounding him had

suddenly grown in size until they towered over him. Many looked immensely strong and powerful.

"Are you good at anything, Vegtam?" Erlik Kahn asked, his voice heavy with sarcasm.

Voden squared his shoulders and looked Erlik Kahn straight in the eyes. "I'm noted to be a fearsome eater in my father Valtam's hall. None has ever eaten more or faster than I."

Erlik Kahn roared with laughter. "Well, that is quite a boast! We'll see about that, we will! Logi! Bring a trencher filled with the best of food!"

A giant of a man, his face split with a huge grin, approached holding one end of a long trencher filled to the brim. The trencher was placed on a table. Logi sat at one end and Voden took the other. At the signal from Erlik Kahn, the two began to eat as fast as they could.

They gobbled and chewed and swallowed. Each devoured as much as he was able, moving his chair forward along the trencher as he ate. They finally met in the middle.

Voden looked back down his half of the trencher. He had eaten every scrap of meat and vegetable, leaving behind only the bones. Then he turned his gaze the other way to see how Logi had done. Logi had eaten not only the meat and vegetables, but the bones and the trencher itself as well! Voden stared in astonishment.

"It looks," Erlik Kahn said sarcastically, "as if Logi has won rather handily." The others gathered around the High Seat shouted their agreement. "Surely," Erlik Kahn continued, "there is something else you're good at, Vegtam?"

"Well," Voden said, "in my father Valtam's hall I am accounted a very swift runner. I wager I can beat anyone here in a race."

"That remains to be seen," Erlik Kahn replied. "Clear a pathway down to the end of the hall and back," he cried out. When that had been accomplished, he called a young man standing near the High Seat, "Hugi, will you run this race for me?"

Hugi and Voden took their places at the foot of the High Seat and made ready to start. "The race will be to the door of the hall and back," Erlik Kahn informed them. "This is a vast hall and the distance is long. Now—go!"

Voden launched himself with all of his strength. Side by side with Hugi he sped down the hall toward the door. His lungs were bursting with the strain. As they neared the end of the hall, he realized that Hugi was pulling slightly ahead. He pushed himself harder and almost made up the gap.

At the far end of the hall they both spun around and headed back toward the High Seat. Voden was several paces behind by now. He put on a burst of speed, but Hugi pulled even farther ahead. By the time Hugi reached the High Seat, Voden wasn't even halfway back down the hall. He nearly collapsed as he reached the finish line. Hugi was barely breathing hard. The Aesir had never seen anyone as swift. Even long-legged Honir couldn't equal Hugi's remarkable performance.

Erlik Kahn sneered at Voden. "Well, Vegtam, you are surely fast, but not fast enough. I'll give you one more chance to prove yourself. Name your game."

Voden thought for several moments. Those surrounding the High Seat were getting restless, and he knew he would have to decide soon. Finally he spoke. "Wrestling. In my father Valtam's hall there isn't one man who can best me in wrestling"

Everyone laughed out loud. Erlik Kahn shook his head. "I doubt anyone here would lower himself to wrestle a puny little thing like you. But let me think. Perhaps one. My old nurse. Yes, she's half crippled, though she was a mighty wrestler in her youth. Yes, she might be willing. Elli!"

A rag-covered old crone came sniffling and shuffling out of the corner. "Aye," she mumbled, a wide grin curving her toothless mouth, "old Elli will wrestle with Vegtam. She's thrown down many a better man than he, she has." She turned to Voden and said, "Well, then, puny Vegtam, lay on!"

Voden stepped up and grabbed the old crone by the shoulders. As soon as he touched her, he realized there was far more power in her shriveled body than he had reckoned. He tried several holds on her, remembering the things Yngvi had taught him so long ago in Folkvang. No matter what he tried, he failed to move Elli. In fact, the harder he struggled, the more easily she was able to resist his efforts.

Then Elli began to try a few holds of her own. Voden was caught by surprise. Elli threw a lock on him and he nearly lost his balance. He struggled mightily, using all his strength, clinging desperately to the ancient crone, trying to take her down with him. For many minutes they stood, frozen in their stances, each straining against the other, neither able to move the other. Then slowly, inexorably, Voden was forced down to one knee.

As his knee touched the floor of the hall, Erlik Kahn called out in a loud voice, "Enough! You've proven you're no better at wrestling than you are at eating or running, Vegtam! I begin to doubt that Vilmeid really sent you. Could it be you are not protected by the dread lord of the Galdar-power! We shall see!"

Erlik Kahn stood and began to wave his hands in the air while muttering a complex spell. A sudden sickness filled Voden's mind and his body was wracked with pain. Pustules broke out all over his skin and his head felt as if it would burst. Waves of heat and nausea washed over him and he nearly fainted. He knew he was dying.

In desperation he fled into his own mind, seeking some way to fight back against the power of Erlik Kahn. Unexpectedly, it was there, waiting for him. He remembered the words Bolthorn had spoken to him when he hung on the tree in the grove of Nerthus. He raised his right hand in front of him while his left closed over the Bones of Audna that hung around his neck in their leather pouch. He began to trace a symbol in the air, a stem with two prongs sticking up to the right at a forty-five-degree angle from it. "This is Feoh," he chanted between fever-cracked lips. "It comforts grief, lessens pain, cures sickness. Its prongs catch and hold your spell." His fingers continued to move, creating a new figure in the air. His voice was stronger now, power flowing back into it as his fever receded. "This is Ur. It is the sign of the healer. Its horns catch and hold your spell." Yet a third time his fingers drew in the air. "This," he cried, his voice echoing in the hall, "is Gen, and it throws your curse back at you!"

There was a bright flash of light and a thunderous explosion. All the pressure Voden had felt was suddenly gone. His body no longer ached, his skin was clear and clean, the fever was gone from his head. He looked over to where Erlik Kahn still sat on the High Seat. The lord of Eljudnir was frowning.

"You have more power than you seemed to have, Vegtam. But do you have enough to best this?" Again Erlik Kahn began to cast a spell. The air between Voden and the High Seat began to quiver, and swords, arrows, spears, and knives appeared. No sooner did they appear than they flung themselves at Voden.

Without pausing to think, Voden began to chant and inscribe symbols in the air. "This is Thurs. It will fetter any foe, blunt the edge of his blade, soften the blow of his staff until it is like the tap of a child. This is Is, slippery, hard, it shields me from danger. This is Eolh. It protects me against evil spells and all danger." The flying weapons fell useless, harmless to the floor of the hall.

Now Erlik Kahn stood, his face transfigured with a scowl of anger and worry. "Can you escape this, then, Vegtam? I bind you in the name of the Unnamable!"

Voden felt a sudden tightening around all his limbs, as if a thousand fetters were being fastened to him. He responded immediately. "This is Os," he cried, drawing the symbol in the air. "If any seek to bind me hand and foot, I speak it and all knots dissolve, all locks spring open, and I walk free!"

The invisible fetters dissolved and Voden stood and stared at Erlik Kahn, his single open eye glowing with power. Erlik Kahn slowly sat down in the High Seat and thoughtfully stroked his chin. "Well," he murmured. "It seems I was wrong about you, Vegtam. You indeed have the Galdarpower, are indeed a servant of Vilmeid. I did not realize you carry the Bones of Audna. My spells have no effect on you, cannot bite and take hold."

He sighed. "I cannot hold you here in Eljudnir, nor even in Niflheim. Your power is too great. I would you were gone, Vegtam, or whatever your real name is. Go."

With a nod, Voden turned on his heel and left Eljudnir. Once outside, he gave cry and leapt into the air, soaring up and up through the dim gray light.

In a few moments he found himself speeding through the dark tunnel he had descended. Suddenly he was back in his own body, sitting in the K'ado Lodge, looking across the circle at the White Bear.

The leader of the Trul nodded to him. "You have returned." Voden nodded by way of reply. "Tell us of your trip."

Voden related his experience in precise detail, leaving nothing out. As he spoke, the others would occasionally grunt in exclamation. When he was done, they all sat silent for some time.

Eventually the White Bear spoke. "You have taken a mighty journey. None I know of have ever gone so far or done so much. Know that Logi is fire, the great devourer, the fever that destroys men, the bane of forests. You could never outeat Logi, but you did not lose to him by much. You can cure men of the fire that would destroy them. This is good.

"Know that Hugi is thought. No man can run faster than thought, but you did very well to stay up with him even for a short while. You can cure men who are troubled by their thoughts, men whose minds are wracked with fear and dread. This is good.

"Know that Elli is old age. No man, no matter how wise or powerful, can resist old age. Yet you only fell to one knee. You can help others resist the ravages of age and teach them to live with it. This is good.

"Voden, know that you have undergone your final trial. Now you must go alone into the wilderness for several days to think on all these things. When you return, you will be a shaman, a follower of Vilmeid, an adept in the Galdar-power.

"Go now. Speak to no one, look on no one, stay with no one. Go far from the haunts of men for nine days and nine nights. Then return and take the name of Har, the High One. For surely you are the most powerful shaman to walk the face of Yggdrasil!"

YNGVI

IV

~~~

"I predict they will make a dramatic attack now, thinking we've been so badly mauled by the Aesir that we won't be able to counter adequately." Hild looked around the table at the four Disir who sat and watched her. Syr was to her left, looking decidedly agitated. Eir, sitting next to Syr, was frowning as if in disapproval of the whole proceedings. Gna was silent, expressionless. Vor, the most ancient of all the Disir, was gazing attentively at Hild as if every word the Valkyrja leader spoke was pure gold. Hild wondered briefly where the other Disir were.

"And were we that badly mauled?" Vor asked quietly.

Hild paused. "Well," she said slowly, " 'mauled' is perhaps too strong a word. But we were beaten, and make no mistake about that. Borr's strategy of pretending to be in retreat lured us out of the forest and gave them the advantage."

"They fought pretty damn well *in* the forest as well," Syr growled. "The few months they had soldiers down here helping Yngvi paid off rather handsomely."

The leader of the Valkyrja nodded. "Yes. They only pretended to be confused in the forest at the beginning. Once we chased them out onto the plain and they counterattacked, we retreated very swiftly and in good order back to the cover of the woods. I'm afraid we were taken by surprise when they followed us and fought so well. It devastated morale. We lost more Valkyrja in the forest then on the plain. I'm ashamed to report that many of their wounds were on their backs."

"But are we as weak as Yngvi thinks we are?" Vor insisted.

"No. I've planted false rumors about the number of dead and wounded and the state of our morale. We were badly hurt, but we can still keep the foresters at bay and even campaign against them fairly effectively. I propose we launch an attack right away before Yngvi can initiate his own offensive."

The four Disir sat in quiet thoughtfulness for several moments. Finally Vor spoke. "No. I think not. It seems likely, as you suggest, that Yngvi will mount some sort of action. Rather than spend our time and resources—now more limited than ever—in trying to chase him down, I suggest we figure out his most likely move and ambush him. If we catch him good and properly, we might be able to deal him a mortal blow."

They all nodded in agreement, except for Eir, who continued to frown. Hild broke into the silence with a question. "And just how do you plan to determine what Yngvi's move will be?"

"Ah." Vor smiled. "I should think that would be obvious."

Hild bowed her head slightly to Vor. "You have the advantage of me, then, for I fail to see the obvious."

Vor chuckled. "Eliminate the possibilities. Will he attack one of our armed camps? Not likely. At best he could kill a few of our Valkyrja, and in all likelihood lose nearly as many foresters doing it. A bad trade, especially since he has fewer to spare than we do. With that option out of consideration, we no longer have to worry about which camp he might attack.

"So what is left? Ambush patrols? Hardly dramatic. What about an attack on Folkvang? Dramatic, indeed, but he simply hasn't the manpower to mount an assault against a fortified city surrounded by camps filled with armed enemy soldiers.

"Which leaves us with the most logical, possible, and dramatic choice of all." The ancient Disir paused and gazed at them all with bright, sardonic eyes, challenging them to complete her thought process. Syr muttered and shook her head in defeat, Gna looked blank, Eir frowned, and Hild returned Vor's gaze with one of mute expectancy.

"Ah, well, then," Vor continued, "the most obvious move is to rescue Freyja from Folkvang and bring her and her household guard to live with the foresters. In one stroke they would legitimize their revolution and pose a very grave threat to the authority of the Distingen. Without the Vanadis . . ." She let the words trail off, knowing they would understand.

Syr looked stunned. "Steal into the city and kidnap Freyja?"

"Kidnap is the wrong word," Vor responded dryly. "Freyja would be more than willing to go. By Audhumla's tits, sister, she's been in contact with the foresters all along through Rota, that Valkyrja captain of hers."

Hild shook her head in admiration. "Brilliant. A brilliant tactic. Bold. Low risk in terms of men. High potential gain. Yes, Disir, I think you may have it. The move smells of Yngvi's style. And I wouldn't be at all surprised if Yngvi himself led a raid like that."

"Nor would I," Vor said softly. "In fact, I'm depending on it, Hild. I'm depending on Yngvi walking into Folkvang and into our trap. And then we will do to him as we did to Jalk. Only we won't send him back out into the forest. We'll keep him for an even darker rite, make him a direct offering to Svarthofdi."

Eir turned sharply to Vor, her frown deeper and more angry than ever. "This is highly questionable," she rasped, her voice tense and hostile. "These decisions should not be made without the rest of the Distingen present, including the Vanadis. Vor, you are presuming too much!"

The expression on Vor's face froze. "The other members of the Distingen are unwilling or unable to make hard decisions. The Vanadis is actually in favor of the foresters. We are the only loyal ones left in Vanaheim. We must make the decisions or they will not be made."

Eir's voice was harsher and angrier than ever. "You who speak so much of tradition, break it to suit your own ends! The things you do are without precedent. I will no longer be party to such blasphemy." She stood and glared at them all. "You work your own wills rather than yield to that of Audhumla. I will have no more to do with you." She stalked from the room, slamming the door as she left.

Syr turned to gaze at Vor. The ancient Disir was looking at the door. "Wheels within wheels," Vor muttered.

"Will she speak to Freyja of all we've been discussing?" Syr asked worriedly.

"No," Vor replied thoughtfully. "Freyja doesn't trust Eir much more than she trusts us, and the healer knows it. Our Vanadis is well aware that it was Eir who administered the mandragora, Eir who was caring for her mother when she died, Eir who was in charge when Freyja herself almost died after Od's departure. The pall of suspicion hangs heavily over the curer's head. I rather imagine she will withdraw from supporting anyone at this point.

"Hmmm," Vor murmured, considering the situation. "Which means that her influence over Hlin will diminish and give us one more vote. Syn and Syofyn will continue to back anything Freyja does, but they will be outnumbered. I wouldn't be at all surprised to see them move into the Vanadis's hall.

"It comes to a head. If Yngvi does as I expect, the whole thing will reach a climax sooner than anyone expected." Vor looked around the table. "We have some planning to do, sisters."

Freyja put the letter down and looked up at Rota. "Do you think it could be done?"

"Yes, my Vanadis, I believe it could. The idea is to move swiftly with a few picked men, secure the gates, bottle up the Valkyrja garrison here in Folkvang in their halls, and then escape quickly by splitting up back in the forest. A group would remain behind to ambush the Folkvang garrison if it set out in pursuit. We don't think it would be possible to rally the nearby garrisons in time to mount an effective chase. The key is secrecy and swiftness."

Freyja sat musing. "If I were out of Folkvang and away from the control of the Disir, do you think people would rally to me?"

"I'm sure of it," Rota replied with enthusiasm. "Even here in Folkvang there are many who side with you against the excessess of Vor and Syr. In the camps there are many Valkyrja who would join you in a minute. And the foresters provide a ready-made army more than willing to fight for you. My Vanadis, all you have to do is say the word and half of Vanaheim will rally to you."

Freyja turned to the young man who stood next to her. He looked remarkably like her, and indeed was her twin brother, Frey. "What do you think, brother? You know Folkvang. Is what Rota says correct?"

Frey frowned and thought for a second. "Many of the younger Vanir back you, sister. But there are others who side with the Distingen and favor the return of the old ways. That's one of the reasons I found it wise to find refuge here with you in your hall. My life was constantly in danger out in the city."

"Is that why Niord fled north to join the Aesir?"

Frey grinned. "Partly. He rather likes the Aesir barbarians, being a rude sort himself. He got on well with them when we were hostages there. But there was also a certain young woman, known as Skadi, whom our older brother got on even better with. I should imagine they're sharing a sleeping cupboard by now."

"But there are those in Folkvang who would rally to me?"

Frey nodded.

Freyja turned to Rota. "And as long as I'm cooped up here in Folkvang, they can't, is that what you're saying?" The Valkyrja nodded. Freyja looked at the letter again, then off into space. "Many could die. It's a dangerous idea."

"Many die already," Rota responded. "Many will continue to die unless something dramatic is done to resolve the situation. The Disir are weak right now. Rumor has it that the Valkyrja are badly demoralized by the beating Borr gave them. Now is the time to act!"

Freyja sat silently for several moments, her countenance thoughtful and sad. She finally sighed and spoke in a soft, faraway voice. "So much has happened so quickly. My poor little baby, my precious Hnoss, has come into a world of turmoil. Where will it all end? When? Only Audhumla knows." She paused again, gazing vacantly into space. "I wonder where Od wanders. I wonder where Voden wanders. I wonder where we all will wander in days to come. I fear the future, Rota. I fear it greatly.

"Tell Yngvi I will consider this thing."

The head of Freyja's personal guard smiled with relief. "Yes, my Vanadis, I'll tell him. He'll be pleased."

Harbard frowned. "I'm thinking it's a crazy idea, I am. Aye, crazy is the right word."

Yngvi smiled. "Old warrior, I agree. And that's exactly why I like it! Something that crazy is the last thing Vor and Syr will be expecting."

"Don't be underestimating them two," Harbard warned. "They have minds deeper than Ginnungagap. You'll be long trying to outplot those damned witches. We'd best be prepared to lose any as is going on this mission. Like suicide, it'll be, mark my words," he said glumly.

"It's dangerous, all right," Yngvi affirmed with a nod.

"No one will have to come. I'll lead it myself and take only volunteers, and only the best of those."

Harbard looked at him sharply. "Lead it yourself? Now there's the stupidest thing I've heard you say in many a month, Yngvi. And what if it fails? What then, eh? Who will be our leader, eh?"

"Any of the others can do it now, Harbard." Yngvi sighed. "Look, old friend, let's face up to the facts. The Valkyrja were badly hurt by Borr. Rumors have it they were totally demoralized. But how long do you really think that will last, if it's even true? A month, two months? And when they're back to normal, what then? You know that we've heard the Aesir went back north to find the Jotun at the gates of Asgard and the whole city ablaze. Borr fought and won two battles. His resources are almost totally drained. We'll get no more help from the north.

"We have no choice. We have to act now, while the Disir are off balance. This chance won't come again. If the plan works, Harbard, we stand a good chance of beating them. With Freyja here we can rally half of Vanaheim to us.

"If the plan fails . . . " He shrugged. "Then we're right back where we were, and it won't make a damn bit of difference whether I'm dead or alive. We probably won't last much past the end of the summer. Maybe through the fall, at best."

Harbard looked grim. "Dammit, I know all that. But to walk right into Folkvang with only a few men—"

Yngvi cut him off. "Honey draws flies. A little honey draws a few flies, a lot of honey draws a lot of flies. The fewer flies we draw, the better our chances of success. We have to move swiftly and secretly, and that's best done with a few men."

Harbard sighed. "Then I'll be going with you."

"No," Yngvi said decisively. "You'll stay outside, in charge of the group that's to ambush the Folkvang garrison if they set off in pursuit. I'm taking twenty men into the city. Fifteen will block the doors of the Valkyrja compound and keep the garrison bottled up until the rest, including Rota's guards, can make their escape from the city. Then Rota's people will cover the retreat of the fifteen. They have the greatest risk, Harbard, those fifteen. I'll lead them."

"You're a damn fool, Yngvi," Harbard said softly.

"Aye," the leader of the foresters agreed.

"Beyla be with you, lad. And all the rest of Vettir too. You'll be needing all the help you can get."

"Believe me, Harbard, it'll work. It has to."

Harbard merely nodded and looked away.

Vor examined the boils on Syr's arm and smiled grimly. "Her power grows, sister. You were warded?"

"I thought so," Syr groaned. "But somehow her spider got through. It was waiting on the ceiling when I came into my room. It dropped as I entered and bit me." She moaned again. "Lucky . . . lucky you came by when you did. I . . . I was trying to counteract it, but the poison clouded my mind. I might not have made it in time."

"Has she attacked any of the others? Gna? Hlin? Hild?"

"Not that I know of. I think she hates me the most and concentrates her efforts against me."

Vor shook her head. "No. She's attempted to breach my wards several times. Mine are more carefully constructed than yours, and she's been unable to break through. I've warned you about sloppiness before. Perhaps now you believe me. The girl is dangerous."

Syr groaned again. "Aye, that she is. Uh, what did you come for, sister?"

"Rota has gone to Yngvi. I think Freyja has agreed to his plan. I was unable to see the message in Rota's mind this time. Freyja has her hedged around with protection. But it seems likely. We must tell Hild to get ready."

"When do you think he'll strike?"

"Soon, sister, soon. He dare not wait very long or his opportunity will pass by. The Valkyrja are pulling themselves together, and he knows it. Yngvi will act within the next few days or he will not act at all. Either way, we will crush him!"

Syr smiled weakly, pain just behind the curve of her withered lips. "Good! I long to perform the rite on him, sister!"

"And so you shall," Vor replied with a leer, "and so you shall!"

Rota's people secured the south and west gates. The twenty approached swiftly and silently, passing through like so many shadows. The guards gave them soundless salutes as they flowed by.

Freyja was waiting, Hnoss in her arms and a nervously

grinning Frey by her side as Yngvi came into her presence.
"Yngvi," she greeted him with a smile.

"Vanadis," he replied, bending his head and knee slightly.

"We must move swiftly," Freyja said. "I've readied a
spell that will help to hide us as we flee, but there's much
magic loose in Folkvang tonight. The Disir mount their own
guard, as always."

"Rota and your guard, with five of my men, will escort
you into the forest to the south, Vanadis. Frey can stay with
you. Once into the forest you'll continue south along the Slid
to a point about two miles from here where Harbard and a
group are waiting. They'll take you across the river and return
to wait for the garrison if they pursue. Another group is ready
to take you across the Hrid."

"And you?"

"I and my fifteen will keep the Valkyrja in their compound
until you're clear of the city and on your way south. Then
we'll flee from the west gate and disperse. Most of us should
make it, since some of Rota's people are going to be in the
forest to help cover our retreat. We'll have to move very
swiftly."

Freyja nodded. "You're very brave, Yngvi. May Audhumla
protect you."

Yngvi bowed slightly again. "Thank you, Vanadis. Now
let us begin."

The fifteen placed themselves so that they could watch every
way in or out of the Valkyrja compound. Each of them stuck
ten arrows into the ground, nock end up, for quick access.
Another ten arrows were in each man's quiver. They also
carried throwing axes and knives for close-quarter fighting.

When they were all in place, Yngvi muttered a quick
prayer to Beyla and gave the signal. One of Rota's people ran
to tell Freyja everyone was ready and it was time to leave.

Now if only they get out of the city unnoticed, Yngvi
prayed, everything will go smoothly and we'll get out too.
There was a nagging suspicion in the back of his mind that he
was wishing for the impossible.

Freyja, with Hnoss strapped on her back, walked silently in
the midst of some fifteen warriors, heading for the south gate.
A cloud of darkness moved with them, hiding their presence

from any casual eye. Would it work against a magical eye? the Vanadis wondered. Surely Vor would have her own watch posted in addition to that of the Valkyrja. But what would it consist of? And how might it be countered? I'm still so new to the Seidar-magic that I can't be sure of the things *I* do, let alone what someone as practiced as Vor might do. If my spell will hold for only a little bit longer, we'll be—

"Now," Vor muttered. "Now!" Syr waved her hands and croaked several words in the elder tongue, then tore the night with a wild laugh of evil glee.

The flash blinded Freyja for a moment. The whole city was as bright as day. A wild laugh, one she recognized as Syr's, rang out, thundering against her ears. She heard shouts of alarm from the Valkyrja guards posted in various parts of the city. Freyja cursed. Discovered! She looked at Frey's shocked face and commanded, "Run for it!"

As she ran, she began to chant a spell and drop acorns on the ground. If the Disir want to involve Svarthofdi in this, she thought, well then, I have a few tricks to play too.

Behind her forest cats, their eyes aglow with hunger, sprang up wherever an acorn lay. They growled softly and lay down to wait for any who might come along.

Yngvi cursed. Damn! That flash and that laugh meant they'd been detected! He gave the cry of a hunting eagle to warn his men. The sound had barely died out when the first Valkyrja came bursting out of the compound. Yngvi let an arrow fly, and one of the brown-clad warrior women tumbled and fell. Quickly he fitted a new arrow to his bow and shot again.

It took three arrows for the Valkyrja to figure out that something was wrong. Yngvi stood waiting, a new arrow ready to fire. He knew they wouldn't give up. They were only trying to figure out what to do, how to—

A volley of fire arrows flew from the center of the compound up and into the streets surrounding it. Light! Now they could see the attackers that had been hidden in the dark! Another volley came, arching into the air and then falling like stars shaken from the heavens. Some hit the halls surrounding the compound.

If the fools don't watch out, Yngvi thought, they'll set all the halls afire. The first volley was enough to let them see, why— It hit him like a rock. They were setting the halls on

fire on purpose! Yngvi and his men would have to withdraw
if the protection they hid behind was ablaze! And the fifteen
of them would make easy targets as they fled through a city
lit by firelight! He was about to whistle for a retreat when he
realized Freyja and the others couldn't possibly have cleared
the city yet. We'll just have to hold out as long as we can, he
decided grimly.

With a shout, the Valkyrja poured out of the compound
again. Their timing was perfect. Yngvi shot two arrows and
then had to drop his bow to pull out his ax and knife. Three
of them closed on him. It would be hand to hand from this
point out.

Bone weary, they stopped to catch their breath. To the north
the glow had decreased. The fire had been put out, or at least
was dying out. Freyja felt hollow. Folkvang was burning. Her
city. She clutched Hnoss to her in anguish.

Rota approached. "We have to move on. Harbard is only
a little farther. We've come on his outposts."

Freyja looked up. "Any word from the city?"

The Valkyrja shook her head. Her face was troubled. "The
garrison hasn't pursued yet. Yngvi must have been able to
hold them. He—"

"No one has made it out?"

"Not that we know of. We've been moving pretty swiftly,
Vanadis. Anyone would be hard pressed to catch up with us."

Frey looked nervously back over his shoulder, then turned
a worried gaze to his sister. "If there is anyone to catch up,"
he muttered.

"Where are the others?" Harbard asked Rota.

"We don't know. The Disir were expecting us," she said
bitterly. "If it hadn't been for Freyja's magic, we never
would have made it out of the city. Someone had planted
groups of Valkyrja in the halls nearest the gates. They poured
out as we approached. Freyja blasted them with . . . with
something horrible. We . . . we fled. Must have lost eight of
our people. The city was on fire. There were forest cats
and—" She choked up, unable to continue.

"Did he make it out?" Harbard asked softly.

"I . . . don't know," Rota replied. "It wouldn't be an
easy thing to do. But maybe . . ."

* * *

Yngvi crouched in the dark, his knife slippery with blood.
His bow and ax were long gone. So were the rest of the
fifteen. He tried to calm his breathing, tried to plan a way
out. Somehow he'd managed to fight his way free of the
Valkyrja. Then he'd fled through the city, heading first to the
south gate. The way had been blocked by Valkyrja patrols
and forest cats which attacked anything that moved.

Finding his retreat in the direction of his friends cut off,
he'd decided to head in the opposite direction. The north gate
had been heavily guarded, and the Valkyrja had the whole
area lit by torches. A lizard couldn't have crept through.

The east gate seemed his only hope. He surveyed it now.
There were guards there, alert, careful, ready. But there were
only four of them. If he was swift and ruthless . . .

He began to move forward. He limped slightly. One of the
Valkyrja had stabbed him in the side. It hurt abominably, but
he couldn't afford to notice it now.

"Yngvi?" Harbard asked the man.

"Saw him go down under about five of 'em." The man
was leaning heavily against the sentry who had brought him
in. He had a nasty gash on his left leg and his right arm had
been broken and slashed deeply. His shirt was stained by a
spreading patch of dark red. He was clearly faint from exhaustion and loss of blood.

"Any others make it out?"

"None as I saw. I waited a few minutes at the edge of the
forest since none of the Valkyrja come after me. I was the
only one that came out. Figured I'd best come down and
report. He coughed, and bloody spittle dribbled from the
corner of his mouth. He grinned quickly. "Figured I'd best
report before I died." He sighed and slumped in the sentry's
arms. His mouth sagged open and blood poured out. The
sentry lowered him gently to the ground.

Harbard looked down at him. "You did right, by Beyla.
You reported before you died."

"If one made it out, others might have," Rota said hopefully. "Perhaps he's just taking a long way around. There are
many Valkyrja out patrolling. Perhaps he . . ."

Freyja met her eyes. "Perhaps."

Rota looked away to hide the tears that suddenly began to

flow. She found she couldn't speak. Freyja moved to Rota's side and put her arms around her. She hugged her gently without saying a word. The Valkyrja tried very hard not to cry.

There was only one guard on the wall. One guard between him and freedom. Summoning every reserve of energy, Yngvi crawled slowly forward, pressing to the shadows as tightly as possible. When he was a few feet from the guard, he carefully rose and prepared to jump, his knife ready.

Before he could move, the guard turned around. Yngvi stopped dead in his tracks, his heart skipping several beats, his knees turning to water. His eyes gazed in horror at the guard's face. Huge demonic eyes glared back at him, lit by hellfire from within. A fanged mouth drooled hungrily at him. Clawed hands reached out to grab him.

Stunned and terrified, he stepped back. Strong arms circled him and held him fast. A net fell over his head, the kind the Disir used to snare forest cats. Before he could react, he was bound and helpless, lying on the ground looking up into the face of the snarling monster.

The hideous face dissolved to be replaced by one he knew all too well. Syr grinned down at him and laughed in evil triumph.

Harbard looked grim. "They never sent no one in pursuit. Only one more come along after the one that died. One messenger with this for you." He held out a small package to Freyja.

The Vanadis took it and looked at it, apprehension growing in her heart. It was wrapped in the same black cloth the Disir used to make their robes.

She uttered a few counterspells over the package before she folded back the cloth. She laid the cloth and what it held on the ground so all could see it. "Do you recognize it?" she asked.

Rota sobbed and Harbard cursed. "Aye. I recognize it," he snarled. "It's Yngvi's. It's Yngvi's right forefinger!"

V

HE awoke to throbbing pain. Slowly, carefully, fearing to
increase the agony that pulsed through his body, he opened
his eyes. Blackness. Did they blind me? he wondered. His
heart pounding with sudden anxiety, he lifted his left hand to
his face and touched his eyes. They were still there. Briefly,
he thanked Beyla. The reason I can't see, he told himself,
trying for calm, is because they've put me in a place where
there's no light. Does that mean I'm no longer in Folkvang?

He tried to remember what had happened. Very little came.
There had been a great deal of pain. Like the sharp pain he
still felt in his finger . . . His finger! He touched his right
hand with his left. The right forefinger was gone. A piece of
memory returned. Syr had cut it off with a flint knife. A
present to Freyja, she'd rasped. She'd cut slowly, maximizing
the pain and shock. He'd passed out toward the end, her
mocking laughter ringing in his ears.

They'd beaten him too. Vor and Syr had watched while
three Valkyrja had whipped him senseless. While he was
being beaten, the two Disir had told him of the things they
were going to do to him, the torture, the mutilation, the
eventual sacrifice to Svarthofdi, the dark goddess of the
Seidar-magic.

Syr had hissed that they'd all been caught—Freyja, Rota,
Harbard, all—and that they were going to suffer the same fate
as Yngvi. Torture, mutilation, sacrifice. Syr said they were
giving special attention to Rota since they knew she was
Yngvi's lover.

He cursed his reviving memory. It had been better when

everything was a haze. Was Syr lying? He thought so but wasn't completely sure. After all, he argued, trying to convince himself, why send his finger to Freyja if she was a captive too? That didn't make sense. No, he decided, the Vanadis and her Valkyrja captain had escaped. Which meant that Harbard was most likely safe as well. Perhaps.

Where was he? The dark was total. Even when he held his hand directly in front of his eyes, he couldn't see a thing. There wasn't a hall in Folkvang so tight there wouldn't be at least some light.

So I'm not in Folkvang, he concluded. Did they take me somewhere outside the city? That didn't seem likely. He didn't remember being taken anywhere that would require a long journey. Again he tried to search his memory for some clue. The only thing that came was a brief bit of consciousness as he was being dragged down stone stairs into a . . . A what? He'd been all over Folkvang and never seen any stone stairs going down to anything.

No, wait. There was *one* place in Folkvang he'd never been: the halls inhabited by the Disir. He only knew one other person who'd ever been there. Jalk. Yngvi shuddered involuntarily.

But he was sure he wasn't in a hall. Could he be beneath one? Had the stairs led down to something beneath the halls of the Disir, something that nobody knew about?

For the first time he noticed the dampness and coolness of the air. He experimented with a low whistle. The darkness swallowed it up. He tried a louder, higher-pitched whistle. A slight echo came back to him. A cavern, he decided. A rather large one.

So, I'm in a cavern somewhere beneath the halls of the Disir in Folkvang. The Disir have tortured me, will torture me again, will mutilate me the way they mutilated Jalk, and then will sacrifice me, probably alive, to Svarthofdi. He shuddered and quailed inwardly. Saying it silently didn't make it any easier to think about. Maybe if he spoke it out loud? "They're going to torture me, mutilate me, and sacrifice me," he said. He was stunned by how weak and hoarse his voice sounded. Every word had quivered with exhaustion and fear.

Slowly he sat up. He ached, and for a moment his head spun. He waited until he felt comfortable. Cautiously he stood up, leaning against the wall on his left as he did. For several minutes he simply stood and tried to stop his head from swinging so wildly. Eventually everything became more normal and he could stand without leaning against the wall.

Can I walk? he wondered. Am I tied to something? He didn't feel any ropes or chains anywhere on his body, but he checked again, just to make sure. No, nothing. He wasn't bound or fettered in any way. Except, of course, that he was in a cavern somewhere beneath the halls of the Disir with no way out.

He took a step, then two. He kept one hand, his left one, on the wall as he moved along. Three steps, four, five . . .

His hand touched something that stirred slightly. He jerked his hand away and stood absolutely still, not even daring to breathe. What had he touched? Was it alive? Was it dangerous?

Nothing happened for several moments, so he carefully reached out to see if he could touch the thing again. His fingers encountered something cool and dry. He moved his fingers over it, noting the indentations, holes, bumps . . .

He jerked his hand back in horror and took two steps backward. A skull! He was touching a skull! He shuddered and cursed beneath his breath. By Audhumla's tits! Where was he?

Gradually his pounding heart returned to normal. A skull, he thought. Perhaps a whole skeleton. A dead man. Dead. No longer dangerous. Perhaps once a prisoner, like me. Perhaps tortured and mutilated. Perhaps offered as a sacrifice. Perhaps . . .

Carefully he continued his search of the place where he found himself. He moved slowly, discovering two more skeletons. He also realized that the cavern was roughly oval in shape, perhaps some thirty feet across the long axis, twenty the short way. There was no evidence of any entrance or exit. He was the only living being in the cavern.

His investigation completed, he went back and sat against the wall at about the same place he'd been when he'd woken up. Hungry, he thought, I'm hungry. He gave a grim chuckle. Things can't be all that bad if I've still got an appetite. If only I had some wood, a fire, water, and a kettle, I could make some broth with all these bones. The very idea made him shudder and laugh at the same time. He laughed for a long time, much longer than was reasonable.

When he stopped, he wondered if he was still sane.

Freyja was coming out of the trance. Rota placed a cool cloth over her forehead and whispered gently in her ear. Harbard leaned forward anxiously. Frey stopped pacing and walked over to join the other three.

The Vanadis sat up, her eyes still vague and blank, like those of someone who has journeyed suddenly from a long distance and left part of herself behind. Eventually it all came together and Freyja's eyes sharpened focus and gained clarity. "He's still alive," she said softly. "They've beaten him badly. He has a couple of cracked ribs. And, of course, they cut off his finger."

"Where is he?" Harbard asked.

Freyja frowned. "Someplace I never knew existed. Beneath the halls the Disir occupy in Folkvang there seems to be a series of caverns. They must have been cut out by the river eons ago. I imagine no one but the Disir, maybe no one but Vor and Syr, are even aware they exist."

"Would they provide a way to get to him and rescue him?" Rota queried.

"I don't think so. There appears to be only one entrance, right beneath the halls. I also sensed that there were things that guarded the place. Things raised by the Seidar-magic. I'll go back and scout the whole situation out more thoroughly later. Right now I'm too exhausted to do it again. I'm not used to using my power yet. I fear I still waste a lot of energy."

"What are they going to do with him?" Frey asked, his voice quivering slightly with fear.

Freyja's face became grim and her voice harsh. "They plan to do to him what they did to Jalk. And then sacrifice him on Svarthofdi's altar. They'll cut his heart out while he's still alive, offer it to the goddess, and then, as her holy votaries, eat it. But they intend to torture him for a while first."

Frey turned pale and looked like he might be sick. Harbard closed his eyes and ran his hand over his face. Rota stared at the ground. "Isn't there anything we can do to rescue him?" she pleaded.

The Vanadis looked pensive. "We'll have to let them torture him. That will give us time. Hopefully we can do something before they castrate him. I'll have to think about it.

I don't know. I have an inkling of a plan, but it will be very dangerous.''

Rota looked up, tears glimmering in her eyes. ''Dangerous? Whatever it is, I'll do it if there's even the tiniest chance!''

Freyja looked at her with a gentle smile playing around her mouth. ''Ah, so you've become fond of Yngvi. Carrying all those messages back and forth . . .''

The Valkyrja straightened up and looked at her mistress. ''Yes,'' she said proudly, ''I love him. I've watched him fight, keep his men together when they would rather just melt away into the forest and give up. I've listened to him talk about the kind of world he wants it to be. I've—'' Her voice caught and she couldn't continue.

Harbard spoke up. ''I'll go too. Whatever it takes, I'll be glad to give it for Yngvi, I will.''

Freyja nodded. ''It will take a great deal. What I—'' She stopped in mid-thought and turned to look at a bundle of furs that lay against the wall of the cave in which they sat. ''Ah, Hnoss is awake.'' She rose and went over to pick up the child, then brought her back to the other two. Hnoss's eyes were wide open, sparkling with intelligence.

Harbard looked away. Those eyes, far too deep and knowing for a baby, disturbed him greatly. There was something in Hnoss's glance that felt wrong, almost frightening. The child was only a little over a year old, a sweet, beautiful, golden little child, yet . . . Why was it so silent? He looked up.

The Vanadis was still sitting with Hnoss in her lap. The two were gazing at each other, tied together by a glance that excluded the rest of the world. Rota was staring at the two of them, her expression one of confusion. ''Freyja?'' she asked timidly. ''Vanadis? Is everything all right?''

Hnoss turned her tiny head toward Rota and said, ''Yes, Rota, everything is all right. My mother and I are working on a plan to save Yngvi. You and Harbard and Frey may go while we discuss it.''

Frey, the Valkyrja, and the forester were all trembling when they walked out of the cave.

''You cannot do such a thing without the approval of the entire Distingen!'' Syofyn was in a rage.

"We can," Vor answered calmly, "if the Vanadis approves it."

"The Vanadis!" Syofyn shouted. "Do you really think Freyja would allow such a . . . a travesty on the will of Audhumla to take place? Do you think she would ever—"

"Freyja is no longer the Vanadis," Vor interrupted coldly. "She has fled Folkvang in disgrace, abandoned her people and her duties, to go into the forest and live with a bunch of foresters who are openly at war with the Distingen and the holy will of Audhumla. Freyja," she repeated with slow emphasis, "is no longer Vanadis."

Syofyn jumped to her feet and shook her fist at Vor. "You can't do this! I'll fight you, rally the people! You can't get away with this . . . this treason!"

"You are the traitorous one," Vor replied with an angry hiss. "Syr is the new Vanadis! And you will go along with us if you know what's good for you!"

"Never!" Syofyn cried out defiantly. "Never! I'll go join Freyja, join them and tell them what you're about! I'll—"

"You'll do nothing," Vor growled. "Guards!"

Four Valkyrja stepped through the door into the room where the Distingen met. They saluted Vor. She pointed to Syofyn. "Take her and put her in the isolation room. But first soften her up. Remember all the times she has demanded things of you, all the petty egoisms, the nasty offenses. Use her roughly. She is a bitch who has earned the wrath of Audhumla!"

The four soldiers grabbed the stunned Disir and dragged her speechless from the room. When the door slammed shut, Vor turned to the others who sat around the table. Her eyes were hard and cold. Eir was missing, refusing to have anything to do with the Distingen until Freyja was back. The old healer didn't matter, Vor decided. She was isolated and had no allies. She would sit the whole thing out without acting. Once it was clear that Vor had won and that the old ways had returned to Vanaheim permanently, Eir would come around.

She gazed around the table again. The rest were so many tools in her hands. Even that fool Syr, who imagined herself Vanadis. Vor laughed inwardly. Vanadis! There was a ritual so old that even Syr didn't know of it! When the time came, she would find out. Aye, find out that Audhumla once had taken not merely the king, but the Vanadis herself to her bosom!

She turned and called out. A Valkyrja stepped into the room. "Tell the Vanadis Syr that the Distingen awaits her. We are ready to discuss the fate of Yngvi and the foresters."

Only one of the brown-clad warriors made it back to the camp, and that one died shortly after telling her story.

The captain in charge of the camp looked down at the limp body and scratched her head. Had the woman been delirious? Her report had made no sense. The part about the foresters attacking had been normal enough. But then she'd said forest cats and wolves fought on the side of the foresters. That was crazy. What was even crazier was the woman's babbling about dead warriors also fighting alongside the foresters. She claimed she'd seen a man she herself had slain a good month ago when she'd cut his throat with a slash from one of her spears. He'd been there, fighting today, his throat wound gaping, his face ghastly and pale, his eyes wide and staring.

The captain frowned and turned away. "Bury her with full honors," she said to the Valkyrja standing around. No sense punishing her for a delirium doubtless born of her wounds.

She began to walk back toward her tent, then stopped and called over the duty officer of the guard. "Mount double guard. Set out forwards twice the usual distance. Keep a sharp look. Something's brewing, and make no mistake about it."

That taken care of, the captain felt better. Yes, something was brewing, no doubt. But whatever it was, it certainly had nothing to do with dead warriors, wolves, or forest cats!

The Valkyrja stopped dead in her tracks as the far-off cry of a hunting wolf reached her ears.

He tried hard not to moan. He gritted the few teeth he had left and choked back the sounds of anguish that rose automatically from deep inside him. I haven't cried out yet, he thought, and I'll be damned if I'll give them the pleasure of hearing me groan now. It was a small victory, but it was all he had.

He didn't even try to sit up or move. He simply let his mind wander around his body, taking stock of the injuries. They'd cut off two more of his fingers. They'd beaten the bottoms of his feet until they were bloody pulp. He couldn't walk at all. Several of his ribs had been cracked. They'd pulled out most of his teeth and all his finger- and toenails.

This last trip to the torture room had been the worst, though. He almost cried aloud as he thought of it. They'd heated several irons until they glowed cherry-red. Then they'd burned him all over, a little here, a little there. Finally they'd taken one of the irons and pushed it into his right eye. His eye!

The pain had been so incredible, he'd bitten right through his own lip with the teeth he still had, trying to hold back his screams. He shuddered. His eye. Syr had said they'd soon come for the other. She'd laughed. Then she told him they were sharpening their knifes. The castration was coming, she'd cackled, taking her own flint knife out and running it lovingly over his sex organs. She cut him ever so slightly, just enough to make a tiny line of blood well up and run down his legs.

How long had he been here? It seemed like forever. They'd given him water, but no food. How long would it take him to starve to death? Too long, he thought grimly. Syr will kill me long before then.

Is anyone coming? he wondered without any real hope. Was it even possible for anyone to come? He knew now that the cavern was indeed beneath the Disir's hall in Folkvang. The entrance was in Vor's quarters. A thing guarded it, a thing he couldn't quite manage to look at. He knew a simple glance at it would drive him raving mad. It was something out of the dark part of an evil mind, a minion of Svarthofdi called by magic to keep the entrance to the cave safe. There were others roaming the cave as well, he realized. They were far more effective than any force of Valkyrja could ever be. He didn't think Harbard, Rota, and all the foresters combined would have a hope against the creatures.

He let a sigh escape his lips. There was no hope, then. He'd never see Rota or Harbard or any of the others again. He'd never run in the forest, the wind whipping the tops of the trees, the dense green filling his heart and mind. He would die here. Alone. In great anguish.

With my last breath, he decided, I'll spit in Syr's face.

• • •

Hild looked frightened. "I tell you, the dead fight with them! Men we've killed before. And wolves and forest cats. I've seen it myself. We're not just fighting men anymore. We're fighting magic!"

Vor and Syr exchanged a glance. "Freyja," Syr suggested. Vor nodded. "Indeed, sister," she said, "little Freyja is using her Seidar-magic. Raising the dead, calling the beasts."

"Two can play that game," Syr replied.

"But is it a game we want to play? Or one we can afford to play? I wonder, sister, I wonder."

"But the Valkyrja—" Hild began to protest.

Vor cut her short. "The whole thing is a diversion. They seek to draw us out, to take our attention from Folkvang and Yngvi. They hope to stall us, to create the time they need to mount a rescue attempt." She paused and looked off into space, a slight smile curving her thin lips. "Yes, yes, a rescue attempt. Who will be in it, I wonder? Harbard for sure. Rota. Perhaps even Freyja. Yes."

Vor's eyes refocused on Hild. "Send out more troops to reinforce your outposts. Use troops quartered in or near the city. Your Valkyrja can fight the dead. Simply kill them again. And forest cats and wolves die as easily as men."

Hild stared at Vor in disbelief. "Send more out from the groups in and around the city? But . . . but that will mean stripping Folkvang of its defenses. The foresters might slip past us and attack. They might—" She stopped and gaped at Vor's vicious smile.

"Just so, Hild. Just so. They might launch a rescue mission. Harbard, Rota, and Freyja might come to save Yngvi."

Vor turned to Syr. "Vanadis, it is time for the double ceremony. We must geld Yngvi and then offer him to Svarthofdi."

Syr rubbed her hands together with glee, then pulled her flint knife from its hiding place in her dark robes. "Yes, yes! It's high time for the knife to drink Yngvi's blood and take his manhood. I'll cut it from him myself and stuff it in his mouth!

"And then I will cut his heart out and offer it to the goddess!"

Hild had turned pale, her eye large with fear. Vor turned to her and smiled slightly. "Let it be known, Hild, that you have heard this. Let the word get out that in two days we will geld and sacrifice Yngvi. Be sure it reaches Freyja.''

They carried Yngvi to a new chamber, one he had never seen before. As he lay on a low pallet, two women entered and took off his old, bloodied, torn clothing and dressed him in a white robe. He was too weak to struggle, and in any case he was saving his energy in case he might need it for . . . He almost laughed. Still hoping for a chance to escape, eh? he asked himself. Damn right, he replied. Escape or die quickly. It came to much the same.

When he was dressed, four Valkyrja came for him. They tied him to a narrow, black litter and carried him down a long corridor to a small empty room. There he lay on the floor for perhaps half an hour.

Suddenly he heard a strange grinding-scraping noise. He turned his head toward the sound and watched with astonishment as a whole section of the floor of the room rose up and back to reveal an opening and steps leading downward.

Vor and Syr came up the steps, accompanied by two hideous creatures that made Yngvi's skin crawl and stomach turn. He closed his eye and forced his face still so the two Disir couldn't see his fear. He felt the two ends of his litter being lifted. In another moment he was being carried down the stairs into a damp, cold passageway. The two Disir had begun to chant softly.

In a short time he felt himself being lowered to the ground. He opened his eye slightly and found himself in a large cavern, lit by numerous torches stuck in slots around the walls. The place had a smell of incredible antiquity to it. He shuddered. It was as ancient as the Vanir themselves.

He turned his head slightly. There were four of them looking down at him from the left. They had their cowls up and pulled forward, so he couldn't see their faces. He was sure one was Syr and another Vor. Who were the other two? Gna and Syn? Perhaps Hlin or Eir?

Beyond the four he saw something that made his heart stop beating for a moment. It was a large stone, roughly squarish in shape. There were iron rings fixed in its sides and chains attached to the rings. The top of the stone was stained a hideous blackish red.

The four lifted him from the litter and carried him effortlessly to the stone. They were all chanting softly under their breaths. They stretched him out, then quickly fastened the chains around his arms and legs.

They stepped back then, as if viewing their handiwork. The chanting grew louder and began to echo strangely off the stone walls, making it sound as if there were hundreds joining in. The volume grew and grew until it roared and thundered around him, battering at his mind and stupefying him.

Suddenly all four drew flint knives from their dark robes. They approached slowly, circling the stone, the chant ringing out with ever greater volume. So loud was it that it thickened and almost took solid shape. It permeated the very stone of the cavern and made everything shake and tremble with its might. Yngvi felt something strange growing within the space of the cavern. It was slowly being filled with a presence, a being that seemed to be forming from the solidity of the chant itself.

Each of the four leaned over him and stabbed him gently in an arm or a leg with their flint knives. The blood welled up and they smeared their blades in it. Then, as they continued to circle and chant, they licked the knife blades clean.

Yngvi quailed. He could feel something there in the cavern, something other than the four Disir and himself. It was vast and dark and utterly evil. It watched him hungrily. His mind gibbered with fear and he clung desperately to his sanity.

One of the Disir stepped up and with her knife cut away the front of the white robe. His whole body was exposed. The other three Disir moved to the foot of the stone. One took hold of each leg and a third placed herself so she could reach his manhood.

The chant turned into a wild howl, a raging storm of fury and anger, a horrible shrieking, screaming madness. Suddenly it stopped and Yngvi heard the dark presence in the cavern snicker with an evil so deep it froze his soul. The knife rose up and slowly began to descend.

Without warning, a terrific explosion literally knocked the four Disir over. It came from the side of the cavern where they had entered. Yngvi turned his head and looked.

Harbard and Rota stood there, covered with strange green ichor and good red blood. The blood was clearly their own. Harbard was holding his side and wincing in pain. Red oozed between his fingers. Rota was dripping blood from several places, the worst a vicious slash on her right thigh.

"Damn," Harbard said, "those things die hard! But they die!" The forester limped a step forward and stopped, his eyes going wide as he looked beyond Yngvi. Rota's hand went to her mouth in horror. She stepped back slightly.

Syr threw back the cowl of her robe and cackled with evil glee. "Yes! You have come into the presence of the Dark One! Quail and quake, little worms, for soon you shall join your friend on this altar! Svarthofdi shall have three!"

Frey appeared behind Harbard and Rota. His sword was also bloody, though he himself was unscathed. Freyja followed on his heels. She was holding Hnoss and smiling slightly. "Ah, yes, Svarthofdi. I know her, too, Syr. And I think it remains to be seen who will be the sacrifice given to her today."

Vor threw back her cowl and smiled smugly at Freyja. "You came, even as I knew you would. And even brought your brother. Loyal to your friends. Do you really think, Freyja, that you are a match for both Syr and myself? You have the Seidar-magic, true, and you have it very strongly. But you lack experience, and you are only one."

"Only one?" Hnoss said, turning her tiny head to gaze at Vor. "Once again, Vor, you show that great age does not necessarily give one great wisdom."

Vor looked stunned. "Hnoss! But . . . but . . . you are a baby, a mere—"

Hnoss laughed. "A baby, yes. A mere baby, no. You created me, Vor, don't you remember? I'm Od's daughter. When Freyja went searching for her husband, I went with her. I, too, came into Svarthofdi's presence and heard her whispers. You caused it all to happen, Vor, you and Syr. Now you must pay the price."

With a curse, Vor raised her hands and pointed them at Freyja and Hnoss. A flash blinded them all. When it died away, Freyja and Hnoss were still there. Freyja spoke two words softly into the air. A dark cloud formed and leapt on Vor and Syr, who had drawn together the better to unite their power. There was another flash and the cloud disappeared.

Freyja moved forward now, motioning to Harbard and Rota. "Free him," she muttered quickly, "while I keep them occupied.'' The two went to the stone and began to undo Yngvi.

Syr howled insanely when she saw what they were doing. She hurled her knife at Harbard. It struck him him in the shoulder and he went down with a grunt. He came up on one knee and threw his ax. It missed Syr and struck one of the other two Disir. She screamed and fell to the floor. Harbard pulled the knife free and threw it to the floor, shattering the flint blade. Then he rose and went to Yngvi.

Vor and Freyja were screaming spells at each other and the air was heavy with the smell of sulfur and rotten flesh. Things kept appearing and disappearing. Monsters met and clashed briefly, only to be replaced by others. Syr clung to Vor, her eyes wide with hatred. Hnoss laughed gaily. Frey covered his face with his hands, his sword falling to the floor.

Rota and Harbard dragged Yngvi from the stone and back to the entrance of the cavern. Vor cried out in a great voice, ''STOP! YOU TAKE THE CONSECRATED OFFERING OF SVARTHOFDI! STOP OR INCUR THE UNDYING WRATH OF THE GODDESS!'' The two paused, stunned, and stared in astonishment as the darkness that had all this time lurked behind the stone took more definite shape and began to move forward. A hideous face, too disgusting and fearsome for thought, leered at them from the center of the blackness.

Freyja drew herself up and confronted the goddess. ''Svarthofdi!'' she cried. ''You wish an offering? Then I give you one! I give you Syr!'' She spun toward the Disir and pointed her fingers at the woman. Syr shrieked and stumbled back, toward the darkness. She screamed to Vor and tried to regain her balance, but it was as if a giant hand were pushing her backward. Vor tried to move toward Syr, but Hnoss fixed her with fiery eyes which held her as if in a vise.

Step by step Syr was forced back, back toward the pulsating, snickering darkness. She screamed and struggled, fighting with every ounce of strength she possessed. The sweat stood out on Freyja's forehead as she concentrated all her power against Syr. Her face was twisted with the strain. Vor and Hnoss remained locked in immobility.

One step and then another. Syr was shrieking and crying, pleading and wailing. Another step. Suddenly the blackness moved forward and enveloped her. Her scream shattered the

air, driving them all to their knees. Freyja almost collapsed.
Hnoss whimpered and passed out. Vor fell as if dead, crashing to the floor. The other Disir crumpled into a shapeless
heap.

Frey stumbled to his feet and picked up his sword. Harbard
and Rota who had been farthest from the magic collision, rose
groggily. Rota moved as if to help Freyja, but the Vanadis
motioned her away. "Get Yngvi out of here," she mumbled
weakly. She was looking down at Hnoss, who lay limp in her
arms. "They've done something to Hnoss. Something's happened to my baby!" She rose to her feet and screamed at the
still form of Vor, "What have you done to my baby!!??"
There was no answer, no movement.

Harbard grabbed Yngvi under the arms and began to drag
him out of the cavern. Rota went to Freyja and touched her
shoulder. The Vanadis turned and looked at Rota without
seeing her. Her eyes were stunned and confused. "They've
done something to my baby," she murmured to Rota. Rota
nodded and patted her on the shoulder. "Come now, Freyja,"
she said gently, her voice catching slightly. "Come. You and
Hnoss need rest, that's all. What you did was so hard. You
just need to rest and everything will be all right."

Freyja's eyes lit up. "Yes. Rest. So tired. Hnoss so tired.
Rest. Yes." She moved forward, meekly following Rota. The
Valkyrja led the way, tears pouring down her face. Frey
stumbled along, bring up the rear, constantly casting worried
glances over his shoulder.

DARK EMPIRE

VI

THE darkness was so intense that it was all but impossible to make out the three cloaked and hooded figures that huddled around the arcane symbols cut into the surface of the rock. The wind swirled past them, moaning with voiceless anguish. Thick, unnatural clouds boiled sullenly a few yards over their heads, shuttering the sky. The barren crag on which they perched fell into emptiness on all sides.

One of them opened glowing eyes and gazed at the other two. "You have seen," came the low murmur from its lips. The other two pairs of eyes opened, shining redly in the gloom. "Yesss," came the soft reply of one. "We have seen," rumbled the other from deep in its throat.

"And do you agree?"

There was a long pause, filled only with the sounds of the night. Finally the deep-voiced one signed and said, "It will be more difficult than you imagine. He is stronger than we thought."

"Yes," responded the first voice. "Stronger. And getting more so every day. Those who answered to the one he defeated now come to his beck and call. They are not the most dangerous denizens of the Kur, but they count, they count. We must stop him before he gains more allies and amasses too much power."

"And yet," the second voice mused, "you are far more powerful and dangerous than he. It would be much to your advantage to have us ally ourselves with you against him. With his minions added to your own, with his armies marching under your banners, you would be almost invincible."

Glaring eyes met and clashed. "Touch the pattern. Feel its texture. See if I lie." The first voice was tense with challenge.

"Ah," came the quiet response, followed by a mirthless chuckle. "Ah, yes, but then, there are many ways to hide a lie, and one of the best is to mask it with truth. I do not trust your sudden honesty. We have sparred too often in the past to become instant allies." The voice paused for a brief moment and then continued thoughtfully. "And yet I felt the same the moment I met him. There is an abyss within him that calls for endless filling. He would swallow the universe if he could."

"Will you join with me, then?"

The soft chuckle came again. "Slowly, slowly. We have more night left. And our shielding is such that even were it broad daylight, none would see us here in this whirl of darkness. How many of the others have you contacted?"

"None. I trust the others even less than I trust you."

The deep-voiced one laughed. "A back-handed compliment at best! What of the one that always stays home in his southern fortress! Surely he and his damned Igigi are dependable. Will he keep out of it if it comes to conflict?"

"He stayed out of the original duel."

"But then backed him in the Anunnaki. If he were to take his side again . . ." He left the words hanging.

"Open confrontation is not the way," the first voice said with calm assurance. "It would make him wary and cause him to put up defenses we might not be able to breach without massing a great deal of force. No, I don't want to alert him. My plan is more subtle than that."

"I would expect no less from you," the soft voice said sarcastically. "Pray, how do you intend to snare the Black One so he will never realize he is trapped?"

"Surround him with barriers and frustrations. Block his every move. Bind those he would make his own. Snatch away as many of his current allies as possible."

"Isolate him," came a deep, musing voice from the darkness.

"Yes. And then slowly, slowly bleed away his power."

"It just might work," agreed the soft voice. "How would you begin?"

"We three must place restraints on as many demons as possible, even ones we have no use for, to keep them from his service. He is actively recruiting, using that damned book he found in the ruins of Badtabira."

"Ah, yes. The *Utukki Limnuti*. Enmeenlu's precious little tome. Seven sevens of demons. Yes, it would be wise to bind as many of them to ourselves as possible. If he were to command them all . . . well . . . hmmm." The soft voice trickled out until it was lost in the rushing of the wind.

"Are you both with me, then?" asked the first voice.

"I suppose so," came a rumble from the night.

"For the moment," said the other voice, "I see no harm in binding a few more demons to my will. It will take some effort, but not so much as to tire me and make me vulnerable to any subplots you may have in mind. And since we are all gaining new allies in the process, we should be able to maintain a balance of force. Yes, I will go along for the moment."

The sound of the wind suddenly rose to a shriek and the night swirled, blackness winding around blackness in two whirlpools of stygian emptiness. In a moment only one figure remained on the crag, gazing silently into the void.

It raised a clenched fist and shook it angrily at the sky. Its eyes glowed redly as if lit from within by flames of blood. "So," it hissed at the night, "it begins. Our final battle, Nergal. I have hated you ever since you tried to snatch Dumuzi from me. I have waited ever since then, ever since the fall of the First Dark Empire, to smash you. Somehow you escaped the destruction at Cuthah when I led the slaughter of your priests. I used too much of my own strength then, burned myself out. For eons I have been too weak to confront you. I have stood by and watched helplessly while you grew again in power, knowing you would come once more for Dumuzi when you were strong enough.

"But I have not been idle. Oh, no! I have gathered my strength, adding to it bit by bit, until I am once more a mighty sorceress. And all the time I have waited, patient as a spider, waited for an opening.

"Now at last I have a way to reach you, to strike directly at you! Your greed for power, your foolish desire to be worshipped once more in Muspellheim, has pulled you forth from the fastness of Aralu. You have opened a portal to Black Surt, that he may serve you and once again establish a priesthood to foul your altar with blood and sacrifice. Yes, Nergal, your precious servant will provide the opening I need. And through that opening I will pour all the power of the Sons of Muspell!

"Oh, yes! I will smash Surt! But only so that I may smash you forever!"

The slender man slammed the door so hard the walls of the room shook. The giant black warrior, resplendent in a gold chased corselet and matching greaves, looked up from the dagger he was carefully sharpening and grunted. "Huh. The Patesi seems out of sorts today. Something his royal evilness ate for breakfast? Or perhaps a small demon thumbed its nose at him?"

Surt threw himself down on a divan in the corner of the room and scowled darkly at Jormungand. "Very humorous, Serpent. But in this case jocularity is the improper response."

Jormungand chuckled. "That's the trouble with you wizards. No sense of humor. Jocularity is *always* the proper response. Take my situation, for example. General of the armies of Borsippa and Maqam Nifl." He chuckled again, mirthlessly this time. "Armies! Ha! Yes, jocularity is the only possible response. One can only laugh at the absurd notion of calling that ragtag collection of inept fools an army." He whipped his hand back and up, then brought it swiftly forward, flinging the dagger through the air. With a thud, it sank several inches into the heavy wooden door of the room.

The giant warrior leapt to his feet and stamped across the room to jerk the blade from the wood. He spun around and glared at Surt, the dagger pointing directly at the slender man's heart. The Black One lounged casually back and returned Jormungand's stare. "I gather Adad was not much of a soldier?"

Jormungand gaped at him for a second, then burst into laughter. He threw his dagger onto a chair and wiped his eyes with the sleeve of the soft shirt he wore beneath his corselet. "I take it back. You do have a sense of humor. Ah, yes, one might well say Adad wasn't much of a soldier. The man was an ass when it came to military matters. Bah! The whole army is a mess! Shot through with rottenness, incompetency, and corruption. Yesterday I had ten men hung, five for gross dereliction of duty and five for selling supplies on the black market. Today I'll probably have to hang ten more. Damn! At this rate there won't be an army in a few months."

Surt looked at Jormungand solemnly. "How long before they are ready to fight, faithful Serpent?"

"Fight?" the giant warrior bellowed. "How long before they're ready to fight? Damn Nergal's balls! They aren't ready to drill, much less ready to fight!" He sat down, suddenly thoughtful at the tone of Surt's voice and the look on his face. "Something's up. It always is when you call me faithful Serpent. Maybe you'd better tell me."

The slender man gazed thoughtfully at the warrior for a few moments. Then he sighed and nodded. "Yes, I suppose that would be best." He shifted his position on the divan, putting his feet firmly on the floor and leaning forward intently. He stared into space for a while, then began to speak softly but surely.

"Things have not gone as smoothly since defeating Adad as I had hoped and assumed they would. The man, as you have surmised, allowed his kingdom to run to ruin. He squandered resources, lost control of many of his allies, allowed others to do as they willed, oppressed the people, failed to develop trade, allowed corruption to creep in at every level . . . in general, made a mess of things.

"I have been so busy trying to straighten matters out that I have had little time to engage in magic, even to bind his demons to my bidding. Some have slipped away, I fear, and others are at the point of rebellion. My own allies are restless because of my lack of attention." Surt sighed and shook his head. "No, it has not been as simple as I had thought.

"But just yesterday I decided it was time to begin again, to call up my allies and begin to assert my power in the Kur. Affairs of state are almost under control. I must concentrate more on magic to both defend what we have and build the resources to gain more.

"So last night I went to my tower, opened the *Utukki Limnuti*, and began to summon demons. My intention was to assert my power over them and bind them as allies." He fell silent for a few moments, his eyes thoughtful and filled with dark secrets.

Jormungand felt the hair on the back of his neck rise. "What . . . has something happened?" he hissed in his soft, silibant voice.

Surt's eyes focused on his, a grim expression settling over his face. "Would that something had. I called on three different demons, Serpent. One that Adad had relations with, one I had called on occasionally in the past, and one new one."

"And?" queried Jormungand.

"Nothing," the slender wizard whispered tensely. "Nothing. They would not come."

The giant warrior sat and stared at his master in stunned disbelief. "They . . . they would not . . . come? But how can that be? You have the *Utukki Limnuti*. You—"

Surt cut him short with a harsh gesture. "They would not come," he growled, his voice deep in his throat. He stood and began to pace back and forth. "They were blocked, bound to someone else. I could not even reach them."

Jormungand felt a sinking sensation in the pit of his stomach. "Bound to someone else? Who . . . ?" The question hung in the air.

"Yes," Surt finally answered, whirling to face the warrior, "who indeed? I wondered the same thing. Something is obviously going on."

"The other Sons—" Jormungand began.

"The other Sons," Surt confirmed. "Yes. The other members of the Anunnaki—Enki, Enlil, An, Marduk, Nannar, perhaps even Utu. Any one of them or even all of them could be behind this."

"But what does it mean? What's the purpose?"

"Purpose? Don't be naive, Serpent. They fear my potential power. They seek to limit me, to isolate me, to weaken and then destroy me. They know quite well the status of Adad's kingdom, they are aware of every weakness, every fault. I am convinced they have been exploiting every opportunity to confound us in our attempt to pull things together. And while we have been getting organized, they have been weaving a barrier of magic around me, stealing my allies, binding demons so I can't call on them, hedging me in on every side. When they think I am weak enough, they will strike."

Surt paused and met Jormungand's eyes. "They would fling us both into the Kur, loyal Serpent. Send us reeling to Tiamat's cave at the edge of Apsu, the Dreadful Abyss, for her and her brood to gnaw for all eternity. We would be lucky to be hung on a stake before Ereshkigal's throne in Aralu."

Jormungand shivered, then straightened, his eyes hard. "I've experienced the stake in Ereshkigal's palace once and have no intention of hanging there again. I've fought Tiamat once, right at the edge of Apsu, and beaten the dragon bitch. I won't return in defeat.

"I have no magic, Surt, other then the strength and skill of my arms. The army will be ready very swiftly," he declared grimly. "I'll smash it into shape. If they come against us as men, they'll have a hard time of it."

"Good." Surt smiled thinly. "That will protect against one threat. But the real danger comes from another place. And the crucial question is who is behind all this. I am convinced it is a carefully laid and managed attack. More than one of the Sons may be involved, but it seems likely only one is in control. Who, dammit, who?"

"Can't you use magic to find out?"

"I am. Just before I came here I sent out Zu, the storm bird with the head of a lion. Zu, hideous, dangerous Zu. How glad I am now that I never let my power over the monster lapse for even a moment! Zu is difficult to control under the best of circumstances and—" Surt stopped speaking and jerked erect, his eyes suddenly going blank. In an instant he turned and headed for the door. As he reached it he looked back over his shoulder at Jormungand, his eyes bright once again. "Zu has returned. Come. Perhaps we will find something out now?"

As the demon disappeared with a flash of sulfurous flame, Surt turned and fixed Jormungand with deeply troubled eyes. "Damn," he muttered softly. "Damn, damn, damn, damn. Innina, Enki, and Marduk! And the entire plot is that bitch's idea!" He began to pace back and forth in the narrow room at the top of the tallest tower of his palace. The room was filled with strange items and old books, the exotic paraphernalia of wizardry. In several cages against one wall poisonous lizards and snakes hissed and writhed, their eyes gleaming with unnatural intelligence and malevolence. The floor was covered with multicolored geometric figures inscribed with words in obscure and long-dead languages. Jormungand stood still, careful to touch nothing and let nothing touch him. The room was filled with nameless menace, and it made him nervous to be there.

"They've blocked me," Surt muttered, "bound me, built walls around me! Damn them! Why? Why does Innina hate me so? Marduk I can understand. He voted against me in the Anunnaki. Enki was hostile from the very moment I entered the Hall of Duku. He wanted to place his flunky Mummu on Adad's throne. But why Innina? I've done nothing to threaten her.

"Two problems. I must break out of this prison they've built. Otherwise they'll slowly squeeze me to death. Second, I must strike back. Strike at Innina, Enki, Marduk. But how? I'm weaker than any of them. There's got to be a way. Got to be a way." He slumped down into a chair shoved into one corner of the room, and sat with his chin in his hands, gazing thoughtfully into the empty air. Jormungand stood warily at attention and watched him.

Innina smiled thinly at Enki. "He knows."

"Ah," Enki replied. "He knows. Rather sooner than you expected, I take it."

She shrugged. "The man is a beginner, but hardly a fool. He has built very adequate defenses in a short time. We won't be able to take anything more from him by magic, I think."

"So Marduk will move?"

"Marduk *is* a fool. He refuses to stage the kind of action that would crush Surt at one blow. Instead, he says he'll 'probe' the defenses of the Black One to 'test' the mettle of his general, that giant Jormungand."

"Perhaps not as foolish as you might think. Marduk is nothing if not a daring and resourceful soldier. I trust his judgment in matters military. He knows his business. Probing might be wisest. If Surt's general fails the test, why then, Marduk's forces will be in Maqam Nifl long before you will be able to breach the Black One's magical defenses. But if Jormungand is as good as he appears to be, it would be foolhardy to commit our forces to combat. A major defeat would be disastrous. Enlil would probably come in on Surt's side. And that would mean Nannar too. Perhaps even Utu. No, the cautious method is best. When does he strike?"

"Soon. His men are on the way."

"Then we shall see."

"The other parties were feints, sir, just as you suspected. The main body's coming through the top of the pass right about now. Must be near a hundred of them."

The giant black warrior grinned wolfishly and rubbed his hands together with evident pleasure. "Good, good. Could you make out whose device they wear?"

"None that I could see. Begging your pardon, sir, but

raiding parties like these seldom wear identification, if you catch my meaning, sir.''

Jormungand nodded. ''Then did you recognize anyone?''

The scout cocked his head to one side in concentration. ''Seems to me a couple of faces were familiar. One big fellow in particular. Seem to remember seeing him before, though I can't quite place him.'' He turned his head to the other side and gave a slight, evil grin. ''If we catch one of them alive, sir, I'm sure we can make him share information with us.''

Jormungand laughed quietly. ''No doubt we can make him sing, dance, and do back flips. See we get a few to play with.'' The scout grinned again, saluted, and slunk away. The giant warrior watched him go with pleasure. If I had an army of fellows like that, I'd feel a lot more comfortable right now, he thought. He turned to the officers, who stood anxiously around him. His eye wandered over them contemptuously. Pathetic! Yet the best he had. Well, they wouldn't last long, most of them. He was requiring them to lead their troops in battle. Those that fought well and were lucky (two critical characteristics for a good soldier) would survive and eventually become real officers. The rest would die. In every platoon he had at least one good man to stay close to the officers and watch them. If they yielded or turned coward, a swift knife between the ribs would end their careers.

''Are the men in position?'' he asked softly, his voice hissing gently in the night. They nodded nervously. ''Then join your troops and be ready for the signal. Remember, there will be a peal of demonic laughter loud enough to shake the hills. When you hear it, attack, and don't stop until you've killed every enemy within reach of your swords.''

They left, melting into the darkness. Jormungand turned and walked back to a group of some ten soldiers dressed in simple black armor like his own. The device on their breastplates was that of Nergal, the Lord of Hosts, King of Aralu. It was the symbol Surt had adopted as his own as Patesi of Borsippa and Maqam Nifl. He looked them over with satisfaction. The best of the lot. The Elite Guard. Only ten now. Someday a hundred. Right now, man for man, they were probably worth a hundred of the other wretches that made up his army. These were fighters, natural-born killers who reveled in the fury and bloodshed of war.

Jormungand signaled, and they gathered around him. "We go down into the valley. Alone. We will take up our post as if we were ordinary border guards. The raiders won't know the difference until they attack."

Low rumbles of grim laughter came from their hard mouths and one muttered, "They'll know better real quick then."

The giant warrior nodded. "Aye. Be efficient. No fancy stuff. Kill quickly and cleanly. And fight like you had your backs to the River Huber, because you do. It'll be a few minutes before the rest arrive, and until they do, it's us against a hundred of them."

"Not bad odds," one of the soldiers quipped. The others chuckled.

Jormungand smiled. "Remember, the Black One has fixed my sword with a spell so that the ninth time it is struck, it will laugh like one of the demons from the Kur. That is the signal for the others. We'll have them surrounded, but we'll be in the middle with them."

"Just means we can get more killing done," one of them responded. The other muttered agreement.

"All right," Jormungand said. "Let's go."

"Guard post. About ten men, mostly sitting around a fire and napping. Three of them were casting bones."

Enkidu smiled. So, Marduk's worries were for naught. This Jormungand wasn't such a great general after all. Only three guards at the top of the pass, easily killed. Only ten at the bottom. Most of the rest of Surt's forces were probably off chasing the groups that had struck earlier to the south. Good. He would kill these ten, then raid swiftly to the east, burn a town or two before Jormungand even knew he was in the country. If Marduk had let me bring more of the army, I could have smashed right through to Maqam Nifl and ended the whole farce in a few days, he thought. Oh, well, at least we have learned that Surt is every bit as vulnerable militarily as I thought he was. Marduk won't need great magic to smash the upstart. He can do it with cold metal instead. He motioned his men forward.

In a few minutes they crested a small rise and saw the guard post below them, an island of dim light in the blackness of the night. Enkidu halted and watched for a few moments to confirm what the scouts had told him. Yes. He counted the men. Three were still casting bones and arguing over the throws. Two were cooking something in a pot over the fire. The other three he could see were sprawled out on the ground at the edge of the firelight, dozing. There might be one or two more in the hut. Eleven at the most. With a grin of pleasure, he drew his sword and motioned his men forward to the kill.

Jormungand saw them coming through the night as soon as they moved over the ridge. He muttered to the others beneath his breath from where he lay outside the firelight, sprawled as if in sleep. He rolled slightly more on his side to free his sword, and casually moved his hand to rest on the pommel. He could hear them now, hear the rustle of their feet on the gravelly soil of the mountain pass. Twenty more steps. Now ten. Now . . .

With a cry, the raiders rushed forward, sure their surprise was complete. From the guard house three arrows flew and found marks in the chests of three raiders. Instantly three more winged their way into flesh. The sleeping guards leapt up, anything but sleepy and confused, their swords in their hands, swiftly finding arms and necks to hack and slash. The men playing at bones already had their weapons out, laying on the ground beside them. One grabbed a knife in each hand, and each one sped to find a throat as he stood with a sudden motion. The cooks leapt over the empty pot and began slashing with unexpected fury.

The raiders were stunned and disorganized for a moment. A giant black warrior strode into their midst, roaring and cursing, his huge sword ripping men apart, sending arms, legs, and heads flying in gory showers through the dark. But the raiders were professionals and regained their equilibrium quickly. With a cry of anger, they closed on the eleven.

Suddenly the very air was shattered with the roar of mighty laughter, a burst of demonic hilarity so tremendous that it deafened every ear and drove several men to their knees. Everyone, raiders and defenders alike, was stunned into immobility for a moment. Then they fell on each other once more, their fury greater than ever.

Jormungand laughed with pleasure. This was work he could understand! The ring of metal on metal, the scream of a dying man, the groans of the wounded, the cries of victory and defeat! Damn all wizardry. This was life!

He looked up and saw a face he recognized. Enkidu! Marduk's chief general and close personal friend. A sudden idea blossomed in Jormungand's mind. With a roar, he leapt toward Enkidu, calling out the man's name, challenging him to battle. Enkidu turned and recognized him. With a cry of rage, he surged to meet the black giant.

They came together with a clash of swords that dimmed the sounds around them and forced those nearby to flinch back and give them room to fight. Enkidu was a mighty warrior, Jormungand knew, a man who had been raised in the wilds like an animal until Marduk had lured him into Muspell and become his friend. Enkidu had run with the desert gazelle and had caught and crushed with his bare hands the giant lions that stalk the wastelands of the west. It was rumored he and Marduk had once fought the demon Humbaba, a giant with a beard of human entrails, and that he had cut off the monster's head.

Enkidu swept his blade back and forth in a blur of razor-sharp death. Jormungand dodged and countered, his massive muscles moving smoothly beneath his black skin. Sparks flew from the clashing of their weapons, and the ringing of the metal set up a terrific din. Both men were strong and experienced warriors. Next to the Aesir Borr, Jormungand knew this was the greatest fighter he had ever encountered. It would be great glory to kill this man.

Yet that was not what the Serpent intended. Dead, Enkidu was just another enemy out of the way. But alive . . .

From the corner of his eye Jormungand could see that the character of the battle around him was changing. Ah, he thought, the rest have come. Marduk's men are surrounded, outnumbered, their retreat cut off. It's only a matter of time until . . .

Enkidu's blade slipped past his guard and slashed him on the upper shoulder. Best pay attention to my own battle, the black warrior realized. He circled slightly to his left. How to get inside the man's guard? he wondered. The battle is easier for him. He simply has to kill me. But I want him alive and unhurt, so I have a much harder task.

He blocked a mighty slash at his head, sidestepped quickly and ripped the flesh on Enkidu's forearm. That should slow him down a bit, he thought, make him a little less aggressive.

Jormungand could see the doubt in his opponent's eyes. The man was no longer so sure of his victory.

But how to take him alive? How to get close enough to grab him? By the balls of Nergal, Jormungand cursed silently, killing the bastard would be far easier than capturing him.

A plan began to form in his mind. It was insanely risky but he could see no other way. He decided. Enkidu slammed Jormungand's sword with a mighty blow and it flew from his grip. With a roar of triumph, Marduk's general raised his sword over his head to deliver the death blow that would cleave the Serpent in two.

Before he could swing his sword downward, however, the giant warrior flew at him and grabbed him around the throat. The impact of his charge knocked Enkidu over backward, and the warrior hit the ground with a stunning crash, Jormungand on top. The Serpent loosened his grip on the other man's throat just enough to let the breath out, then he tightened it more firmly than ever. Enkidu let go of his sword and wrapped his arms around Jormungand. He had crushed lions. Now he would crush a serpent.

The two men rolled silently on the ground, straining with every muscle in their bodies. Enkidu could feel himself losing strength as his lungs tried to draw in badly needed air. His head reeled and the night turned red and filled with rushing noise. Jormungand clung on for dear life as the other man's grip tightened. He could feel his ribs bending and beginning to give. Soon they would snap and pierce his lungs. He would die. The night turned red for him as well, and he thought he could hear the sound of the River Huber once again.

In desperation the black giant tightened his grip with the last bit of strength he possessed. It was his last hope, his final gamble. He knew his ribs were about to shatter.

Suddenly, unexpectedly, he was laying on top of a limp mound of flesh. His head reeling, he staggered to his feet, drawing in painful gulps of air. His chest and sides hurt abominably. He looked down. Enkidu lay there, his face contorted, his eyes rolled up and bugging out, his tongue lolling from his mouth. With a groan, Jormungand knelt next to him and grabbed his wrist. There was still a pulse, but it was very weak.

Quickly he rolled the man over, pulled a strong strap from his belt and bound Enkidu's wrists behind him. Then he

bound the man's ankles with a second strap. He tested the
bonds. Satisfied they would hold, he bent to place his mouth
over his captive's. Slowly, steadily, he breathed out, filling
the other's lungs with life-giving air, forcing it past the closed
throat. After a few moments he felt the pulse again. Good.
Stronger. Enkidu would live. At least he would until Surt got
hold of him. Then only the Black One and Nergal knew what
his fate would be.

For an instant Jormungand pitied the man. Then he shrugged
and looked around to see how the battle was going. It was all
but over. His elite guard, every one bearing several wounds,
but not one of them missing, stood around him in a circle,
informally guarding their leader. He nodded at them and they
grinned back.

Jormungand was unable to control himself. His face split
with a grin that matched their own and he laughed out loud.

For twelve days Surt wove spells around the ever-weakening
body of Enkidu. Fever and sickness wracked the semicon-
scious warrior. At times he cried out to Marduk, pleading
with his lord and friend to come and save him. He wept
bitterly because he was to die in shame, not in battle as befit a
mighty warrior. Enkidu cursed the day he had left the wilderness and entered the city of Muspell.

Every day Jormungand came and watched for a while. As
Enkidu became weaker, the general of the armies of Borsippa
and Maqam Nifl became increasingly restless. On the twelfth
day he could no longer hold his peace. "By Neti's talons,
Surt, quit playing with him! Kill him and get it over with!"

The Patesi looked up in surprise at his servant. "Playing
with him? That's hardly what I'm doing, loyal Serpent. Enkidu
is no ordinary man, you know. He was born and raised in the
wilds by animals, and he has the strength and endurance of
the beast. What's more, Marduk has protected him with many
spells. No, I'm hardly playing with him. Quite the contrary.
I'm having a very difficult time of dealing with him. But it's
almost over, Serpent, it's almost over."

With that Surt turned back to Enkidu, who lay awake now,
gazing at him with feverish, fear-filled eyes. Surt spread his
arms wide and began to chant. "I have draped your body
with clean clothes. Let the Guardians come against you like
an enemy. I have anointed you with the beaker's sweet oil. Let

them smell it and crowd around you. I have thrown your throw-stick into the nether world. Let those whom it struck surround you. I place your staff in your hand. Let the shades flutter all about you. I have tied fine sandals on your feet. You will raise a cry in the nether world. You have kissed the wife you love. You have struck the wife you hate. You have kissed the child you love. You have struck the child you hate. Let the cry of the nether world hold you fast. Let the cry for her who is sleeping, for the mother of Ninazu, whose holy body no garment covers, whose holy breast no veil drapes, rise up and hold you fast.''

As Surt completed the chant, Enkidu gave a great cry and fell back, his eyes rolling up into his head, his tongue lolling out of his slack mouth. He lay, limp and lifeless. Surt went to him and took his wrist in his hand. He felt for a pulse, considered, and then finally nodded in satisfaction. ''Excellent, most excellent,'' he said softly.

He stepped back and gazed at Enkidu's still body. ''Not even Enlil could bring you back now,'' he murmured. ''But Marduk will try, the fool. So we will send you to him to distract him. And then there will only be two to contend with.'' He waved his arms in a strange pattern, his fingers weaving obscene words in the air while he muttered the twisted syllables beneath his breath. Two minor demons appeared suddenly. ''Take this offal to the door of Marduk's palace in Muspell and dump it there.'' They snarled compliance, and suddenly Surt stood alone inside the magic circle. Weary now, he turned to face Jormungand. ''Innina is next,'' he said softly. ''Enki is too strong. But Innina has a weak spot.'' He smiled grimly. ''Yes, a weak spot she is well aware of and has surrounded with many spells. Many, many spells. But I wonder if she has ever even thought of what I intend to do? Ah, well, we shall see, we shall see.''

Marduk looked up from where he sat next to the body stretched out on the pallet. His gaze was dull and listless, his shoulders stooped in weariness, his back bowed with grief. When he spoke, his voice was weak and halting. ''I have sat by his side, weeping, for six days and seven nights. Dreams have assailed my frantic mind. The heavens groaned aloud, the earth echoed the agony. Alone, I stood between them and wept bitter tears. A man came to me. His paws were the paws of the lion, his talons the talons of the eagle. He leapt upon me, bearing me down, his talons twined in my hair, overpowering me, smothering me. He transformed me, made my arms into feathered bird wings. Then he seized me and dragged me down to the house of darkness, the dread palace of Aralu, the cold dry dwelling of Ereshkigal and Nergal. It is the house where one who goes in never comes out again, the road that, if one sets foot on it, one never comes back. It is the house where light never reaches, where those who dwell there must live on dust, and mud is their food. They have no clothes, only a covering of bird feathers, and they sit always in the dark.

"Into that house of ashes I entered." He groaned deeply, the fear and anguish overflowing from his mind to his voice. "I entered and I saw the mighty, their crowns fallen and rolling in the dust, their robes scattered and covered with dust. All their glory becomes ashes, dirt, dust, dust, dust." He looked up, his eyes haunted by memory and despair. "And there, on a stake, I saw Enkidu. Next to the throne on which Ereshkigal sat. Namtaru knelt before her, his tablet in his hands, and on it was written Enkidu's name. Ereshkigal lifted her head and looked directly at me. 'Who has brought this one here?' she asked. I . . . I woke and the dream was done."

Marduk's weary, haunted eyes wandered back to the still face of Enkidu. "Six days and seven nights I sat here, weeping by his side. Like an eagle I circled over him. Like a lioness whose whelps are swept away in a sudden flood, I paced back and forth. 'What is this sleep that has taken hold of you?' I cried. 'You've become dark and cannot hear me when I call your name.' I touched his heart but it did not beat. And then I saw a worm crawl from his nose. I covered his face like a bride's."

He stood, his eyes suddenly wild. "It is not fate that holds him fast. It is not sickness that holds him fast. It is the nether world. It is not Nergal, the unsparing, that holds him fast. It is the nether world. He did not fall in battle, in the place of manliness. He fell in the nether world, and it holds him fast. Death! Death! Death holds him fast, and none may loosen that grip!"

With a deep moan of horror, Marduk sank back into his chair, his head on his hands. "My friend, my beloved friend who underwent all kinds of hardships with me, Enkidu, whom I lured from out of the wilds to be by my side in all things, Enkidu who fought Humbaba with me, Enkidu has been overtaken by the fate of mankind.''

He looked up again, his eyes filled with pleading and fear. ''Six days and seven nights I wept over him, chanting every spell I knew. Six days and seven nights. Until a worm fell out of his nose.

''I am afraid,'' he whispered. ''My mind wanders in a wilderness of terror. The fate of my friend lies heavy on me. On remote paths I wander empty places of horror. The fate of Enkidu weighs on my soul. I wander the lonely, windswept steppe. How can I rest? How keep still and silent? The friend I loved so dearly has turned to dust.'' His voice dropped even lower. ''And someday shall I not lie down like him, never to move again?'' His head dropped and he stared blankly at the floor.

Innina turned to Enki and frowned. ''This is Surt's doing.''

Enki nodded. ''Partly. Enkidu wanted to lead the raid, and Marduk let him. Jormungand recognized him and managed to take him alive. From that point on, indeed, it is all Surt's doing.''

The sorceress gestured toward Marduk in disgust. ''This one is useless to us now.''

Enki snorted. ''I believe he was useless from the beginning. A good soldier, but beyond that, a fool at best. Never managed to master more than a small portion of the *Shurpu*. Yet he served a purpose. At least we know the Patesi of Borsippa and Maqam Nifl is not an easy target militarily.''

''We still have him isolated magically,'' Innina said. ''We must see to it he doesn't break out. The two of us can surely manage that.''

''Surely? I'm not so certain of that as you seem to be, my dear. The Black One is trickier than I had thought. And I begin to sense that there is more to this than meets the eye.''

Innina looked at him, a question in her eyes. She spoke it softly. ''You think perhaps one of the other Sons is in league with him?'' She considered. ''It's possible, but who?''

''Who knows? But if that is indeed the case, then with Marduk effectively out of the way, there are no more than four of us to resist him.''

With a sudden cry, Marduk sprang to his feet, his eyes

wild and unfocused. He tore at his hair and ripped the rich robe he wore from his body. He threw it on the floor and trampled it beneath his feet. Then he turned to look at Enki and Innina. There was no recognition in his stare. His mouth began to work and he cried out, "I will make a statue of alabaster in the shape of Enkidu's body! I will cover it with gold, and the chest will be made of lapis lazuli. I will inlay it with carnelian. Before it I will place a wide table made of elammakum wood, and upon the table there will be a lapis lazuli bowl always filled with cream.

"But I will shed my fine robes. I will leave my bright palaces, leave the luxurious bed of my consort, Zarpanit. I will loosen my wide belt and drop it to the ground.

"Then I will cover my body with unshorn hair. I will don a dog skin and roam the endless waste in search of Utnapishtim, who has stood in the assembly of the Igigi and has found eternal life. I will go to him and he will teach me of life and of death." He crouched suddenly, his eyes haunted once more. "For I am afraid. Sorrow has come to my belly. Will I die like Enkidu?"

He pulled himself upright again. "I will search out the house of Utnapishtim, the offspring of Ubaratutu. Siduri, she who is Sabitu, will point the way, she will show me the path, tell me of the landmarks. And Urshanabi, the boatman to Utnapishtim, he who has the things of stone with him, he who picks up the Urnu-snakes, he will take me across the Me Muti, the Waters of Death." Marduk slumped back into his chair again and gazed vacantly into the air, muttering ferociously, planning his trip.

Innina shook her head in disgust. "He's totally broken down."

Enki smiled ironically. "Seems as good as ever to me. Yes, Surt has done his job well." He turned to face the sorceress. "I'm going back to Eengurra. The place is so well warded, even the Black One couldn't break in. I'll be safe there. And right now the idea of being safe is very appealing." There was a slight pop of imploding air as Enki disappeared.

For a few moments Innina watched the mumbling Marduk, then she, too, disappeared.

LAO-KEE

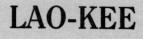

VII

HRODVITNIR sat with his chin in his left hand and looked pensive. "The Risar become more and more of a problem. Especially Fenrir. His ambitions and mine clash. There must be some way to stop him."

"Why not just put a knife between his ribs?" Lao-Kee asked.

"Eventually it will come to that. But I'd lose even the small amount of support I've gained among the Risar if it was known I was the one who attacked first. I'll have to kill Fenrir at some point, that's sure. But I'd rather do it in a way that will make him carry most of the blame."

"Then if we can't strike directly at Fenrir, why not indirectly through some of the fools that support him?"

Hrodvitnir nodded. "Yes, of course. But again, it cannot seem as if I'm directly involved, or I risk loss of Risar support."

"Hmmmm," Lao-Kee mused. "What if a situation was created where . . . hmmm." The slender warrior smiled slightly. "Yes, I think I have an idea."

"I thought you might," Hrodvitnir replied. "You generally do. And generally they're very good ones."

"Ah, this is one of the best!" Lao-Kee paused for a moment, looking down at the ground, then shot a quick sideways glance at the other Jotun. "One of the best, but also one of the more dangerous. A great trick, a wonderful joke. But it involves using the Aesir."

Hrodvitnir was silent for several moments as he considered what Lao-Kee had said. "Is there danger to their lives? Yes?

Well, you realize that if they were to die or even be seriously injured here in Utgard, it would mean a bitter war to the death with the Aesir. That's a war I'd rather avoid until we're much, much stronger.''

Lao-Kee shrugged. "How badly do you want to be Warlord? You haven't let the lives of a few Jotun stand in your way. Why treat the Aesir any differently than your own people?"

"Because they're *not* my own people." Hrodvitnir sighed. "They're a very powerful and determined enemy. The whole point to bringing Voden and his group here to Utgard was to throw them off guard and make them think I'd be willing to deal peacefully with them if I became Warlord. We need more breathing time, Lao-Kee. Breathing time to gather our strength so we can sweep them from the face of Yggdrasil. If one of them dies by our fault—"

"I understand," Lao-Kee interrupted. "I think, though, that a little risk is worth running. What I propose would put them in a dangerous situation, but one I'm sure I could control. And the beauty is, if things come out well, you'll be rid of one of Fenrir's strongest supporters, and perhaps even Fenrir himself. If it goes wrong"—the slender warrior shrugged—"you could still kill Fenrir's friends in revenge for the death of your 'guests.' "

Hrdovitnir was silent for several moments. Then he said softly, "Tell me of this scheme, Lao-Kee. It interests me."

Lao-Kee smiled smugly. "Hreidmir, with his three sons—Fafnir, Reginir, and Ottar—is one of the most powerful of the Risar and a great friend and ally of Fenrir. . . ."

Step by step, Lao-Kee laid out the plan. In the end, Hrodvitnir reluctantly agreed.

The storm rose swiftly in the west, the clouds towering into the sky until their tops were lost in darkness. It burst over the travelers with an elemental fury that forced them to stop and wait until it passed. When it had, they found everything they carried with them was utterly drenched and sodden, and the air a good ten degrees colder.

"This grand tour of Jotunheim isn't as exciting or interesting as I'd been led to expect," Tror complained as he wrung the water out of his cloak. "Most of the time we haven't even had one of your damned, uncomfortable wagons to spend the night in." He glowered at Lao-Kee. "Instead we've been sleeping on the ground like wild animals. But tonight will be worse yet. Thanks to that damn storm we'll be damp as well as cold. Oh, how I long for my warm fire and dry, cozy hall in Asgard!"

Honir shivered. "I'm already cold."

Voden turned to Leo-Kee. "Is there a Jotun camp nearby? Tror's right. It would be pleasant to spend the night on the floor of a nice, dry wagon."

The Jotun warrior nodded. "Yes. We're not too far from the camp where Hreidmir lives. He's a member of the Risar clan and none too friendly to Hrodvitnir, but you're guests of the Trul as well as of Hrodvitnir, so he'd be obliged to treat you well, if grudgingly. He's grasping and miserly, so it might be best if we brought him a little something extra by way of a gift. He loves fish. There's a small river not far from here. The rain will have roiled the waters, but perhaps we can catch a few trout and take them along."

The land became more broken as they approached the river. The ravines were sharper and deeper, and outcroppings of rock appeared here and there. Lao-Kee rode well in advance to scout the way.

The Jotun walked carefully up the last ridge before the river and peered surreptitiously over the crest. There below, only a few yards away, Lao-Kee saw a sight that promised everything the slender warrior had hoped for to carry out the plan against the Risar clan. Hreidmir's youngest son, Ottar, stood waist deep in the water, catching trout with a net. Already some nine or ten good-sized fish lay gasping on the shore.

As the others approached, Lao-Kee wiggled back from the crest, signaling for them to be silent. When they finally arrived, the Jotun whispered to them. "There's a lad on the other side of the ridge. He's fishing in the river and has already done our job for us! We'll just take his fish and—"

"Is he likely to give them to us?" Tror asked in his hoarse whisper.

Lao-Kee shrugged. "We won't ask."

"Oh, fine. Just steal them, eh?" Tror grumbled. "What if he's from this Hreidmir's camp and tells on us? What then? You said Hreidmir's not all that friendly to begin with. Surely stealing fish from one of his people isn't going to make him any friendlier.''

Voden nodded. "Tror's point is a good one. Best we catch our own fish.''

Lao-Kee looked from one to the other and laughed softly. "Pah! Don't be fools! The trout are there on the bank, waiting for us to take them. Why wade into that ice-cold river and hope to grab a slippery trout or two when someone else has already done the work for you? He'll never even know we took them.''

"And how do you hope to accomplish that?'' Tror asked, raising his bushy red eyebrows in query.

The Jotun picked up a smooth stone that lay right by Tror's feet. "This will do the trick. I'll knock that lad out with it before he can see me. He'll never know what hit him! When he wakes up, his fish will be gone. He'll just catch some more and assume some animal took them.''

"Can you really throw a stone that well?'' Honir asked in wonder.

Lao-Kee nodded in solemn assurance. "Well,'' Tror grumbled, "I still don't like it, stealing this way. But I guess it is better than wading in a freezing river. Trout are damned hard to catch by hand anyway.'' They turned to Voden, who simply shrugged.

With a grin, Lao-Kee crept back up the ridge. For several moments the Jotun lay still, peering over the crest. Then, in one fluid motion, the slender warrior stood, threw, and raced over the top. In a rush, the others followed.

Lao-Kee was already dragging the limp body to the bank of the river. "Wouldn't want him to drown,'' the Jotun called out by way of explanation. "This way he'll simply wake up on the bank with a headache and a goose egg on the side of his head and wonder what happened.''

Tror was holding up the fish, admiring them. Honir suddenly cried out, "Look!'' and pointed to the water. A long, dark, furry form was just emerging from the water, a fish in its mouth.

So swiftly none of them could even follow the motion, Lao-Kee picked up another stone and threw it with deadly accuracy at the creature. It dropped on the spot, and Jotun swooped down on it with a cry of glee. The slender warrior held up the body to show it to them all. "An otter! What luck! The fish and the pelt of this beauty will be sure to make us welcome at Hreidmir's! We'll get a very special greeting, I guarantee!''

"He's dead," Voden said, his voice cutting through their excitement. They all turned to the leader of the Aesir, who stood over the body of the fisherman. "You didn't knock him out, Lao-Kee. You killed him.''

Still holding the otter, Lao-Kee came over and gazed down at the still form on the river bank. "I believe you're right.'' The warrior sighed. "Sometimes I'm just a bit too accurate. Well, no use dithering over it now. Here, help me dump him back in the river. If anyone ever finds him, they'll assume he got caught in the river in the middle of the storm, lost his footing and drowned.'' Lao-Kee put down the otter and grabbed the young fisherman's arms. With a slow, deep glance from his single eye, Voden gazed for a moment at the upturned face of the Jotun warrior, then bent and took the dead man's feet. Together they set him adrift in the river. The current caught him and, tumbling him over and over, carried him away.

They arrived at Hreidmir's circle of wagons as dusk was turning to night. Leo-Kee went in advance. Hreidmir himself came out to meet them.

"Ho, Hreidmir," Lao-Kee called out. "Can you give us a wagon to sleep in tonight? We'd rather not have a dew bed on a cool, damp night like this.''

"Lao-Kee," Hreidmir muttered as if the word were distasteful. "And three I don't know. But I do know I don't like their looks even a little bit.''

"They're Aesir. Here with the protection of Hrodvitnir and the White Bear of the Trul.''

Hreidmir spat on the ground. "Hrodvitnir, bah! But I bow to the will of the Trul. I've no wish to run afoul of that lot.''

"We can pay for our beds. We've had luck hunting and fishing today. We've enough for everyone.''

"Enough for all? Even Fafnir and Reginir? Even for Lyngheid and Lofnheid and their husbands?'' Leo-Kee nodded. "Huh. Then I guess I've not much choice," Hreidmir said sourly.

Lao-Kee grinned and motioned the other three forward. "Here are your guests, Hreidmir." The slender warrior chortled. "And here is dinner, plus a little extra present!" Tror and Honir held up the string of trout and the otter.

When Hreidmir saw the fish and the otter, he stiffened and his eyes became cold and hard. He stood staring at them for a moment, then turned on his heel and stalked off without a word.

"What's wrong with him?" Tror asked, looking from the retreating back to Lao-Kee's grinning face.

Lao-Kee shrugged. "A cool welcome is better than a cold bed under the stars."

"I wonder," Voden said softly.

The four of them rode into the circle of wagons and dismounted. There seemed to be no one around. Lao-Kee seemed mystified, and went to find their host. When the Jotun failed to return after a few moments, Honir went to see what had happened.

Tror was looking around nervously when suddenly five fully armed Jotun warriors, including Hreidmir, appeared between the wagons. Two held Honir, with a knife pressed firmly against the young Aesir's throat. For a brief second the confrontation was silent, then Hreidmir spoke. "One move and your friend feels the taste of my knife Aesir!"

From the corner of his eye Voden could see Tror's body tense for action and his hand tighten around the haft of his hammer. He spoke so quietly that only Tror could hear, but his voice was firm and full of command. "No. Hreidmir means what he says. This isn't the time for fighting."

"Then you'd better use your magic," the red-bearded giant growled in response, his body relaxing slightly, "or else we're in for it."

"Magic?" Voden replied with a shake of his head. "Magic isn't something you use quickly or casually, old friend. It's tricky, dangerous stuff, and you need time to prepare before you let it loose. No, I'd only use magic as a last resort. We have better weapons."

"Like what?" the other man asked, keeping his voice low.

"Like patience and cunning. Follow my lead. And whatever you do, don't raise Mjollnir."

Voden lifted his eye to meet Hreidmir's and spoke out loud, his voice stiff with suppressed anger. "We came as guests, with the guarantee of safe passage from Hrodvitnir and the Trul. Are those of the Risar clan so low they don't recognize the rights of guests?''

Hreidmir spat on the ground. "Guests? Bah! Murderers! Those fish you offer as food were caught by my son, Ottar. And the otter you bring as a gift was his pet. It went everywhere with him, helping him fish. He loved the river and fishing, my boy did. He was my youngest son, and you killed him. You killed him, and now I will kill you all for vengeance! Even the Trul will not stand in my way where blood vengeance is concerned.''

Voden looked calmly at Hreidmir. "We didn't know the fisherman was your son. And we certainly didn't mean to kill him. That should be obvious. Would we have come to his father's camp if we'd known what we had done?''

"Nevertheless, he's dead and you must pay the price!''

Voden nodded. "True. We must pay the price. But you must give us a chance to pay a wergild, a blood ransom, before killing us, since the murder was not intentional. If you don't do that much, you will incur the wrath of the Trul, and you know it.''

Hreidmir gazed at Voden and said nothing. He knew the Aesir was right.

"I'll speak for all of us, for I've passed the tests of the Trul and I'm now partially one of them. Name Ottar's wergild, Hreidmir. Whatever it is, we'll undertake to pay it.''

Hreidmir thought for a long time. Finally he spoke. "You have the right of it, Aesir.'' He turned to one of his men and said, "Fafnir, bring Lao-Kee out to hear this too. And you, Reginir, bring me your brother Ottar's robe.''

When the slender Jotun was brought, tied and still gagged, and the robe had been handed to Hreidmir, he began to speak. "First, you'll all swear that you'll meet the wergild I ask or willingly forfeit your heads.'' They swore.

"Now," Hreidmir continued, holding up the robe, "this is the robe of my youngest son, Ottar. He made it from the pelt of the largest otter ever caught in Jotunheim. The head is still attached, so you can see how huge it was. It contains the pelts of several other otters as well. We will add that of the one you killed.

"The wergild will be to fill this robe with red gold. Then, after it has been filled, you will cover the outside with red gold, so that not even a whisker of the otter's head is showing. Do you agree?''

"You like gold a good deal," Voden said sarcastically.

Hreidmir stiffened. "You have taken away my youngest son. I ask but a small price compared to your own lives. Do you agree?"

Lao-Kee was nodding furiously, trying to speak through the gag. Voden looked at Hreidmir, who gestured to have the gag removed. When it was out, Lao-Kee spoke. "You ask for a lot of gold, Hreidmir, more than most men in Jotunheim possess. But I would like to talk to Voden before he agrees to anything."

Hreidmir glowered but finally nodded. "No tricks now," he rumbled angrily.

Lao-Kee whispered in Voden's ear for several moments. Finally the Aesir nodded and turned to Hreidmir. "We agree. On the condition you set Lao-Kee free to go and gather the gold. The rest of us will stay here as your prisoners until Lao-Kee returns."

Hreidmir looked at Fafnir and Reginir. The two brothers nodded their assent. "Agreed. Cut Lao-Kee loose. Go now, little one, and if you wish to see your friends alive again, hurry back. We won't wait forever for our revenge."

Lao-Kee leapt into the saddle, gave them all a slight bow and a mocking smile, and then with a jeering laugh that made everyone uneasy, spurred out of the wagon circle and onto the horizon-girt grasslands of Jotunheim.

To the north and west of Hreidmir's camp, lay one of the great wonders of Jotunheim. Eons ago, long before the Sons of Ymir had come to the vast grasslands to the north of the River Iving, the ground had suddenly collapsed and a giant sinkhole had opened up. Steam and mist rose from it constantly, so that no man had ever seen its bottom. It was rumored it went straight to the realm of Glitnis Gna and Erlik Khan. Most of the Jotun avoided it, often riding miles out of their way to pass it by.

But there was another story about the sinkhole, one that greatly interested Lao-Kee. In the days after the fall of the First Dark Empire, when the Dverg had had to abandon their great city of Alvis—the ruins of which now lay in the Great Eastern Waste—most of the gray men had gone westward and settled in Nidavellir. One group, following Svarin, had gone even farther toward the setting sun and founded the legendary city of Auravangar, somewhere near the western edge of the Western Forest.

There was an ancient rumor that told of yet another group, led by Andvari, that had gotten separated from the others in a snowstorm and had wandered far to the north and west, eventually settling in the caverns along the banks of a vast underground river. They had supposedly entered the caverns by way of a huge hole in the ground caused by the collapse of the roof of one of the caverns carved by the river. This story was especially intriguing to Leo-Kee because it hinted that Andvari had vast amounts of gold.

Lao-Kee was in no hurry to reach the sinkhole and rode slowly, chuckling and grinning the whole time. The Jotun thought about how uncomfortable Tror, Honir, and Voden must be, tied and kept closely guarded in a wagon all day and all night. The slender warrior knew they were in no real danger, for Hreidmir would not harm them as long as he had hopes of getting so much gold. The Risar was undoubtedly already planning how to use it to back Fenrir against Hrodvitnir. If Fenrir won the Warlordship of the Horde, Hreidmir would be very powerful, probably the next most powerful Jotun after the White Bear and Fenrir. No, Hreidmir would do nothing to jeopardize his chances. The three Aesir were safe for a good while.

And what if the legend of Andvari was false? Well then, Lao-Kee smiled, I'll just have to think of something else. Or perhaps find a way to take advantage of the death of three important Aesir at the hands of the Risar.

The plume of steam and mist that rose from the sinkhole was visible a long way off. Lao-Kee reached the hole itself about noon. The Jotun cautiously approached the lip of the hole and gazed downward in wonder. It was perhaps two hundred yards across, and the bottom was hidden completely in darkness and swirling mist.

As Lao-Kee studied the sides of the hole, the slender warrior saw that a way down could be gained by moving from ledge to ledge, crack to crack. It would be precarious but . . . what an adventure! Taking all the food in the saddle bags and putting it in a sack slung across the bank, Lao-Kee hobbled the horse and without another look around began to descend into the hole.

The descent took longer than expected. It was already dark when Lao-Kee finally reached the uneven, boulder-filled floor of the hole. Deciding discretion was the better part of valor, the Jotun camped for the night on the spot. Morning would be soon enough to find the actual opening to the caverns.

Morning dawned dimly in the hole. Lao-Kee ate quickly and began to search the jumbled floor for the opening. The warrior simply clambered to the hottest, mistiest spot and carefully felt around in the blinding whiteness. After more than an hour of searching, Lao-Kee found an opening large enough to crawl through, and entered head first. The rushing hiss of steam and mist escaping past the Jotun's ears was deafening.

After a few yards the passageway opened up enough for the explorer to stand. Like most of the night-riding Jotun, Lao-Kee saw exceptionally well in the dark. And strangely enough, the passageway was not as dark as might be expected. Lao-Kee felt a thrill of excitement. Could that mean that indeed Andvari was here?

The dull roar of moving water could soon be heard, echoing up from deep in the earth. Lao-Kee moved forward carefully.

Suddenly the Jotun entered a cavern so immense it took the breath away in wonder. Huge stalactites hung in curtains from the ceiling, yearning down toward equally gigantic stalagmites which rose from every surface. Off to the left a river tumbled out of the rock and fell with a roar into a misty darkness far below. Water dripped from every surface.

It took Lao-Kee several hours to reach the banks of the river at the bottom of the cavern, but eventually the explorer came to a medium-sized cavern lit by a shaft of light that came through a hole in the ceiling. The light shone directly on a pool of still water in the middle of the cavern. Next to the pool was the sign Lao-Kee sought—the bones of fish. The Jotun went to the pool and looked in. As the Jotun had suspected, it was stocked with trout. Andvari doubtless caught the creatures in the river and then brought them here as a source of food. All Lao-Kee had to do was hide and wait for the Dverg to get hungry and come for a fish.

The wait was longer than Lao-Kee had expected, but eventually a Dverg appeared, gray-skinned, gray-bearded, and shuffled over to the pool. Its eyes gleaming yellow in the light, it gazed at the fish, then suddenly leaned over and grabbed one. Without pausing, it began to eat the wriggling creature, tearing off mouthfuls of living flesh.

Lao-Kee crept up silently while the Dverg was tearing at its meal and placed the point of a knife at the base of its skull. The Dverg felt the blade and stiffened in response. "Turn around very carefully," the Jotun said softly. When the gray man had turned and was staring at the keen edge and sharp point of the weapon pointed directly between his eyes, the Jotun spoke again. "I'm here to see Andvari."

"What do you want?" The Dverg rumbled in a voice rusty with disuse. "What do you want with Andvari?"

"I want his gold."

The Dverg tensed, and Lao-Kee laughed. "Don't move. Don't twist or turn or breath too strongly. And above all, don't try to escape. If you don't take me straight to Andvari, you'll be one old Dverg that won't get any older. Now where is he?"

For a moment the Dverg was stubbornly silent. Lao-Kee grinned and touched the tip of the creature's drooping nose with the point of the knife. "Do you need encouragement, gray one?"

The Dverg shook his head slowly and then with a sigh said, "I am Andvari."

Lao-Kee chuckled. "I suspected as much. Well then, Andvari, old friend, if you value your head and wish to avoid Niflheim, take me to your gold!"

"You want all of it?"

"All."

Grumbling, the Dverg turned and began to shuffle off. Lao-Kee followed close behind, knife ready for instant use if the creature tried to escape.

They went down a narrow passageway that twisted and turned, until it opened into a small chamber made even smaller by the presence of a great forge glowing with heat. Gold was piled everywhere the Jotun looked.

Lao-Kee grinned hugely. "Excellent! Gather it all up, Andvari, and be quick! Don't miss a mote of it!"

Complaining bitterly beneath his breath, the Dverg began

to stuff the gold into two sacks. There were chunks of gold, splinters of gold, shavings of gold, disks of gold, rings, bracelets, brooches, pins, daggers, things barely begun and things almost completed.

When the two sacks were full, Lao-Kee made a quick inspection of the room to make sure the Dverg had not held anything back. The Jotun nodded, then turned to Andvari and said, "And now the ring."

Andvari shrank back, thrusting his hands behind his back. "Not the ring too! Leave me the ring at least. Then I can get more gold. Leave me the ring."

"I said all of it and I meant all of it. What do I care if you can or can't get more gold? I won't be needing any more, so it's of no interest to me whatsoever."

"Please, not the ring," Andvari moaned.

Lao-Kee stepped quickly forward and held the knife to the Dverg's throat, pricking the gray skin slightly. "I said everything. Now hand it over before I cut your stupid throat and take it off your dead body. Now!"

Moaning and sighing, Andvari took the ring off his right hand and gave it to Lao-Kee. The Jotun looked at it carefully. It was wonderfully crafted, with tiny animals running around it in a wild tumult. The slender warrior slipped it over a little finger and admired it again, holding it up so Andvari could see it. "Looks good on me, don't you think?" The Dverg only scowled and moaned again.

Lao-Kee told Andvari to pick up the two sacks and carry them back to the opening of the cavern in the sinkhole. When they finally got there, Lao-Kee shoved in the two sacks filled with gold and then turned to the Dverg. "Back into your cavern now, gray one. I've got what I came for and I'm taking it."

"Take it, then!" Andvari screamed in frustrated anger. "And take my curse with it! That ring and that gold will destroy whoever owns them!"

Lao-Kee grinned at Andvari and this unexpected but welcome twist to the developing plan. "So much the better, fool," the Jotun said. "I'll tell those who get your treasure of the curse you've placed on it to make sure it comes true. Good-bye, and thanks for your hospitality!" With a mocking bow, Lao-Kee ducked into the passageway.

• • •

"You certainly took your time," Tror grumbled when Lao-Kee finally rode into the circle of wagons that made up Hreidmir's camp. Like the other two Aesir, his hands and feet were firmly tied with rope made from rawhide. Hreidmir had brought all three of them out of the wagon where they had been kept prisoners as soon as Lao-Kee was seen approaching across the plain.

The Jotun laughed and gestured to the two bulging bags tied behind the saddle. "It takes time to find good red gold in the middle of Jotunheim, Tror! But I've found it, and we'll soon be on our way again." Lao-Kee jumped lightly from the horse's back and helped Fafnir unload the bags.

Hreidmir stood by, his eyes gleaming with avarice, as Lao-Kee poured one bag of the gold into the otter cape. It totally filled the cape. The slender Jotun wrapped the gold in the cape, turned it over, and then dumped the other bag of gold over the robe, covering every inch of it with the gleaming metal.

Hreidmir walked up when Lao-Kee had finished and carefully surveyed the result. "Hmmm, hmmm," he murmured. "It looks like enough. Ah! What's this? Here, here, this whisker of the otter's head isn't covered! See it sticks out! Ha! You haven't kept your bargain, Lao-Kee!"

The warrior ambled slowly over to stand next to Hreidmir. The man was pointing to the whisker, which did indeed protrude from beneath the gold heaped over the cape. "Well, well," Lao-Kee said, "so it does remain uncovered. Surely, though, Hreidmir, all this gold is enough. You wouldn't hold the promise broken because one tiny whisker is showing."

Hreidmir crossed his arms over his chest and glowered smugly. "A bargain is a bargain. My son is dead, and you agreed to the ransom. Your heads are all forfeit."

Lao-Kee sighed. "Very well, then." The slender warrior looked over at Voden and shrugged, then removed the gold ring taken from Andvari and placed it over the whisker. "There," Lao-Kee said. "A bargain's a bargain, true enough. And we've met our part. Now you must turn us loose."

Grumbling, Hreidmir gestured to his sons to cut the bonds from Voden, Tror, and Honir. When the three were free, Fafnir brought their horses and their packs. Tror checked his gear, then with a curse, checked it again. "My hammer,

Mjollnir! It's missing!'' He turned on Hreidmir, his fists bunched, his face red with anger. "Where is my hammer!"

Hreidmir looked uncomfortable. "Uh, well, it's, ummm, you see . . ." Tror took a menacing step toward the man. Both his sons' hands went to the hilts of their swords. Hreidmir held up his hands to forestall them. "No bloodshed. The hammer is gone. I traded it to Thrymir for three horses. I thought Lao-Kee was never coming back, and it was getting expensive feeding you all, so I traded it and then traded the horses for five cows. You've eaten two of them already."

Tror looked stunned. "Mjollnir, traded for horses? My hammer? I . . . I . . ."

Voden stepped up quickly and laid a calming hand on his friend's shoulder. "We'll get it back, Tror. Let's leave here first, and then we'll send Lao-Kee to talk to this Thrymir and get it back."

Tror took several deep breaths and then nodded. The red began to recede from his face, and he became calmer. "All right," he said. "All right. But we'll have to get it back, even if it means killing Thrymir and everyone in his damned camp." He turned to Lao-Kee. "Do you know this Thrymir?" Lao-Kee nodded. "And will he give back the hammer?" Lao-Kee shrugged noncommittally.

When they were finally mounted and ready to leave, Lao-Kee turned and addressed Hreidmir in a sneering tone. "Listen carefully, Risar! You have gained a great weregild so that my friends and I might keep our heads. But you and your sons are not fated to thrive, for this treasure shall be a bane to you all. Know that the ring and that gold were stolen from the Dverg Andvari. When I took it from him, he also gave me something else. Now I give that to you with the gold." Lao-Kee's voice became low and compelling. "Andvari said to me, and I say to you, 'Take it then! And take my curse with it! That ring and that gold will destroy whoever owns them!' Much pleasure may you have of Andvari's treasure, Hreidmir!"

Voden glanced at Lao-Kee, his single eye glittering from the shadows beneath his hood. The Jotun smiled at him, a smile filled with sly knowledge. They nodded to each other and spurred their horses in the flanks. With a clatter of hoofs and gear, the four rode swiftly from the circle of Hreidmir's camp.

VIII

~~~

"WELL, what does he want?" Tror demanded. "More gold, like that avaricious bastard Hreidmir?"

Lao-Kee smiled slyly and sat down opposite the red-bearded giant. Voden and Honir leaned forward to hear what the Jotun would say. The slender warrior paused and held out chilled hands to the fire that glowed between them. "Ahhh," Lao-Kee murmured, "that feels good! It's a chilly night, for sure."

"Dammit!" Tror exploded. "Stop stalling! Tell me what Thrymir said! You're doing this on purpose just to spite me, you little . . . little . . ."

The Jotun held up a hand in protest. "I'll tell you, Tror, but by Ymir's left leg, man, it's a cold night and I'm half frozen with the ride. Give me a chance to thaw out!

"That's a bit better. Well, let's see—Thrymir. Yes. I found the old bastard relaxing after having combed his horses manes until they were smooth as silk. He was sitting on a mound of green pillows and braiding collars and leashes for some of his favorite hunting hounds.

"When he looked up and saw me, it was plain he wasn't any too pleased. He's a Risar, like Hreidmir, and is no friend of Hrodvitnir's nor of any who support my half brother.

"For a while we talked of the weather and of the doings in Utgard and things inconsequential. Then I casually mentioned the hammer. Well, he'd obviously been expecting that all along because he chuckled and said, 'That hammer might as well be buried eight miles down for all the chance you have of getting it back, Lao-Kee.' I asked why, and he replied,

'Because that's Tror's hammer, and I've no intention of giving an enemy like that damn Aesir his weapon back. He's already crushed enough Jotun skulls with it. I've seen him battling in front of Asgard and I know.'

"I continued to prod him gently and he finally admitted there was one thing he would trade the hammer for. One thing and only one thing."

"Well what in Fornjot's name is it, damn you!" Tror bellowed. "Quit stalling and get to the point! Whatever it is, I'll get it for him!"

Lao-Kee sat back and grinned mischievously at Tror. "You might have a little trouble with this request, red beard."

"Dammit! Tell me what it is! I'll get him anything!"

"He wants an Aesir woman to be his bride."

Tror was utterly silent for a moment, his jaw slack and his eyes confused. "He . . . he wants what?"

"An Aesir woman to be his bride."

"But . . . but . . . that's impossible!" Tror howled in fury. "Did you offer him gold, horses, cattle, dogs—"

"I offered him anything in the world, and he chose an Aesir woman as bride. He says he once raped an Aesir woman while raiding across the River Iving and enjoyed the experience so much he wants one for a wife now. He was positively drooling when he talked about it.

"Yes, an Aesir bride is the only thing he wants. He has more cattle, horses, and dogs then he knows what to do with. Even a herd of black bulls. He has enough gold and precious jewels to have paid our ransom to Hreidmir ten times over. And he's had seven different Jotun wives. He's had most everything he's ever wanted. Except an Aesir bride."

Tror exploded. "Where in the name of Fornjot's icy balls will I find an Aesir woman who's willing to marry an old Jotun?"

Lao-Kee shrugged. "Asaheim? I really don't know what to tell you, Tror. I only know that's what he wants."

Tror turned stricken eyes to Voden. "What am I going to do? I must get Mjollnir back, but where am I going to find an Aesir woman for Thrymir?"

Voden had been keeping his eye on Lao-Kee during the entire conversation. A slight smile played over his lips. He turned his gaze to Tror and said, "I think Lao-Kee has a plan."

Tror turned back to the Jotun. "Please, Lao-Kee, if you have any ideas at all, I'd—" He broke off, surprised by the slender warrior's smile.

"As so often, Voden is correct," Lao-Kee said with a nod toward the chieftain of the Aesir. "He sees deeper with one eye than most men do with two.

"Thrymir hasn't seen too many Aesir women, Tror. So we could disguise someone who spoke the common tongue with an Aesir accent as a woman and then bring him to Thrymir and pretend it was a woman. A Jotun bride has the right to ask any gift of her husband before they're married. If the disguised Aesir asked to be allowed to hold the hammer, then . . ."

Honir said softly, "If the disguised Aesir was Tror, then he could get his hammer that way."

Lao-Kee feigned surprise. "Brilliant! Why didn't I think of that twist? Yes, that's it, Tror! We'll dress you up in a bridal dress and a bridal veil and pretend—"

Tror jumped to his feet with a roar, his face red and his beard bristling with anger. "By Fornjot's frozen cock! I'll be damned if I'll dress like a bride! Why I'll—"

Lao-Kee was laughing heartily. Voden was chuckling. Even Honir was unable to suppress a furtive giggle. Tror stopped bellowing and stared at the three of them. "Funny! You all think it's a great joke! That's just wonderful!"

"But Tror," Lao-Kee gasped, "it's the only way to get your hammer back. You said you'd give anything." The Jotun lapsed into a new round of laughter and was unable to continue.

Tror turned to appeal to Voden but stopped when he saw his old friend was laughing almost as hard as Lao-Kee. "I think you'll look wonderful in a dress and veil, Tror," the chief of the Aesir said between bursts of hilarity. "Though it had best be a long dress to hide those thick legs, and a big veil to cover your beard!" That set the three of them off again, and all Tror could do was stand there, his fists clenched, fuming.

When they had calmed down, Lao-Kee began to spell out a plan in great detail. The Jotun would tell Thrymir that indeed he could have an Aesir bride, but not for eight days, since it would take a while to fetch one from Asaheim. Then Lao-Kee would escort the disguised Tror to the Jotun's camp to see that everything went well. When Tror had the hammer, they could escape from the camp on their horses and join Voden and Honir. Once the four of them were together again, even if Thrymir did give chase, he'd have to think twice before attacking such a large party.

They discussed the plan until long after the moon had set, but by the end, even Tror had grudgingly agreed to go along with Lao-Kee's suggestions. The slender Jotun was smiling smugly when they finally rolled up in their blankets and went to sleep.

Nine days later, in the early evening, two riders approached the camp of Thrymir. When the old Jotun saw them coming across the plain, he called all his people together and told them to ready the welcome and the feast. They already had several oxen roasting and had put two succulent dogs into a trench lined with hot coals early that morning. Thrymir himself was literally trembling with excitement at the thought of having an Aesir bride he could rape whenever he wished.

When he saw the bride up close, though, he had a moment's misgiving. She was so big and strong looking! But then, he liked a good tussle and hated passive women. This one would surely give him a lusty time of it!

Thrymir had set up a special chair for the bride in the center of the circle of wagons and covered it with the hides of several black bulls. The bride, her face almost completely covered with a heavy veil (which Lao-Kee explained was the custom among the Aesir), sat there and glowered around at the proceedings. The old Jotun was surprised at the ferocity of the glare and asked Lao-Kee what was wrong. "Her eyes, they're like burning coals!" he whispered.

"What can you expect?" Lao-Kee reassured him with a sly smile. "The poor dear hasn't slept for the last eight nights, so great was her desire for her wedding night! The burning you see in those eyes is that of lust!"

Thrymir was mollified, and ordered food and drink brought for the bride. The bride quickly gulped down two mugs of ale and gobbled a whole hind leg of one of the dogs. The old Jotun was stunned by how much and how swiftly his bride-to-be ate and drank. He sidled up to Lao-Kee and exclaimed, "Whoever heard of a bride who ate and drank so much, so quickly?"

The slender warrior smiled and winked at him. "The poor dear," Lao-Kee whispered to him, "she hasn't been able to take hardly a mouthful, she's been so crazy with desire for her wedding night! Now she's just getting back her strength for later, when I'm sure she'll need plenty to satisfy a lusty old bull like you!"

Thrymir chuckled appreciatively and looked with burning fondness on his bride-to-be. No doubt he was in for a good time with this one! He rubbed his hands together gleefully.

But then he heard the bride say something to Lao-Kee and was stunned at how deep and hoarse her voice was. He rushed up to the slender warrior and asked, "Why is her voice so deep? Whoever heard of a tender maid with a voice like that?"

"Ah, lucky man," Lao-Kee said with a sigh. "Your bride's voice is hoarse because for eight days and nights she's been sighing with desire for her wedding night!"

Thrymir was somewhat reassured. "What did she ask you?" he queried.

"She told me her bridal wish."

"And what was it? I'll fulfill it right away so we can consummate the marriage as soon as possible!"

"Well, of course she knows you have Tror's hammer, Mjollnir, and that's why she's to become your bride. She says she wants to hold the hammer between her knees for a moment before she gives you what is yours by bridal right."

"Bring the hammer!" Thrymir bellowed. "Bring it right away and place it between my bride's knees! Ha! Then I'll put my hammer there and it won't be any smaller!"

It took two men to drag the hammer up and place it between the bride's knees. As soon as it was there, the bride grabbed it and stood up. The veil was swept off with one hand and the other raised the hammer aloft. "Here's your bride, Thrymir!" Tror bellowed, his red beard bristling with fury. "And here's your bridal right!" Without another word the Aesir slammed Mjollnir down on Thrymir's head. The old Jotun fell like a log.

"Oh, no," Lao-Kee said softly into the stunned silence that followed. The slender warrior grabbed Tror by the arm and dragged him quickly away. "Let's get out of here before they recover!"

The two ran for their horses and sprang into the saddles,

though Tror had to hitch the dress up around his waist to do so. Then they rode for all they were worth.

The fire leapt and twisted, casting bizarre and constantly changing shadows into the night. The wind blew steadily out of the northwest, bringing the chill of the Icerealm with it. Overhead, the stars shone, beautiful, hard, uncaring. Beneath their vast indifference four figures clung to the firelight in the midst of the endless, dark plain.

Tror roared with hilarity. Honir could barely sit upright, he was laughing so hard. Voden was weeping from his single eye, hardly able to catch his breath. None of them could even lift the mugs of Jotun ale they held in their hands.

Lao-Kee was standing in front of the three Aesir, acting out the recent episode for their benefit. The Jotun first played the part of Thrymir worriedly asking, then that of Lao-Kee cleverly replying. "Then he asked why the bride's voice was so deep, and I replied it was because the sweetling had been sighing with desire for eight days in anticipation of her wedding night! You should have seen him drool!" With a single gulp, the slender warrior drained the rest of a mug.

"Ah, by the gods, Lao-Kee, stop, stop! My sides hurt so much I can't take any more! Oh, Voden, you should have seen it! Lao-Kee was wonderful! Had Thrymir by the nose and led the old bull all around the ring! Took two of them to bring the hammer. As soon as it touched my hand, ah, the power just flowed and I struck!" Tror took a long swallow of the ale.

Lao-Kee looked up from refilling a mug and frowned. "Wish you hadn't done that, Tror." The Jotun's speech was slightly slurred. "Could get both of us in a bit of trouble, you know. You were a guest. Bride's a guest. Ate Thrymir's food, drank his ale. An' you killed him. No need for that." The Jotun took a long draught.

"Trouble? What kind of trouble?" Tror said, blinking his eyes and blurring his words. The Jotun ale was every bit as powerful as Aesir ale, and they had all been drinking it for some time now.

"Blood feud. Thrymir's sons have a right to demand revenge. Like with Ottar and Hreidmir. His cousin does too. Hrungnir. Mean bastard. Real killer. Big. Fast. Would'n wanna mess with old Hrungnir. He'd squash poor little Lao-Kee like a bug.''

"Aw, I wouldn't let 'im do that to you! You're my frien'd. Right, Voden? Lao-Kee's our special friend. Even if he is a bastard of a Jotun, he's our friend. Right, Honir? By Fornjot's icy balls, Lao-Kee, you can depend on us. We'll defend you against anybody. Right? Right?'' Voden and Honir both nodded.

Lao-Kee looked up at the three of them. "Really? You swear it? You'd defend me? Be my blood brothers? Really?''

"Sure,'' Tror said expansively, a big grin on his face. "Blood brothers to the end!''

Lao-Kee pulled out a dagger and took a wavering step toward Tror. "Let's do it! Blood brothers!'' The Jotun quickly cut a finger and held it out to Tror. For a second the Aesir stared dumbly at the oozing blood, then blinked, drew out his own dagger, and slashed his finger. He looked at Honir and Voden, a question on his flushed face. Reluctantly, Honir pulled out his knife and cut his finger. Slowly, thoughtfully, Voden followed suit. They all held out their fingers, and Lao-Kee held a full mug of ale beneath each finger in turn, allowing four drops of blood to fall into the frothy liquid.

When each of them had contributed their blood, the Jotun first held the mug up to the sky and called out, "Witness, Father Gymir!'' Then he thrust it down toward the ground and cried, "Witness, Mother Nerthus!'' Lao-Kee took a deep drink and then passed the mug to Tror. After Tror, each in turn drank, passing the mug around until it was empty.

"Now,'' Lao-Kee said jovially when they had finished, "we're blood brothers! Your feuds are my feuds and my feuds are your feuds. Your enemies are my enemies and my enemies are your enemies. Your wagon is my wagon and my wagon is your wagon. Your—oh, it goes on like that forever. You get the idea.''

Tror clapped the slender warrior on the back, nearly knocking the unsteady Jotun sprawling. "Brother! Damn right! To Niflheim with Thrymir and his sons and brothers! I've got Mjollnir back and a new brother to boot!'' Tror drained his mug with one gulp and staggered over to get more.

Lao-Kee watched him go, a strange smile curving enigmatic lips, a strange light gleaming in veiled eyes.

From where he sat, Voden saw the smile and the light, and nodded slightly. For sometime now he'd realized Lao-Kee was only pretending to be drunk, while plying the three of them with mug after mug. At first he'd been unable to understand the Jotun's purpose, but now he knew that this blood oath had been the goal all along. Why? What did it mean?

For several moments he thought about it, then shrugged. Time would tell. But best to be on the lookout. *I like Lao-Kee*, he admitted. *But I don't trust him. There's something . . . not quite right. . . .* He lifted his mug and drank a little, pretending to drink more. *Yes, best to keep alert.*

When they finally arrived back in Utgard, the coolness of fall was in the air. They'd been gone almost a month and a half and had seen more of Jotunheim than any of them really cared to see. But they'd managed to meet many Jotun, and had found them to be almost universally hospitable after a short-lived period of suspicion and hostility. Tror moaned that he hoped he never saw another pipe as long as he lived, and claimed he'd never get the smell of kinnikinnick smoke out of his clothes. Honir had enjoyed the trip immensely and made instant friends with the Jotun children everywhere he'd gone. They would always follow him around any camp in troops, vying for his attention and the right to hold his hand. Voden had asked endless questions about everything he'd seen, and had nodded enigmatically over every answer received.

Heimdall was waiting for them when they arrived. Kao-Shir and Anhur, however, had gone back to Asgard after a month of discussions with the White Bear. The yellow-robed old man had told Heimdall he was thinking of going back to spend the winter in Nidavellir again in hopes of meeting the Dverg. On the other hand, he might also go to Alfheim in hopes of finding the equally elusive Alfar. He promised to leave word with Gagnrad as to his decision. He had also promised to return by next summer.

Hrodvitnir frowned. "A little too effective, I fear. Fenrir has challenged me to a personal duel to revenge the affront to his relatives."

Lao-Kee frowned. "Andvari's curse. What happened?"

"The family fell apart, quarreling over the gold. They are all dead now, and the gold gone, taken by young Sygyrd, foster son to Reginir. No doubt the curse has gone with him."

Lao-Kee whistled softly. "No wonder Fenrir's angry. He's lost five Risar supporters at one fell swoop: Hreidmir, Fafnir, Reginir, Ottar, and Sygyrd! Not to mention a hoard of gold! And I suppose he blames you for all of it?"

Hrodvitnir gave Lao-Kee an appraising look. "Yes. He knows you were behind the whole thing and assumes I put you up to it. He demands blood right for all five. Of course, Lao-Kee, you had no idea all of this would happen when you proposed . . ." He left the words hanging.

The slender warrior's eyes widened innocently. "You don't think . . . ? But how could I know all that would happen? Of course I intended to kill Ottar and create an incident with Hreidmir. We'd discussed that before I left. That was the whole idea of taking the Aesir around—hoping to create incidents among the Risar we could take advantage of. But I had no idea—"

Hrodvitnir held up his hand to bring Lao-Kee's protestations of innocence to a halt. "Enough, little one. I know you too well. Save the posturing for someone who wasn't raised in the same wagons. It doesn't matter whether you knew or not. It's done now, and probably will work out for the best."

He paused and mused for a moment. "The challenge is for knives." He looked at the slender warrior to judge the reaction.

Again Lao-Kee whistled. "Knives? In the Circle? To first blood or death?"

"Death, what else? This thing must be decided once and for all. We are not fighting over weregild for a few Risar fools, and both of us know it. This fight will decide which of us will become the Warlord of the Horde. Of course, whichever of us wins will have other enemies to kill off, but none so dangerous."

The slender warrior gave Hrodvitnir an appraising look. "He's good with a knife, you know. Damn good."

Hrodvitnir nodded. "I know. But so am I. What would you say the odds are? Objectively."

Lao-Kee considered for a moment. "I'd give you a slight edge. He's taller than you are and has the reach on you. You're stronger and perhaps a bit faster. And you have a year or so more experience. But it'll be close, damn close." The slender warrior paused, then continued. "Are you sure it's wise to bring this whole thing to a head right now? Are you really ready for such a total move? Perhaps it would be best to find another way out. Perhaps if I—''

Hrodvitnir shook his head firmly. "No. No more of your schemes. This will be. We will fight beneath the eye of Father Gymir, and Mother Nerthus will drink the heart blood of the loser. I have waited long enough. It is time.''

Lao-Kee nodded solemnly. "When will this take place?''

"In one week's time, when Ymir's finger touches the horizon just before the eye of Gymir opens. That day we fight in the Circle at high noon. Two will enter the Circle. Only one will leave it. Alive.''

"I don't see why an Aesir has to know all about this damn knife fighting,'' Tror grumbled. "Give me a sword or an ax or my hammer any time. This damn knife stuff seems sneaky.''

"Huh,'' Lao-Kee snorted. "All of that's fine when you're three feet away. But what about three inches? Not much you can do with a sword or ax or hammer then.'' The Jotun wagged an admonishing finger at the red-bearded giant. "Many an Aesir has died in grappling with a Jotun he thought was finished because his sword was gone, Tror. Besides, personal duels between Jotun are almost always fought with knives, and unless you understand what's going on, you won't be able to appreciate the fight between Hrodvitnir and Fenrir. So pay attention.

"Now, the Jotun knife has a dagger-style blade. It's relatively narrow, tapers from the hilt to the point, and is edged on both sides. This makes it good for both slashing and stabbing.

"There are three ways to hold a knife. One, with your fingers wrapped around the hilt and your thumb over your fingers so that the blade sticks out from the top of the fist. That's the most natural way.

"Next,'' the slender warrior continued, shifting the knife slightly so that the thumb was on the hilt above the fingers, "is this grip—call it sword grip—either with the thumb on the narrow side of the hilt so that the blade is up and down in the hand, or on the wide part of the hilt so the blade is sideways.

"Finally there's this grip, one I call the stabbing grip.'' Lao-Kee flipped the knife so that the blade was reversed, sticking downward from the hand. "It's best when you're striking down, though it can be used for stabbing backhanded.

"You always hold the knife lightly, like you'd hold a live bird. Squeeze too tightly and the bird dies. Hold too lightly, and the bird will break free and fly away. Any knife fighter of worth can shift from one grip to the other faster than you can follow. Watch." The knife spun in the slender warrior's hand, flowing from one position to the other as smoothly and as quickly as thought.

"The reason for the different grips is that they're good for different attacks. Let's review the attacks.

"Basically there are slashes and thrusts. We'll start with slashes. The simplest is the full slash, like this." Lao-Kee darted forward, and holding the knife in the sword grip, slashed across Tror's body from his left shoulder to his right hip. The red giant stepped back in surprise. The Jotun grinned. "Don't worry, I won't cut you. Only demonstrating." Lao-Kee turned and spoke to Voden. "See? Very powerful. You can open an enemy from crop to crotch with a good slash. Also hard to deliver because it's a big movement, easy to block, and requires you to commit yourself. If you're careful and well-controlled, though, you can slash with surprising strength in a fairly small area.

"A second kind of slash is the jerk-slash. You slash out with the wrist cocked back, like this, and then at the last moment before the blade reaches the target, you jerk the wrist forward and slash the blade across. Much more controlled and harder to block, though it's not as powerful as the full slash. I like to use this one on the hands." Lao-Kee turned and gave Honir a feral grin. The Aesir turned pale and looked slightly ill.

"The last slash is the pull-slash. Tricky. You aim to the side of the target, go slightly past it, and then with a snap of the wrist, hook the blade back toward yourself, slashing as you pull back. Good to use on the hamstrings to cripple people." Lao-Kee made a quick movement and demonstrated the move on the back of Tror's right leg. Then the Jotun leered up at the giant Aesir warrior. Tror returned the glance with a thin, discomfited smile. He nodded weakly and swallowed.

"Now we come to the thrusts or stabs. First, and quickest, the jab. You snap the knife directly out at the target and snap it back even quicker. You aren't trying to penetrate more than an inch or two. Speed is the issue here, not the depth of the wound. Nevertheless, it can be a pretty nasty wound—especially in the gut, and if you spit on the blade or dip it in horse shit. This isn't really a powerful, killing stab, but it shakes an opponent. It's very hard to block, and if you hit a couple of times, it softens your opponent up for bigger things.

"The full stab or thrust is delivered with the whole weight of the body behind it. It can penetrate all the way up to the hilt of the knife, especially in soft places like the gut. If you twist as you bring the blade out, it leaves a big hole.

"Probably the sneakiest move of all is the hook. You can really confuse an opponent with one." Lao-Kee moved toward Tror again, knife ready, face intent. The Jotun made a few tentative jabs which Tror worriedly tried to block. "This one works especially for someone who puts up a good defense." The slender warrior moved in closer. "You deliver it like this." Almost quicker than they could follow, Lao-Kee thrust to Tror's left side. The giant warrior instinctively blocked with his left forearm. As soon as Tror's arm touched Lao-Kee's, the Jotun hooked the thrust to the right by bending wrist and elbow and lightly touched the left side of Tror's stomach, just below the floating ribs. Tror's face became red and then pale.

Lao-Kee stepped back and graced them all with a sly grin. "Technique is only part of it, though. You also have to know where to slash or stab to do the most damage. Basically there are three types of wounds you can inflict. First are the kind that cause rapid loss of blood. Slashing arteries is best for that kind of thing. Weakens your opponent gradually, but surely. Cut them enough that way and you can just stand back until they can't stand anymore, then step in an deliver a killer blow.

"That's the second kind—killer blows. Very special places. Like a slash across the jugular; in the eye to reach the brain; upward under the ear, especially if you pump the handle a little; directly into the temple; the heart, though that's hard to hit; upward into the solar plexus. That's most of them.

"And finally, what we call the cripplers. Slashing muscles, tendons, the backs of the hands, the arms. Score enough of those, and your opponent won't be able to move when you step in to cut his throat.

"So," the slender warrior said brightly, stepping back to grin impishly at the three of them, "now you know something about Jotun knife fighting. Not enough to appreciate the fine points, but at least enough to be able to follow the duel."

Honir was looking paler than ever. "I'm not too sure I want to, Lao-Kee."

"Oh, but of course you do!" the Jotun practically crowed. "After all, you really want to give Hrodvitnir all the support you can. It's very important for your future, you know."

Voden cocked his head to one side and fixed Lao-Kee with the keen-eyed stare of his single open eye. "How so?"

"Well," the Jotun drawled, "you're Hrodvitnir's guests and under his protection. If he should die in the duel, Fenrir isn't bound to protect you. Indeed, he has plenty of reason to hate you since you were all involved in the mess over Ottar and Hreidmir. He could easily decide to have you killed."

"But," Tror sputtered, "we're guests of the White Bear too."

"Oh," Lao-Kee replied offhandedly, "I don't imagine the Trul would pay too much attention to something the man most likely to be the next Warlord of the Horde might do to a couple of Aesir. I'm sure they'd cluck their tongues over the bodies afterward and wag their fingers at him in reprimand. But as for stopping him . . ." Lao-Kee shrugged and began to walk away, then stopped and turned back to them. "So if I were you, I'd be there, and I'd be cheering very hard for Hrodvitnir. After all, if he loses, so do you."

IX

HRODVITNIR was having a strip of leather about two inches wide wound around and around his middle from just above his floating ribs down to his hips. "Not too tight," he murmured to the man who was doing it. "I still have to be able to dodge and move freely."

The man grunted in reply. "Huh. Still, it's got to be tight or it won't keep your guts from spilling on the ground if you're cut across the stomach."

"If he's cut that badly across the stomach," Lao-Kee commented sarcastically, "the leather will be cut, too, so how will it hold his guts in?" The man doing the winding just looked up and grunted again, shrugging slightly.

Hrodvitnir turned his head to Lao-Kee and said, "It's always done this way for a duel. Tradition. Perhaps it works. By the way, are their horses saddled and ready to go?"

Lao-Kee nodded. "But I don't see why they have to go back to Asaheim if you win. If you lose, of course. I doubt they'd even make it out of Utgard. But why if you win?"

"When—not 'if'—I kill Fenrir, my struggle for the Warlordship of the Horde enters its final and most dangerous stage. My enemies will be desperate and will stop at nothing to destroy me or my allies. It will be their last chance to defeat me. Voden and his friends will be obvious targets. I don't want them to die here in Utgard. I will be much too busy battling my Jotun enemies to have vengeful Aesir attacking me from behind. Warn them, Lao-Kee. Make it quite clear they must leave and return to Asgard as swiftly as possible. No delaying or they might die."

120

Lao-Kee nodded and chuckled. "Oh, they're warned! Honir looks terrified when any Jotun turns in his direction. Tror never lets go of that damn hammer of his. Heimdall's eyes and ears are always open. And Voden . . . ah, Voden is Voden. I'll stay by their sides during the duel to make sure they leave the instant the outcome is obvious."

The man finished the winding and stepped back, gesturing to Hrodvitnir to try moving about. The warrior went into a knife fighter's crouch and made several practice passes. "Hmmm," he finally said, straightening up, "seems fine. Can't bend down quite as far, but turning is fine."

"If you win, what do you intend to do about the Aesir?" Lao-Kee asked casually.

Hrodvitnir laughed harshly. "I've already told you. Do everything I can to keep them off my back for a year or two."

"And then?"

"And then, when my control is total and the Horde is sufficiently powerful, I will sweep southward and wipe them from the face of Yggdrasil."

"You'll kill them all?" Hrodvitnir nodded. "Even the women and children?"

Hrodvitnir nodded again. "I want no half-breed bastards among the Jotun," he snarled.

Lao-Kee smiled ironically. "Ah, then am I to go back to the Sunrise Empire? Or do you intend to wipe me from the face of Yggdrasil as well?"

Hrodvitnir laughed. "The blood of the Sunrise Empire and of the Jotun are very close. And in any case, I'm sure there will be tolerance for those who share the blood of the Warlord."

"Tolerance, yes. But acceptance? I wonder, brother, I wonder." Lao-Kee mused quietly as Hrodvitnir finished dressing by putting on a pair of leather leggings and a beautifully beaded and fringed shirt. "Will you kill Voden as well?" the slender warrior asked finally.

"Especially Voden."

"Why?"

"Why?" Hrodvitnir responded angrily. "You ask why I wish to kill the most dangerous Aesir ever to live? The one man in all of Yggdrasil who could defeat my plans?"

"Ah, yes," Lao-Kee replied in a voice dripping with sarcasm, "your plans! I had forgotten about your plans to conquer everything from the Sunrise Empire to the Western Forest, from the Icerealm to the Smoking Lands.''

Hrodvitnir's face became cold and hard. His voice dropped into a feral growl. ''Don't push too hard, little one. Even full blood can assure only so much. Half blood should assume half as much. My patience is long but not endless.'' For a moment he was silent and menacing. Then his face broke into a smile and he laughed. ''Perhaps we'll keep some to the Aesir and the Vanir alive after all! They might make good slaves. Would you like to have Voden as your slave?''

Lao-Kee smiled slyly and nodded. ''Very much, brother. Very much.''

In Nerthus's Grove, not far from the tree where Voden had hung for nine days and nine nights, lay a large ring of beaten earth, perhaps twenty-five feet across, marked with ash wands around its circumference. This was the Circle of Judgment, where men brought their differences before Nerthus and Gymir. The trial was by combat, and the gods decided who the winner was to be. The loser lay in the Circle, his blood soaking the holy ground.

Those who entered the Circle were clothed only in a breech-clout of pure white skin. Their ribs were wrapped in a strip of hide to offer some protection and to make it possible to keep going if they received stomach wounds. When they entered the Circle, a rawhide cord about twenty feet long was tied around each man's ankle. The cord could only be cut by the man who had cut his opponent's throat. The rules were simple: they fought with naked blades, and there was no fair nor foul; once two men stepped into the Circle, only one man was allowed to step back out again. How he accomplished it was up to him.

A crowd of more than a hundred Jotun had already gathered at the Circle before the parties of supporters accompanying the two fighters arrived. Each group vied with the other in richness of dress and ornamentation. Both Hrodvitnir and Fenrir had the wolf as their Fylgjur, and both wore elaborate wolf capes crowned with wolf's-head helmets. Upon seeing each other across the Circle, both broke into lupine snarls and howls.

Two of the Trul undressed each man, stripping him to his

breechclout. The White Bear took Hrodvitnir's knife and examined it, checking to make sure the blade had not been poisoned. Nodding, he handed it back and then went across the circle to check Fenrir. Satisfied that both men bore nothing but naked blades, he returned to the center of the Circle and waited for the opponents to get ready.

From where he stood, Voden scrutinized Fenrir. Hrodvitnir's opponent was taller and looked strong. His face was darker than Hrodvitnir's, his eyes more ferociously slanted and yellow in color, not unlike those of an actual wolf. He had drawn a wolf's paw on his face, crossing the bridge of his hooked nose. His hair was lustrous black, greased with wolf grease and braided into a short braid. Voden watched the man move as he warmed up and was impressed with his grace and power.

He turned his eyes to the nearby Hrodvitnir and watched the Jotun preparing himself. Shorter, thicker, with massive shoulders, Hrodvitnir was lighter and quicker on his feet. He seemed to flow rather than move. He handled his knife as if it were an extension of his arm. Voden watched him flip it around in his hand and then toss it back and forth between hands. He was equally adept with either hand.

The Jotun around the Circle were more subdued than Voden had expected. They were clearly in two separate groups, almost equal in size. Between them was a small open space on either side of the Circle. Across the gap they eyed each other with open suspicion and hostility. Lao-Kee is right, Voden thought. The situation is highly explosive. I'm glad the horses are saddled and ready to go. He looked over to where the slender warrior stood next to Hrodvitnir, giving him last-minute advice.

When both men had signaled their readiness, the White Bear raised his hand over his head and called out in a loud voice,

> "Ho, Gymir, open your eye to see!
> Ho, Nerthus, open your ear to hear!
> Ho, Father, come to judge for us!
> Ho, Mother, come to judge for us!"

As he spoke, he began to move around the circumference of the Circle with a shuffling step. From somewhere beneath his

bear robe he pulled a drum and began to beat lightly on it.
His feet moved in time with the tempo.

> *"Ho, Ymir, we are your sons.*
> *Ho, Ymir, we are your children.*
> *Ho, Ymir, come to judge for us!"*

Completing once around the circle, he turned and went in the
other direction.

> *"Ho, we are the Kaigwu, the People.*
> *Ho, we are the Kata, the Biters.*
> *Ho, we are the Kogui, the Horned Ones.*
> *Ho, we are the Kingep, the Big Shields.*
> *Ho, we are the Semat, the Thieves.*
> *Ho, we are the Kongtalyui, the Black Boys.*
> *Ho, we are the Kuato, the Dead Ones."*

He finished his second circuit and returned to the center of the
circle. His drumming picked up in speed, even though he
now stood stock still.

> *"Ho, let the Ten Grandmothers come and watch!*
> *Ho, let the Tai-me guard the ways!*
> *Ho, let Gadombitsouhi, Old Woman Under the*
> *Ground, be ready to receive the blood!"*

The drumming ceased suddenly and an absolute silence fell
over the Circle of Judgment. The White Bear shattered it with
a vast growl that shook the ground and made everyone sway
back in fear. "Let the two who seek the Judgment come into
the Circle!" he cried in a mighty voice. "Let the two come
into the Circle, and let only one leave it alive!"

Hrodvitnir and Fenrir moved swiftly and silently to stand
on either side of the White Bear. Two of the Trul came with
the cord and fastened it around their ankles. When they were
done and had left the Circle, the White Bear raised his eyes
toward the sky and said "Gymir!" in a soft but penetrating
voice. He then looked toward the earth and said "Nerthus!"
in a similar voice. With that, he stepped back out of the
circle, his arms folded across his chest, his deep, burning

eyes watching the two men facing each other across the space he had abandoned.

Fenrir was the first to move, reaching down swiftly to grab his end of the cord and hold it in his left hand. Hrodvitnir did the same, wrapping the cord twice around his left wrist, giving himself plenty of slack so he could move his left hand and arm freely. They both went into a knife-fighter's crouch, head erect, feet about shoulder width apart, back leg bent slightly, front foot lightly on the ground, knife held close to the body about waist high, free hand extended slightly in front of the body. The center of gravity for each of them was somewhere in the lower part of the abdomen. Their feet moved carefully, keeping contact with the ground through every part of every step.

The two men stepped toward each other cautiously, each watching how the other moved. They knew each other, had even fought the Aesir together. Now they were face to face, and only one would survive.

Hrodvitnir feinted a slash across Fenrir's front, from lower left to upper right. As the hand rose past the halfway mark, Fenrir stepped in and feinted a jab. The slash snicked out and downward, aiming at the wrist, and the jab converted into a slash toward the right, avoiding the attack.

They stepped back now and judged each other. Fenrir was bigger and had the reach. Hrodvitnir was lighter and had the speed. Although overall Hrodvitnir was stronger, Fenrir's powerful shoulders gave him nearly as much stabbing and slashing power. It was a very even match.

Voden felt a presence by his side and looked down. Lao-Kee looked up at him, a mocking smile curving the Jotun's lips. ''Notice how they protect their knife arm,'' the slender warrior said, nodding toward the contestants in the circle. ''That move of Hrodvitnir's was to draw out Fenrir's knife arm, not to go for his gut. Gut cutting is later. Right now they both want to cut the other's hands and arms. Cut the hand that holds the knife badly enough, and it can't hold it anymore. Then you can just step in and cut the throat.'' Lao-Kee grinned viciously and drew an imaginary blade across an imaginary throat. Voden merely nodded and turned his attention back to the duelists.

A series of feints, almost too fast to track, followed in

swift succession. The knife blades sparkled in the early sunlight, sending off sudden flashes which surprised the eyes.

Lao-Kee continued a running narrative in a soft voice.
"They're both going for immobilizing wounds. They'll aim
at places like the shoulder muscles, those on the back of the
arm, the back of the forearm, the backs of the hands, the
front and back of the knee, and the ankles. If they can score a
bleeder, they'll do it. Inside of the wrist is good for that. So
is the inside of the arm, right by the elbow. Throat's great,
but tricky and hard to get at. The artery on the inside of the
thigh works well, lots of bleeding. But it's hard to get, too.
Once either one thinks he's done enough damage with immo-
bilizers and bleeders, he'll go for a killing blow. That's
dangerous, though. Got to be real sure your opponent's not
pretending. Get too close and you might get a nasty surprise.
Best to stay back and kick his head in."

Hrodvitnir jabbed toward Fenrir's left arm. As the other
man moved his own knife to counter with a slash to the
forearm, Hrodvitnir suddenly stepped in and kicked out with
his left foot, hitting Fenrir's right knee. Fenrir took the blow
lightly, moving his leg just in time to soften the kick. His
shift in concentration, however, allowed Hrodvitnir to change
his jab into a slash and rake his blade across the back of
Fenrir's knife hand. The blood flowed swift and red.

Hrodvitnir's triumph was short-lived. Rather than stepping
back in confusion, Fenrir attacked. He suddenly shifted the
knife to his other hand and slashed out, catching Hrodvitnir
on the forearm, just above the elbow. More blood flowed.

The two circled again, looking for openings. Suddenly
Fenrir moved, stepping in and to one side, then instantly
shifting his weight to the left and sweeping his blade in a
swift arc. It ripped into Hrodvitnir's shoulder, opening a deep
gash. Hrodvitnir spun with the blow and countered with a
slash of his own that opened Fenrir's right arm from shoulder
to elbow.

Both men were panting heavily now and blood covered
their arms, making their knife hands slippery and their grips
tenuous. Hrodvitnir stepped to the left and jabbed. Voden
could see it coming and almost cried out. Hrodvitnir had
placed his foot directly on the cord. With a swift jerk, Fenrir
pulled upward on the cord, which he now held in his badly
bleeding right hand. Hrodvitnir lost his balance and fell back-

ward. He was instantly back on his feet, but not before Fenrir had slashed the back of his calf and almost severed the tendon of his right leg.

Now Fenrir moved better and more swiftly than his shorter opponent. His superior reach began to prove its value as he darted in and out, jabbing and slashing. Both men scored, but it was obvious to everyone that Fenrir was having the better of it now that Hrodvitnir was partially crippled and could no longer move as swiftly as before.

Soon they were covered with blood, heaving in great gulps of air, and their movements had slowed down considerably. Both had already lost a good deal of blood.

But the fact was that neither one had yet scored a truly killing blow. Fenrir, feeling his superior speed and reach, was becoming impatient and more daring. It was clear to everyone that he was convinced he was going to defeat his shorter and now slower foe. Hrodvitnir looked very much like an animal brought to bay, his head down and bloody, his gaze wild and frightened, his whole stance one of exhaustion and defeat.

Fenrir decided, and moved in for the kill. He feinted to the left, trying to cut the inside of Hrodvitnir's knife-holding hand, then changed the jab into a slash for the other's throat. Hrodvitnir stepped to his own left and suddenly flipped his knife from his right hand to his left. His left hand was already moving as he did, and the blade plunged deep into the side of Fenrir's neck, just below the ear. Hrodvitnir took Fenrir's slash on his shoulder. The blow was slightly off, but it still flung him backward and knocked him down.

As he rose, Fenrir was on his knees, trying to get up. Everyone gasped to realize Hrodvitnir's hands were empty! His knife was gone, lying on the ground next to Fenrir. Fenrir tried to stand, but sank back to his knees, his eyes dazed and fixed on Hrodvitnir. The latter moved quickly forward and kicked out with his wounded leg, slamming his foot into the other man's temple.

Fenrir went down, the blood suddenly gushing from the wound the other man had delivered to his neck. Hrodvitnir stood, swaying on both feet, watching as his opponent slowly crumpled forward, his knife falling from his fingers as his hands went out to hold him from the ground. Hrodvitnir stepped in and kicked again. Fenrir went down in a heap. Hrodvitnir picked up his own knife and slashed Fenrir's throat. The blood gushed out the man's mouth and nose as well as from the wound. His eyes glazed and he was dead.

Hrodvitnir fell to his knees, grabbed the cord and cut it. Then, slowly and painfully, he crawled to the edge of the Circle. He got across before he collapsed.

Lao-Kee grabbed Voden's arm and whispered harshly, "Let's get out of here! All hell's going to break loose!" The Aesir and his companions pushed quickly through the stunned crowd and ran for their wagon where their horses were tethered, ready to ride.

The White Bear was the only one who bothered to look up as they rode from Utgard. Then he went into the Circle and checked on Fenrir. The man was dead. Next he moved to Hrodvitnir's side. Alive. He stood and spread his arms toward the sky. "Ho, Gymir," he cried, "you have judged this one right!" He dropped his hands toward the earth. "Ho, Nerthus, you have judged this one right!" Then he gestured to Hrodvitnir's supporters. "He lives. Come and take him to his wagon. I will follow and attend to his wounds." He turned to Fenrir's supporters. "He is dead. Wait until his blood has drained into the earth and then take the body and throw it to the dogs."

The crowd dispersed until only the White Bear and a slender Jotun warrior remained. They were both looking in the direction the departing Aesir had taken.

"They are gone," the White Bear said.

"Gone," Lao-Kee sighed.

"Your feelings for Voden are dangerous," the White Bear commented casually.

Lao-Kee looked up sharply. "It is no business of yours, Trul."

"Oh, but you are wrong. The half sister of the next Warlord of the Horde cannot afford to be in love with the chieftain of the Aesir. Whom will you serve, Lao-Kee? Your brother and your people, or the man you love?"

"Lao-Kee will serve Lao-Kee!" the slender warrior said angrily. "I don't need your advice!"

"They do not even know you are a woman, do they?" the White Bear asked in a musing tone.

"No."

"And how do you suppose they will react when they discover how you have tricked them?"

Lao-Kee barked a harsh laugh. "I don't care how they react! Voden will keep his blood oath to me. I don't give a damn about the rest."

"Do not be too sure of what Voden will and won't do, little one," the White Bear said sharply. "He is deeper than you imagine, and his destiny leaves no room for trifling. He will do what he must, and best you not be in the way when he does it!"

Lao-Kee gave the White Bear a sour look. "Hadn't we best be attending the next Warlord of the Horde? He has many wounds. If he lives, things will be bloody and chaotic for a while. But if he dies, they'll be much, much worse. Coming?" Lao-Kee turned and stalked off in the direction of Hrodvitnir's wagon.

For a brief moment the White Bear stood and watched her go. There is great ambiguity in that one, he thought. So much love and so much hate. A devious nature, both a friend and a foe, an ally and an enemy. Whom would she end up serving? And whom destroying?

They rode without stopping until they crossed the Iving at Bifrosti's Ford. When they rode into Asgard, Gagnrad was waiting for them in the Warrior's Hall. They related what had happened until late into the night.

The next morning Gagnrad told them that Kao-Shir and Anhur had passed through on their way to Nidavellir and by chance had arrived at the same time an emissary had come from the Alfar. This was the first time in memory one of the Alfar had come out of their forest fastness. The creature had wanted to speak with Voden, but had decided not to wait. Fascinated, Kao-Shir and Anhur had volunteered to return with the Alfar to Alfheim and find out what the hidden people of the realm between the River Vid and the Bones of Ymir wanted. They promised to return the following spring.

But the most interesting news had come from Vanaheim with Niord. The young Vanir warrior came himself to talk with Voden and tell him of the state of open civil war that reigned in the forests of the south. "Freyja has fled Folkvang and joined Yngvi in the woods. The lines are clearly drawn now. It's total war."

Voden sat quietly, a strange look coming over his face at

the mention of Freyja. "Ah," he finally said when Niord had finished his narrative, "Freyja. Who will win this war, Niord?"

Niord scowled thoughtfully. "That's a hard call. Yngvi and Freyja probably have the numbers on their side. But Vor has the better fighting force. I'd call it pretty well balanced. It'll be a long and bloody struggle, mark my words."

Voden looked at Gagnrad. The older man grinned and said, "Aye, and that makes one enemy out of commission. Our backs are safe for the moment."

The chief of the Aesir let his gaze wander over Gagnrad's features. It dawned on him that his father's closest friend was an old man. Gagnrad's hair was snow white. His beard was grizzled and bristling. His frame was shrunken and twisted by age and by the multitude of wounds he'd received during his many years as an Aesir warrior. His eyes were rimmed with dark pouches and looked infinitely tired. There was pain lurking just beneath their surface. His breathing was laborious. He won't live through many more winters, Voden suddenly realized. And when he dies, he'll be the last of my father's generation to go.

The last. Voden sat up and looked into the distance. The last of the old generation. It was a new time, a time for new ideas, new approaches. He'd already begun to walk that road by going to Jotunheim against the advice of Gagnrad and the other old men. He would continue that way.

"Yes," he said softly, "our back is covered. But is that really enough? I know it was always my father's fondest wish to see the Vanir neutralized, but I wonder if that is still the best policy. Know, friend of my father, that Hrodvitnir will soon be Warlord of the Jotun Horde. I've watched this nephew of Bergelmir closely, and I trust him not. He makes the sounds of peace with his mouth, but his eyes are filled with war and death. He waits, like the lone wolf stalking the caribou, for enough of his kind to gather before he attacks. It'll be a few years before he gathers his numbers and his strength, but when he does, I doubt not he'll cross the Iving and attack.

"Is a neutralized Vanaheim enough in the face of such an onslaught? I wonder. Perhaps we need something more."

Niord was nodding. "Aye, that's the truth of it! With the Horde united under one leader, could you hold the Ford? Could you keep the Sons of Ymir from sweeping south? And after they'd finished the Aesir, would they stop short of the Smoking Lands?

"Like it or not, Aesir and Vanir are in this together! If we stand separately, we'll die separately. Voden, we must band together, form a solid truce! Only that way can we stand against the Horde!"

Voden nodded, a strange smile playing across his lips, his single eye gleaming hotly from the depths of his hood. "More than a truce, Niord. This time we must join together, blend into one people. Only as one people can we stand firm against an enemy like the Jotun Horde."

He was silent for a moment. Then he spoke again, his voice deep and hollow, ringing with vague threat. "There are more things loose in Yggdrasil than Hrodvitnir. Powers are gathering. We must match them with other powers.

"Let us think on this thing. And then we will act."

A council was called and riders went out across the Himinborg, Idavoll, and Aesir plains, even as far as the Valaskialf Plateau, to summon all those who wished to participate. It would take a month for everyone to gather.

While he waited for the leaders of the Aesir to come together, Voden spent his time wandering about Asgard, renewing old acquaintances and meeting those he didn't know. Tyr was there, and Thrud, Tror's sister.

Most important of all, though, was Vili, his own sister. At first she was shy around her grim, one-eyed brother. But soon her natural friendliness and vivacious spirit cut through her shyness and his reserve. In the end they went everywhere together, and Voden found himself charmed by the bright-eyed young woman who reminded him of their mother in so many ways and yet was always herself. He quickly grew to understand why everyone loved her so dearly. No matter how heavily his foreboding weighed on his mind, Vili could always raise a smile to his lips.

They often rode far out on the Himinborg Plain. Vili loved to ride, the wind blowing through her long blond hair. She especially loved the small stands of woods that dotted the plain here and there. She would race to them and then ride slowly beneath their green branches, looking for apple trees. When she found one, she would leap from her horse and climb lightly into the tree, picking and throwing the golden, ripe fruit down to Voden until he could hold no more. When they came to a farmstead, Vili would ride in and make a gift of the fruit to the woman of the hall, sometimes even joining with her in her household tasks.

When they wandered Asgard together, Voden never ceased to wonder at the way children would swarm to her. Somehow she always managed to have a golden apple hidden in her robe for almost every one of them. If she ran out, she remembered who had been left out and made sure to give them an extra apple the next time around.

Every now and then Voden was surprised to find himself thinking of Lao-Kee and Hrodvitnir, not as enemies, but as people he both liked and admired. He especially missed the slender warrior's mischievous grin and sly wit. When he thought of some of the scrapes Lao-Kee had gotten them into, rather than being angry, he found himself laughing. Tror grumbled when he mentioned the Jotun, but it was plain the red-haired giant felt much the same way. Heimdall was the only one who frowned unpleasantly when he heard them talking of Lao-Kee. It was plain that the strange pale man had little use for the Jotun.

Even more often, Voden's thoughts turned to someone else. Then his mood would turn dark and quiet and he would leave Asgard and go out to the mound where his grandfather, father, and mother were buried. There he would sit for hours, gazing southward, an odd smile filled with longing and despair twisting his face. Everyone was disturbed by his smile and his mood, and gave him wide berth at those times. Everyone, that is, except Honir. Voden's long-legged friend would sit near him on the mound, sharing his silent thoughts, remembering the smile and the woman it was for.

Eventually the Aesir gathered and the council began. For a full week they sat in the Warrior's Hall, allowing every man who cared to speak to have his say. Hrodvitnir's likely rise to power worried them all. Yngvi's plight reached their sympathy, and many of those who had gone to fight with him spoke for joining the fight on his side. "Now is the time to act," Hinar declared. "While the Jotun are caught up in their own struggles, we can turn to the south and help Yngvi and Freyja smash Vor and her damn brown-clad killers! I've fought side by side with those forest lads and I've watched our own go down beneath the Valkyrja. I say we fight!''

Others were fearful of getting involved. ''We'll lose good men we cannot spare,'' Gagnrad warned. ''We've lost enough lately as it is. The last two battles have bled us white. We need time to regain our strength. We can't afford to lose men in the south whom we need to guard against the enemy in the north.''

On and on it went, round and round. Slowly, though, a consensus began to form. Finally, when it had become clear to most of them what the general feeling was, Voden stood and held up his hands. ''Aesir,'' he said, his voice calm and soft but reaching every ear, ''have fought Vanir since any can remember. It is time to end that fighting. Yngvi is not our enemy. Freyja is not our enemy. Vor is our enemy. We will join with Yngvi to defeat the rule of the Disir. Now is the time to act, while the Jotun are occupied with the struggle over the Warlordship.'' He turned to Niord. ''You will be our emissary to Yngvi and Freyja. Carry our offer of alliance to them. We are ready to fight by their side. We are ready to become one with them in war and in peace.''

A roar of agreement greeted his words. He sat back down in the High Seat and let the cheering ring on. His eye met Heimdall's, and suddenly the cheers sounded like war cries and the screams of the dying. Behind it all he thought he could hear the deep notes of a fateful horn ringing out through the many lands of Yggdrasil. It is coming, he thought. It is coming.

DARK EMPIRE

X

THE hair on the hound's back rose stiffly. A growl rumbled deep in its throat, and its lips curled back in a snarl that showed long, sharp teeth. It was massive, with powerful shoulders, well-muscled legs, and jaws built for crushing bones. Standing waist-high at the front shoulders, it was all black except from some dark brown markings on the chest, muzzle, and just above the eyes.

Jormungand held the leash tightly. "I agree wholeheartedly, Garm," he muttered to the growling dog. "This place stinks of evil. Why have we come here again, Surt? The first time was enough to last me forever."

The Black One was gazing intently around the ruins. "The only entrance to Gnipa Cave is somewhere here in the temple of Nergal." He paused in his search and looked at Jormungand. "Be calm, faithful Serpent. We are in no danger here in Cuthah. At least not very much. I admit I don't like to be here any more than you do, but it is necessary. Innina and Enki have me hedged in no matter which way I turn. I must break out, and this is the only way."

"Well, why don't you at least tell me what you are looking for. I don't mind standing here trying to keep Garm under control, but if it would shorten this expedition, I'd be willing to help search too. By the pen of Namtaru, I'd be more than willing."

"Then look for some sort of entrance, something marked with the ensign of Aralu. It must be here somewhere. It leads to a secret place known as Gnipa Cave. The cave itself guards one of the entrances to the nether world."

Jormungand frowned and shook his head. "What in the name of the tits of Ereshkigal do you want with a cave that leads to Aralu? If you haven't had enough of that damn place, I have. Why not find another cave? One that doesn't lead anywhere."

Surt smiled slightly and sighed. "Gnipa Cave is within the domains ruled by Nergal. That means it is secure from the likes of Innina. Which in turn means that anything I do there will remain hidden from her." He walked up to Jormungand and the hound and laid a calming hand on the dog's head. "That's why Garm is with us."

"Ah, of course, that's why Garm is with us!" Jormungand exclaimed, his voice heavy with sarcasm. "Of course, it's all clear as can be now. We're looking for Gnipa Cave, which is secure from Innina, and that's why Garm is here. Dammit, Surt, make sense for once, will you?"

The Black One looked around as if half expecting to see someone peering at them over the broken and tumbled piles of stone. The ruins were empty except for the sense of dread that hung heavily to every shattered stone. "I suppose the temple of Cuthah is a safe place to reveal what I intend to do. Well, sit down and I'll tell you." Grumbling, Jormungand found a fairly flat stone and sat, Garm laying down at his feet, his lips curled in a constant snarl, his black eyes darting from shadow to shadow in search of the things that made him so uneasy. Surt sat too, leaning forward.

"Innina, Enki, and Marduk have built a wall of magic around me, cutting me off from the possible allies I might have summoned with the *Utukki Limnuti*. What's more, they've been draining off the power I have already accumulated and attempting to loosen the ties I have established over my allies. Know, Serpent, that the storm demon Abubu no longer comes when I call. Lahamu comes only grudgingly and performs her tasks with surly indifference. Even Ningishzida, who has always guarded my door, is disaffected and answers my summons slowly.

"Without doubt, your capture of Enkidu has saved us. Though Marduk was far from being the most powerful or effective of the three, the fact that I was able to neutralize him has lessened the pressure against us. Enki has seen fit to remove himself to his palace, Eengurra, where he feels safe. Yes, Marduk's defeat has thrown my enemies off balance. I must act swiftly and keep them that way.

"But how? Enki, locked away in his stronghold, built on a rock in the sea near Eridu, is unreachable. As is Innina, safe within the mighty walls of noble Uruk, surrounded by both her own power and that of the ancient An. Yet somehow I must act against at least one of them.

"Should it be Enki? My magic is limited, my power circumscribed, my allies few and weak. I could never stand up to the power he wields through use of both the *Nimeqi* and the *Shipti*.

"Innina, then? She is very powerful in her own right. And I more than half suspect she has access to An's magical book, the *Maqlu*. I have nothing to match her.

"Is there no way? Am I doomed? It would seem so. But wait, let us think about Innina again. An's lovely consort. Sister of Ereshkigal. Sister of Dumuzi. Ah. Merely the sister of Dumuzi? No, hardly. An is old, too old to be of much use to a lustful bitch like Innina. Yet the consort of one of the Sons must be cautious. Not just any lover will do. It must be someone special, someone who could be trusted. But who? One of the other Sons? Not likely. A commoner? Even less likely.

"There is a tale, Serpent, a rumor that says Dumuzi is more than brother to Innina. Dumuzi. Bull, ram, stud. Is he Innina's lover? And if so, is it possible to strike there, much the same way we struck at Marduk through his friend Enkidu?

"An interesting possibility. One worthy of investigating. So I sniffed around Dumuzi, and what did I find but a maze of protecting spells, a wall of magic the likes of which I have only found around the persons of the Sons themselves. And all of it, every little piece, smelled of Innina. Obviously the rumor is true. Why else would Innina expend so much time and energy? She is hardly the type to spend such resources to protect someone simply because they happened to come from the same womb.

"Dumuzi's protection was so powerful and complete that at first I despaired. There seemed to be no way, no hope. Yet I sensed that he was my only chance, the only weak point at which I might be able to attack Innina. So I persisted, circled Dumuzi, studied him from every angle. I discovered an odd fact, one that seemed insignificant yet intrigued me. Many sars ago Dumuzi was Enki's shepherd, in charge of all his flocks. When he was Enki's shepherd, he had wonderful dogs to help him herd the sheep, the goats, the cattle. Large, black dogs they were, the dogs of his shepherdship, and he loved them greatly. When he left Enki's employ, he had to leave the dogs behind. Innina had no love for the beasts and made him abandon them.

"Aside from Innina's frequent and passionate visits, Dumuzi now lives all alone, isolated in the midst of his sister/lover's spells. He pines for his dogs, faithful Serpent, pines for his black dogs, the dogs of his carefree days as a shepherd."

Surt stopped and gazed intently at Garm for a few moments. Then he began to speak again, seemingly addressing the hound. "So we will send him a dog. A black dog. And in his loneliness he will accept it and clasp it to him. But it will be a dog such as he has never clasped before."

A vicious smile spread slowly over the face of the Patesi of Borsippa and Maqam Nifl. "We will find Gnipa Cave, loyal Serpent. There we will place Garm. And there I will construct something new, something unlike anything that has ever walked the face of Yggdrasil before. With my magic I will transform Garm into a hellhound, a demon of great power, a monster that will do my bidding, loyal to me alone as its creator. And I will send that monster to Dumuzi, I will send that black dog, that dog of shepherdship, to the lonely brother and lover of Innina."

Surt's voice dropped to a harsh whisper. His eyes glowed with a vile, sulfurous light. "And that dog will drag him down to the Kur." The Black One looked up to see the stunned face of Jormungand. His smile grew even wider, showing his teeth in a feral snarl. "Yes, faithful Serpent, I will make a monster of Garm and cast Dumuzi into the realm of demons! I will strike Innina from behind! And with both her and Marduk out of the way, no one will be able to stop me!"

His wild laughter echoed from the shattered ruins that lay tumbled about them.

• • •

They bound Garm in Gnipa Cave with thick ropes made from gleipnir, the same material Surt had used to make the net with which they had entangled and defeated the demon Tiamat. When they were sure the hound was securely tethered, Surt began the arduous task of opening a Bab-Apsi, a magical doorway to the demon world. He kept the opening small and easily controllable because he no longer trusted the extent of his own powers.

After many hours of chanting, burning various powders, and sacrificing two pure black cocks that had never crowed, the dark, slender wizard turned and smiled at Jormungand with grim satisfaction. "I must rest and gather strength for a few hours before I begin the next stage. It will be long and difficult, requiring several visits. I must move slowly and surely. One misstep and I could lose control of the whole process."

Jormungand gave Surt an appraising look. "Lose control? And what, pray tell, would that mean?"

Surt frowned. "Nothing good. What I am attempting is something that has never been done before, so far as I know. Generally, when one opens a Bab-Apsi to demonkind, it is for the purpose of calling up demons and forcing them to take physical shapes. Though demons dwell on the spiritual plane, they do have corresponding physical manifestations on the material plane. If a wizard knows a demon's True Name, if he has a strong enough will, and if he has sufficient knowledge to circumscribe and control the demon, he can summon the demon, neutralize its strength, and force it to do his bidding. I have been doing such things for many years now, beginning long ago with simple Gallas-demons and slowly working my way up to more powerful ones like the Saghulhaza or the Utukku. My mastery of the mighty storm demon Zu is my greatest accomplishment to date.

"But all this is the kind of thing every wizard does, even pathetic Kishpu sorcerers." He looked proudly around the cave. "What I am trying to do here . . . no, what I am *going* to do here, is something much vaster, more difficult . . . something no other wizard has ever even thought of doing before."

Surt began to pace back and forth as he talked. Every now and then he would gesture with his hands. Occasionally, as he passed near Garm's head, he would give the tethered beast a quick pat. "As I've told you, faithful Serpent, existence consists of three planes. The lower two—the material and the spiritual—are merely aspects of the highest, the sacred—or the Utterly Other, as I prefer to call it. This highest plane is the true reality, and everything on the lower two merely reflects the ultimate reality.

"I've also mentioned that all existence is of a piece, that the diversity we seem to perceive in the world about us is simply a failure to see correctly, a failure to see the unity that underlies and transcends multiplicity and joins it in ultimate oneness. Thus the three planes are really just one, and all the myriad existences on each plane are really unity. Everything dissolves into the Utterly Other.

"This unity in diversity is expressed in another way on the two lower planes, the material and the spiritual. The two planes interpenetrate each other. All material bodies have a spiritual aspect, and all spiritual existences have a corresponding physical emanation. Spirit and matter are inextricably bound together as thoroughly as both are bound to the higher unity.

"That means, loyal Serpent, that everything in the world about us has its spiritual counterpart, or as some writers prefer to call it, a soul. These rocks, for example, have a soul, and that is why they seem to emanate such evil. Trees, plants, rivers, lakes, birds, animals, all have a spiritual aspect. Each is different and shaped in accordance with its physical manifestation, and vice versa.

"It is precisely this interpenetration of spirit and matter that makes magic possible. And this is the deeper meaning of the phrase, 'That which is below is like that which is above, and that which is above is like that which is below.' The only reason a sorcerer can summon up a demon is because he has a spiritual aspect to his corporeal nature, a spiritual aspect that he can project into the spiritual plane to force another spiritual aspect to assume its corresponding corporeal form. And when, brave Serpent, you battle a demon or a dragon, as you have on several occasions, you are fighting not only with your body, but with your spirit as well. It is the combined strength of the two that allows you to triumph over the monster.

"Yes, this intermingling of spirit and matter, of soul and body, is what makes magic possible. Without it, the two planes would be separate and you could not move from one to the other. If the two ever ceased to interpretrate, or if men ever came to believe they did not, then, indeed, magic would be impossible." He paused for a moment, musing. "What a strange, cold, sterile world that would be," he murmured thoughtfully.

"Now, as I said, demons, being spirits, have their own corresponding physical manifestations. In general the only way a spirit can enter the material plane is in its own corporeal form. Since most spiritual beings have an aversion to the material plane, and since the taking of a physical shape requires the expenditure of a great deal of energy, very few spiritual entities ever cross between the two planes. Indeed, only the most powerful are even capable of it.

"Now, when a wizard conjures up a spirit, what he is doing is tricking or forcing it to take its physical form. Once it has done so, he can place restraints upon that form to control the spirit. As you have doubtless noticed, brave Serpent, this is a difficult procedure and requires both great knowledge and great strength.

"Occasionally, however, the two planes come very close to each other and it is possible for an entity from the spiritual plane to cross on its own and enter into an already existing physical form. This phenomenon is known as demonic possession, because the spirit possesses a material form that is not its own."

Surt stopped his pacing and stood looking at Garm. He talked directly to the animal as he continued. "What I intend to do is a combination of both procedures. I plan to call up several demons, but not in their own physical forms. I will summon them to come and inhabit the form of Garm. I will cram them in together, forcing them to blend, to interpenetrate, to mix. The result should be much the same as when you mix certain physical things together. They will interact, be transformed by the interaction, and the result will be something totally new. The whole will be greater and different from the mere sum of the parts."

The slender wizard turned suddenly and fixed Jormungand with excited, glowing eyes. "Yes, faithful Serpent! I, Surt the Black One, will create something new! A monster in the shape of a hound, a demon from the Kur that can pass as a simple dog. Innina won't have protected Dumuzi from such a creature because such a creature has never existed before.

There will be no need to batter down the wall of magic she has built around her brother. Garm will simply walk through it!"

"Be calm, my love. Tell me of your dream. Perhaps I can help explain it or understand it if it has meaning."

Dumuzi shuddered. "I don't even like to think about it, sister. It was . . . frightening. I was walking down by the river. It was a warm day and I became drowsy, so I laid down among the buds and the rushes and dozed off.

"It seemed as though I never even closed my eyes. Suddenly the rushes began to rise and grow tall and thick all about me. I noticed one reed growing by itself, and it trembled and moaned as I looked on it. Then I saw a double reed, and first one part, then the other disappeared.

"Without any transition I found myself in this grove, here where my little house and sheepfold are, where we sit even now. I gazed at the trees and they rose up around me, leaning in, threatening, whispering. Terror rose in my throat and I cried out.

"From nowhere a swift deluge of water came and poured over my hearth, snuffing out the fire, hissing horribly as it turned the coals from living cherry red to dull dead black. My drinking cup, made of clay for me by Ninmah, fell from the peg where I always hang it. It shattered into a million pieces. I turned to find my shepherd's crook, but it had disappeared.

"I heard a cry of anguish and rushed to the window. Out in the sheepfold I saw an eagle seizing a lamb. And on the reed fence, a falcon had caught a sparrow and was pecking its head, killing it."

He paused and looked at Innina, his large dark eyes filled with fear. "And then," he continued, his voice dropping to a whisper, as if he was reluctant to give voice to his next words, "I heard a voice call out, a dark voice, one that came from deep in the earth. It said 'Cold lies the hearth. No fire burns. Shattered lies the cup. Dumuzi is no more. The sheepfold is given to the winds.' "

Innina sat silent and thoughtful. The dream was disturbing, far more so than Dumuzi realized. The rushes that rose around him symbolized demons that would come to attack him. The reed that grew alone stood for his mother, Sirtur, and it trembled because it wept for some terrible fate that awaited him. The double reed stood for the two of them, Dumuzi and Innina. It meant they would be separated and both would be taken away somewhere.

The rest was even grimmer. The rising up of the trees around Dumuzi's house and sheepfold was the rising up of Gallas-demons. The quenching of the hearth fire meant desolation, the falling of the clay drinking cup from its peg symbolized the falling of Dumuzi to the ground in defeat, and the disappearance of the shepherd's crook indicated that everything Dumuzi owned, every hope he had, would wither. The eagle that seized the lamb was a Gallas-demon seizing him and scratching his cheek. The falcon catching the sparrow on the fence was a Gallas-demon that climbed the fence to come and take him away. And the voice . . . ah, the voice came from below, from Aralu or the Kur. It was the voice of Nergal.

She didn't like it. This was the tenth day of the month known as Tammuz, and the constellation of the Scorpion drew near the moon. If the moon appeared tonight and the Scorpion stood by its right horn, it mean dire things. Locusts would pour forth during the harvest and eat up all the grain, bringing hunger and desolation to the land. A king would lose his throne and an enemy go forth to plunder his land. And more.

But how could there be any danger to Dumuzi? She had hedged him round with so many spells and magical protections that no demon known to her, much less some miserable Gallas-demon, could ever hope to break into his sheepfold and quench his hearth or shatter his drinking cup.

She felt a sudden chill of premonition. Surt. The Black One had struck at Marduk through Enkidu. Would he strike at her through Dumuzi? Likely, all too likely. Yes, the whole situation smelled of the man.

Yet what could he do? He didn't command any demons powerful enough to smash through the protections she had built around Dumuzi. And there was no possibility he had managed to figure out all the interlocking spells and neutralize them. She let her awareness spread out around her for a moment to check. Yes, everything was in place. Nothing had been tampered with.

Then what could it be? The dream was frightening and

prophetic. Dumuzi was in terrible danger. This, she realized, requires serious thought.

She looked at Dumuzi. His eyes were bigger and darker than usual. Her gaze moved over his smooth, muscled limbs, and finally rested on his kilt. He was erect. His fear excited him sexually. She felt a warmth growing between her own legs as she thought of the size and vigor of him. Her mouth was suddenly dry, and she licked her lips. She would only stay a while, and then go back to her tower and see what she could find out about this situation. Only a little while, only a little enjoyment. She reached her hand out and moved his kilt aside. Gently she stroked him as he pulled down her skirt with feverish fingers. Yes, yes, later she would study this. But now . . . now . . .

The dog appeared at his door while the sun yet clung to the western horizon. It was black except for some dark brown markings on its chest, muzzle, and just above the eyes. It had the same regal bearing as the dogs he had once had when he had been in charge of Enki's flocks. There was a light in its black eyes that spoke of intelligence far beyond that of an ordinary dog.

Dumuzi was lonely and frightened. He had kept Innina with him most of the day, giving her orgasm after orgasm, until she lay panting and exhausted, her whole body loose and relaxed, her skin glowing, her eyes soft and deep. He had expected her to stay the night, indeed had pleaded with her, for he feared being alone with the memory of his dream. But she had risen from their bed and gone back to her palace, determined to find out what—or who—was behind the dream.

When he first saw the dog, he was afraid. It was so massive and strong. How had it gotten here? Innina had always refused to let him keep a dog, even though he had asked several times. He missed the dogs of his shepherdship. Then he wondered if perhaps she had not sent it to him, to keep him company and give him strength against the dream. How else could he explain the dog's arrival at this moment? Besides, he knew he was surrounded with magic and that nothing dangerous could get through to him. So finally he opened the door and let the dog in. It smiled up at him as it crossed the threshold, but its tail was strangely still.

As night fell, the crescent moon rose in a clear sky. By its

right horn the Scorpion stood, its tail stinging the horizon.
Deep in the earth locust eggs began to hatch.

He fled from the house to the sheepfold and cowered
among the milling animals. The dog climbed the reed fence
and leapt on him, its claws raking his cheek with piercing
nails, leaving bloody wounds behind. It knocked the shepherd's crook from his hand and the tip hit his other cheek a
bruising blow that made him stagger. He wailed in despair.
The monster had knocked over the kettle that hung above the
fire in his hearth and drowned it, turning the cherry-red coals
to dead black lumps. It had slammed into the wall, and his
clay drinking cup had fallen from its peg and tumbled to the
floor, shattering into a million shards. While he stood in the
middle of the sheepfold, dazed by the blows the beast had
given him, he saw it seize his ewes, his lambs, his goats, his
kids, and slaughter them. Then it ripped the cap from his
head, tore the garments from his body, and pulled the sandals
from his feet. Naked, he stood before it, helpless, speechless,
hopeless. It bound his hands. It bound his shoulders. And
then it dragged him into darkness deeper than any night.
    Cold lies the hearth. No fire burns. Shattered lies the cup.
Dumuzi is no more. The sheepfold is given to the winds.

Enki stared in amazement. Innina's eyes were painted large
and dark with stibium, and a cloak made of interwoven
boughs of sweet-smelling cedar covered her shoulders. She
was dressed in a shining robe and a diadem of rich stones
gleamed on her head.
    He looked more closely and saw the lines at the corners of
her mouth and eyes. The eyes themselves were red from weeping. When she spoke, her voice was hoarse from crying out in
anguish. "He is gone. My love, my sweet love is gone.
Dumuzi, the wild bull, the shepherd, lives no more. The ram,
the stud, Dumuzi, lives no more. No longer can I serve him
food or drink. No longer can I stroke his strong body, make
him rise in endless lust. The jackal lies in the bed, the
croaking raven alone huddles in his sheepfold. He cannot
move his hands across my body. He cannot move his feet in
dance to heat my blood. He cannot sing his gentle songs so
full of love and longing. Now the wind must sing for him."
    "Dumuzi's gone? How? What's happened, Innina?"

A flicker of anger and hatred lit up the dark sadness in her eyes. "Surt. He sent seven Gallas-demons blended into one. They were incarnated in a dog. A black dog like those of Dumuzi's shepherdship. He . . . he let it in, and it dragged him away."

Enki shook his head in wonder. "Surt? The Black One did that? By all eleven of Tiamat's brood, the man's cleverer by half than any of us ever could have conceived! First Enkidu and now Dumuzi." He looked nervously around, as if fearing Surt would suddenly materialize and attack him. "What are you going to do, Innina? Do you know where Dumuzi is?"

Innina turned her solemn gaze on him. "Do? I will go to get Dumuzi back. I rescued him once before from the very clutches of Ereshkigal and Nergal. Now I will save him once again. I asked the holy fly, the fly that dwells among the talk of the wise ones, that dwells amidst the songs of the minstrels, if it had heard word of my brother. It told me it had seen a giant black dog that was seven and yet one. In its jaws it held a shepherd. It plunged into the Kur and there, at the edge of a vast steppe, in a place called Arali, it holds him. Dumuzi.

"I will go to the Kur, Enki. I will search for this place called Arali. And when I find it, I will slay the hound and free Dumuzi. Then I will come back and wreak my vengeance on Surt. And a terrible vengeance it will be!" Without another word Innina turned and walked away. After several steps she simply melted into thin air.

Enki sat and thought of many things. Foremost, though, was Surt and a careful consideration of whether or not it wasn't time to become the man's ally.

"Utu, as usual, did not attend. Marduk is away on ummm . . . business. An was indisposed and chose not to be there. It is rumored that Innina is gone for the moment. That left Enlil, Enki, Nannar, and myself. Enki sided with me in everything. Nannar, of course, backed Enlil. The result is that Marduk's army is neutralized until he returns. Our left flank is secure. It was decided that we could indeed recruit among his idle soldiers. The *Shurpu* will remain in the hands of Zarpanit until Marduk returns. Enlil tried to get it for Nannar, but we stopped him cold."

Jormungand shook his head in amazed respect. "I've got to

admit, Surt, I never thought you could do it. Not only did you escape the prison those three built for you, you turned things around on them, trapped two and got the third as an ally. You're clearly more powerful than Nannar and probably the equal of Enki now. Huh. I guess the only one with more power is Enlil. But then he has the Tupsimati and is Ellilutu.''

Surt's eyes gleamed. "Yes, Enlil. He and he alone stands in my way now.''

"Stands in your way? You don't mean you're thinking of . . . ? By Sedu's horns, Surt, are you crazy? No, don't answer. I already know. You want to be Ellilutu.''

"Long ago, long before it even seemed possible, I said that someday I would be Ellilutu, faithful Serpent. I must be! For only as leader of all Muspellheim can I marshal the forces of the Dark Empire to my command.''

"The forces of the Dark Empire? Surt, the Empire fell so many sars ago, the Igigi themselves lost count. You can't rally the Empire's forces. They're gone.''

"I refer not to the First Dark Empire, but rather to the new Dark Empire that will rise when I call it into being. For call it into existence I will, once I am the Ellilutu. The other Sons of Muspell will bend the knee to me and do as I command. I will join all their respective armies into one, Serpent, one vast invincible army which you will command. And then we will strike.''

"Strike? Against who? The scorpion men of the Maqlu mountains? The waves of the Western Sea? Once you've brought all the Muspellheim under control, who's left to strike? What direction will you go? South?'' Jormungand paused suddenly, an idea crossing his mind. He gazed thoughtfully at Surt. "North?'' he murmured in wonder. "You'd strike north?''

Surt grinned and nodded eagerly. "Yes! North to the lands of the barbarians, to the plains where the cursed Aesir and his rotten brood foul the land and water! I will be avenged on Borr, Serpent, avenged on the man who left me to die on the Vigrid! I will destroy him and his entire race, wipe their scum from the face of Yggdrasil. They are not even worthy of slavehood. I will put them all to the sword and let Nergal drink their blood!

"Years ago I placed a curse on Borr. I was sorely wounded in that raid on the caravan, Serpent, the same one in which

Borr nearly killed you. Borr refused to take me with him, refused to give me a chance to heal. He deserted me, left me lying there among the dead and dying, walked away without a backward glance.

"I survived." His voice dropped to a bare whisper. "The Igigi help me, but I had no choice. I . . . I didn't want to die, didn't want to hang on a stake in Aralu. So I made a pact with Nergal. A pact—" His voice cracked and he fell silent.

"Borr forced me to it," he finally managed to continue, his voice tight with anger. "Forced me to the very thing that will make my revenge possible!

"I have learned that Borr himself escaped me while I was trapped by the three. He died old, honored, a warrior-hero to his people. This is bitter for me to know. I sent minor demons to haunt his dreams, but he is beyond me now. He has entered the hall of his barbarian god, Fornjot the Destroyer, and I cannot touch him now.

"But he has a son and a daughter who yet live in Asaheim. I will find them, Serpent, find them and wreak a horrible vengeance on them. And not only on them, but on every Aesir that lives.

"Only Enlil stands between me and the consummation of my desire. So I will destroy Enlil."

"Today, as the sun drew near the western horizon, it shrank to a dull red ball, while on the eastern horizon the moon rose, equal in size and color. Between them, on the mountaintop by the temple of Cuthah, I stood, balanced between their power and light.

"I faced the rising moon, full, round, a thing of constantly changing beauty, a thing ever dying, ever being born anew. Movement, transciency, renewal, life and death—the moon is all these things. Imperfect yet ever striving, it reflects the life we live here on earth. It permeates our every act, controls the tides within our bodies as surely as those within the seas.

"I faced the setting sun, full, round, a thing of never-changing beauty. It gives light and life to our world. The moon reflects its glory. It is the endless, the source of all, the transcendent, the eternal.

"Between the two I stood in wondering tension, feeling the power of both surging through me. The temporal and eternal, the transient and the everlasting, the here and now and the always. Our lives are lived in a movement from one toward the other, from the moon toward the sun and back again from the sun toward the moon. We never quite reach the blinding glory of the sun, for we are the finite children of the moon. We never quite achieve peace with the moon, for we are the restless, longing children of the sun.''

Surt stood wrapped in silent contemplation for several moments. Then he sighed deeply and said quietly, ''There are times, Serpent, when I long to cast myself into the cleansing fire of the eternal and burn away all the dross of the temporal.

''But such was not meant to be my fate, nor that of men. We cannot resolve the tension of our lives, the pulling between the sun and the moon. Living is a constant contradiction, an endless confusion of ought and is. I begin to doubt if even death resolves the conflict.''

He held his hands before his face and looked at them, turning them this way and that. ''Every step taken in one direction,'' he continued, ''is a step away from every other direction. The very exercise of the will is a limiting of it. Choosing takes away choice.'' He dropped his hands to his sides and chuckled ruefully.

''Today I went to a place where I could gain the knowledge I needed to defeat Enlil. Long have I prepared for this day, for this revelation. Alone I climbed to the top of the mountain and chanted spells to the four corners of the earth. I . . . ah, but what do all the details matter?

''Eventually the winds whispered the secret I sought. I now know where Enlil keeps the *Tupsimati* hidden. And where he keeps his secret name, scratched on a bloodred ruby.''

His gaze became soft and unfocused. His voice took on a singsong quality as he continued. ''Once a tree grew on the banks of a mighty river known as the Hepr. It was well-nurtured by the waters of that river and grew lustily. But one day the South Wind saw it growing so well and strongly, and it became angry that the river should produce such beauty and health. So it attacked the tree and tore at its roots and crown. It whipped up the waters of the river in its fury and flooded the roots, washing them loose. The tree toppled, stricken, and was swept away.

''For many days it floated along, until the flood receded and it was left high and dry on the desert sands. There it languished until Ninshubur, the messenger of Geshtinanna,

found it one day and brought it to Enlil as an offering. 'Here
is the huluppu tree that was nurtured by the mighty Hepr and
torn by the South Wind. Plant it in your garden to give you
shade. One day, when it is grown to the right size, you can
make a chair and a couch from its wood. You can make a
pukku and a mikku and drum up the power of the Hepr and
the South Wind.'

"So Enlil planted the huluppu in the garden of his
castle, the mountainous Ekur. Ninlil, his escort, watered it
every day, and it grew mighty. Enlil grew fond of the tree
and decided to give it magical protection. At its base he made
a nest for the snake that knows no charm. In its middle he
made a home for Lilith, the maid of desolation. On its crown
he allowed the fierce Imdugud bird to place its young. Then,
knowing the tree was well-guarded, he placed the Tupsimati
in a crack along with the ruby that bore his secret name.
There, safe against all intruders, they have remained to this
day."

Surt paused, his eyes coming back into focus as he turned
his gaze to rest on Jormungand's face. "Safe to this day," he
repeated, his voice hard. "To *this* day, Serpent, the day on
which the wind whispered Enlil's secret to me. I will send Zu
to steal them both."

Elil raged, wept, and wrung his hands. His eyes ached
from the sight of the huluppu tree. At its base the snake that
knew no charm lay dead, mangled by the claws of Zu. Lilith
had left its middle in fear to make her home in the waste
places of the world. And the Imdugud bird had been driven
from its crown and forced to flee to the mountains with its
young. The tree itself was shattered and broken, its trunk split
open by a single blow from Zu's beak. The crevice that once
had hidden the Tupsimati and a bloodred ruby lay empty. The
mighty storm bird, Surt's ally, had flown away with them
tightly clutched in its claws. Zu had stolen the Tablets of
Destiny, the very ones that Marduk had wrested from the
dying hands of the rebellious Kingu so many sars ago. In
doing so, the monster had stolen the power that gave Enlil
preeminence among the Sons of Muspell and made it possible
for him to hold the title of the Ellilutu, the Overlord of
Muspellheim.

•   •   •

Surt started up from the table in astonishment. "How . . ." he blurted, unable to believe his eyes. Before him stood the slight, smiling form of Utu.

"You . . . how did you . . . this place is warded, completely warded. There is no way in or out. Not even Zu could—"

Utu waved a hand in dismissal. "You ward against what you know. Demons from the Kur. I did not come through a Bab-Apsi, Surt. I came through a Dur-An-Ki, one I opened myself. And however much you may know about openings to the demon world of the Kur, Black One, you are utterly ignorant about openings to the realm of the Igigi."

The dark, slender wizard raised his hands, his fingers weaving bizarre patterns, and he began to chant. Utu snorted disgustedly. "Don't bother, Surt, nothing will come. This whole room is inside the Dur-An-Ki I created. Your demon allies can't enter it. They can't even hear you call out of it.

"In any case, you have nothing to fear. I didn't come here to confront you or do battle."

Surt glared at him defiantly. "Why else would you come? I have defeated the rest. Marduk, Innina, Enlil. Soon I will be Ellilutu. Only you stand in my way."

"Nonsense. I don't stand in your way at all. By the Three Hundred, Surt, you can be the damned Ellilutu for all I care. If you need my vote in the Anunnaki, I'll be happy to give it."

The Black One stared cautiously at Utu. "You don't care?" The Patesi of Sippar and Larsa shrugged and shook his head. "You'd give me your vote in the Anunnaki? I don't believe it. It doesn't make sense."

"Not to you, of course not. But let me whisper some names to you. Dimmer-an-ki-a. Ashgirbabbar. Nudimund. Duranki." Surt started and his eyes went wide with surprise. "You've heard them whispered like that before, eh? By the wind?"

"You!" Surt hissed in wonder and terror. "You . . . you were the breeze that whispered those names in my ears! You who told me of Dumuzi's weakness and where Enlil kept the Tupsimati! You who suggested I send Zu! You—"

Utu laughed harshly. "Not all that, no! You did a fair share of the plotting yourself. Credit given where credit due,

Surt. I merely whispered things to the breeze. You went on your own to seek them out.''

"But why?" Surt's eyes narrowed in suspicion. "What is in it for you? If you don't want the Ellilutu what do you want?"

Utu smiled slightly. "You'd never understand. I want what I must want, what must be wanted so that something else not to be wanted cannot be. I am the curer who cuts off the limb to save the body. Or better, the one who kills the body that the soul might live."

"I . . . I don't understand."

"Naturally. That's why you are such a willing and useful tool. As am I. We both do the bidding of a greater force, Black One. We both dance to the tune the *Baru* sings."

"The *Baru*! Then you *do* have it!"

"Oh, yes. Or rather, it has me. But enough of this chatter. Soon you will be the Ellilutu. I only come to warn you of one thing. The son of Borr is more than you bargained for. He is no barbarian dolt. Do not underestimate him. Yet also know that no mortal man may slay you, nor will you ever die. You are destined to fling fire into the nine worlds, to carry the Bane of Forests northward into battle. You will meet the son as once you met the father, and there the issue of the worlds will be decided. Do not tremble at the thought of it. Your destiny calls, and you must give it answer." With a slight smile, Utu disappeared.

When the Anunnaki met, Utu was there and voted with Enki and Enlil to pass the Ellilutuship to Surt. When Nannar realized what was happening, he also cast his vote in favor of the Black One. An and Marduk never even came.

FREYJA

XI

~~~~

It was Hild herself who came into Freyja's presence under protection of the white flag. The Valkyrja leader looked drawn and exhausted. She had been wounded in several places, and her uniform was soiled and torn. The fighting had been intense for many weeks now, and every one of the brown-clad warrior women of Vanaheim had been engaged in the combat on an almost continual basis.

Our people don't look any better, Freyja thought sadly. Almost every forester wears a bandage, and even those who have joined us from Folkvang have wounds to show for their efforts. Even sadder are the number of fresh graves dotted throughout the woods. I wonder if the Aesir are doing any better?

Niord had returned from Asaheim late in the fall with news that the Aesir wanted an alliance with the Vanir under Yngvi and Freyja. They pledged their active support in the war against Vor and the forces that backed the rule of the Distingen. He had borne a letter for Freyja, a letter from Voden.

She remembered how strangely her heart had pounded as she opened it. Her eyes blurred so that she had had to wait a few moments, blindly staring at the page, pretending to read, until her vision cleared. Then the message had been simple and straightforward. The Aesir proposed alliance, indeed a merging, between the two people—both to defeat Vor and to prepare for the inevitable onslaught of the Jotun Horde under Hrodvitnir. Simple, straightforward, impersonal, unemotional. An unexpected feeling of disappointment had washed over her for a brief moment. Angrily, she had pushed it aside,

157

harshly reminding herself that the past was gone forever and that it was the present that needed tending to.

She looked up to notice Hild kneeling in front of her, a cloth-wrapped bundle in her outstretched hands. Freyja shook her head to clear her thoughts. I must pay attention, she chided herself. I tend to drift away from the present too much lately. Ever since poor Hnoss . . . Forcefully she pulled her mind back to the matter at hand. There was nothing to be done for Hnoss. She had tried everything a grieving mother could try, and nothing had brought the child back. Her little daughter still lay in a coma, alive but not alive.

"Hild," she said softly, "why are you here? You come under the white flag. For what purpose?"

"Vanadis," Hild said, her voice breaking with emotion, "I bring something for you. This . . . this package will . . . speak for itself. I . . . Open it. Or have one of your people open it. I . . ."

Freyja gestured to Frey, who was lounging nearby. Her brother moved to Hild and took the cloth-wrapped package from her hands. He carried it to Freyja, a strange look of foreboding dawning on his face. Frey looked up at his sister. "Would you have me open it, Vanadis?" She nodded. He placed it on the floor and began to unwrap it slowly.

As the cloth fell back, everyone in the cave gave a slight gasp. There, nestled in the cloth, was something they all recognized. It was a head. Vor's head.

Freyja gazed at Vor's closed eyes, wrinkled mouth, and lank gray hair for several moments before lifting her eyes to meet those of Hild. "Who has done this thing?" she asked, her voice soft but demanding.

Hild threw herself forward onto her face and mumbled into the dirt floor of the cave. She managed to say, "I did, my Vanadis," and then broke into wracking sobs.

Freyja rose and walked to the Valkyrja. She leaned down and touched the top of Hild's head. "Why have you done such a thing?"

Hild looked up, her face soiled by tears mingled with the dirt from the cave floor. Her eyes were filled with misery. "I . . . I . . . so many were dying . . . my Valkyrja . . . forester lads . . . so many . . . I couldn't stand it any longer . . . I'm a soldier, not a butcher . . . I just couldn't stand it any longer—" She choked on her emotions for a moment, then summoned up her soldierly self-control and came to a kneeling position. She took Freyja's hand and pressed it against her forehead. "My Vanadis, I had Vor executed. I had her head struck from her body and placed on a pole in the center of many-seated Sessrymnyr. I called all the people of embattled Folkvang to come and see the head of the traitoress who had betrayed her Vanadis and plunged us into this dreadful war to satisfy her own ego and desire for absolute power. I told them that Audhumla was angry with us, that she was angry that we were shedding the blood of other Vanir, of our own people. I told them I was going to take the head of the traitoress and offer it to our Vanadis, our rightful ruler, and unconditionally surrender myself, the Valkyrja, Folkvang, and everyone and everything in it to her, and to throw myself and everything on her mercy.

"I . . . They cheered, Vanadis. They cheered and wept with joy. I . . . deserve nothing better than death. But spare them, Vanadis. Show your mercy to those others Vor led astray. Audhumla would be pleased by such generosity. I ask nothing for myself, but spare the others." With that she crumpled back down to the ground again and lay there motionless.

For a moment Freyja stood and looked down at her prostrate form. Then she turned and walked slowly back to her chair. She sat down and leaned forward, her chin in her hands, her elbows on her knees as she stared fixedly at Vor's head.

Finally she spoke. Her voice was soft and sad, filled with the pain of things she would rather not have remembered. "Vor killed my mother, Hild. I know that now. And it was she who was behind the disappearance of Od, my king. She also it was who destroyed Hnoss and made her the lifeless thing she is today.

"Yet my personal grief is as nothing when compared to that of Vanaheim as a whole. How many have died, forester and Valkyrja? How many are crippled forever? How far have we fallen from a once great and powerful people? We have bled ourselves until we are so weak that the only way we can even solve our own dilemma is to call in the Aesir to aid us. We did not break Vor's power. The warrior's from the north broke it. They are the ones who surrounded Folkvang and cut it off from the rest of Vanaheim. They are the ones who breached the walls and carried the fighting into the very streets of the city. We joined their legions, but we were not in charge, not in control. We lost control over ourselves long, long ago. This may all be as Audhumla has willed it. I don't know, I just don't know anymore.

"You come to me to surrender. You should have gone to Tyr, the one who heads the Aesir force. Or to his master, Voden, who stays in Asgard." She paused and lifted her eyes, gazing around at those who stood silently in the cave. Her glance finally dropped again to Vor's head. Her nose wrinkled in disgust. She gestured to Frey and said, "Take that thing away and throw it to the forest wolves. And Rota, send a runner to Yngvi to tell him of the surrender. There is no need for any more to die."

Her eyes moved to Hild. "No need for *any* more to die. Not even you, Hild. I forgive you. Vengeance would be a poor satisfaction at best. Living to see fully what you have done will be punishment enough."

Yngvi clasped Voden's arm. The two men regarded each other silently, their faces serious and filled with questions. "Your eye—" Yngvi began.

"And yours," Voden interrupted. "We could almost be a grim set of twins."

Yngvi smiled mirthlessly. "I hope your loss wasn't as painful as mine. I bear other scars that went with it."

Voden nodded. "I too. But most of mine cannot be seen unless you look deep in the good eye. And that isn't really an advisible thing to do.

"Is it over then?" he asked, stepping back and changing the subject. "Has Folkvang fallen?"

"Aye," Yngvi replied. "The walls are rubble, and many of the halls charred skeletons. It took a winter, a spring, a summer, a fall, another winter, and half a second spring, but the power of Vor and the Distingen is broken." He paused and looked thoughtfully at Voden. "And so is the power of the Vanir, old friend. You wouldn't recognize us any longer."

"And Freyja, how is she?"

Yngvi looked down at the floor of the Warrior's Hall for several seconds before raising questioning countenance to Voden. "What do you intend for Freyja, Voden? I know what happened between you. After all, I was the one who rescued you from Folkvang and the mandragora. I remember how you . . ." He paused and shook his head to clear away the memory. "Ah. So long ago. But Freyja . . . she's suffered a lot, Voden. And she's a good Vanadis.

"Many of us love her. We . . . we wonder what you'll do. None of us are deceived as to the nature of our alliance. You're the strong member, the dominant one. We've bled ourselves into weakness. We're at your mercy. What will you do with Freyja?"

Voden turned and went to sit in the High Seat. He looked vacantly off into the distance of the empty hall. "Freyja," he said quietly, his voice filled with strange longing. "How often I called her name as you and your men held me down. I remember it well, Yngvi. I called it many times after that too. She was in my dreams." He shook his head as if to clear it. "Even when I wasn't dreaming, she was in my mind. Freyja.

"I've changed, friend. I've done things other men have never done, been places where other feet have never trod. I've changed. And yet . . . Freyja is in my mind."

Yes, he thought silently, in my mind, always in my mind. He thought back to the first time he'd ever seen her, there in Fiorgynn's hall in Folkvang. Everything about her had intrigued him. And when she'd made a fool of him in front of the other children, his interest had only grown.

He remembered the look of her, the sense of her, the endless mystery of her. Being with her, even in the practice yard learning the Thiodnuma, had been a pleasure and had sent strange shivers up his spine. Walking with her, talking with her, sitting with her, he'd felt something he couldn't give a name to.

And then suddenly he'd known what it was called. It was love, or at least as much love as a young boy was capable of. It burned in him and haunted his dreams. It built up inside of him, increasing its pressure until . . .

The mandragora. Ah, he remembered it well. They'd made endless love, and he'd known a joy transcending anything he'd ever felt before or since. Was it only the drug? Once he'd thought so. But then he'd been bitter and angry. Later he'd discovered that Freyja had cried out for him even as he'd cried out for her. Yes, the cursed mandragora had had something to do with it. But it had only reinforced the feelings that were already there. Reinforced them and removed any barriers to their expression. The result had been explosive for both of them. They'd nearly died because of it.

And yet, and yet . . . Everything he remembered was how *he* had felt. How could he be sure that it had been that way for her too? Of course he realized that Freyja's reactions had been as natural and as unrehearsed as his own had. She'd had nothing to do with the plot involving the mandragora. She'd been as much a victim as he had. Perhaps even more.

But how could he know what she'd felt? Had it been love, or merely lust heightened by the drug? Even more importantly, how could he know what she felt now? Had the mandragora burned away any love she might have felt? Was nothing but a bitter ash left behind?

It struck him that he really knew very little about Freyja. He'd carried a memory of her around with him for years, but now he began to wonder if his image was a true picture of the way she'd been or whether it was merely a fantasy he'd created from his own need. The looks, the touches, even the words that he held in his mind were all—he had to admit—ambiguous proofs at best, and could be interpreted in many different ways. What made his interpretation more valid than any other?

He couldn't know. He could only trust in the truth of his own recollection. But trust was something he'd had little practice in. Love even less. Both were dangerous to a man in a position like his. Did he dare expose himself so deeply to another human being? Could he ever afford to lower his defenses that far? If he did, what dangers would he face? He'd been betrayed by his love once. Could it happen again?

A great sadness filled him. I'm utterly alone, he thought bleakly. Even if I wanted to reach out and touch Freyja, I dare not. I must wait and see, try to find out how she feels, before I open myself again. Too much depends on me to create a weakness, an avenue of attack.

And yet, he admitted, I can't deny how much I want to love her and to have her love me. He hardened his heart. I must remain silent, he sternly commanded himself. And hope she can hear my heart crying out, a small voice deep within him added gently.

Voden refocused his attention outward and saw that Yngvi

wished to say something. Unable yet to speak himself, he nodded encouragement.

"For all our sakes, it would be best to make this alliance as complete as possible, Voden."

The Aesir chieftain looked hard at his friend. "Speak clearly, Yngvi. I would not have you talk in riddles to me. What do you mean?"

"I mean Freyja should become your wife and you should become her king. The Aesir and the Vanir should become one people."

"My wife?" Voden said softly, wonder in his voice. "My wife?"

Yngvi nodded. "Aye, and more than that. Our two people should build a new city where our two lands meet. And you and Freyja should live there as a symbol of our unity."

"Would you abandon Asgard and Folkvang?"

"No. But I would make them secondary cities. The new one would be the center of our united peoples."

"My wife," Voden mused. He looked at Yngvi. "You know that I already have a wife, an Aesir wife? This winter I was given the daughter of one of the most important chieftains of the Valaskialf Plateau as wife. She comes from Lidskialf at the upper end of the Gate. Her name is Frigida. This coming winter she'll bear my child. It will be a boy, and we'll name it Baldur. She's seen this. She has the power given by Vidlof, though she almost never speaks what the goddess whispers to her."

"If she's that wise," Yngvi said slowly, "she'll realize the need of what I say." He paused as if unsure whether to continue or not. He looked at Voden, and the leader of the Aesir nodded for him to go on. Yngvi drew himself up boldly and asked, "Can the Aesir have two wives?"

Voden shrugged. "It has been done."

"Then it should be done again. Frigida and Freyja. Frigida should reign here in Asgard. Freyja in the new city. Only that way will you be able to tie the two people together, Voden. Only that way will you be able to create the unified force you'll need to face the threat of the Jotun Horde."

Voden's single eye burned into Yngvi's for long moments. The forester felt the power of the look but stood and stared back, refusing to drop his glance. Finally Voden nodded and smiled strangely. "I will think on these things."

• • •

Syofyn bowed her head, but not before Freyja could see how gaunt and worn her face had become. She was thinner than Freyja had ever seen her, and her skin was the pasty, unhealthy color of one who had not seen the sun in many months. Indeed, the Vanadis thought, she hasn't. Vor threw her into a cell for daring to stand up for me in the Distingen.

Her eyes roamed over the other two who stood, heads bowed in homage, on either side of and slightly behind Syofyn. One of the heads was pure white. That was Eir, the ancient healer who had also refused to go along with Vor and had simply withdrawn from the entire situation. The final one was Gna.

Freyja's voice was gentle when she spoke. "So then, Syofyn, this is all that is left of the Distingen?"

Syofyn nodded and lifted haunted eyes. "Yes, my Vanadis. The rest are dead. Only three. Never in all the history of the Vanir have there been so few Desir. Our ancient way is broken. You see only the shards."

"How strange the world is," Freyja mused aloud. "Vor meant to bring back the old ways. Instead she destroyed them forever."

Syofyn bowed her head. "It is as Audhumla wills."

Freyja turned her attention to Eir. "Have you looked at Hnoss, healer?"

Eir glanced up, her eyes disturbed. "Aye."

"And what have you to say?"

The ancient healer paused, arranging her thoughts. "I do not understand what has happened to Hnoss. She is here and yet somewhere else. I fear . . . I fear there is nothing I can do for her. I have no magic, only the arts of healing. Hnoss's body is here, but her spirit is somewhere else."

"Where?" Freyja demanded.

Again Eir paused, uncertain of exactly how much to tell Freyja. "I'm not sure, but I think . . ." She hesitated and her voice broke. Fear glimmered swiftly in her eyes. When she spoke again, her voice was a hoarse whisper. "I think she may be with Glitnis Gna in Niflheim."

Freyja breathed in sharply. "How can this be?"

Eir sighed, the fear remaining in her eyes. "There was a great deal of magic flying about when you rescued Yngvi. Hnoss was right in the middle of it, deep in contest with Vor and her power. Vor was calling on Svarthofdi, and perhaps the backwash of the death of Syr . . .'' Her words trailed off.

Freyja was silent, her eyes blank with shock. Finally, light and life came back into them. "Yes" she whispered softly, "yes, what you say might be true. Hnoss's spirit may well be in Niflheim with Glitnis Gna and Erlik Kahn. Her body is still here because she isn't really dead. She's trapped between Niflheim and Vanaheim, between two worlds.''

"She cannot remain so trapped for long, Freyja." Eir's voice was gentle. "Her body weakens day by day without the spirit to guide it. Soon it will waste away and she will slide wholly into the realm of death. She will join those who sit on the benches in Eljudnir.''

Freyja stood suddenly. "No! This cannot be! I won't let it be!" Tears started from her eyes and flowed down her cheeks. "Vor has taken everything from me! She took my mother and my king. And now she reaches out from her grave to take my child! I won't stand for it! There must be some way!''

Eir hung her head and stared at the ground. The other Disir turned away, unable to meet Freyja's intense glare. In the silence that hung over them, all that could be heard was the panting anguish of the grieving mother.

Finally, after they had gone, Freyja cried aloud.

Gagnrad frowned. "Would you abandon Asgard and Frigida? And what of your son, when he is born? Will you leave him behind too?" He paused, as if unsure exactly how much he dared to say. "Are you certain this taking Freyja as your wife is wise? Is it really necessary? Or is it just to satisfy an old lust? Think carefully, Voden. The fate of the Aesir rests in your hands.''

Voden's single eye flashed red in the depths of his hood. Gagnrad, seeing it, shrank back in fear. Voden was so different. Ever since coming back from the Jotun the lad had changed. No, the change was even before that. When he'd come back from wandering Fornjot knew where, he'd been a strange and mysterious creature the likes of which Gagnrad had never seen. Now he was given to solitary rides across the plain or long periods sitting all alone on the mound where his parents and grandfather were buried. Gagnrad and the other chieftains had hoped that marrying him to Frigida would bring him out of his solitude, but now Gagnrad realized the problem went deeper than any of them could comprehend.

Voden sighed and smiled slightly. "Look north on a clear day, old friend of my father. In the distance you'll see the glint that comes off the River Iving. On the other side lie the wagons of the Jotun. More wagons than you can believe, old man. I've been there, and I've witnessed the potential might of the Sons of Ymir. All they need is a leader, a Warlord capable of uniting them and forging their raw power into a finely honed weapon.

"That man exists. Him, too have I seen. Hrodvitnir. He's almost Warlord even as we speak. He killed Fenrir in personal combat in the Circle of Judgment. I saw that to. Now he's taken the name of Fenrir as well as everything that belonged to him—wagons, cattle, horses, dogs, weapons, robes, women, everything, even his membership in the Risar clan.

"The result is open warfare in Jotunheim between those who support Hrodvitnir-Fenrir and those who oppose him. His enemies are fierce and desperate. He pursues them with the feral intenseness of the great wolf he's named after. It won't be long before he wins. Then it will be only a little longer until he's strong enough to turn his eyes southward.

"I've often ridden northward and sat on my horse gazing across the broad waters of the Iving. And I've wracked my brain for a way to stop what is coming. I can find nothing.

"But there's worse, old friend of my father's. I've also sat on the mound above my father and let my thoughts turn to him and the ways he fought both the Jotun and the Vanir." Voden's voice dropped now to a husky whisper, one so filled with dire threat that it made Gagnrad look over his own shoulder at the shadows that gathered in the empty corners of the Warrior's Hall. "And there at my father's grave I've discovered yet another danger, one that may make even that of the Jotun pale by comparison.

"Know, Gagnrad, that in the land far to the south where once Borr raided, where on the desolate Vigrid he slaughtered and pillaged the caravan that held my mother, know that south even of that a new power grows. It rises on the ashes of the Dark Empire and promises to rival it in evil.

"Its leader is one called Surt, the Black One." Gagnrad drew a sharp breath. He knew that name! Voden nodded.

"Yes. It's the same one. The cutthroat that raided with my father and whom he left behind on the Vigrid to die of his wounds. Somehow he survived, and now he's determined to carry out the curse he flung at my father's back.

"It was Surt who so haunted my father's dreams with demons and visions of horror. It was the Black One's sendings that robbed him of peace in the last few years of his life. Surt sought revenge for what my father had done to him so long ago."

"But surely, now that Borr is dead . . ." Gagnrad's words hung in the air between them.

Voden laughed silently, his eye glowing strangely. "Surt's hatred goes beyond Borr. It goes to all of his blood, all of his race. He's risen to the chieftainship of Muspellheim. His power is vastly greater than ever. He burns with a mad desire for revenge. Borr has escaped him, but he only turns his hatred on the rests of us. On me. On Vili. On you. On every man, woman, and child in Asaheim.

"Already he's moved against me, sending things to haunt my dreams as he did my father's. But I'm too strong for him. I hurled them back in his face and sent some things of my own to haunt him! He was startled. Now he's quiet. But I know this peace is a false one and only temporary. He's planning something. He'll strike again. And when he does, it will be with all the dreadful strength he possesses. He's a wizard, Gagnrad, an evil magician in league with demons. And he has armies at his command that number like the leaves in the forests of Vanaheim.

"So, old friend of my father's, we're surrounded! The Jotun to the north and the power of the Dark Empire to the south.

"Do you still think my desire to merge the Aesir and the Vanir into one people, one fighting force, is so foolish?"

Gagnrad shook his head in wonder. His mind spun with the things Voden had revealed to him. Surrounded! Enemies on all sides! The odds were frightening. Suddenly he felt his age, every year of his life weighing heavily all over his limbs, pulling at him, pressing him down. The simple world he had always known had disappeared into the past. The present was too complicated to understand. And the future was too frightening to contemplate. His shoulder sagged. He looked up at Voden and saw a stranger, a man he didn't comprehend. The

world has gone past me, he thought. I should have died next
to Borr that day. Then I would have died happy. Now . . .

Voden smiled sadly. "I will marry Freyja, not because of
old lust, but because of new necessity. I will not abandon
either Frigida, my son, or Asgard. But I will build a new city
where the River Gunnthro and the River Svol meet, just north
of the forests of Vanaheim. I will call the city Gladsheim. It
will be a shining place, filled with the golden light of the
Idavoll Plain."

Voden's eye began to glow with enthusiasm and his voice
rose and took on a rhythm that made it sound as if he were
chanting a song of wonder. "There I will raise a great hall,
larger than any ever built in Yggdrasil. The Vanir will provide the roof beam, even as Buri once wished them to do for
his own hall. I will call it Valholl, and it will have room on
its benches for six hundred forty warriors. Those six hundred
forty I will hand pick from the best in Asaheim and Vanaheim.
They will be my elite guard, and I will call them the Einherjar.
Every day they will drill and practice their warlike arts in the
courtyard of Valholl, and I will watch them. Every night they
will feast and drink the finest mead. When the final hour
comes, they will storm forth from Valholl, their armor shining brightly, their voices raised in battle cries that will pierce
the very heavens and bring dread to—"

He stopped and shook his head. He looked around at the
empty hall and then down at the amazed face of Gagnrad. He
chuckled softly. "Ah, old friend of my father, I almost forgot
where I was! Forgive me. I speak of things you cannot
understand."

Voden sat down in the High Seat and gazed off into the
emptiness of the hall. Gagnrad found himself suddenly alone.
Weary, his shoulders sagging with foreboding and age, he
stumbled from the hall. Outside, night was falling.

"And when will this marriage take place?" Freyja asked
Yngvi.

The one-eyed forester blinked once and looked uneasily at
Rota. "Uh, the day of the summer solstice, when the sun is at
the height of its power, when day is longest and night shortest."

"The day when the Vanadis used to wed her king," Freyja
muttered beneath her breath. "The day I took Od as my
husband. The day Hnoss was conceived."

"My Vanadis, there is no other way," Rota said softly.

Freyja smiled bitterly. "Perhaps there never has been."
She paused and looked toward the ceiling. "Once, long ago,
I would have welcomed this marriage. Now . . . 'there is no
other way.' Bitter words to take the place of what was once
love."

Yngvi swallowed hard. "Perhaps . . . perhaps your love
for Voden hasn't died completely. Perhaps his hasn't died for
you either."

"Perhaps, perhaps, perhaps," Freyja said wearily. "I cannot deal with so many possibilities. Let the wedding be when
it will. I care about only one thing."

"Hnoss?" Rota asked in a breathless whisper.

"Hnoss," Freyja affirmed with a curt nod. "My little
treasure wastes away while I stand by helpless. If only I had
magic enough . . . Ah, by Audhumla, what wouldn't I do!"

Yngvi looked thoughtful. "Magic? Voden has magic. He
has the Galdar-power. Could that help?"

Freyja stood and stared at him. "The Galdar-power? Voden
has the magic of Vilmeid?"

The forester nodded. "Aye, it shines from his eye. Surely
you know of it? But then, how could you? He went and drank
from Mimir's Well. And then he hung on Nerthus's Tree for
nine days and nights. He even made a vision quest to . . ."
he paused, his voice suddenly filled with wonder, "to Niflheim!
He contested with Erlik Kahn in Eljudnir itself!"

Freyja sat down suddenly, all strength gone from her legs.
Her voice was filled with tears. "For the sake of Audhumla,
Yngvi, go to Voden! Beg him, promise him anything, if only
he'll go to Niflheim and save Hnoss!

"No, wait!" She held up her hand and then pressed it hard
against her forehead. "I must think!" she muttered to herself.
"No. Don't tell him why I need him. Just tell him I do. Tell
him it's urgent. He . . . might come for me. I'm not sure he'd
come for Hnoss. Or that he'd be willing to return to Niflheim
for any reason," she finished in a hoarse whisper.

Yngvi looked at Rota, then bowed and strode from the hall.
Freyja sat in her chair, her eyes closed, her breath coming in
quick gasps. Occasionally a groan escaped her lips, a groan
that sounded vaguely like the word "please." Rota stood and
watched over her mistress, the word "please" echoing through
her own thoughts as well.

• • •

The air between them was electric with power. Voden's eye was burning from deep within his hood. Freyja's eyes burned no less fiercely. Yngvi, Harbard, Rota, Frey, Syofyn, and Eir stood grouped behind their Vanadis. Heimdall, Tyr, Niord, and Honir stood behind Voden. Voden spoke first. His voice was soft and gentle. "Hello, little forest cat."

Freyja smiled with unexpected shyness. "Hello cattle-shit barbarian."

Voden smiled in return, and the two of them simply stood there for several moments, grinning at each other, completely ignoring the existence of the others. Finally Voden cleared his throat and spoke. "Ummm. Yngvi tells me you have a problem I may be able to help with."

The Vanadis dropped her eyes. "It's my baby, my Hnoss."

"Ah, yes." There was a strange hollowness in Voden's voice. "Your child. Od's child."

"She was no ordinary child," Freyja said quickly. "When I was carrying her, Vor placed a wandering curse on Od. I . . . I went in search of him. I went inward, into places I should not have gone. There I met Svarthofdi and learned much. Hnoss went with me. She was not ordinary after that. She . . . she had power.

"Without her we never could have rescued Yngvi. She helped me hold Vor at bay, helped me force Syr into the arms of the Dark Goddess. She . . .

"Something happened. She lies unconscious now. Eir says her spirit may be with Glitnis Gna in Niflheim. She will die if her spirit doesn't return soon. She's so thin now, so thin and . . ." Freyja's voice ran down into a sob.

Voden's jaw was firmly set, although one muscle in his cheek was twitching slightly. He nodded. "Niflheim. Yes, it could be. Perhaps something Vor did blasted her spirit and sent it to Glitnis Gna."

Freyja looked at him, hope struggling with despair in her eyes. "You've been to Niflheim. You've even been to Eljudnir, stood in it, battled with Erlik Kahn. Yngvi told me. It's true, isn't it?" Voden nodded reluctantly. Freyja rushed on. "Voden, you must help Hnoss. I know she's there, captive, held against her will! You must save her! I'll do anything—" She stopped and covered her mouth with her hand, stunned into silence by the look that twisted Voden's face.

"You ask me to go to Niflheim to rescue Od's child?" His voice hissed out from between tight teeth. He gave a harsh bark of a laugh. "You've never been there, have you? You've never felt the dread oppression of the mists that fill the gray air. Never heard the endless wail of despair that echoes from every corner." A bitter laugh rose to his lips. "No, you've never gazed in horror as Nidhogg and his brood writhe and squirm as they devour corpses. Never walked down the middle of Eljudnir, the rotting corpses on all sides, all grinning at you and reaching for you, wanting to make you one of them, their empty eyes yearning, their—" He stopped, his breath coming in short gasps. Slowly, he brought his breathing back under control. "It's a horrible place."

Freyja dropped her eyes to the floor and moaned softly. "I have no right to ask it of you," she whispered, her voice full of desperate pleading. "Another man's child. And yet mine too. I love Hnoss, Voden! I have no right to ask it." Her voice dropped until it was all but inaudible. "And yet I do."

Voden gazed at her bowed head. Many emotions raged across his features so swiftly, everyone had to turn away in fear. "And yet you ask it," he replied as softly as she. He drew himself up at last, his face calm. "And yet you ask it," he repeated, his voice normal once more.

She nodded and looked up, something in his tone giving her hope. His eyes was cold and emotionless, his face stiff with control. The calm, she realized, was only surface deep. She smiled tentatively.

His return smile was harsh. "Yet you ask it," he said a third time. "And for some reason which I can't even fathom, I'm going to do it." He sounded amazed at himself. "I'm going to journey to Niflheim in search of Hnoss. And even if she's in Eljudnir, I'll go there and stand before Erlik Kahn and Glitnis Gna once more. I'll demand they release her and let her spirit return to its body here in Vanaheim."

Freyja's face was radiant. Voden had to look away. There was so much hope and love there, but he didn't know who it was for, so it burned his heart as surely as hatred. He felt both angry and confused all at once. Her face . . . her face, he thought, his mind echoing the words endlessly. When first he had seen her, it had been as if he had stepped back years and years. It was Freyja, his Freyja! But then she had turned slightly and the light had illuminated her features from an unexpected angle. And suddenly he was staring at a total stranger! A stranger who lurked just beneath the surface of the face he knew!

How could such a thing be? One moment the Freyja he knew and longed for, the next an utterly foreign person? Do I appear the same to her? he wondered. I must. I have only on eye. And my face shows the pain I have been through. The Voden she sees both is and is not the one she knew.

That was the key, he realized. The face that lies behind the face I know is the Freyja that has come to be since last I saw her. Like me, she has experienced many things, things I know nothing of. Suddenly the years they had been apart opened before him like a vast gulf. How much living lies between us? he wondered, trying helplessly to estimate the depth and width of the chasm. Could it be bridged? Should it be?

With a wrench, he pulled himself back into the present. My mind is in turmoil, he admitted. I'm not sure that what I'm saying and doing is really the right thing. He winced inwardly, gathered his will around him, and hardened his heart.

"I will go to Niflheim," he finally declared. "And as you promised, you will do anything I ask."

"Yes!" Freyja cried out in ecstasy. "Yes! Anything!"

Voden's face froze as he spoke, all emotion leaving it as though it were dead. "What I wish is for Hnoss to be *my* child. I will bring her back to life, give her a new birth. As such, she is my child by all rights. As much as she is Od's."

Freyja's mouth was hanging open in astonishment. She grasped for words but none would come. "Hear me out," Voden demanded, holding his hand up to forestall her voice. "Hear me out. Hnoss will become my child because I will bring her back. As my child, I will give her a new name, a name of my choosing. She will be raised as I choose, raised as an Aesir. Do you agree?"

The Vanadis looked helplessly around her. All eyes were turned away in confusion. No one had ever heard of such a thing. She swallowed several times. Then, unable to speak, she nodded her head twice.

Voden smiled slowly, his lips curving into what was as much a grimace of pain as a sign of humor. His voice came from his mouth but seemed almost to come from another place, infinitely far away. "Vidar will be Hnoss's name, and she will dress like an Aesir warrior and learn to fight like one. I myself will buckle on her shoes, and they will have thick soles so that some day she will trod on the wolf's jaw without the teeth cutting through. Then she will avenge me."

Without another word he turned and strode from the hall. Behind, he left utter silence.

XII

Dusty emptiness stretched away forever. The light was a uniform gray that didn't cast shadows. Silence pressed against his ears. Could Hnoss be in such a place? he wondered.

Geri stirred restlessly by his right leg. Freki, who was standing on his left, sat down with a sigh. "I don't like this place, little brother," the giant gray beast rumbled. "It smells of death." Voden nodded wordlessly in agreement.

Hugin sat heavily on his right shoulder, Munin on his left. "It looks empty," he said to them. "Brothers, could you fly about and see if there is anything of interest?"

Hugin ruffled dusky feathers and croaked, "Thought cannot fly where life is no more." Munin muttered, "Memory comes not from beyond the grave. We cannot take wing here, little brother."

"Have any of you any idea of where to look for Hnoss?" Voden asked. "One direction looks as good, or as bad, as any to me."

Geri growled. "In death, right and left, up and down, mean very little. This place makes me uneasy, little brother. I smell and sense things I cannot see." The hair along the back of the black wolf had risen slightly.

"I hear something now myself," Voden responded, cocking his head to one side. "A dry rustling noise. Like old leaves rubbing lightly together." He smiled oddly. "I think something dwells over there, to the left. Let's go and see."

The man and the two wolves walked slowly and warily over toward the rustling sound. It became louder as they went. They finally stopped and gazed around.

"I sense a hall," Freki said. "And we stand by its east door. Yet I see nothing."

"Nor do I," Voden responded. "But I sense more. There is a Volva, a seeress, buried here. She was mighty long ago. I will call her up and speak with her." He fixed the gaze of his one glowing eye on the spot where the rustling noise seemed to be coming from and began to mutter a charm of calling. After a few moments, a gray specter rose from the earth and hovered in the air before Voden and his companions.

"Who wakens me?" came a hissing, empty voice. "The snow has fallen on me, the rain soaked me, and dew seeped through me. Long, long have I lain dead."

Voden pulled his hood even farther over his face. "I am Grimnir."

"Who, then, is your father? And what is your ancestry?"

"My father is Vindkald. He was the son of Varkald, whose father was Fjolkald. That is enough to know."

"Enough?" the specter moaned. "It is enough to fill me with cold and hopelessness. Why have you wakened me to sorrow once more?"

"There are things I would know."

"I do not wish to speak, but I have not the power to resist you. Ask and let me go back to my endless rest."

"I seek news of one called Hnoss."

"The shining one has passed this way, carried by a minion of dark Svarthofdi. She cannot enter Eljudnir, for her soul has not yet won free of her body. I will go. I was unwilling to speak, and I will speak no more."

"Stay yet a while, seeress, and answer what I ask. If Hnoss is not in Eljudnir, where is she?"

"She is here on this dusty plain, a wandering shade, drifting, moaning, sighing, knowing no peace, knowing such longing. Ah, I was unwilling to speak, and I will speak no more."

"Stay yet a while, seeress, and answer what I ask. How are we to find her in all this vastness?"

"Pour some blood in a trough. The shades will come to drink. Watch for her. When she drinks, grab her, for with the blood in her, she will be solid enough to hold. I was unwilling to speak and I will speak no more."

"Stay yet a while, seeress, and answer what I ask. Once I have her in my grip, what must I do?"

The specter paused and pulsed slightly. "You are not Grimnir," she hissed in sudden anger. "You have the Galdar-power and are as old as time. I would curse your name, and you have many and all are powerful."

"Beware, answer or risk my curse! If I am not Grimnir, then you are no seeress, nor are you wise. You are a triple monster—"

"Do not bother with your curses, Har. We have tangled before, and you cannot harm me more." Her voice rose and filled with a vague semblance of gloating life. "Yes, we have battled, you and I, Jafanhar. But now I will go back to my rest. And no one will raise me again until the Great Wolf shatters his fetters and Bane of Forests marches north to set the whole world aflame. The forces of the night gather, Thridi, and twilight comes swiftly." The specter, shimmering grayly, slowly sank back beneath the dusty plain. Voden stood for several moments and gazed with a heavy heart at the spot where she had disappeared.

Freki whined and licked his lips. Geri growled and said, "I like it not, little brother."

Voden shrugged and walked away. After moving some fifty paces, he stopped and dug a trough in the ground with his heel. "This will do as well as anything," he muttered. He took the iron dagger given him by his grandfather from his belt and made a cut in his forearm. The blood spurted out and into the trough. When he thought there was enough, he muttered a spell and the wound stopped bleeding and closed quickly.

They heard them coming from every direction. The rustling, moaning sound of their approach filled the gray air with a sound like that which fills the forest on a still day late in autumn when the last of the leaves are falling from the trees.

They watched carefully as the shades drank of the blood and gained the slightest bit of solidity. Suddenly Voden pointed, "There! That's Hnoss!" Geri leapt forward, scattering the gibbering shades in all directions. He caught Hnoss in his mouth before she could escape.

Voden took her from him and held her carefully. "She doesn't know me," he muttered. "She's probably afraid I've come to take her to Eljudnir. Is there any way to talk to her, to tell her?"

Hugin shook his black head. "None. The shades cannot

talk, cannot think. There is no thought, no memory here in this place. You must take her swiftly away. The solidity the blood has given her will fade. You won't be able to hold her. She'll just drift away again.''

Voden nodded and turned to leave. As he moved off, Geri and Freki suddenly stopped dead in their tracks and growled fearfully at the ground. It had suddenly come alive. Everywhere one looked, the whole dusty plain was writhing with poisonous vipers, their mouths gaping open, their fangs dripping death.

The leader of the Aesir paused and gazed about. "So, Erlik Kahn," he muttered, "you don't want Hnoss to escape. Or is it you, Svarthofdi?" He muttered a quick spell and began to walk forward. His gait was otherworldly, swift yet slow, smooth yet sudden, he flowed like a natural thing, a rivulet of water, now this way, now that. The bobbing and weaving serpents' heads failed to even notice him as he passed.

Soon he was beyond the serpents, but found himself at a vast gate. He tried to open it but it would not yield. "What is it?" Freki muttered with a snarl.

Voden half closed his eyes and thought. "This," he finally said, "is Thrymgjol. It was made by the three sons of the Dverg Solblindi." He raised his left hand and drew a vertical line in the air. From its upper end he drew a short line down toward the right at a forty-five-degree angle. Then, just below that, he drew another, parallel and of the same length. *"Ansuz asur oss,"* he chanted, his voice deep and hollow. "Lord of Asgard, mouth of men, source of all command. I order lock to spring open, fetter to fall, gate to give way." As he finished, the gate slowly opened wide. Voden gestured to the two wolves, and they all hurried through.

Before they had taken many more steps, a curtain of flame suddenly sprang up directly in front of them. Voden stopped and laughed out loud. "Fire? A curtain of fire? This is almost a joke! Svarthofdi, Glitnis Gna, Erlik Kahn! Fools! You think to stop me with such ridiculous barriers? There was a time when such a thing would have daunted me. But my power grows every day, and now this is but child's play!"

Geri was cringing back from the flames. "Child's play for you, perhaps, little brother. But the damn thing singed my whiskers. And it's hurting my eyes. For the sake of my black fur, get rid of this fire as quickly as you can!"

Voden drew another vertical line in the air. From about a third of the way up from the bottom, he drew a second line downward to the right at a forty-five-degree angle. Then he drew a second symbol over the first: a vertical line with a short line from its top down toward the right at a forty-five-degree angle. While he drew he muttered, "*Kenaz, kaun, cen. Laguz, logr, lagu.* Blinding, brilliant, living torch, I know the charm to quench the flame, no matter how fierce it be. Water comes, for life, for death, to quench, to drown, and to renew." The flames sputtered for a moment and then died.

He threw back his head and laughed. "I come, Freyja! I carry Hnoss with me! But she'll be Hnoss no more. I've defeated Od. We've wrestled one last time and I've won!"

The two bodies lay side by side in many-seated Sessrymnyr. Freyja herself had laid Hnoss out, covering her with the finest and richest piece of cloth in Folkvang. Then she had sat in wonder and watched as Voden had drummed and sung himself into a trance state. They had placed him alongside Hnoss, their hands intertwined as Voden had instructed.

At first Voden had tossed and muttered in his trance. But gradually he had gone deeper and deeper into the Alterjinga, as he called it, the world where the spirits dwelt and where he expected to find Hnoss. "She may not be in Eljudnir. She's not dead yet. She could be someplace else in Niflheim. I don't know exactly where. I'll have to search."

"Shouldn't I come with you?" Freyja had asked. "I'm adept in the Seidar-magic, one of Svarthofdi's own. You might be able to use my power. I'm willing to come."

Voden had looked at her with a musing smile on his lips. "No. Traveling in the spirit realm is not part of the Seidar. It belongs to the Galdar-power. Besides, I may have to do battle with Svarthofdi or one of her minions. Could you stand against her? No, I thought not. She is the source of your magic. You could no more oppose her than I could do battle with Vilmeid."

He'd paused then and considered for several moments. Finally he'd spoken thoughtfully. "Though it might be wise if you were to keep watch. You have a tie with Hnoss. If something were to go wrong, you might be able to reach us if we weren't too far into the Alterjinga. Some of the gravest dangers lie near the borders. If . . . if worse came to worst, you might be able to pull Hnoss back. Keep watch, Freyja. Guard us both.''

She sat next to Hnoss now and watched them both. She'd been watching for several hours. So still, she thought, as still as death. Perhaps Voden was wrong. Perhaps Hnoss was already in Eljudnir. If so, was it too late?

Her eyes moved to gaze at Voden's face. He had his hood pulled forward as far as possible. Only one eye, she mused. And such a stern look. There is power in his countenance. That and a great deal of weariness.

What do I feel for him? There was a time when . . . No, that was long ago. Is there any of that left? And would it apply to *this* man in any case? So different, so frighteningly different. Could I love this man?

And yet, is he really so different? He has vast power, but I thought I detected an unsureness when we first met. Yes, there was almost a yearning, a reaching out, a . . . For me? For the Freyja that is? Or for the girl that was?

She sighed. I've changed too. She shuddered as she thought of the things that had happened in the last few years. So much. Yet have I really changed all that much myself? Inside I still feel very much the same. Frightened, unsure, aching for love, for someone to hold me when things become frightening and confusing. I wonder if Voden—

Voden tossed suddenly in his trance and grunted hoarsely. His face twisted as though in pain. Hnoss arched her back and cried out sharply. Freyja sat rigid, her eyes wide with fear. Audhumla! Something's going wrong! What should I do?

He didn't see the thing approaching until it was too late. Freki gave a sudden growl and yelp of fright and it was on them. Voden had never seen anything like it. It was huge, hairy, and had a beard made of human entrails. It carried a giant club which it swung at him, barely missing as he stumbled back in astonishment.

"In the name of Vilmeid," Voden cried, "who and what are you?"

The monster stepped back, eyeing Geri and Freki, who had spread out to be able to attack from two sides at once. When it spoke, its voice shook the air and made the dust rise from the ground. "I am Humbaba, guardian of the cedar forest, mighty demon. I can hear the heifer as she stirs sixty leagues away. My teeth are like dragons' fangs. My countenance is like the lion's. My charge is like the rushing of a flooded river. With my look I crush the trees of the forest. I have the nod and the eye of death. I fasten my eye on you now. You are doomed, little worm.''

Humbaba fixed a glaring stare on Voden. Voden tried to return it, but found himself suddenly very tired. His arms weighed too much to lift, too much to raise in defense. His eyelids were so heavy they began to droop. He cradled Hnoss's shade to him and felt his knees begin to buckle. To sleep, to sleep, to . . .

Hugin pecked one ear, Munin the other. "Wake up, little brother, or you die! As your eyes close, Humbaba raises his club again. He will smash you into pulp."

Voden heard the whistle of the wind as the monster swung. He threw himself sideways, but not quite swiftly enough. The club caught him on the very edge of his left shoulder and sent him flying. He hit the ground with a crash and grunted with pain.

Quickly he sprang to his feet and dodged another blow. His left arm refused to work. Broken, he realized. Geri and Freki were darting in now, nipping at the monster's legs. Humbaba took a few swings at them, but they were like smoke and were never there when he struck.

Their attack gave Voden time to gather his wits about him again. Don't look the giant in the eye, he told himself. His gaze has the power to put you to sleep . . . permanently. How do I fight this thing? he wondered. I've never seen anything like it. Where can it have come from?

As if the creature had heard his thought, it spoke. "I am the ally of Surt, the Black One. He watches every move you make, son of Borr the Aesir. When you came here to the spirit world at the very edge of the Kur, he sent me to kill you. He sent me, for you are of the forests and I am Guardian of the Forests. Here in the Kur you are vulnerable. You have power, but not enough, not of the right kind. I will kill you for my master." With a roar, Humbaba leapt forward again.

Voden dodged. Surt! He knew the man had gained great power in Muspellheim, for he'd been able to haunt his father's dreams for years. Once he'd even tried to attack Voden himself, but the Galdar-power had been too strong for him.

He'd been watching, waiting. Voden cursed his own carelessness. Here in Alterjinga I'm more vulnerable than back home in Asaheim, he thought. Plus I've already been here for some time, using my power to overcome the barriers Svarthofdi, Glitnis Gna, and Erlik Kahn have been throwing in my way. He felt Hnoss's shade stir. Damn, he thought, I almost forgot about Hnoss. If I don't get back soon—

He leapt to the side. Soon? If I get back at all, I'll be fortunate, he realized. How long can I leap around, avoiding Humbaba's blows? If even one lands, I'm finished. The worst of it is, he doesn't even give me time to rist the necessary runes for a counterspell. I'm not powerful enough to cast the runes without writing them. Visualizing them isn't adequate. Perhaps with a few more years practice I'll be able to . . . Years? I'll be lucky if I get a few more minutes!

He dodged and stepped to the right. Humbaba read his intentions before he moved and swept his club back swiftly. He caught Voden a glancing blow on the left side that sent him sprawling into the dust. With a roar of triumph, he raised his club on high and stepped in to give the death blow.

There was a sudden flash of light. Humbaba was dazed by its brilliancy. Even Voden's eye was stunned, but the depth of the hood saved him somewhat. Humbaba roared, momentarily blinded.

Voden looked up and saw Freyja. "Quickly," she said, panting with effort. "I'm trying to hold this thing. I can't last forever. His eyes will clear any moment."

The Aesir raised himself from the dust into a sitting position. He lifted his good arm, wincing against the pain that paralyzed his left side. He quickly traced a symbol in the air that resembled a three-pronged fork, the points toward Humbaba. "*Algiz, eolh, algir,*" he chanted, "hold back my enemy, blunt his sword, soften his club." Humbaba roared, but appeared unable to move. Voden quickly drew another figure in the air, an upside down U with the right leg shorter than the left. "*Uruz, ur, urur*—horn fighter, moor stamper, strike for me, lend me your strength!" He rose from the ground now and gestured once more. This was a simple spearlike symbol, its point toward the giant. As he muttered his chant, the symbol solidified in the air, glowing with a dark light, becoming long and deadly looking. "*Teiwaz, tir, tiwar*—I invoke you to aid my victory, to strike my enemy!"

Voden made a throwing gesture with his arm and the glowing spear shot forward, striking Humbaba full on the chest. The giant roared in agony, fell backward, and disappeared in an explosion that knocked them all flat.

Geri and Freki were the first on their feet. They limped to Voden and Freyja and tugged at them to get them to rise. "Hurry, little brother," Geri growled, "there are more things on the way."

"I . . . I don't know the way out," Voden muttered in dismay.

"Follow me," Freyja said. "I still have touch with the other world. Follow me, oh, quickly! Hnoss's shade is fading!"

Voden stood, holding tight to Geri's back, and stumbled forward. Without warning, he felt himself stumble and fall to the floor of Sessrymnyr. He raised himself slightly and looked up at Hnoss's body. Freyja was standing next to it, looking down anxiously. The small figure stirred and the child opened her eyes. Freyja cried out with joy and threw herself on her daughter, gathering her up. She turned to Voden. She was glowing with joy, even though tears were pouring down her face. Such joy for Hnoss, Voden thought bitterly, and nothing for me.

"Voden," Freyja said, her voice breaking with emotion, "you did it! You brought Hnoss back!"

"Vidar," he said harshly, and collapsed.

It was a full month before Voden had mended enough to mount his horse and head back north again. In the time he spent in Folkvang, he made arrangements with Yngvi to send the foresters out to find the largest tree in all of Vanaheim. They would girdle it and then let it stand until early spring. Before the snows melted, they would cut it down, trim it, and then pull it over the snow northwards to where Voden wanted to use it as the beam for his new hall in his new city.

His relations with Freyja were friendly but formal. All the details for their forthcoming wedding were worked out. Freyja would come north to Gladsheim once it was completed. She would have her own hall, called Vingolf, and though it would not be as grand as Voden's Valholl, it would be large enough to hold Freyja and her entire household, including her personal Valkyrja guard, led by Rota.

At times when the two of them sat together and planned, a

sudden pause would settle between them. Then they would look shyly at each other out of the corners of their eyes, refusing to allow their glances to meet directly. Only Rota and Honir, who were often in these sessions and knew them both so well, could see their longing and confusion.

Hnoss-Vidar was doing well, but now seemed a normal child. The wisdom that had once dwelt deep in her dark eyes no longer appeared. The child's glance was a child's glance, and her laugh that of a normal infant. She would play gaily with her mother or any of the other women. Even Honir was the object of gleeful games. But whenever Voden appeared, Hnoss-Vidar became silent and thoughtful. She looked as if she were trying to remember something. She wasn't afraid of the one-eyed Aesir, as were most of the children of Folkvang. She was just very silent in his presence. Occasionally she would walk slowly up to him and climb into his lap, all the while looking up into his face with a slight frown on her own. Voden, for his part, was always gentle and kind to the child and always called her Vidar.

Voden arrived back in Asgard to find Kao-Shir and Anhur waiting for him. Anhur grumpily told him that the old yellow robe had wanted to hurry off to Nidavellir again but that he had refused to go until they had had a chance to see Voden once more. "Who knows when the next time will be, the way this ancient refugee from the Sunrise Empire wanders? Next he'll decide to see what lies on the other side of the Western Forest."

"Not a bad thought," Kao-Shir said with a chuckle. "If we can't find any Dverg in Nidavellir this time, perhaps we should head west and see if we can find Joruvellir and Svarin's great city, Aurvangar."

Anhur groaned, but Voden smiled and said, "Wasn't that mountain you were hunting for supposed to be in the west too? What was it called . . . ?"

"Hsu-Mi Lou, where Hsi Wang Mu lives," Kao-Shir answered promptly.

"Yes, and where she grows the peaches of immortality, if I remember correctly."

Kao-Shir cocked his head to one side and gave Voden an appraising glance. "You have an excellent memory."

"Wait a minute," Anhur interrupted. "I've got a good

memory too. Doesn't this Hsi Wang Whatsit have tiger's teeth and a leopard's tail? And doesn't it take a thousand years for the peaches to ripen?''

Kao-Shir nodded. "Yes, indeed! Would you like to go there with me, Anhur? If the peaches were ripe—''

Anhur growled. "Bah! We'll go back for Dverg in Nidavellir. It's a dull thing to do, but it's better than wandering around looking for silly peaches!''

"I knew you'd agree," Kao-Shir said smugly. "And just to show you my heart's in the right place, after we find the Dverg, I'll personally search for Horus!''

Voden stiffened. "Be careful what you promise, old man. If Horus is in the Alterjinga, the journey in search of him isn't one you'd want to make. Promises relating to the dead often come true in ways we least expect.''

Anhur looked uncomfortable. "I appreciate the offer, Kao-Shir. I'd give anything to find my lord Horus. But I don't know how he would react to being found by an ancient from the Sunrise Empire. Best someone from Svartalfheim find him.''

Kao-Shir nodded and turned to Voden, suddenly serious. "In any case, lad, we go again as soon as I have spoken to you." He gestured for Voden to follow him, and walked off toward the gate of Asgard, leaving a curious Anhur behind.

Silent, they walked together out of Asgard and to the mound where Voden's family lay buried. The two men sat and gazed westward. It was late afternoon.

Eventually Kao-Shir spoke. "I have been to Alfheim and to Vidblain, the 'main place' of the Alfar. The road to the land of the Alfar is a hard one, fraught with many perils. Nothing to be lightly embarked upon, I can tell you!''

He paused for a moment as if remembering, then continued. "Vidblain itself is a strange place, Voden, unlike anything I've ever seen before. Not so much a city as a place where they gather from time to time. It's an open clearing, very large. Scattered about it are massive stone columns, sometimes alone, sometimes in a group, sometimes one lying atop two others. In its center is the hall known as Gimle. There are a few other halls as well, but none as large as Gimle." He shook his head. "Vidblain is a beautiful place. Yet ineffably sad.

"The Alfar are a dying race, Voden. I don't know why,

but they are. When I asked those I met, they just shrugged and smiled sadly, saying 'It is the will of the Huldre.' They're an incredibly ancient race. I think they may even have preceded the San Miao.''

The old man paused for a moment, his eyes filled with musing. Then his eyes cleared and he spoke again. ''I spoke with Gymirling and his radiant daughter, Idun. He . . . I guess the word is 'speaks' for many of the other Alfar. They have sensed something dreadful in the offing, something to do with a thing they call Fimbulvetter, an endless winter, a time of killing cold, to be followed by a great disaster. When Gymirling heard of you and what you have done, he became very pensive. Finally he said he would come and see you, perhaps during your wedding to Freyja.

''They are a strange people, Voden. I'm glad I had a chance to learn something of them, even though it was nowhere near enough.'' He paused and looked quizzically at the leader of the Aesir. ''You make changes in Asaheim.'' Voden nodded and waited for him to continue. He sighed and went on. ''Voden, ruling a country is like cooking small fish. The less you stir them, the better.''

Voden smiled and replied, ''True, but changes larger than those I make are coming, as even the Alfar seem to sense. I but change to meet them. My people need a leader right now. I must lead them as best I know how.''

''The worst kind of leader,'' Kao-Shir mused, ''is the one whose people fear and hate him. The next best kind is the one the people love and revere. But the very best is the one of whom, when he is gone, his people say, 'We did this ourselves.' ''

XIII

VODEN stood in the middle of Valholl and looked around. It was truly magnificent. The roof beam was the biggest ever seen in Asaheim or Vanaheim. It stretched for six hundred forty feet, carefully shaped to be thicker in the middle and thinner at each end. It was supported by six great pillars, each bigger than two large men could put their arms around, each soaring some thirty-five feet into the air. From the beam, rafters came down at about a fifty-degree angle and sank deep into the ground. About eight feet in from their lower ends, a wall almost ten feet tall rose to meet the rafters. Along it, running for approximately six hundred feet on both sides, were broad benches. More than two hundred men could sleep on the benches; at feast time by bringing in extra benches and crowding together, the hall could hold nearly five hundred. There was a huge door, more than ten feet wide, at the end of the hall, and two smaller doors in the walls halfway down.

The High Seat was the largest any man had ever seen. Voden called it Hlidskjalf in honor of the chieftains from the Valaskialf Plateau who had sent the exotic dark wood from which it was built. It could easily hold three full-grown men at the same time.

Behind the High Seat was a wall that divided Voden's personal quarters from the rest of the hall. There were sleeping cupboards for himself and Freyja; for Yngvi, Honir, and Heimdall; benches for the servants; a cooking area and storage rooms for both food and clothes. The walls were covered with rich furs.

Voden turned to the small group around him and smiled. "Do you like it?" he asked Gagnrad.

The grizzled old Aesir shook his head. "Big it is. Bigger than anything Buri or Borr ever had or even dreamed of. Yet . . ."

Voden laughed. "Yet it isn't in Asgard, and it should be! I know how you feel, old friend of my father's. I should not abandon Asgard. But I'm not, you see. You'll be there to guard the ford. And Heimdall will be just to the north and west of you at the edge of the Himinborg, watching to see what the Jotun are up to. If they move southward toward the Iving, you can move out to hold Bifrosti's Ford and I and my Einherjar will be there within a few hours."

Gagnrad grumbled. "Aye, your Einherjar."

"Yes, six hundred forty of the best fighters in Vanaheim and Asaheim. Trained by Tyr with the spear, by Ull with the bow, and each a swords- or axeman of renown. All day they practice their skills, all night they feast. There is no better army anywhere."

"Mayhap not better, but there are far more Jotun than there are Einherjar," Gagnrad grumbled. "You spend so much time with them, you neglect the others."

"Neglect? Each chieftain has agreed to form his own Einherjar. There will be a group of six hundred forty formed from among the Aesir of the Himinborg Plain, six hundred forty from those of the Aesir Plain, six hundred forty from the Idavoll, and six hundred forty from the Valaskialf Plateau. The Vanir will also form Einherjar among their own people. The best from each group will enter my Einherjar here in Gladsheim. We will have more and better trained warriors at our command than ever before. How could you not like that, old war dog?"

Gagnrad looked away for a moment, then mumbled, "It's not our way." He turned to Voden and spoke more forcefully. "Aesir have always been warriors, but never soldiers. We've been men of peace as well as men of war, herders and farmers as well as swordsmen and axemen. We've always enjoyed the fruits of living calmly as well as the joy of the wolf work. But"—he spat on the ground—"these Einherjar, they do nothing but fight and get ready to fight. I like it not."

Voden's look became sober. "Nor I, Gagnrad. But it is as it must be. Yngvi tells me parties of strange black warriors have been seen at the edges of the Smoking Lands in the far south and east of Vanaheim. They creep cautiously through the passes made by the rivers Non and Thyn, looking, exploring. They have made no hostile moves as yet.''

Gagnrad's bushy white eyebrows rose. "Who are these dark men?'' he asked, looking toward Yngvi.

The forester shrugged. "I haven't seen them myself, but they sound to me like men from Muspellheim.''

Gagnrad looked stunned. "Muspellheim? But . . .''

Voden chuckled grimly, "Aye, 'but'. It looks as though the Dark Empire rises yet again, old friend of my father's. And Borr's raiding partner, Black Surt, is at its head. These scouting parties but pave the way for war parties.

"But that's not all. Heimdall watches the north and sees how Hrodvitnir-Fenrir builds his strength. He's quiet now, abiding by the peace we two agreed to. But that will only last until he's become Warlord of the Horde and has gathered his forces.

"The Einherjar are necessary. The old ways must change to meet the new threats.''

Gagnrad looked into Voden's face for a few moments, then muttered something and turned away. Voden was the only one who heard what the old man said. "If the old ways die, what is there left to fight for?''

The day of Voden and Freyja's wedding approached and men poured into Gladsheim from all over. Vanir came from the farthest reaches of their forest, some from so deep into the green fastness that they had never seen the plains nor the Aesir. Outlandishly dressed chieftains arrived from the far eastern edge of the Valaskialf Plateau. They wore garish robes they had gained by raiding southward on the caravan routes that ran from Kara Khitai and Prin through the Oasis of Kath to Muspellheim.

One of the most interesting arrivals, though, was that of Lao-Kee attended by five other Jotun warriors. As Heimdall had predicted, Hrodvitnir-Fenrir had not come.

Lao-Kee brought a gift for Voden. It was a wonderful horse named Sleipnir. The slender warrior presented it to him with a deep bow. "This horse is the best of all those among the Jotun. Better than Gyllir, Glen, Skeidbrimir, Silfrintopp, Sinir, Gils, or Falhofnir. It's the swiftest ever to run the grasslands of Jotunheim. So fast is Sleipnir that he seems to have eight legs. I raised him myself, as if I'd been his mother.''

Voden was deeply touched by Lao-Kee's gift. He was surprised, though, by the chilly greeting the Jotun gave Freyja, and at the lack of any gift for his bride-to-be. He was also a bit dismayed at the evident greedy interest Lao-Kee took in Brisingamen, the necklace Freyja had inherited from her mother, Fiorgynn. It was the very same one Borr had gifted Fiorgynn with so long ago, when Voden had first been sent to Folkvang. Lao-Kee had stared at it during the entire interview with Freyja and had finally boldly asked to touch it and even put it on. The Vanadis had been nonplussed and had not known how to respond. Reluctantly she had finally let the Jotun both touch and put the necklace on. Lao-Kee's face had been transfused with light, but when asked to give Brisingamen back, the slender warrior's face had gone rigid and the eyes had turned hard and filled with hatred and envy. Voden had felt uncomfortable and had hinted to Heimdall to keep a close watch on the necklace.

Lao-Kee readily confirmed what Heimdall had heard about the situation in Utgard. ''Hrodvitnir is very close to winning. But his enemies are that much more dangerous and determined. They're desperate and would stop at nothing to defeat him. That's why he sent me here. To keep me out of harm's way. I make a wonderful target for the Risar. They hate me after the incident with Hriedmir and Ottar.''

Although Lao-Kee didn't get on with Freyja, the Jotun and Vili became instant friends. The two of them could be seen everywhere, dashing about on their horses, challenging other riders to races and generally leaving them in the dust.

The second interesting arrival was that of Gymirling and his daughter Idun from Alfheim. The Alfar were slender creatures, tall and pale, with long narrow faces, delicate features, and almost translucent skin that seemed to glow with inner light. Their hair was white and their eyes deepest black with flecks of purple. Gymirling didn't look a day older than his daughter. Idun was stunningly beautiful.

They brought gifts that no one understood. For Voden they offered a small, oval rock covered with lichen, one side of which bore a mark that looked for all the world like the whorls on a man's thumb. Voden could sense that it was incredibly ancient and had a certain power, but he couldn't reach it or comprehend it. It was as if the thing was somehow on the other side of an invisible curtain he couldn't pull aside because he didn't know how to grasp it.

Freyja's gift was even odder. It was a small flower, intensely blue, unlike any blossom anyone had ever seen before. It didn't fade or wilt, looking freshly picked all the time. When asked where it had come from, Idun smiled slightly and whispered, "From the Sidhe." The word had meant nothing to any of them, and the lovely Alfar had said nothing further.

Both the Alfar spoke the common tongue, but in a strangely inflected form that made them very hard to understand. They seemed to be incapable of pronouncing the letter P and simply dropped it, especially at the beginning of words. They also changed J to D, giving many words an odd sound.

Their clothes were light and airy, consisting of baggy pantaloons and a loose blouse, both of soft, thin material which moved as fluidly as they did. Every garment was edged with exquisite embroidery in gold thread. Strangely, though, nothing natural was depicted in the embroidery, which was made up of pure sweeping curves and undulations with close-set spirals. Both wore jewelry of a type never seen before. It was made of some substance poured on a heated brass base to which it adhered and became as hard as stone. The patterns were intricate, like those of the embroidery, and were in bright, shining colors. The Alfar called it "enameling" and promised to show the Aesir how to do it.

Idun gave several pieces of the enameled jewelry to Vili. In turn, Voden's sister gifted her with a rich robe of silk that had once belonged to Vestla. Idun didn't join Vili and Lao-Kee in their rides across the plain, but in the evenings she and the other two could generally be found huddled in a group near the fire in Valholl, talking and whispering.

Gymirling spoke often with Voden and told him of the Fimbulvetter the Alfar feared. "Snow," he said, "will drive endlessly from all quarters. There will be hard frosts on even the warmest days, and biting winds will never cease to blow. The sun will be no use. This winter will last three years and cause every river, including the Iving, to freeze to its very bottom. Men and animals will freeze solid, and many will perish. No fire will be hot enough to warm even the smallest hall. The best place to be then," he continued softly, "will be Gimle, though the hall called Brimir in Okolnir would be fine, as would Sindri in Nidafjoll. These are all in Alfheim and very hard to find.

"When the Fimbulvetter is over, the Bane of Forests will come northward from the flaming land of the south and the whole world will catch fire."

Voden listened to his dire words and nodded solemnly. "This is part of what I, too, have seen," he said finally. "We will need every man to meet the threat. Can we count on the Alfar to stand by our side when the time comes?"

Gymirling was silent for several moments. When he finally spoke, his voice was far-off. "Few are the Alfar. We have not fought for many turnings of the earth. The last time we took up arms was against the First Dark Empire." He paused, then began again. "We fear no man. There is nothing to fear. We fear only that the sky will fall on us." He stopped, shook his head, and continued. "The day will come when three cocks crow. The red cock misses nothing and will crow from bird wood. The gold-combed one will lift his voice from south of the Iving. And a third cock, rust red like dried blood, will call the dead from Niflheim.

"Then Yggdrasil will tremble and moan. How will it fare with the Aesir? How with the Alfar? All Jotunheim will resound. The Dverg in their hillside homes will creep forth in awe and weep beside their doorways of stone." He stopped and sat silently for a long time. "I cannot say further," he spoke in a voice barely above a whisper. "But when that time comes, the Alfar that live in this world will take up their swords and spears and fight by your side. To the end."

"Thank you," Voden said simply. The two of them sat in silence until Gymirling finally rose, bowed, and left. Voden continued sitting, his chin in his hand, the Alfar's words ringing in his mind. They had loosened other words, spoken long ago by his dying mother. They came back to him now.

> "An axe-age, a sword age,
> shields will be battered;
> a wind-age, a wolf age,
> before the world is shattered!

> *The sun goes black,*
> *Earth sinks from sight,*
> *the heaven's lack*
> *their starry light!*

> *Smoke billows high*
> *by fire driven,*
> *flames lick the sky*
> *and heaven's riven.''*

The day came. From early in the morning until noon, every pot in Gladsheim bubbled, every spit turned and every oven baked. The air was filled with the aromas of a vast feast. Mead was everywhere in clay jars. The drinking started early and was in jolly earnest. People sang and danced whenever and wherever the notion took them. Every man considered himself a skald and made up verses on the spot.

Valholl was one center of activity. Freyja's hall, Vingolf, was the other. Women poured in and out of it, bearing costly garments, priceless jewelry, soft leather shoes, cloaks, brooches, sashes, ribbons, more things than one could count. Inside was a scene of hilarious confusion, gay chatter, and ceaseless movement. Women tried things on only to take them off and put something new on a few moments later. They called to each other, exclaimed over bracelets, compared fabrics.

In the middle of it all, calm, solemn, and thoughtful, sat Freyja. Rota helped her dress, bringing the things she asked for, commenting when asked to. Freyja chose a long, white, pleated petticoat of the softest, finest linen anyone had ever seen. Threads of gold were woven into it so that it shimmered whenever she moved.

Over the petticoat she finally decided to wear a long rectangular garment made of fine silk interwoven with threads of silver. It was made of two panels and fastened together at the top with braids of silver set with rubies. On top of that Freyja put a shawl of the most exquisite material, made from the fur of a small forest rabbit, dyed a rich purple, and edged with a fringe of marten fur. The shawl was triangular, and fastened at her neck with a large brooch that was a masterpiece of the goldsmith's art. It bore the face of a forest cat in its middle, the cat's eyes made from two incredible emeralds, the teeth from whitest ivory. All around the cat's face were intertwined figures of more forest cats, gripping each other's legs. Each had emerald eyes and ivory teeth. Around her neck Freyja wore Brisingamen, and her arms were loaded with heavy rings of red gold, intricately carved.

On her feet she drew boots of cat skin dyed deep blue and fastened with small brooches of silver studded with diamonds.

Exactly at noon she and Voden met in the center of Gladsheim, halfway between Valholl and Vingolf, in a wide plaza covered with cloth of gold. Voden was dressed simply in trousers of black silk and a hooded jacket of gray linen, washed until it was as soft as a baby's skin. He wore no jewelry at all. His ancient iron knife was in a simple leather scabbard hanging from his belt on the left.

The ceremony was short and simple. Freyja approached Voden and knelt in front of him, offering him her hands. He took them in his own and promised to protect her from all harm, even at cost of his own life. Then she stood and he knelt. She asked him if he had defeated all the wrestlers in Folkvang and thus deserved to be king of the Vanir. He replied that he had. She touched his head and bade him rise.

The two of them walked arm in arm to Valholl and mounted the High Seat. The guests poured into the hall, cramming themselves onto the benches along the walls and the others that had been brought in along with the tables. Then the servants began to serve food and mead and the noise became deafening.

The feasting went on long into the night. Through a haze of mead Voden looked over the throng, spotting his old friends. Yngvi was there, Gagnrad, Honir, Tror, Tyr, Heimdall, Lao-Kee, Rota, and many others. They were all laughing and enjoying themselves. Everyone was having a fine—

His eye stopped and focused on a single figure that sat quietly and gazed in his direction. The form was hooded and seemed oddly vague, as if out of focus. He stared harder, trying to make it out more clearly. The hood was not of any type he had ever seen before. It was more pointed at the top than the Aesir and Vanir hoods, and it fastened differently at the front.

A sudden chill swept over Voden as he caught a look into the darkness of the hood. Two red eyes glowed there, eyes that did not belong at a wedding feast, indeed did not belong

anywhere on this earth. With a curse he leapt from the High
Seat and drew the runes of protection in the air.

Every guest stopped eating and drinking and stared at him.
He was panting, the sweat pouring from him, his single eye
blazing with fury and power. Those nearest shrank away in
fear. His voice was quivering with dire energy when he spoke
to the hooded figure. "Who are you and why have you come
here?"

The thing stayed silent, but stood in its place. Slowly it
lifted both its hands at him, fingers pointing. Voden stood
aghast at the power of it, feeling the energy flowing toward
him from its fingertips. He battled that power, weaving more
runes into the air between them. The thing in the hood began
to moan or chant, Voden was not sure which. The force that
flowed from it increased, and Voden felt himself being pressed
back toward the High Seat.

Behind him he vaguely heard Freyja calling to him. "What
. . . what is it? What do you see? What are you fighting?"

He had no time or strength to answer her for he could feel
that a climax was coming. He threw the last of his energy into
a new barrier of runes. As he did so, the creature's hood fell
back and he found himself staring into the dark eyes of a
slender man with black skin. He knew in an instant that this
was Surt, the Black One, the wizard who ruled in Muspellheim.
But how could that be? How could Surt be here in Asaheim?

Instantly he knew that this wasn't really Surt, but merely a
sending, a projection of the wizard, who was doubtless still in
his tower in Muspellheim. Nonetheless, the creature he faced
was deadly and had the same strength that Surt had, indeed
was no doubt directly controlled by the wizard. It could kill
him. And if he could kill it, perhaps the backlash would kill
Surt as well!

A sudden twitch came from the figure's fingers, and Voden
was knocked backward into the High Seat. There was a
terrific flash and a stunning crash as Surt's power slammed
into the barrier of runes Voden had built. The barrier groaned
and bulged inward, but held. The force of the attack re-
bounded, and the figure disappeared with a shriek and a flash.

The unexpected release of the pressure was so great that
Voden fell forward and nearly crashed into the nearest table.
He looked up. The entire hall was dead silent, every eye fixed
on him. Freyja was by his side holding his arm, talking softly

and gently to him. "Whatever it was, it's gone now, isn't it? Come back to the High Seat." She raised her voice to the guests. "Begin to eat and drink, my friends. It's nothing. Please forgive him. He's sometimes like this. A temporary fever brought on by the mead and all the excitement."

She pulled him down into the seat and sat close to him. "What did you see?" she hissed in his ear.

He looked at her in amazement. "You . . . didn't you see it too? The hooded figure, sitting over there. It—"

He stopped, looking deep into her sober eyes. "I saw nothing," she said softly, firmly. "Only you leaping from the High Seat, staring like a madman at that spot, weaving symbols into the air, stumbling back and forth and finally almost collapsing on the table. That was all."

Voden shook his head. "No explosion? You felt no force, no magic, nothing?"

"Nothing."

He sat and stared at her. "Yet there was something," he said slowly. "Surt was there. Not really there, but a sending of him was there. He tried to destroy me, but I sent him reeling back into Muspellheim." He paused. "I destroyed his sending, but I wonder what would have happened if it had really been him? He used a great deal of his power for the sending. I only bore the brunt of what was left over. If he were here in person, I would have had to bear it all. Could I have done it?"

He shook his head and looked grim. "The Einherjar are not enough. It appears I must become stronger in the Galdarpower if I'm to resist this ancient enemy of my father's. I must go deeper into those places I would rather not be."

Freyja looked at him without speaking. After a few moments he rose and went into his own quarters. She stepped down from the High Seat and began to circulate among the guests.

Dawn had not yet touched the sky when Lao-Kee crept through the hall. The Jotun moved so softly and smoothly that none of those sprawled across the tables, benches, or the floor noticed the slender warrior's passage.

Lao-Kee passed the High Seat and went swiftly to the door that gave entrance to Voden's private chambers. Gently the

Jotun opened the door, making sure not a sound was heard, and then with a last look around, slipped inside.

Once inside, Lao-Kee paused and gazed about. On the right was Voden's own sleeping cupboard. Freyja had eventually left the feast, as Voden had earlier, and gone through the door into the private quarters. Doubtless, Lao-Kee thought, she'd joined Voden in the cupboard. The Jotun grinned slyly and crept forward.

Ever so quietly, Lao-Kee opened the door to the cupboard and looked within. Voden was there against the far wall. Freyja lay next to him on her back, his arm around her shoulders. Lao-Kee quietly sniffed. There was no smell of lovemaking in the air. Could it be that Voden and Freyja had been too drunk or too tired to consummate the marriage? The slender warrior laughed with silent pleasure.

Lao-Kee's eyes went back to Freyja sprawled in sleep. She still had Brisingamen on! With a pleased grin, the Jotun slipped into the cupboard and closed the door.

The slender warrior sat, eyes adjusting to the dark and schemed. Freyja lay on top of the clasp. How could she be turned without waking her? Lao-Kee thought about it then smiled, leaning forward to gently take a tiny bit of the skin on Freyja's neck between forefinger and thumb. Then Lao-Kee pinched, just hard enough to mimic a flea bite.

Freyja moaned in her sleep and turned to her left. The clasp was exposed! Lao-kee sat silently, waiting for Freyja to go fully back to sleep. Finally, sure everything was safe, the slender warrior reached out and skillfully undid the clasp, then gently, slowly, with infinite care, slid the necklace off Freyja's neck.

Without making a sound, Lao-Kee left.

Gladsheim was in an uproar. Brisingamen was missing! Someone had stolen it from Freyja's neck as she had slept! No one had ever heard of such a thing. Freyja was pale and Voden red with anger. Everyone wondered who could have done such a thing.

Heimdall was standing next to Voden when the visitors from Jotunheim arrived to take their leave. Lao-Kee bowed low and said gaily, "It's been a wonderful party, but it's time I was getting back to Utgard to see how Hrodvitnir-Fenrir is faring. Who knows, he may need my help with the Risar!"

Voden thanked Lao-Kee for coming and for the gift of Sleipnir. He then gestured to Heimdall and asked that gifts be brought to be taken back to Utgard for Hrodvitnir-Fenrir. Lao-Kee held up a forestalling hand. "No, please! No more gifts! Our saddlebags are already weighted down with your generosity! I have all I ever wanted, and will share my trove with my half brother."

The chieftain of the Aesir smiled graciously and asked Lao-Kee if it was really necessary to leave so suddenly. Lao-Kee considered and replied, "Well, perhaps I could send the others back with the gifts and stay awhile?" Both Tror and Honir applauded this idea and begged Lao-Kee to stay. They had all gotten gloriously drunk together the night before, and hated to lose such a good drinking companion. "Besides," Honir bashfully reminded the slender warrior, "we've already had several adventures together in Jotunheim. Perhaps we could have some here in Asaheim."

While this conversation was going on, Heimdall was staring at Lao-Kee, a musing look in his strange eyes. Suddenly he stood rigidly upright and tilted his head as if listening. Without warning he leapt at Lao-Kee, crying out, "I can hear it rustling!"

The two of them rolled around the floor in front of the High Seat, struggling and bellowing at each other. Everyone else stood back in astonishment, uncertain what to do.

Suddenly there was a rip of fabric and Heimdall jumped up and back with a triumphant cry. He thrust his hand into the air toward Freyja. Brisingamen gleamed in his grasp.

All eyes swung to Lao-Kee, who was hastily trying to put the ripped shirt back together. Honir gasped out loud and Trot cursed. "By Fornjot's icy balls, he's a girl!" Between the shreds of the shirts, small but unmistakable breasts were visible.

Realizing there was no longer anything to hide, Lao-Kee stood with a lopsided grin and answered Trot. "Brilliant, you red-faced dolt! What was your first clue?"

Tror could hardly reply. "But . . . but . . . I . . . we drank blood oath with you. . . . We thought . . . I mean . . ."

Lao-Kee laughed and turned to Voden. "Did you know? There were times when I thought you did."

Voden smiled slightly. "There were times when I wondered exactly what you were, but I wouldn't limit my doubts to just male or female.''

Heimdall was furious. "Why do you bandy words with this . . . this criminal? She should be punished. She stole Brisingamen from Freyja. She is a thief—''

"Stop, Heimdall," Lao-Kee sneered. "I wasn't going to keep it. I only stole it to see how it looked on me. That, and for the fun of it. I intended to stay around for a while and put it back on her some night when she was sound asleep. What a trick that would have been! What a mystery you all would have had to solve then!" Lao-Kee laughed at Heimdall's expression.

"Besides," she continued, "Voden can't punish me. He and Tror and Honir all swore blood oath with me. They can't harm me without breaking their oath. And finally," the Jotun concluded triumphantly, "how would it appear to my brother if you gallant Aesir punished a harmless prank by a girl?''

For several moments everyone simply stared at the grinning countenance of Lao-Kee. Then Voden began to laugh. In a moment Tror joined in, bellowing and whooping. Even Honir managed a giggle. Heimdall continued to scowl, and Freyja wasn't certain what to do. She just held Brisingamen and looked in dismay at Voden and the others.

Voden was the first to get himself under control again. "Ah, Lao-Kee, you are a rogue! I sense you don't wish to hurry back to Utgard. Is that true?''

Lao-Kee nodded. "Jotunheim is a dangerous place for me right now. I have enemies that even Hrodvitnir-Fenrir may not be able to protect me from. I'd rather stay here for a while, if I may. I once saved you—''

"Only after getting us into the mess in the first place!" Tror interrupted with a roar of laughter.

The slender Jotun continued calmly. ". . . from Hreidmir and his vengence. I also got Mjollnir back for Tror.'' They all grinned while Tror flushed bright red and grumbled. "I have a right to claim asylum.''

"That you do," Voden agreed. "But you must promise that you'll refrain from tricks like this one with Brisingamen, or you'll soon have as many enemies here in Asaheim as you have in Jotunheim! Will you take that oath?''

Lao-Kee smiled sarcastically. "Not even one little joke? My, but things will be dull here in Gladsheim! All right. I've

no choice. I promise. I won't steal any more necklaces."
With that, Lao-Kee turned and walked away. For the first
time Voden noticed that the slender warrior walked with a
slight sway to her hips. He almost broke out laughing again.

Gymirling and Idun came next to say good-bye. Voden was
sorry to see the Alfar leave, and promised to send someone to
them soon by way of an embassy to work out the details of
military cooperation in case of an attack against either of their
realms. Idun bowed low as she received a gift of golden
apples from Vili. The two friends had tears in their eyes as
they parted.

Then the Alfar departed, and Voden sat alone, gazing into
the uncertain future.

TROR

XIV

WINTER slammed into Asaheim with a power and violence that left everyone stunned. The first storms struck in the middle of what was ordinarily fall, and before the oaks could even lose their leaves, snow covered the land. The temperature dropped so sharply that many of the Aesir claimed to have seen birds freeze in midflight, fall to the earth, and shatter like dropped icicles. Every hall, no matter how tightly built, was cold. The people suffered greatly, and frostbite was common.

Immediately on the heels of the snow, large packs of ferocious wolves appeared out of the northwest. Several travelers disappeared without a trace, and people soon took to going about in large groups. Children were never allowed out of sight of their parents, for the great, shaggy beasts came right into the yards of the farmsteads. In two cases they actually broke into isolated halls and slaughtered the inhabitants.

Even more frightening and amazing than the appearance of the wolf packs were sightings of the great white bears that ordinarily dwelt exclusively on the fringes of the Icerealm. So vicious and deadly were the white monsters that men fled before them in utter terror. They actually stalked humans with an almost supernatural cunning and skill. More than one solitary hunter disappeared, leaving behind nothing but a bloody stain on the snow, surrounded by massive paw prints.

Voden began to wonder if this wasn't the beginning of the Fimbulvetter, the three-year-long winter that Gymirling had foreseen. Since he was the only one the Alfar had mentioned it to, he decided to remain silent. Time would tell.

On the very day of the winter solstice, Voden's Aesir wife, Frigida, gave birth to twin boys. The twins were a great surprise to everyone since Frigida had only foreseen a single child. One was the most beautiful child anyone had ever seen. They named him Baldur. The other was perfect in every way except that when he opened his eyes, they were white as milk. The child was blind. They named him Hod.

One cold winter's evening in Asgard, Tror went to the hall of Billing, a man he knew only vaguely. Billing had moved to Asgard that fall. Previously he had lived on the northern Aesir Plain, just south of the Iving and east of the Fimbulthul. Despite the fact that the truce between the Jotun and the Aesir held for the most part, there were still occasional raids set in motion by hot-blooded Jotun youths. Lying so close to Jotunheim, his farmstead had been an easy target for one such raid. The raiders had set his hall on fire, but Billing and Ull, his son-in-law, had managed to drive them off, killing two in the process. Ull had died later of his wounds, and Billing's wife succumbed to a fever she had caught when she had been driven from the burning hall into the subzero weather in her sleeping shift. Discouraged at the prospect of trying to rebuild his hall in the middle of the winter, and unable to see how he could live in its ruins during such a harsh time, he had packed his daughter Sif and her infant son, named Ull after his father, onto his sled and come to Asgard. There he had taken over the hall of a family that had moved to Gladsheim. He was meeting with Tror in an attempt to sell some of his livestock.

When Tror arrived at the hall, his host ushered him in, holding a hand to his lips, begging his silence. He took his guest to the High Seat and showed him the reason for the request for quiet. There, Ull cradled in her arms, was Sif, sound asleep. "She works so hard around the hall," Billing whispered. "We can't afford many servants now, so she has to do both her own work and her mother's. She fell asleep after dinner and I haven't the heart to wake her."

Tror stood and gazed at Sif in open-mouthed wonder. Never had he seen so beautiful a woman! She glowed and shimmered with light. Her hair, a mass of golden glory, was spread around her. Her skin was so white and so soft, he yearned to reach out and touch it. Instantly he knew that the earth would be a desolate place unless he could lie with her in his arms.

That night he bargained poorly and yet bought all Billing had to sell. When he returned to his own hall, he lay awake in his sleeping cupboard until dawn colored the sky. Then he rose and found he had no appetite.

For several nights running he returned to Billing's hall. Mostly he just talked to Billing, his mind and conversation wandering loosely since he was constantly following every motion Sif made. Billing saw what was happening and smiled to himself. A marriage between his daughter and Tror would be very advantageous. He would suddenly find himself secure again and be sure of a good home for Sif and his grand-child, Ull. Yes, it would be a good thing, he decided. He rose and excused himself on some pretext, leaving Tror and Sif alone.

Tror was too tongue-tied to utter a word. Sif smiled at him and tossed her head. Her hair shone and rippled with golden light. The red-bearded giant felt all the strength leave his limbs, and a massive lump rose into his throat. Without a sound Tror stood and walked with a wobbly step to the door of the hall. As he left, Sif smiled contentedly. She knew he would be back.

"What am I going to do?" Tror wailed. "Everytime I see her, I get so hard I can't stand up. And when she tosses that hair of hers, by Fornjot's icy balls, I melt! I can't talk or think or— "

Voden laughed. "You're in love, Tror. Or at least in lust."

"Is there any cure?"

"Aye," Voden replied with a sly wink of his single eye. "Aye, that there is. You must win her, red-beard. Convince her you can't live without her. Then bed her and get rid of the hardness that bothers you so."

"But . . . but what then?"

"What then? Why, then you've satisfied your desire and can relax again."

"But that's faithless! I mean, it isn't right. I mean—"

Voden laughed again. "Believe what I say, Tror. I know both men and women well. Men don't keep faith with women. We speak fair words even while we're thinking most falsely in an attempt to bewilder their wits. We give them pleasing words and offer presents to win their love. We flatter their looks because we know full well that praise will gain its prize. Oh, yes, we act in bad faith, to be sure!

"But they're no better than we! Never trust what a woman tells you nor count on her constancy. I swear, their hearts are turned on a potter's wheel and their minds are made for change. Praise the day when night falls, Tror, a friend when he's dead, a sword that's been proven in battle, a maiden once she's married, ice only after you've crossed it, and mead when it's been drunk. But a bow that creaks when drawn, a smiling wolf, a shallow-rooted tree, a grunting wild boar, mounting seas, a coiled snake, a playful bear, a sword with a hairline crack, new ice, kind words from your brother's murderer, or a woman's promises—ah, a man's too trusting who takes chances on these!"

Tror moved uncomfortably, his eyes disturbed. "Don't you trust anyone, Voden?"

Voden's face became instantly serious, though a hint of humor still lurked in his eye. He gave his friend a long look. "Trust anyone? No, I guess I don't. In my position I'm not sure it would make much sense to trust anyone."

"Don't you even trust me?"

"Mostly," Voden replied, and then fell silent without expanding on his answer.

"Mostly," Tror repeated sadly. "When don't you trust me?"

Voden smiled suddenly and laughed. "When it comes to beautiful women with shimmering hair!"

"You're making fun of me," Tror grumbled. "By Fornjot's icy balls, Voden, I think I'm really in love. I don't just want to sleep with her once. I . . . I want to marry her."

Voden became truly serious. "I'm sorry. No man should ever mock another man's love. No one, however wise, is immune to love's folly. Indeed, more than one wise man has been made a fool by the lures of love. Only you can know what lives near your own heart. And for the man who sees clearly into himself, there's no greater sorrow than being without love.

"Yet take my advice. Test the virtue of Sif. See what you can get for mere words and promises before you commit to marriage. Perhaps you can get satisfaction. Perhaps it will be enough. If not"—he shrugged—"then marry her."

Tror slammed one fist into the palm of the other. "By Fornjot, that's what I'll do! I'll test her!" He rose and stumped out of Valholl without looking right or left or even saying good-bye.

Voden sat on the High Seat and watched his friend's back as he left. "Aye," he said to himself, laughing quietly, "test her. Though who will be tested remains to be seen."

Sif's face was flushed by Tror's words. She shook her head so that the light shimmered from her golden hair, and looked down at the floor of her father's hall. Her voice was soft but firm. "This is no way to woo me, Tror. Here in the bright daylight there are too many eyes to witness my weakness. No, if you wish to woo me, come after dark when none can see. Perhaps then we can reach an understanding."

The rest of the day Tror quivered with anticipation. How the hours dragged by! Ah, he sighed silently, Sif is both body and soul to me, but no more mine for all that. Yet tonight . . . Ah, tonight we will see if Voden was right!

When the hour came, he crept through the darkened streets of Asgard, one shadow among others. The clouds hung heavily in the sky, blocking out light from the moon or the stars. A perfect night for an assignation!

As he approached Billing's hall, though, he began to grow apprehensive. The light seemed to be increasing all about him. He peered around the corner of another hall and discovered its origin. Billing's hall was ablaze with light! The few warrior friends that Billing had were walking around and around it, blazing torches and sharpened spears in their hands. Billing himself stood at the door to the hall, a torch in one hand, his sword in the other.

Tror watched for a while and then turned and slunk back to his own hall. Sif's message was loud and clear. They had indeed reached an understanding that night. There was only one way he was going to satisfy his love. He would have to marry her.

Spring didn't arrive until very late that year. There was a snowstorm in the early summer, and though it melted swiftly, it harmed many budding plants. The Aesir worried about the crop they would harvest in the fall.

Tror married Sif and adopted Ull as his son. The marriage

feast was a gay one, and everyone commented on the beauty of the bride with the golden hair.

Sif wanted to live in Gladsheim, and it wasn't long before she'd convinced Tror it was the only thing to do. He decided to build a hall there, and chose a spot near Valholl, just across a small stream known as the Thund. The hall he built was modest in size, and he called it Bilskirnir. He moved into it with his wife Sif, his adopted son Ull, and his sister Thrud, who had never married. Thrud loved Ull and spent many hours playing with the child. Sif was delighted with the arrangement and spent the spare time it gave her having her maids plait her long, golden hair to create stunning and unusual hairdos. She especially loved twining silver and gold wires into her tresses.

Tror and the other men were drinking in Valholl. The talk and the play had turned rougher than usual, and Tror had ordered—no, had bodily thrown—Lao-Kee out. "No place for a damned girl!" he'd bellowed with drunken laughter, and slammed the door behind her.

Now she sat in total silence, gazing at the sleeping features and dazzling hair of Sif. It's so easy to find one's way into these Aesir sleeping cupboards, the slender Jotun thought with a leer. Try creeping into a Jotun wagon and you'll find it's a whole different thing. Damn wagons move whenever you do, so you have to creep ever so slowly, shifting your weight carefully, carefully . . .

Sif muttered in her sleep and rolled away from Lao-Kee onto her left side. The Jotun frowned. That drunken bastard Tror! Not that I'm not damn near as drunk as he is, she giggled under her breath, but to throw me out after all I've done for him. Without me he'd be rotting under the ground near Hreidmir's wagons. Or still trying to get his damn hammer back from Thrymir. No gratitude. Typical of all damn men—Aesir, Vanir, Jotun, whatever.

Except Voden. He's different, she silently proclaimed. Pity he's married to that bitch Freyja. Frigida wouldn't be any problem. Dumb Aesir cow. I could make Voden forget all about her. But Freyja—now, Freyja's a different story. Too much between them. Can see it in their eyes whenever they look at each other.

Sif stirred again, her hair rippling in the dim light. Lao-Kee gazed at her, a sneer on her face. You, on the other hand, are a bitch, she thought. I see you making eyes at Voden. Virtuous, my ass! You'd have him if you could!

She turned away, a tear in her eye. Worse yet, she admitted, I see the way Voden looks at you. Oh, yes, I can see the fire grow in that eye of his! Bastard! Why won't he ever look at me that way? But he wouldn't touch you, Sif, you stupid bitch! Oh, no, not my Voden. You're Tror's wife. Your golden hair and white body belong to that red-haired, red-faced oaf! Voden would never betray a friend over a foolish creature like you.

But why won't Voden ever look at me that way?

She sat for a few moments, battling the mead for control of her thoughts. Then an idea occurred to her. Sif. There was a way to get back at both Thor and Voden at the same time. Sif.

With a sly grin the slender Jotun pulled out her razor sharp knife and leaned toward Tror's soundly sleeping wife. Gently, she took hold of Sif's golden hair and with quick strokes cut it off. Sif murmured but didn't wake up. The hair left on her head stuck up in short, stubbly clumps. Lao-Kee picked up the shining tresses, grinned at them, and threw them on the floor.

Let's see how many men look at you now, my pretty one, she thought with glee. Then she crept noiselessly from the cupboard and from Bilskirnir.

"Put her down, Tror," Voden said sternly for the second time.

"But . . . but . . . she did it and you know it! There's no one else in Gladsheim who would have done such a thing! It had to be this little Jotun bitch! She's always hated Sif, you think I can't see that?"

"Lao-Kee will be punished. Now put her down," the leader of the Aesir demanded firmly. With a rumble Tror released his grip around the slender Jotun's neck and she tumbled to the ground.

For a few moments Lao-Kee was unable to speak. She rubbed her throat, trying to get her voice and her breath back. The livid marks of Tror's fingers showed against her skin. Voden felt sorry for her but refused to alter the harsh look on his face. She had done this thing. There was no doubt about it.

"Th-thank you," she finally managed to gasp. "Thought I was finished there." She stood shakily and glared defiantly at Tror. "It was only a joke. Her hair will grow back."

"Only a joke!" Tror bellowed, stepping forward as if to grab Lao-Kee again. "I'll show you a joke! I'll smash your head in and laugh like Fornjot, damn you!"

Lao-Kee leapt out of Tror's way and scurried behind Voden. "I didn't mean any harm by it," Lao-Kee said quickly. "I mean, I could have slit her silly throat. I just got so damn tired of her stupid hair. All those shakings and tossings. All those idiotic hairdos with wire and junk. By Nerthus! And the way all you men kept gawking at her. It'll grow back."

Tror groaned and slumped to a bench. "Grow back! By Fornjot's icy balls, of course it'll grow back. But have you any idea of the crying and weeping that went on this morning? And do you know that Sif has refused to even come out of the cupboard or let anyone in to see her until it's all grown back? It'll be months!" He leapt to his feet again and glowered at Lao-Kee. "I'm going to break every bone in your body!"

Voden held up his hand. "Enough. This is getting us nowhere. Lao-Kee admits cutting Sif's hair. I agree she must be punished. The question is how?" He turned to the Jotun girl hiding behind him and asked, "What do you think the punishment should be?"

"Look," she began, "you don't need to punish me at all. I'll make the whole thing good. To both Sif and to Tror."

Voden raised his eyebrows. "And just how do you propose to do that?"

Lao-Kee gazed at Voden, then at Tror. She licked her lips. "Well," she began, "everyone always says Sif's hair looks like spun gold. But no gold has ever been seen spun that fine. At least it's never been seen by anyone but me.

"Just to the south and the west of the place where the Sid and the Gopul meet is a hill that's one of the last of those belonging to the Himinborg. In that hill two Dverg, the sons of Ivaldi, live. They know the way to spin gold as fine as hair. To my knowledge they're the only ones in all of Yggdrasil to know that secret. I've been there and seen it for myself.

"I'll go there and have them make a wig of gold for Sif. She can wear it until her hair grows out." She snorted. "If I know the sons of Ivaldi, the damn thing will be so beautiful, she'll keep her hair short and wear it all the time. There won't be anything else like it anywhere in Yggdrasil. How does that sound to you, Tror?''

Tror's mouth had opened in wonder at Lao-Kee's tale. Gold spun as fine as hair? A wig made of such gold for Sif to wear? Surely that would please his wife! He hesitated, frowning. Don't give in too quickly, he advised himself. Lao-Kee's tricky. ''Well,'' he grumbled, ''it might do for Sif. But you said you'd do something for me too. What?''

Lao-Kee looked slyly at Voden and Tror. Her voice took on a conspiritorial tone. ''Years ago, when the Jotun attacked and burned Asgard, Tror, a Jotun raped Thrud, your sister. At that time, as you've often told me yourself, you swore vengeance against him. Surely you haven't forgotten your pledge?''

Tror's face darkened and he scowled harshly. ''No, I haven't forgotten. And it galls me deeply that I haven't been able to carry out my promise!''

''Well,'' Lao-Kee drawled, ''I can help you. I know the Jotun who did it. His name is Hrungnir. I've got a grudge against him myself for something he did to me. He's a mean bastard, and I've always hated him. But he's one of my half brother's supporters, so I've never had a chance to get even with him.''

She moved around from behind Voden and sat down on a bench, motioning the two men to sit on either side of her. ''Here's what I'll do. First, I'll go to the sons of Ivaldi and get the golden wig for Sif. Then I'll go to Jotunheim and lure Hrungnir to Gladsheim.''

''How will you do that?'' Tror asked, his face suffused with grim pleasure.

''Hrungnir's crazy about horse racing. He's got a horse, Gullfaxi by name, that's one of the fastest in all Jotunheim. If I go back, I can brag about Voden's horse, Sleipnir, and claim he could beat Gullfaxi. Hrungnir won't be able to resist the challenge. The very idea that an Aesir could have a horse faster than a Jotun's . . . Well, he'll fall for it.''

''But he'll be suspicious if he thinks Tror is here. . . .''

''We could pretend I'm somewhere else,'' Tror suggested.

Lao-Kee snapped her fingers. ''Perfect! I'll say you've gone south to investigate the rumors that the Dark Empire is sending scouting parties north of the Smoking Lands. He won't be able to resist! Perfect!'' She stood up. ''I'll get my

gear together right away and head off for the sons of Ivaldi.
Then I'll bring back the golden wig and—''

Tror stood and grabbed Lao-Kee by the throat again. He
squeezed ever so gently, a dark scowl on his face. "Just don't
try any more tricks, Jotun. You'd best come back with the
wig and with Hrungnir. Because if you don't, I'll track you
down and smash your skull with Mjollnir.''

"Don't worry,'' Lao-Kee said hoarsely. "I'll keep my
word. I always do.''

The sons of Ivaldi lived in a great cave deep in the heart of an
isolated hill to the south and west of the River Sid. For years
the two brothers had made jewelry to sell to the Jotun. Their
work was beautiful and very much in demand. It was also
very expensive.

Lao-Kee had been to see them on several occasions, so she
had no trouble finding the opening to their abode nor in
gaining entrance. The two Dverg rubbed their hands together
when they saw her, knowing she was the half sister of
Hrodvitnir. Surely the almost-Warlord of the Jotun Horde
would want special jewels and armlets to mark his status. No
doubt he could be charged a good price as well. And who
knew what golden wonders his half sister would want to
adorn her person?

When Lao-Kee explained her needs, the two brothers stared
at each other and scowled. "And what will you pay us for
this wondrous wig, eh?'' They asked, speaking as one.

Lao-Kee smiled coldly. "First, you will gain the friendship
of Lao-Kee, sister of Hrodvitnir-Fenrir. Don't frown so at the
idea. Without that friendship you could lose everything.'' She
grinned, baring her teeth threateningly. "Second, you will
gain the patronage of Sif, Tror, and Voden. There's a good
market for golden brooches and arm rings among the Aesir.
You'd be the only Dverg to have it.'' They grunted in mild
interest.

"But there's something more,'' she said slyly. "I have a
secret to tell you, one two of your cousins will pay dearly
for.''

The sons of Ivaldi leaned forward, their interest piqued by
the promise of payment coming from other Dverg. "And
what is that secret?'' they asked in unison.

"Ah,'' Lao-Kee said with a wag of her finger, "promise

first. I'll tell you this much. It involves a man who carries a great treasure with him. He's in Nidavellir right now, probably in the area where your two cousins, Falar and Galar, live. Promise to make the golden hair and I'll tell you.''

"We promise,'' they said together.

Lao-Kee smiled broadly. "Well,'' she began in a low, secretive tone, "his name is Kao-Shir and he comes from the Sunrise Empire. He's traveling with a Svartalfar by the name of Anhur. He wants to meet some of the Dverg.''

They nodded. "We know,'' they chorused. "He wandered around here for a while. We had no interest in an old man with long ears and no gold or jewels. He's a poor Yellow Robe.''

"Ah,'' Lao-Kee chuckled, "that's what he *appears* to be, for sure. But Voden himself has told me that Lao-Kee carries with him the greatest treasure known to man. One he said he himself would give a great deal to possess!''

The sons of Ivaldi rubbed their hands together with avaricious glee. "Yes, Falar and Galar would trade good gold for such information! They're terribly greedy fellows. What, pray tell, is this treasure beyond compare?''

Lao-Kee had everything to do to keep from laughing out loud. What a wonderful double joke on both that stuffy, pompous old man from the Sunrise Empire and on the Dverg! "That, Voden would never tell me,'' she replied with great seriousness. "I think it's so special that he didn't even dare mention it for fear others might find out Kao-Shir has it and try to take it from him. The old man is a great friend of Voden's, or else the Aesir chieftain would take it for himself. But Falar and Galar— ''

"Aren't anybody's friends!'' chorused the two Dverg, completing Lao-Kee's thought. "And you're right. They'll pay dearly for information about such a treasure. They're such greedy fellows! Yes, Lao-Kee, we'll make the wig you requested!''

They turned and scurried to their great forge. The fire was always smoldering in it, so they simply piled on more wood. While one of them worked the bellows, the other took an ingot of pure gold and placed it in a crucible to be heated. Then, when the gold was soft, they began to work it, beating and spinning it out into an incredibly thin thread. Out and out it stretched until it nearly filled the cavern.

When they had completed the thread of gold, they made a

cap of skin-thin gold cloth and cut the gold thread into thousands of strands. They passed each strand through the cap and knotted its under end. Then they smoothed the underside out with a hot, flat iron, fusing it into one flexible piece, totally connected with the cap.

Finished, they held up the wig for Lao-Kee to see. The slender Jotun was stunned. She'd never seen anything so beautiful. The gold hairs shimmered and flowed with every movement, every breath of air. They seemed alive with glowing, shining life. By all the gods, this wig makes Sif's original hair seem a dull thing indeed! she thought. For a brief moment Lao-Kee was so dazzled by the beauty of the golden wig that she considered keeping it for herself. Then she pictured in her mind's eye how ridiculous she'd look with long, golden tresses, and she laughed out loud.

Bowing low to the sons of Ivaldi, she left with the wig of golden hair.

Sif reached her hand out of the sleeping cupboard to take the wig. Everyone in the hall could hear her gasp of wonder as she saw it. Then there was a moment's pause as she tried it on.

The cupboard door slid back and Sif stepped out, her head held high, her eyes glowing, her cheeks flushed with excitement. The light flickered off her hair and filled Bilskirnir with a golden glow. Everyone in the hall was too stunned to speak. None of them had ever dreamt such a thing could exist.

Sif came over to Lao-Kee and took both the Jotun's hands in her own. "It's everything you promised it would be," she said, her voice almost breaking with emotion. "Oh, thank you! I forgive you for your horrid trick!"

Tror came up and stood next to his wife. "Yes, Lao-Kee, I agree. You've thoroughly kept this part of your bargain. Sif is happy. Now all that remains is for you to keep the second half. My half." His eyes glowed with excitement at the thought of his revenge.

Lao-Kee nodded and grinned. "I'll be back on my horse and heading north to Jotunheim as soon as I have a chance to change my clothes! Don't worry, Tror. I'll trick Hrungnir into coming right here to Gladsheim. He won't be able to resist the lure of a horse race. And you'll get your chance to take vengeance on the man who raped Thrud."

• • •

Lao-Kee didn't bother to go to Utgard. In fact, she decided it would be safer if as few people as possible knew she was back in Jotunheim at all. If she went to Utgard, hundreds of pairs of eyes, both friendly and unfriendly, would see her and know she had returned. As long as she stayed right by her half brother's side, she was at least as safe as he was, though even that was no sure thing since the Risar had not yet yielded and there was always the possibility of an assassination attempt. But once she was away from Hrodvitnir-Fenrir's protection, even for the short trip to visit Hrungnir, she would be fair game. More than one of his supporters had been found with a slit throat. The mere fact she was a girl would make no difference to the Risar. No, it would be best if no one knew of her presence in Jotunheim, not even Hrodvitnir-Fenrir. That way she could go in and out freely, swiftly, silently, invisibly.

There was another reason for stealth as well. She didn't want anyone to discover what she was up to. Hrungnir was stupid and would probably fall for the trick. But someone with more intelligence might see through it.

So she crossed the Iving at Bifrosti's Ford in the middle of the night and rode directly to Hrungnir's camp. The Jotun was surprised and not at all pleased to see her. But since she was Hrodvitnir's half sister, he made her welcome, throwing a visiting cousin out of the guest wagon and installing her in his place.

As they sat around the next night, Lao-Kee began telling tales of Asaheim. She described Voden and Freyja's wedding in terms that had the Jotun roaring with laughter. Eventually she got around to describing Voden's possessions, including the great hall Valholl and his horse Sleipnir.

"I raised and trained that horse myself," Lao-Kee bragged, "and there isn't a faster horse in all of Yggdrasil!"

Hrungnir bristled. "Fool. Don't you remember Gullfaxi?"

"Gullfaxi?" Lao-Kee said, feigning ignorance. "Who's Gullfaxi?"

"Why, my horse, you cretin! The best damn horse in the whole of Yggdrasil! However fast Sleipnir may be, Gullfaxi could run him into the ground without half trying!"

"Pooh!" the slender Jotun scoffed. "I've seen your old nag run. Fast, no doubt. But I've seen Sleipnir run too. He goes so fast you'd swear he had eight legs rather than just four. Can Gullfaxi go that fast?''

"That fast?" Hrungnir sputtered in anger. "That fast? Why, damn you, Gullfaxi can go as if she had sixteen legs instead of only eight! Ha!''

"Talk, talk, talk," Lao-Kee muttered scornfully.

Hrungnir came to his feet with a roar. "Talk, eh? Just talk, you say? Why, damn your eyes, I'll pit Gullfaxi against any damn Aesir nag any day! And give you any odds you ask for into the bargain!''

"Faugh," Lao-Kee snorted derisively. "Do you mean you'd be willing to go to Asaheim and try Gullfaxi against Sleipnir? Surely, you're not brave enough to do that?''

"Brave enough? Brave enough? By Gymir's Eye, I'll go to Niflheim to match Gullfaxi against Sleipnir!''

"That will hardly be necessary," Lao-Kee sniffed. "Gladsheim will be far enough.''

Hrungnir was suddenly silent, realizing what he'd promised. He silently cursed his own foolish pride. "Ummm," he muttered, "there is one little problem, now that I think of it.''

"Oh?" Lao-Kee asked sweetly, "and what might that be?''

"Well, I know that we have a truce with the Aesir right now. Ummm, but there's one Aesir that truce wouldn't be enough to satisfy. Ummm, you see, Tror . . . I mean his sister . . . I mean—''

Lao-Kee brushed the objection aside. "Tror isn't even in Gladsheim right now. he's way off to the south in a part of the Vanir forest known as Iron Wood. It's near the Smoking Lands. Voden sent him there to check out the rumors that the Dark Empire is sending scouting parties north. So if you're not afraid that Gullfaxi can't beat Sleipnir—''

"Afraid! Damn you! Go and tell Voden I'll be there in a week. And then we'll see who has the fastest horse in Yggdrasil!''

"Indeed we will," Lao-Kee muttered with a secret smile. "Indeed we will.''

XV

HRUNGNIR arrived in Gladsheim with several of his most trusted warriors and two mounts for each man. Gullfaxi came without burden, but the Jotun still demanded the horse be given a day's rest before the race. Voden agreed as he inspected Hrungnir's horse. "A beautiful beast," he said admiringly. "Looks fast too."

"Fast?" Hrungnir puffed himself up. "Fast isn't the word for Gullfaxi. Why this horse is so swift, sometimes she meets herself going when she's coming back on the second lap! On a bright day her shadow has everything it can do to keep up with her! Ha! There isn't a faster horse in all Yggdrasil! I'd stake my head on that!"

Voden laughed. "I'd take that wager if I had any use for your head. But as I have none, let's each bet a bag of gold the size of my head. Winner takes all."

"Done!" Hrungnir roared.

The next morning Lao-Kee laid out the track for them to run. "Due east," she said. "I've set out markers of red cloth. About five miles out I built a cairn with a red flag flying from its top. That's where you turn to come back."

Hrungnir readied Gullfaxi as Voden prepared Sleipnir. Lao-Kee sidled over to the leader of the Aesir and asked, "Are you positive you wouldn't rather have me ride for you? I'm a lot lighter. Plus I know all the Jotun tricks."

"No thanks," Voden replied, tightening and testing the girth. "My horse, my challenge, my race."

Lao-Kee scowled and shook her head. "Your loss too!

Well, just be careful. Hrungnir's a mean bastard. There won't be anybody out there on the plain to see how he wins, and he damn well intends to win. Jotun don't always play fair in a horse race, you know.''

"Or in anything else," Voden said, and laughed as he jumped up on Sleipnir's back. "Don't worry. I don't always play fair myself."

The two men walked their horses up to the starting line, barely able to restrain the two animals. Gullfaxi and Sleipnir had taken an immediate dislike to each other and were more than eager for the contest.

"Ready to lose?" Hrungnir said between his teeth.

"As ready as you are," Voden replied calmly.

They both watched Lao-Kee intently as the slender Jotun dramatically raised her hand. Then, with a sudden jerk, she swept it downward and cried, "Go!"

The two horses exploded from the starting line, their bunched muscles stretching out with incredible power. The turf sprayed out behind them as they raced off across the plain. In a few short moments they were already over the first rise and out of sight. Lao-Kee sat down nonchalantly on the grass to await their return. The other Jotun and Aesir who had come to watch the race milled about in uneasy confusion.

The slender Jotun grinned to herself. It's going well, she thought. Tror's kept himself hidden. Hrungnir doesn't even suspect he's around. She chuckled, thinking of how the red-bearded giant must be pacing back and forth in his hall, waiting impatiently for the signal to come out and confront the man who had raped his sister.

A sudden thought occurred to Lao-Kee. What if I let him stew a little longer? What if, in fact, I change the whole plan without letting anyone know? Things had been arranged so that as soon as the race was over, when Hrungnir would be tired and his men off guard, Lao-Kee was to call Tror. He would rush forth from Bilskirnir, Mjollnir in his grasp, and attack the Jotun, slaughtering him like a dog, right in front of his own men. A fitting death for the bastard, Lao-Kee agreed. The only trouble was that it would cut her fun short.

What if she prolonged the joke? What if rather than calling Tror right away, she convinced Voden to bring Hrungnir into Valholl for a bit of mead to clear his dusty throat? How delicious! To let Hrungnir get drunk and silly before Tror killed him! Maybe he'd even lose control so thoroughly that he'd beg for mercy! I'd dearly love to see that, she thought, remembering again how Hrungnir had laughed at her own pleas.

Could she improve on the plan even more? An idea crept into her mind. An idea so convoluted and tricky that she gasped as she met it. Not only would it revenge her against Hrungnir, but against Tror and Hrodvitnir as well! Three with one!

A sly grin on her face, she began to work out the details of her new plot.

Far across the plain to the east, Voden and Hrungnir were neck and neck. They'd been that way for some time now. Gullfaxi was every bit as swift as her owner had bragged. But Sleipnir was her equal. The difference, then, would lie in the riders.

Hrungnir was a Jotun and hence born and bred in the saddle. The Aesir started riding when they were very young, but they were no match for the Jotun. Voden had an advantage over most Aesir, though. Lao-Kee had been coaching him, showing him how to get the most out of Sleipnir.

The Jotun suddenly swerved his horse into Voden's, trying to knock him and his mount off balance. Sleipnir was too quick, though, and without breaking stride, leapt lightly to the side. Hrungnir closed the gap and slashed at Voden with his whip. He missed and tried again. Voden raised his arm and took the blow on his forearm. He slashed back at Hrungnir and connected against the other man's hand.

They rounded the turning point, slashing and striking back and forth, each trying to ram the other with his horse. Even Sleipnir and Gullfaxi tried to bite each other whenever they came in range.

Without warning, Hrungnir spurred Gullfaxi to a sudden burst of speed that put her slightly ahead of Sleipnir. Before Voden could respond, the Jotun took a handful of dust from his pocket and threw it into Sleipnir's eyes. The horse cried out in fury and began to slow, shaking its head to rid itself of the stinging dust.

Voden was furious. He pulled Sleipnir to a halt and leapt from the saddle. He grabbed the water bag he carried against thirst and splashed its contents over Sleipnir's eyes. The horse shook its head again and whinnied, declaring it was ready to run. Voden vaulted back into the saddle and Sleipnir shot away like an arrow released from a tightly drawn bow.

They'd lost a lot of ground to Hrungnir, but Sleipnir stretched out and began to gain it back. The Jotun looked over his shoulder and was stunned to see that his opponent was rapidly gaining on him. He had no dust left. Only a throwing knife. If it comes to that, he decided, I'll use it.

They were neck and neck again for a few moments, but then Voden began to pull ahead. First he led by only a head, then a full neck, and finally by a full length. When his back was thoroughly to Hrungnir, the Jotun slipped the knife from his belt and got ready to throw it.

Voden felt a strange pricking as he passed the Jotun. Never let an enemy get close behind you, he suddenly remembered. He swerved Sleipnir to the right. The knife whizzed by him, grazing Sleipnir's neck and drawing a bright line of blood behind it.

Angrily, Voden turned in his saddle and thrust out his left hand, making a sign in the air, a straight vertical line with a shorter line beginning about halfway down the right side and going diagonally down to the right. "*Kenaz, cen, kauna,*" he cried in a thunderous voice, "The torch, the living flame, is blinding and brilliant!" The rune he had written in the air suddenly glowed with intense light. There was a flash and an explosion. Even in the bright daylight, sudden, abnormal shadows fled in all directions. Hrungnir gave a shout of anguish and Gullfaxi whinnied in fear. Voden grinned in victory as he looked back to see the two of them standing still, dazed and momentarily blinded.

Voden crossed the finish line well ahead of the Jotun challenger. When Hrungnir thundered across, his face flushed and angry, the chief of the Aesir was already off his horse, his sword strapped to his side, surrounded by an armed group of the Einherjar. He held a horn of mead in his hands.

When Hrungnir jumped from Gullfaxi's back, Voden held out the horn to him with a cynical smile. "A good race, Hrungnir. Well and fairly run." The Jotun eyed him carefully, waiting to see where this train of thought would lead. "Here," Voden continued, holding out the drinking horn, "drink, for you must be thirsty after such a ride. I know I used all of my water, and assume you must have done the same.''

Voden turned to all those who were crowding around, both Jotun and Aesir. "Hrungnir ran a good race. But Sleipnir is the faster horse, even if I'm not the better rider. I honor my Jotun friend in the name of the truce that is between our people." He turned back to Hrungnir. "Here, take the horn, drink deep. Let Gullfaxi rest and drink her fill from the Thund. And come with all your men to Valholl. There we will feast and drink in honor of this great race between the two fastest horses ever to stride the face of Yggdrasil.''

Somewhat mollified by Voden's conciliatory words, and realizing that he had no real choice, Hrungnir took the horn and growled his assent. As he took a deep drink, everyone, Aesir and Jotun, heaved a sigh of relief and gave a cheer. Lao-Kee, standing apart from the crowd, smiled with pleasure.

Hrist and Mist, two of Voden's favorite serving maids, brought horns of mead to Hrungnir as he sprawled on the High Seat next to his host. Voden raised his own horn. "Drink! Test your mettle against the finest drinkers in all of Asaheim!'' The Jotun all raised their horns with a roar and drank deeply. The Aesir responded in kind.

None, though, drank more deeply nor more often than Hrungnir. The Jotun was still smoldering with resentment over his humiliating defeat. He cast a baleful eye over all the Aesir in the hall. Every time his glance happened to fall on Freyja or Sif, however, his eyes glowed with the hot light of lust.

"By Gymir, I will!'' he shouted suddenly.

"Surely not,'' Voden said quietly, his single eye burning intently deep within his hood.

"Dammit, I will!'' Hrungnir jumped up unsteadily and gestured to the entire hall. "I'll take this whole damn hall back to Jotunheim with me!''

The Aesir laughed uncomfortably, and the Jotun put down their horns, moving subtly to free their weapons in case of sudden need.

Voden smiled slightly and asked, "Whatever will become of us if you take Valholl with you?''

"You?'' Hrungnir roared. "Who gives a dog's ass for all of you? I'll kill every damn Aesir in here.'' He turned to glare evilly at Freyja and Sif. "Except for you two. I'll take you back with me. I've got plenty of use for you!"

The hall was utterly quiet. Freyja stood and smiled. Taking a horn of ale from the motionless hands of an Aesir warrior, she flowed toward Hrungnir. "Here," she said softly, "calm yourself. Drink this."

Hrungnir grabbed the horn and sat on an empty bench. "Drink it? By the tits of Nerthus, you're damn right I'll drink it! I'll drink all the mead in Asaheim! And then rape all the women!" He put the horn to his lips and slobbered it down in one long draught.

No sooner had he finished than Sif, taking her cue from Freyja, was standing ready with another horn. She smiled at him and placed it in his hand with a slight bow.

Voden's smile was mocking as he turned and nodded to Lao-Kee. With an answering smile, the slender Jotun left the hall.

Valholl's massive door slammed open as Tror entered, Mjollnir gripped in his hand, his face red with anger, his flaming beard bristling. Thrud was beside him. Lao-Kee slipped in behind them and closed the door securely. As he saw Thrud and Tror, Hrungnir stopped drinking, the horn he had raised to his lips slowly dropping down until it fell to the floor from limp fingers. The color drained from his face.

Thrud walked slowly forward until she was not ten paces from the Jotun. She gave him a cold, searching look and nodded, turning to her brother. "That's the one, Tror. That's the Jotun who raped me." Without another word she turned and left the hall, her shoulders shaking as she cried softly.

Tror moved up the hall until he stood in front of Hrungnir. "What in the name of Fornjot's icy balls do you think you're doing here? How dare you drink mead in the presence of Aesir warriors? You, a weak and cowardly raper of girls! How dare you take mead from Freyja or cast lustful eyes on Sif, you bastard!"

The Jotun sank back and waved one arm in the direction of Voden and the High Seat. "He said it was alright," he claimed, a slight whine creeping into his voice. "He was the one that guaranteed us safe conduct." His words were slurred both by all the mead he had drunk and by his fear. "Voden invited me in, that's who."

Tror scowled more deeply than ever and tightened his grip on Mjollnir. "It's easy to get in, but much harder to get out. You may have walked in, raper of girls, but I think they'll have to carry you out when I've taken my vengeance!"

Hrungnir was rapidly becoming sober, his mind working furiously. He knew that the next few moments were crucial. If he said the wrong thing or made the wrong move, both he and his followers would be slaughtered. But for the life of him he couldn't see a way out.

He was about to spit in Tror's face and accept his death beneath the crushing might of Mjollnir when Lao-Kee spoke up. "Wait a minute, Tror." All eyes turned to the slender Jotun who stood near Voden, a mocking smile curving her lips. "Hrungnir's unarmed. He left his sword here in the High Seat. If you kill him now, it won't add much to the glory of your name. That's not the kind of deed the skalds sing of."

"That's right," Hrungnir agreed quickly. "Killing me that way won't do much for your fame. In fact, it'd earn you a name for foul play, that's what it would do." He looked toward Lao-Kee, wondering what came next.

"A better test of your bravery, Tror, and one that would redound to your glory forever, would be to fight a fair duel with Hrungnir," Lao-Kee continued. "Now that's the kind of thing the skalds can't resist!"

Tror looked confused. "A duel?" He thought about it for a moment. No one had ever challenged him to a duel before. In fact, duels were uncommon among the Aesir. They had an institution, known as the Holmganga, which was the same as a duel, though it was seldom used any longer. The Aesir had plenty of enemies to fight outside Asaheim, and saw little sense in killing each other. Generally disputes involving honor were resolved by the chieftains. On those rare occasions where no accommodation between the parties could be arranged, however, they could only resort to the Holmganga. The two enemies would meet on a field marked out with ash wands. The fight was usually to the death, and the winner received all the property of the loser as compensation.

But in all his years in Asaheim, Tror had only heard of one Holmganga being fought. Tror had heard the story of that fight several times by the skalds. Lao-Kee was indeed right, a duel was precisely the kind of thing skalds did sing about. "A duel," he muttered thoughtfully.

"Yes," Lao-Kee urged. "Why, it'd be the biggest event in years! Tror versus Hrungnir. The greatest warrior of the Aesir pitted against the greatest of the Jotun! What a fight! And since it would be a fight between two individuals, it wouldn't even be a breach of the truce."

"Yes," Tror nodded, lowering Mjollnir, "a duel would suit me very well."

"Good," Lao-Kee said, rubbing her hands together. "Let's see. How about a week from today? Excellent. Now all we need to do is pick a spot convenient to both parties. Ah, how about Grjotunagardar. It lies just on the other side of the Iving, where the Fimbulthul joins it. There's a good-sized flat area there and a large, natural wall of stone for spectators to sit on. Yes, that would be the perfect place to hold an event of this importance."

"Well," Hrungnir said, puffing himself up, "that's settled, then. It's a pity I wasn't wearing my sword or we could have taken care of it right away. But Lao-Kee's right, it would be cowardly of you to attack me while I'm drunk and unarmed." The other Jotun all rose and began to head cautiously for the door. Hrungnir followed them. "Now, don't forget to come a week from now to Grjotunagardar."

"Depend on it," Tror growled. "Make sure *you're* there. I always keep my word. See to it you keep yours."

The Jotun scurried out the door of Valholl. A strange silence fell over the hall. Lao-Kee walked up to Tror, an innocent look on her face, Hrungnir's sword in her hands. She held it out to Tror and said, "It seems Hrungnir forgot his sword in his haste to go and get ready for the duel."

The whole place exploded with laughter, Tror's bellow being the loudest of all. Even Voden laughed until tears streamed down his single eye. One and all, they praised Lao-Kee for her cleverness. The slender Jotun smiled sardonically.

Near Grjotunagardar there was a small stream that emptied into the Iving. One of its banks was made of clay. As the Jotun prepared for the forthcoming duel between Tror and Hrungnir, one of the younger men had the idea of building a statue out of the clay. "It'll scare Tror! We'll make it huge," he declared, "and dress it like a Jotun warrior. The red-beard will think it's a giant and piss in his pants!" They all laughed heartily and set about building the monster.

When it was finished, it was nine feet tall and three feet across the chest from armpit to armpit. They dressed it in bits and pieces of old armor and built a shield for it out of wicker. Then they decided that every Jotun warrior had to have a heart, so they killed an old war stallion that could no longer stand the rigors of raiding and put its heart into the clay body. Finally, with hilarious solemnity, they dubbed their giant Mist Calf and made extravagant claims for its prowess.

Tror chose Thialfi, one of the most promising young men of his household, to second him in the duel. Thialfi was to accompany him, hold his shield, help strap on his armor and be generally useful. "Maybe," the youth said, "I'll even get to fight one of the Jotun!"

"You're a bit young yet for that," Tror rumbled pleasantly. "But keep a sharp eye out for my technique. Though I use a hammer, an ax is much the same. And from what I've seen, you seem to favor that weapon."

When they rode from Gladsheim a few days later, a group of some fifty Einherjar accompanied them, Voden at their head. The group was fully armed, but a festive atmosphere ruled the day and everyone was laughing and cheering as they rode northward.

They arrived before noon and found themselves places on the stone wall. The sight of the clay giant caused much comment and a great deal of joking. "Perhaps," Tyr suggested, "if Hrungnir can't beat you, that clay man can!"

Thialfi had a brilliant idea and begged Honir to lend him his sword. "I'll stand in front of that silly clay man and every time Tror strikes Hrungnir, I'll strike the clay man! That way everyone can keep a tally of how the battle is going."

"By the time it's over," Tyr suggested with a laugh, "you'll be stirring a pile of dust with your sword!" They all chuckled, and Honir gave Thialfi his sword.

"Just don't get it too bloody," he said with a shy smile.

"You mean muddy!" Tyr guffawed.

Hrungnir appeared from the north, surrounded by a large group of Jotun. Voden recognized Hrodvitnir-Fenrir among them. He strode forward to greet him, and Hrodvitnir sprang from his horse with a whoop and ran to embrace Voden. The other Jotun quickly arranged themselves along the wall.

Lao-Kee stood and talked with her half brother while the two duelists got ready for the battle. "Fine mess you've created," Hrodvitnir said quietly. "The whole truce is in jeopardy. If Hrungnir wins, I'll be hard pressed to keep the hotheads from starting the raids again."

"He won't win," Lao-Kee said brightly. "And don't worry about the Aesir going to war when Tror triumphs. They see this strictly as a grudge duel between Tror and the man who raped his sister."

"If Hrungnir loses, little one, I have a different problem. I lose one of my strongest supporters. I've always counted on him and his brother Geirrodmir and all their followers if it ever comes to open warfare. This weakens me, Lao-Kee, and I'm not pleased about it at all."

The slender Jotun looked at her half brother and smiled. "When Hrungnir loses, brother, I'll tell you of a plot to rid yourself of several very important Risar. This is just the first step in a scheme bigger than anyone realizes. It could break the deadlock between you and the Risar. So be patient and trust me."

"Trust you?" Hrodvitnir snorted. "Ha! I'd sooner trust the smile of a White Bear! I know you too well, little sister." He paused, giving her a considering look. "But I also know you scheme exceedingly well. So, *if* Hrungnir loses, we'll talk further of this 'plot,' eh?"

Lao-Kee nodded and left.

Hrungnir was armed with the small, circular shield and curved sword typical of the Jotun. Tror held Mjollnir in one hand, an Aesir shield in the other. They stalked toward each other in the center of the flat area. "Raper of girls, I come to kill you!" Tror cried out as he stopped and stood his ground.

"Bah, Aesir dog," the Jotun replied with scorn. "I'll rape you as I raped your sister! Only I'll stick my sword in you instead of my cock!"

With a mutual roar of anger, they launched themselves at each other. Tror swung Mjollnir and slammed the hammer into the center of the Jotun's shield. The blow was so powerful, Hrungnir staggered back under it, almost losing his footing. With a shout of joy, Thialfi slammed Honir's sword into the shield held by Mist Calf, the clay giant.

Hrungnir was quick to return Tror's blow. He slashed and hacked at the Aesir's shield, carving away great chunks of it. The wild flurry of blows caused Tror to back up two steps in surprise. The Jotun roared their approval.

For a time the two warriors traded blows. Soon their shields hung in tatters and both men flung them aside. The battle became more bloody now as Tror smashed Hrungnir's left forearm and Hrungnir opened a large gash in Tror's right thigh.

Round and round they went, slashing and parrying, hacking and dodging. It was hard to tell who was winning, both men bled so freely. On the sidelines Thialfi had all but hacked the clay statue to dust.

Suddenly Tror slipped in the mud that had been created from the dirt and blood mixed up by their feet. He landed heavily on his back and Hrungnir leapt in, his sword high, to deliver the death stroke.

But as the sword swept down, Tror met it with Mjollnir. The dense solidity of the massive hammer was too much for the thin Jotun blade, and it shattered into a thousand pieces. Tror rose up swiftly from the ground, almost as if coming from underneath it, and Hrungnir tumbled back, thrown off balance.

As the Jotun fell, his hand found a large stone. From his back he hurled the stone at Tror's head with all his might. Again Mjollnir intervened, and the stone shattered against the hammer's iron head. The pieces sprayed across the area, causing Aesir and Jotun alike to duck in fear. One piece struck Tror in the forehead and sank deep into his skull.

For a moment the red-bearded giant tottered as if about to fall. But with a roar, he brought Mjollnir down on Hrungnir's skull and dashed the Jotun's brains out across the ground. Then he stumbled to his knees and fell face down on the ground beside his dead opponent.

Thialfi was the first one to him. He tried to turn Tror over but was unable to budge him. Tyr joined him, and together they were still unable to move the red-bearded warrior. Finally Voden came and all by himself turned his friend onto his back.

The blood was pouring down Tror's face from where the

piece of rock was lodged in his forehead, but his eyes were open and there was a slight smile on his face. "Killed him, didn't I?" he asked his old friend in a hoarse voice. Voden nodded solemnly. "Bit tougher than I expected," Tror said as he licked dry lips. "Gave me a bit of a headache." He reached up to feel his wound.

"I wouldn't touch that if I were you," Voden said softly. "Best to leave it where it is, Tror. Trying to take it out could be more dangerous than letting it alone."

Tror grunted. "Uh. Hurts like all Niflheim. Guess it'll get better?" Voden nodded again. "I think I can get up. Give me your hand, will you?" Voden bent over and held out his hand. Tror gripped it tightly and pulled himself erect. He wavered and almost collapsed. Voden gripped his arm securely to keep his friend from falling. As Tror stood, everyone else, Jotun and Aesir alike, stood to honor him. It had been a good, fair fight. Tror had revenged the rape of his sister, and Hrungnir had paid for his brutality and braggadocio.

Hrodvitnir approached and greeted Tror. "A good fight, Aesir. You have a right to everything Hrungnir owned. That's the standard wager in case of a duel among the Jotun as well as among the Aesir. You can even take his name if you want."

Tror grunted. "I want nothing for myself. I only sought revenge for my sister. Hrungnir's wife and children can keep what they have, all the wagons, cattle, dogs, all that. I don't want to beggar them. I'll only take one thing, and that not for myself."

"And what will that be?" Hrodvitnir asked, his curiosity peaked by Tror's strange request.

"I'd like Gullfaxi, the damn horse that started all this. Give it to Thialfi. He fought almost as good a battle as I did! Mist Calf is nothing but a pile of dust, while Hrungnir is still whole!"

They all roared with laughter and cheered Tror's decision. Thialfi blushed, but puffed his chest out proudly as Gullfaxi was led to him.

As the Aesir made ready to return to Galdsheim, Voden watched Lao-Kee conferring in secret tones with her half brother. He sighed, wondering what deviltry the slender Jotun was up to now. He liked Lao-Kee. Indeed, he enjoyed her

company more than that of most other men or women. She
was witty and quick, always ready with a story or a jibe. She
could make up poetry on the spot as well as any skald. She
could ride better than any Aesir, and was a deadly shot with
the short Jotun bow. With a knife, she was the equal of any
man.

Yes, he liked Lao-Kee. And yet . . . And yet, he didn't
trust her. Her schemes and jokes were endless, convoluted,
and, it seemed to him, increasingly dangerous. No doubt
she's hatching one right now, he thought, even as she's
talking to her half brother. Who will this one involve?
Hrodvitnir? Me? Tror? He couldn't know, but it worried him
nonetheless. Some day she'd go too far. Already Tror dis-
trusted her. Once they were great friends, but ever since the
cutting of Sif's hair, Voden had noticed a considerable cool-
ing in the red-bearded giant's manner, even though Lao-Kee
had kept her promises. Heimdall already hated her. Would
Tror soon hate her as well?

She left her half-brother and approached the Aesir. As she
caught Voden's eye, she winked and flashed him a conspiratorial grin. She mouthed the word "later" and pointed surreptitiously toward where Hrodvitnir-Fenrir was mounting his
horse.

The Jotun rode north, the Aesir south. Lao-Kee rode in the
midst of the Aesir, next to Tror, and kept up a constant
stream of chatter.

Voden rode by himself, cloaked in gloomy foreboding.

A shout of alarm snapped Voden out of his reverie. Tror had
fallen from his horse!

The others were crowded around him as Voden rode up.
Tror was sitting up, looking dazed. "I . . . I can't see," he
said, his voice small and frightened. Voden bent down and
looked into his open eyes. They were staring and unfocused,
but other than that, nothing seemed to be wrong.

"How does your head feel?" Voden asked.

"Worse than the iron under the hammer," Tror grunted.

"It's that damn piece of stone in his forehead," Tyr muttered.

Voden nodded agreement. "Yes. Maybe we should take it
out after all." He examined it closely, then sat back. "I'm
afraid I'm not up to it, Tror. We need a real healer for this."

"How about Groa?" Honir asked.

"Groa?" Voden replied in surprise. "I thought she was

dead years ago! I didn't see her when I returned from Mimir's Well, and just assumed—''

"Oh, she left Asgard," Honir explained. "She has a small hut way out on the Himinborg Plain east of the city. Hardly anyone ever goes there unless they need a love spell or something to cure a sick cow. But she's still alive. Says she's waiting for her husband Aurvandil to come back home again."

Voden thought for a moment. "Groa might be just the one to help Tror. In any case, she's probably the closest healer. Let's try. Lead the way, Honir."

It was night when they finally arrived at Groa's hut. Tror had been unconscious for several hours. Tyr had ridden behind him in the saddle and held him up.

Groa, as ancient and wizened as ever, cackled out loud when she saw them ride up. "Ah, ah, look at all the fine warriors! Come to visit Groa again. Just like when they were kidlings. Tyr and Honir and Voden and, ah, ah, Tror with a rock in his head." She cocked her head to one side and fixed Voden with a birdlike stare. "And Voden with only one eye in his." She gripped Voden's arm in a surprisingly strong grasp. "Went to Mimir's Well, he did. And gave even more than Groa, he did. Did it make him happy? Ah, ah, Groa thought not. She warned him, she did." She leered at him and snickered.

They laid their unconscious friend out in her cluttered hut, pushing aside bundles of herbs, dried bat wings, mummified snakes, and some things none of them looked at too closely. Then Groa shooed them all out into the night and began to burn foul-smelling powders and mumble strange spells over Tror.

As she chanted, Tror became conscious and gazed up at her. "Ah, ah, and how does your head feel now, bristle-face?" she asked.

"Much better," Tror said softly, not daring to speak too loudly for fear he might bring back the pain. "And I can see."

"Good, good," Groa muttered. "The stone's beginning to work loose." She began to mumble and chant spells again.

Tror frowned. "I've been having the strangest dreams." The old hag cocked an eyebrow at him and continued to chant. "Yes, very strange. Groa, I dreamt I was far to the

north and that I met your husband Aurvandil there.'' Groa
stopped chanting and stared at him. "Strange," he continued.
"He needed help, so I put him in a basket I was carrying on
my back and brought him across this dreadful river, the
Elivagar, the one made by the slaver of Fornjot's wolves.
One of his toes stuck out of the basket and it froze as we were
crossing. I broke it off and hurled it up into the sky. It
became a new star."

Like someone in a trance, Groa gripped his arm and forced
him to rise. She pulled him outside the hut with her. "Where?"
she asked. "Where did you hurl Aurvandil's toe?"

Tror looked up and pointed. "There. Right there where
that star is shining."

The other Aesir gathered around. "I've never seen that star
before," Tyr said in soft wonder.

"Nor I," Honir and Voden both admitted.

"That's Aurvandil's toe," Groa murmured to herself. "And
he's not far behind. Coming home at last, he is." She turned
and went back into her hut, closing the door behind her.

"Wait!" Tror cried out. "The stone. It's still in my forehead. You didn't finish taking it out!"

Groa opened the door a crack and peered out at them.
"Pain's stopped, eh?"

Tror nodded carefully. "Why, yes, it has."

"And you can see." The old hag closed the door. "That's
good enough, then. Aurvandil's coming back. I've no more
time to waste on the likes of you. Leave the stone where it is.
Aurvandil's coming home, and it won't make a bit of difference for what's going to happen to you. Not a bit of
difference."

Groa fell silent, and no matter how they yelled and banged
on her door, she refused to acknowledge their presence any
longer. Eventually they gave up, mounted their horses and
rode off, Tror with the stone still in his head and Voden with
some very strange thoughts whirling around in his.

XVI

━━━◆━━━

HEIMDALL scowled, Tror looked thoughtful, Tyr grinned eagerly, Voden's expression was hidden in the depths of his hood, and Honir looked anxiously from one face to the other. "Well," Lao-Kee asked in an annoyed tone, "is that all you have to say? Nothing? What's the matter with the lot of you?"

"Patience, Lao-Kee," Voden replied softly. "This is a rather difficult idea to deal with. Give us a few moments to absorb it."

Surprisingly, Honir was the first to respond. "Do you really think Hrodvitnir would believe it?"

The slender Jotun nodded emphatically. "I've already broached the idea to him, and he was very interested. Look, things haven't exactly been going his way in Jotunheim, you know. He expected a quick win against the Risar. But they've held out a lot longer than he ever thought possible. He never realized how much their chief men hated and feared him.

"Also, the loss of Hrungnir has hurt him more than he'd calculated. Geirrodmir, Hrungnir's brother, has withdrawn his support, says he won't back anybody. Claims Hrodvitnir never should have let the duel take place." Lao-Kee paused for effect and looked around the group. "The result is that Hrodvitnir is getting anxious. He's ready to try a bold stroke, to risk the whole thing on one pass with the knife."

Heimdall nodded. "Please go through it one more time, if you do not mind. I wish to make sure I understand the whole scheme from beginning to end."

Lao-Kee made a sour face, sighed, and nodded. "All right.

One more time for the slow learners. I've hinted to Hrodvitnir that some of the Aesir have been talking privately to the Risar. In particular, I indicated that Heimdall and Tror have been negotiating with Loddfafnir and Hodmir. The talks deal with two things. First, the Risar want Aesir help against Hrodvitnir. Second, the Aesir want guarantees against Jotun attacks. If the Aesir help the Risar, the Risar pledge to help the Aesir.

"I've also told him that some of the Aesir are against these talks. Voden doesn't even know they're taking place. Tyr and Honir are opposed and want to maintain the status quo.

"So, I suggested that he and two of his most trusted men meet with Voden, Tyr, and Honir, and that together you catch Heimdall, Tror, Loddfafnir, and Hodmir in the act. I've convinced him that Voden would probably banish both Tror and Heimdall for scheming behind his back. He'd be happy to be rid of the two of you, that's for sure. Plus, he'd be able to kill Loddfafnir and Hodmir for committing treason against the Horde. He could make a real object lesson of the two of them, and probably weaken the Risar so badly that victory would be easy."

Heimdall nodded again. "And so you want to dress up two Aesir who are about the same height and shape as Loddfafnir and Hodmir and stage this meeting on the shores of the Amsvartnir Sea between Utgard and the River Sid."

"Your mental prowess never ceases to amaze me," Lao-Kee replied sarcastically. "Yes. And then when Hrodvitnir and the other five come to surprise you, we turn the surprise around. It'll be seven against three. They won't have a chance."

"You would have us kill your half brother and his two men," Heimdall said coldly.

Lao-Kee shrugged. "Kill or be killed. With Hrodvitnir out of the way, the Aesir will enjoy many years of peace. What are three lives when compared to the number of your women and children who will be saved by such a death?"

They were all silent for several moments, each doing his own version of mental and moral arithmetic. Then Voden spoke a single word, dropping it like a rock in their midst. "No."

The slender Jotun turned and stared at him. "No?" she echoed. "Did I hear you say no? You won't take advantage of this opportunity to make Asaheim secure against the Jotun?"

Voden shook his head slowly. "I meant, 'No, I won't kill Hrodvitnir.' It would be a thoroughly dishonorable act. We've sworn blood brotherhood and friendship to each other, and there's a truce between our people."

"By Gymir's left nut, that's stupid," Lao-Kee snarled. "Hrodvitnir's friendship is a sham! So is the damn truce! He uses the two to stall for time until he's ready to sweep you and your honor off the face of Yggdrasil." Her voice became intense and persuasive. "He told me so himself. He's only biding his time, building his strength. Then he'll strike across the Iving and kill you all. He'll burn every hall, level every farmstead, make this whole land a smoking desert. Hrodvitnir neither has nor wants any honor but that which comes from the triumph of utterly destroying his enemies. Don't be fools."

Voden's smile was strangely twisted. "You didn't listen. I said I didn't want to kill Hrodvitnir. There are other ways to get rid of him without working the wolf's joy."

They all leaned forward. "Almost opposite the place where the Sid leaves the Amsvartnir Sea," Voden explained, "there's an island called Lyngvi. On a clear day you can just see it from the western shore. I don't think it's ever visible from the eastern shore. It's a good-sized island filled with animals and birds. The waters around it are rich with fish. A single man could live there alone if he was clever and resourceful. Yes, he could live there a long time."

Lao-Kee's eyes were shining. "Maroon him! Yes! Kill the other two, but not Hrodvitnir. Maroon him on Lyngvi!" She rubbed her hands together with glee. Maroon him, she thought. Leave him all by himself in the middle of nowhere. He'd live there for years, thinking constantly of what could have been! His agony would be long and drawn out!

She laughed out loud. "Yes! I even know where there's a boat we can use to take him out there. It belongs to the sons of Ivaldi and they call it Skidbladnir. It's a well-founded boat, perfect for a trip out to Lyngvi. I'm sure they'll be happy to loan it to me for a little gold."

Voden ignored Lao-Kee. "What do you think, Heimdall?"

The strange white man paused and looked into Voden's eye before speaking. "The plan is devious and typical of Lao-Kee. It is fraught with danger. And yet it just might work. If it does, it would be even as she says. The danger of a united

Horde would disappear and the Aesir would be able to live in relative peace for many years.''

He paused again and looked at each one of them individually. ''That may be more important than any of you realize. I see and hear things that are far away. And lately I have been seeing and hearing strange things from out of the far south. The Dark Empire appears to be on the move again. Its soldiers already probing northward in ever growing numbers. And behind them, at the very core of Muspellheim itself, a darkness grows and grows.

''I do not trust Lao-Kee. But I can see nothing wrong with her scheme. Marooning Hrodvitnir-Fenrir on Lyngvi would be very much to our benefit.''

Voden nodded slowly. ''I agree. We'll do this thing.'' He turned to Lao-Kee and nodded curtly. ''Arrange it.''

A half-moon and a million stars played hide and seek behind a fast-moving scud of clouds. Although the four hooded figures could be dimly made out huddled together down by the shore, it was nearly impossible to tell one from the other.

Lao-Kee pointed off to the left. Two Aesir horses stood there, nervously pawing the ground. Then she pointed to the right. Two Jotun ponies stood quietly. Hrodvitnir nodded.

They moved swiftly and silently back down the hill from the crest. ''They're there,'' Hrodvitnir whispered softly. ''One must be Tror. No Jotun could be that big! The other two are about the size and shape of Loddfafnir and Hodmir. I thought I caught a glimpse of white hair. That would be Heimdall. It looks as though what Lao-Kee has told us is true, Voden.''

The single eye glowed deep within the hood. ''They scheme against both of us. Though I still find it hard to believe this of Tror and Heimdall, I'm with you. Do we kill them or capture them alive?''

''Alive.'' Hrodvitnir grinned with lupine pleasure. ''I intend to try both Loddfafnir and Hodmir in public by torture. They'll die screaming their crimes and begging for mercy. Their deaths will be a salutary lesson for all the Risar!''

Voden sighed deeply. ''I'll merely banish Tror and Heimdall. I've known the red-beard since I was a child. And Heimdall saved my life after I'd drunk from Mimir's Well.''

Hrodvitnir shrugged. ''Do what you like. We Jotun believe

in killing our enemies. That way only their ghosts will ever come back to haunt us. And we don't believe in ghosts.''

They sent Honir and one of the other Jotun off to the right to circle around and secure Loddfafnir's and Hodmir's horses in order to cut off their escape. Voden and the other Jotun went to capture the Aesir horses. Hrodvitnir, Tyr, and Lao-Kee crept directly toward the four schemers.

As they came near the Aesir horses, Voden gestured to the Jotun to move ahead. The man nodded and crawled almost to the point where the two beasts were tethered. Voden picked a good-sized rock from the ground and held it in his hand. The Jotun rose slowly from the grass, his gaze intent on the two horses. Voden rose directly behind him. As the man stood fully erect, Voden swung the rock up and then down on the top of his head. The Jotun crumpled to the ground with a soft moan. Now it's seven to two, the leader of the Aesir thought with grim satisfaction. Hurriedly he bent over the man and tied his arms and legs with stout leather thongs. Then he stuffed a piece of horsehide in the Jotun's mouth as a gag. You'll have a terrible headache when you wake up, Voden chuckled to himself. And it'll take you most of a day to work your way out of these bonds, but you'll survive.

Leaving the Jotun and the horses, he crept toward the four standing figures. A night bird cried, was answered by a second and then a third. Silence settled over the grasslands of Jotunheim again, broken only by the sound of the wind in the grass and the gentle shush of wavelets breaking on the shore of the Amsvartnir Sea.

Suddenly a shout split the silence and six men holding swords leapt to their feet. The four figures by the shore spun around in surprise and pulled their weapons out.

Almost immediately there was a second cry, one of fury and betrayal, as Hrodvitnir and the other Jotun realized that two of the shrouded figures were not Loddfafnir and Hodmir. They were Aesir!

Hrodvitnir spun around and leapt back in an attempt to escape. Tyr launched himself at the Jotun, his hands out to grasp him and wrestle him to the ground. Hrodvitnir's curved sword swept down and sliced into Tyr's right wrist, cutting the hand clean off. Tyr slammed into him and the two went down in a tangle. Before Hrodvitnir could regain his feet, four Aesir had him pinned. Voden was bent over Tyr, holding his right arm and chanting softly as he tied a piece of cloth around it to stop the bleeding.

When they had tied Hrodvitnir securely, Heimdall asked about the other two Jotun. "One's by the horses," Voden replied. "He should wake up sometime in the morning."

"The other one won't wake up in the morning," Lao-Kee said blandly. "He tried to grab me for a shield. I stuck a knife between his ribs and twisted it two or three times. We should take his body with us in Skidbladnir and dump it far from shore."

Hrodvitnir was raging, struggling wildly against the cords that bound him. He spit at Lao-Kee. "Bitch!" he screamed. "I'll cut your liver out and stuff it down your fucking throat!"

Lao-Kee sneered and spit in his face. "You'll spend the rest of your life talking to the birds and the fish out on Lyngvi, dear half brother! I've always hated you and your disgusting father! Bastards! Both of you! Bastards! I'm your half sister because your filthy father raped my mother! I hate you and I laugh with joy to see you tied and helpless!"

She was panting so hard she could barely speak. "You used to laugh when he beat me. And then you'd hit me a couple more times for good measure. You think I don't remember every blow? And the bastard raped me, too, did you know that? Him and Hrungnir and . . ." She had to pause for a moment to catch her breath. "If I had my way, I'd cut your fucking throat!" she screamed, her voice breaking. She hit him twice and spit at him again. Then she broke down, sobbing wildly. Voden put his arms around her and led her away from Hrodvitnir.

"Heimdall, Tror," he called back over his shoulder, "load him in Skidbladnir. Take the body too. Honir, go with them. Take him to Lyngvi and leave him there." His arm around Lao-Kee, he disappeared into the dark.

The meeting in Valholl was subdued. "It is accomplished," Heimdall said quietly. Voden nodded and glanced at Tror.

The red-bearded giant looked down at the floor. "He tried to swim out after the boat. Doesn't swim too well. Nearly drowned. He stood on the shore after that, just watching us sail off. There were tears pouring down his face. He called us every damn name you can imagine." He looked up at Voden, his eyes troubled. "That's no way for a warrior to end his life. No way at all." He shook his head sadly.

To everyone's surprise, Lao-Kee didn't say a thing. She just sat and stared stubbornly at the floor, ignoring all attempts to speak with her. A single tear glistened on one cheek.

The reaction of Jotunheim to the disappearance of Hrodvitnir was even more violent than they had expected. The Jotun Voden had bound claimed the Risar had overpowered them and killed both Hrodvitnir and the other Jotun. The Risar claimed it was all a plot to justify an attack against them. Both sides began to skirmish, and before long Jotunheim was in a virtual state of civil war. The danger of a united Horde receded rapidly into the background. The Aesir were able to turn their attention southward to the growing number of incursions from Muspellheim.

It was late fall when Anhur appeared alone at the door to Valholl. In one hand he carried a staff. In the other, cradled against his body, he held a vaguely spherical package wrapped in cloth. "I have a tale to tell Voden," he said, and would speak to no one else.

When Voden came and saw his friend, his face became grave and troubled. Anhur walked up to him and handed him a staff made of strange black wood bound with iron strips and iron end caps. The leader of the Aesir took it and held it gently in his hands, gazing at it with sad fondness. "He would have wanted you to have it," Anhur said softly, tears in his eyes.

"How?" Voden asked.

Anhur sighed. "It's a long tale." Voden gestured for horns of mead and walked to the High Seat, Anhur by his side. They sat next to each other. Anhur put the package he carried between his knees. One of the serving maids handed Voden and him full drinking horns, and they both took long draughts of the mead.

"We left Asgard," the Svartalfar began, his eyes vague with reminiscence, "and headed west. You stood on the mound and watched us go. I saw you there.

"We crossed the Gopul south of the Himinborg and wandered around that area for a month, looking for Dverg. Kao-

Shir was determined to find some. But the harder we looked, the less sign of them we saw.

"The old Yellow Robe was almost beside himself with frustration." Anhur chuckled. "We spent the winter in a nice warm cave. He could hardly sit still! Then in the spring we wandered southwest. He kept quoting Yao Fang Whatsit and Ding Ping Whosit about this and that. Ah, endless, pointless stories! Kao-Shir at his best. And his worst!

"Then one day, out of the clear blue, we found two Dverg! We were almost to that spur of the Smoking Lands that thrusts north toward the Amsvartnir Sea. The land is pretty rugged there. Lots of rock outcroppings, caves, that sort of thing. Well, sitting right there in the shade of a big rock were two Dverg. They introduced themselves as Falar and Galar and said they'd been waiting for us. Just like that! After all those months of looking!

"They invited us to join them and some of their brother Dverg in a large feast. Naturally, Kao-Shir accepted with delight. At last he was going to meet and talk with the mysterious Dverg! What couldn't he learn now!

"Well, the hall where they held the feast was a large cavern. Rather than rich carpets, the floor was covered with a sandy grit. Instead of bright hangings, the walls were decorated with glistening stalactites. The table was a huge slab of rough rock placed on four stalagmites.

"The conversation was unbelievably dull. All they talked about was profit and loss, mining and smithing, iron and gold, spite and petty revenge. I was bored to tears, but Kao-Shir drank it all in as though the gray men were the wittiest and wisest hosts he'd ever broken bread with.

"Ah, yes, the meal. That, at least, was worthy of comment. The plates and dinnerware were all of the finest gold, beautifully worked. The food itself was excellently prepared. And there was plenty of it! But what did the Dverg do? Ha! They commented on the price of each dish and fork, each bowl and spoon. They bemoaned the cost of the roast, the amount spent on the pudding, the price of good beer. Ah, it was endless!

"After the meal Falar and Galar took us on a tour of the place. We went from one gloomy, clammy cavern to the next. We passed dark, cold, underground lakes, frothing, rushing torrents, still pools. Everywhere we went we heard the ceaseless drip, drip, drip of water.

"But the gold we saw! And the jewels! And the wondrous things they'd crafted! I'll never forget a little ship of gold, perfect in every detail. The sail was the finest cloth of gold. Even the pegs that held the golden planks together were of gold! And there was a miniature boar they called Gullinbursti, with hundreds of tiny bristles, all of gold. His eyes were smoky rubies and his tusks of the finest ivory. Incredible!

"As we walked, Falar and Galar ceaselessly questioned Kao-Shir. Where was he from? What was it like there? Did they have much gold? Was there any work the equal of theirs there? Why had he come to the west? Did he have any treasure on him? On and on it went until my head fairly spun with all the words. But through it all Kao-Shir kept up a rapid fire of answers, never faltering, never appearing weary. He knows so much, I thought with amazement. The man's mind is a treasure trove of knowledge!"

Anhur paused and took a long drink of mead. He shook his head and sighed. "The Dverg were impressed too. But they kept coming around to the same questions again and again. Did he have a treasure with him and what was it? Kao-Shir would laugh and say that the only treasure he possessed was in his head. Ah, by Sekhmet, I wish he'd never said that!" The Svartalfar gazed broodingly into the mead that still half filled his horn. Lao-Kee and several of the Aesir had entered Valholl and now sat quietly listening to Anhur's tale. He acknowledged them with a slight nod.

"They feasted us again, this time just the two of them and the two of us. Kao-Shir talked and talked, told tale after tale. Falar and Galar seemed to eat it up. Now and then the old Yellow Robe would ask them questions. They'd answer, and you could just see him storing the information, nodding, hmmming, and pulling at his long ears as if to make them even longer.

"This went on for a good month, maybe more. It's hard to tell time in those damn caverns. As the weeks passed, the Dverg became less hospitable and shorter of temper. Their questions about treasures became more pointed and demanding. They became impatient with Kao-Shir's display of wisdom.''

Anhur's face took on a look of melancholy so profound it

moved all his listeners. His grief was palpable and affected them all. "One day, or night, I never knew which, they gave us a meal that was stingy and poor. The plates were cheap iron, rusty and crudely made. The service was dented and bent. After we'd choked the foul slop down and swallowed as much of the sour ale as we could stomach, Falar and Galar sat frowning at us. Falar asked again about Kao-Shir's treasure. The old man laughed and told them once more that the only treasure he owned was in his head. Galar nodded grimly and said they would like to show him something they were sure would interest him. He rose to go with them. I rose, too, but they curtly told me to stay where I was. Kao-Shir gestured for me to mind our hosts and not to worry.

"Worry! Oh, by the paws of Sekhmet, how I wish I'd ignored his command! Worry! I . . . I failed him, failed him at the most important moment! When I should have been by his side, I was not!" He paused in his narration, sitting calmly but miserably, tears coursing down his dark cheeks. "I failed my friend."

"What happened, Anhur?" Voden gently asked.

"Falar and Galar took Kao-Shir into another cavern. There they pulled out knives they'd concealed on their persons and stabbed him to death. Then they cut off his head to search for the treasure he said he carried there." His voice was flat, declarative, and filled with utter misery.

Dense silence filled Valholl. No one moved. All thoughts were on the yellow-robed wanderer they had known and loved.

Anhur broke the silence. "They came back after a long time, looking very discontented. Falar carried Kao-Shir's staff. I was fully armed and ready. They stopped and stared at me, suddenly afraid. 'Where is he?' I demanded. 'What's happened to Kao-Shir?'

"Galar looked at the ground and muttered that Kao-Shir had choked to death. Falar sneered and said, 'Choked on his own knowledge. He was so full of it, it overflowed and got stuck in his throat and he choked.' Galar laughed evilly then and said, 'Aye, that's the truth of it. There was no one in all the nine worlds smart enough to understand him or help him. No one knew what to do with all the knowledge when it got stuck in his throat, and he just choked.'

"I stuck one spear through Galar's rotten mouth before he

could close it on his lying words. The point came out the back of his head. I skewered Falar with two more, one in the guts, the other through one of his deceitful gray eyes. Then I picked up Kao-Shir's staff and went in search of him.

"I . . . I found the body, drained of blood through the many wounds the Dverg had gashed him with. I also found his head." He lifted the cloth-wrapped bundle that he held between his knees and passed it to Voden. "Here it is. I . . . I thought you might want it. I . . . I . . ." Anhur could speak no further.

Voden took the bundle and slowly unwrapped it. Kao-Shir's face looked up at him. There was a slight smile on his lips. Though the eyes were closed, Voden almost had the feeling the head was about to open them, blink at him, and begin some tale of wonder with an important lesson lurking at its core. Voden felt the tears rising to his eyes. He blinked them back and held Kao-Shir's head up so the others could see. Lao-Kee took one look, stifled a sob, and ran from the hall. The others gazed in wonder and sorrow. Kao-Shir was truly dead. Voden placed the head on the High Seat next to him. "If only it could speak," he said gently, "what wondrous things, what endless wisdom, it could tell us. Ah, old friend, now you no longer have to worry about eternal life. You've found it."

The Svartalfar looked from the head to Voden. The chief of the Aesir turned to him and asked, "What will you do now, Anhur? Return to Ro-Setau?"

Anhur laughed harshly. "Hardly. Something is stirring in Svartalfheim. Something that bodes evil. We got wind of it in Nidavellir. The Dverg were muttering about it. Khamuas is up to no good. You know how he feared you, Voden. Thought you were the Upuatu, the Opener of the Ways. I'm sure you remember how he sent the four and seven Uamemtiu serpent demons after us. No, I don't dare go back to Svartalfheim."

"Then stay here in Gladsheim with us. You're more than welcome, old friend."

The Svartalfar looked around at the faces of the Aesir. He could see the welcome in their eyes, but still he shook his head. "No," he said slowly, "no, mine is a different fate.

"If Khamuas is stirring again, prodding the evil things of the Tuat, he must be gathering strength for some test. I've heard the name of Dark Empire mentioned more than once lately. Khamuas was their ally a long time ago and could easily become so again.

"If the Dark Empire is on the move once more, then it's time for her enemies to be moving as well. So I have my task cut out for me. I must go and find Horus. If indeed the time of the Opener of the Ways approaches, it's time Horus was set free so that those who are loyal to him can rally and fight by his side against the evil that spreads like a cancer across Yggdrasil.

"I go to find my lord Horus. Wherever I have to go, I'll go, even into Tuat itself." His voice became strong and resonant. "I'll find him and set him free. Then we'll return and raise the army of the true Svartalfari. We'll fight whatever evil has to be fought. If we triumph, we'll lead our suffering people back south to the banks of the holy Hepr. If we fail . . ." He shrugged.

Voden nodded. "I understand," he said softly. "May all the gods be with you, Anhur." He picked up Kao-Shir's staff. "I never learned to fight the old man's way. But his staff will become my weapon all the same. Tror, you know the art of forging. You learned it from your father, Volund. Make me a spear head for this staff. I'll carry it into battle. It will be known as Gungnir, and I'll add a new name to the ones I already carry: Hnikar, Spear Thruster. When I shake Gungnir in battle lust, let our enemies tremble!"

The leader of the Aesir stood and stepped down from the High Seat. He handed Tror the staff and then turned and picked up Kao-Shir's head. Without looking at them again, he walked slowly and sadly to the door that led to his own quarters. After the door closed behind him, they all sat in silence for a long time. Then, one by one, they rose and left without a word.

DARK EMPIRE

XVII

THE two sat in total silence. The wind moaned, whipping the thick, black clouds past them, yet unable to so much as ruffle the stygian robes that cloaked their forms. Their hoods were pulled far forward, hiding their features from any intruding eyes. First one and then the other leaned forward and traced the symbols that were cut into the rock between them.

Finally a voice came from the depths of one hood. It was drawling and sarcastic. "So, we meet again. I must say you're back earlier than expected. But still far too late."

"Then he's in complete control?" came a sad, deep voice.

"Yes," the first replied. "He holds the Tupsimati and the *Utukki Limnuti*. Enlil and Nannar fawn on him. An is mostly silent but submissive. I play my role. And Utu, as usual, stays home."

"Are we safe here?"

"As safe as anywhere. I doubt he's looking for you, Marduk. You're no longer a threat."

Marduk pulled his hood back and gazed thoughtfully at Enki. "Still, I'd rather he didn't know."

Enki shrugged. "Have it your way. By the way, you look positively haggard. Your strength is wasted, your cheeks hollow and starved, and your face is drawn and lined. You look like someone back from a long, hard journey. Yes, your skin is weathered by heat and cold as if you'd been wandering over the wilderness in search of the wind. Wandering for years."

Marduk smiled sadly. "I *have* wandered the wilderness for years. But that isn't what's aged me so, Enki. No. Rather it's that Enkidu, my friend, my loved one, my Ibru, is dead and can never live again."

He sighed hugely. "And more, even, than that. So much more. It's the realization that I, too, must die someday, as he has."

"Ah," Enki said smugly, "then your wandering was for nothing. You never found Utnapishtim."

"I found him. I spent many days with the Atra-Hasis, the Utterly Wise, there in his refuge on the other side of the Me Muti, the Waters of Death. Urshanabi, his boatman, ferried me across, though I did most of the work. I cut the poles, one hundred twenty of them, I painted them with bitumen, and I used them to propel the boat across the Me Muti."

"But if you found him, surely he must have told you his secret? He knows the Pirista Sa Ilani, the Secret of the Gods, the key to everlasting life!"

Marduk shook his head. "The secret of Ki Ilani Nasima, the Way of Living Like the Gods, cannot be given to a mortal by any but the Igigi themselves. And they would never give it to one who has dealt with the Kur. I'm afraid we're cut off from that hope forever, Enki."

He sighed. "Oh, I tried, believe me I tried. I got down on my hands and knees and groveled in the dust. I heaped ashes on my head. I wailed and howled and begged. I cried out to him, questioning him about the living and the dead. 'How,' I sobbed, 'can I find the life I seek?'

"But Utnapishtim just scowled and said, 'There is no permanence. Does any house, no matter how carefully built, stand forever? Do promises, made with even the most solemn oaths, hold forever? Does friendship or enmity last forever? Does any river, no matter how vast, stay at flood level forever? How, then, does Marduk hope to live forever?'

"His words burned me like the desert sun. I cried out, 'I look at your face, at your body, and you are no different from me. We're the same. How, then, will you not suffer death as I will?'

"He shook his head. 'I rendered the Igigi a great service many sars ago in ancient Shurippak, long before the First Dark Empire rose to foul the land. I cannot even tell you of it. There is no hope, Marduk. Unless . . .'

"I leapt from the ground and grasped his hand, covering it with kisses. 'Anything,' I promised, 'anything!'

"He smiled coldly. 'Just this—stay awake for seven days and nights.'

" 'Nothing easier!' I laughed with joy. 'Since Enkidu has died, I've been utterly unable to sleep, for fear of the specters that haunt my dreams.' I sat down prepared to stay awake seven years if necessary." Marduk paused and gave Enki a weary smile. "It seemed such an easy challenge."

"Well?" Enki coached. "What happened?"

"Utnapishtim shook me. 'Ah,' I cried, surprised. 'I must have closed my eyes for a second.' But the Atra-Hasis shook his head and pointed to the ground in front of me. Seven small loaves of bread lay there. The first loaf was hard as a rock, the second like leather, the third was soggy, the crust of the fourth was moldy, the fifth was mildewed, the sixth was fresh, and the seventh still warm." He paused and gave Enki a long look. "Utnapishtim's wife had baked a loaf for every day I slept.

"Realizing what had happened, I cried out in pain and fear, 'What can I do, Atra-Hasis? Where can I go? A vile thief has stolen my very own flesh. Now death dwells in the house where my bed is. Wherever I walk, there Death walks by my side!' Utnapishtim had no answer. There was no hope."

"So," Enki said after a pause, "that's the tale of your misfortune. Then you gave up and came back, eh?"

Marduk laughed hollowly. "Ah, no, there was yet more to suffer, more to learn. Utnapishtim's wife took pity on me. Just as Urshanabi was about to push off and take me back across the Me Muti, she turned to the Atra-Hasis and said, 'Marduk has strained and toiled long and hard to reach this faraway shore. What have you given him as guest-gift before he returns to his own land? Surely you would not be so ungracious a host as to send him away empty-handed?'

"Utnapishtim scowled at his wife, but his brow creased in thought. 'Yes' he said, 'you are right. It would be ungracious, especially after all he has suffered. Well, then .. .' He paused and looked at me: 'Marduk,' he continued, 'I will uncover one secret of the Igigi for you to repay you for your labors. There is a plant called the Sibu Issahir Amelu. Its roots go deep and it is covered with sharp thorns which will prick and tear your hands when you grab it. But if you endure the pain in your hands and pluck it out, then your hands will hold a way to give a man back his lost youth. You cannot achieve eternal life, but perhaps you will enjoy regaining your youth.''

"I praised Utnapishtim's generosity to the skies. 'And where is this wondrous plant, this Sibu Issahir Amelu, to be found?'

"The Atra-Hasis smiled and pointed down into the water. 'It grows there, at the bottom of the abyss.'

"As you can imagine, I wasted no time! I tied two heavy stones to my feet, had Urshanabi row me out over the abyss, and jumped in. I sank down, down, down into the water. I saw the plant and grabbed it. It cut my hands and made them bleed. The pain was terrible. But I hung on, pulled with all my might, and uprooted it. Then I quickly cut the stones from my feet, and the sea cast me up on the shore with the Sibu Issahir Amelu in my bleeding hands.

"Urshanabi poled me away from the shore where Utnapishtim dwells. I clutched the Sibu Issahir Amelu to my chest.

"That night, when we rested on the opposite shore, I found a pool of crystal clear water and decided to take a bath to rinse the grime of my long journey from my skin. I was returning in triumph and wished to be fresh and clean when I arrived. I took off my robe and carefully wrapped the Sibu Issahir Amelu in it. Then I put it on the ground and placed a large rock over it. Feeling it was secure, I dove into the pool.

"Ah, what I fool I was! While I was sporting about in the water, dreaming of eternal youth, a serpent smelled the plant. The sweet fragrance drew the creature. It slithered up, squeezed under the rock, into my robe, and carried the Sibu Issahir Amelu off to its own lair, deep beneath the water! As it went, it sloughed its skin. Forever young!

"Then, oh, then how I wept! My eyes opened floods of tears which matched those I spilled when Enkidu died! Urshanabi offered me his hand in comfort. 'Ah,' I wailed, 'for whom have my arms toiled? For whom have I wrung out the last drop of my heart's blood? For whom have I suffered? All my efforts have been utterly wasted. I have not brought Enkidu back to life. I have not gained eternal life. I have not even regained my lost youth. I have not won any good for myself.'

"Eventually I stopped crying. I rose and walked off alone. And here I am.''

"Very sad." Enki's sympathy was ironical. "And what will you do now? Slink back to Muspell and your consort Zarpanit? Bend the knee in submission to Surt? Or slither off into hiding?"

Marduk was thoughtful. "What happened to Innina? Why isn't she with you?"

"Ah," Enki said with feigned sadness, "Surt outmaneuvered her too. Sent a hellhound after Dumuzi. Innina went off to find her brother and lover and bring him back."

"And she hasn't returned yet?"

"Not yet," Enki sighed. He gestured listlessly. "It's been three years, and I have my doubts. Her Sukkal, Ninshubur, came to see me the other day, begging me to help find her mistress and bring her back. I refused, of course. No sense in taking undue risk. Besides, even if she *does* come back, it's too late anyway. Surt is the Ellilutu now, and there's no question about it. None of us have enough power to oppose the Black One any longer."

"Not even if we all worked together?" Marduk asked, his eyes narrowing thoughtfully.

Enki laughed. "Not unless Surt isn't looking! The man's immensely powerful, Marduk. This isn't the old Surt you remember. We're not talking about some minor Kishpu sorcerer. Or a beginner with potential. The Black One commands all seven sevens of the demons listed in the *Utukki Limnuti*. Plus Zu and a whole assortment of others. You might as well bend the knee to the new Ellilutu, Marduk."

Marduk was silent for long moments. Then he shook his head. "No, I think I'll wait until Innina comes back. She'll have some ideas, you can be assured of that. And who knows, some time Surt might not be looking."

"First time wasn't enough, huh, Surt?" Jormungand asked sarcastically, looking down at the slender wizard. "He blasted you right back into your tower that time. You had a headache for two weeks. Even if you don't remember it, I do. I had to play nursemaid the whole time! At least now you've got Sinmora."

"Softly, Serpent, softly. Don't raise your voice so," Surt said weakly, wincing at the sound of his own words. He moved his head slowly and carefully to look around the room. "Where is she? Where is my consort, Sinmora?" His voice held the whining quality common to sick children. "She was supposed to bring me some warm juice of Balata Tesu."

The door opened soundlessly and Sinmora swayed in. Jormungand shook his head with admiration. Even carrying a cup of hot Balata Tesu, Sinmora was seductive. The way her hips moved! Her dark eyes sparkled with a mixture of lust and humor. And her breasts, ah, her breasts jiggled just ever so slightly to let you know they were naked beneath the thin robe of silk. The giant warrior sighed. Sinmora was Surt's consort. He had to settle with lesser women. He grinned to himself. Some of those who had graced his bed would hardly be called settling, he thought with a chuckle.

"How is my Bel?" Sinmora asked, her voice throaty with concern and lust. Lust, Jormungand thought—everything she does, she does with lust! By Neti's nostrils, I'll bet she spits with lust!

Surt sighed dramatically and took the cup of Balata Tesu. "Awful, but getting better." She helped guide it to his lips, and he swallowed it in short gulps. When he had finished, he lay back and gestured her out. She bowed low, her breasts bulging against the fabric of her robe, and left.

"What are you grinning at, Serpent?" Surt asked sharply after the door had closed behind her.

Jormungand guffawed. "You!" He raised a theatrical hand to his forehead and said in a voice exaggeratedly mimicking Surt's, "Awful, but getting better." He laughed again. "If that sigh had been any deeper, your toenails would have been showing between your teeth!"

Surt scowled. "Taking care of me is her purpose."

Jormungand bowed deeply with mock respect. "Most assuredly, my noble Ellilutu." He grinned as he straightened up. "But then I remember you from when a two-bit whore wouldn't have let you blow a kiss at her hand! Ah, well, I guess you deserve it as much as anyone." He paused and looked at Surt with concern. "Does it really feel better? I found you all in a heap, you know. You were bleeding out of the mouth, nose, and ears."

The Black One nodded. "I'm better. Nothing really dangerous happened. I just . . . ran into something surprising."

"Huh," Jormungand grunted. "Looked to me like you ran into a wall going full speed."

Surt grinned slightly, wincing as he did. "That's about

what happened. It seems that after my last visit to his wedding feast, the Aesir has somewhat improved his defenses. I wasn't expecting it, that's all.''

"Yes, that's all." The giant warrior paused. "While you were out, I got a report from Thiazi, the man who's been leading the scouting expeditions across the Smoking Lands."

"Ah," Surt replied, his interest peaked. "And?"

"There are two good passes over the first range. They lead to a high plateau. From there another pass leads to the head of the River Non. There's also a fourth pass, much more rugged and treacherous than the others, that leads directly to the head of the River Thyn. It could be used in a pinch, but I'd not want to take too many green men on it."

"And the raids?"

"Well," Jormungand said, "they didn't go as well as the scouts. Those forest people, the Vanir, knew we were there all along, Surt. We never saw them, but they saw us. I'm . . . hmmm . . . I'm afraid two of the three raiding parties suffered rather heavy loses.''

"Any prisoners?"

The giant warrior shook his head. "None. But I fear they may have gotten one or two of ours."

Surt considered. "Then it appears that Voden's military defenses are as good as his magical ones. Hmmm."

Jormungand waited a moment, then said, "Uh, Surt, that Svartalfar is still here. I think you might want to see him after all."

The Ellilutu of Muspellheim nodded slowly. "Yes, it might be best. What's his name, Khamuas?" Jormungand nodded. Surt sighed. "Well, I guess I'm feeling up to seeing him now. That's what you want me to do, isn't it? That's why you refuse to go away and let me suffer in peace?"

Jormungand grinned and went to the door. He opened it and spoke briefly to someone standing outside. In a few minutes the door swung open and a short figure dressed in a pure white robe stepped through. He seemed to be a young boy with smooth, black skin and large, dark, liquid eyes. His features were simple and straight, though the lips were full and pouting. He gave them both a smile full of dazzling white teeth, bowed low and spread his arms wide. "I am Khamuas, at your service."

"I am Surt, Ellilutu of Muspellheim. And this is—"

"Jormungand, I know, I know," Khamuas said lightly, a boyish grin splitting his features. "I'm so delighted to meet you both at long last. Oh, I forgot to mention, I'm the Kheri Heb of the Svartalfar. Ah, sort of their king-priest. Or is it priest-king? I never could decide."

Surt and Jormungand exchanged glances. "Uh, what can I do for you, Kheri Heb of the Svartalfar?" Surt asked, beginning to wonder if he wasn't wasting his time.

Khamuas wagged a finger at him. "It's not so much what you can do for me as what I can do for you."

The Dark One's left eyebrow rose. "Oh, really?"

"Yes, yes, yes. You see, it seems we have a mutual enemy. A certain young man by the name of Voden. He's an Aesir, one of those barbarian races that snuck down out of the north after that terrible mess following the tragic fall of the, um, First Dark Empire. I understand that you put a curse on his father and now have extended it to the son. Very wise. No good riffraff, the whole family. I knew it the moment I set eyes on him." He shivered slightly. "He has those two big wolves, you know. Nasty, hungry things." His voice dropped to a confidential whisper and he continued. "What's more, I suspect he is none other than the Upuatu, the Opener of the Ways. It's all because of that dreadful little mouse. I saw it on the twelfth day of the first winter month. Horrid thing!"

Surt sat quietly. "Voden. You know something of Voden, the son of Borr?"

The Kheri Heb stopped talking and smiled. "Yes. Indeed, yes. You see, between you, me, and the Jotun, we surround him."

The two men of Muspellheim traded glances again. Then Surt smiled at Khamuas and nodded. "Ah. Tell me more."

"Gladly," Khamuas said, rubbing his hands together gleefully. "Gladly. Ah, yes, but it's good to be working with the Bel of the Dark Empire once more!"

Enki sat and stared out the window. "You went to Utu and he said you should return and ask me again?" Ninshubur nodded. "Because things had changed?" She nodded again. "Hmmm." He sighed. "I only wish I knew whose game he's playing."

He turned his eyes to Ninshubur. "He's right, you know. Things have changed. New forces seem to be coming together from unexpected directions.'' He smiled and gave his head a short, affirmative nod. "Yes, Ninshubur, I will help find and bring Innina back.

"Now the question is how? It's not all that easy. I suspect she's the unwilling guest of her sister Ereshkigal. Ah, yes.'' He thought for a moment, then began to studiously clean his fingernails. He took the dirt he had scraped from beneath them and molded two tiny creatures. "These are the Arragruk and the Rutalag. I will give the Food of Life to the Arragruk and the Water of Life to the Rutalag. Then I will send them to Aralu.

"Once there, they will creep through the first gate like flies, right past Neti. Through all seven of the gates they will creep, stopping at none.

"At the center of Aralu they will find Ereshkigal, moaning and crying out loud. There will be no linen covering her body. Her breasts will be uncovered. Her hair will swirl around her head like unruly weeds growing wild.

"When she cries 'Oh, my pain, my stomach!' they will cry 'Oh, my pain, my stomach!' When she cries 'Ah, my pain, my back!' they will cry 'Ah, my pain, my back!' When she sees that they are moaning and wailing and crying with her, she will ask them who they are and offer them a gift.

"They will reject everything she offers them. Eventually they will ask for the corpse that hangs from a hook on the wall. It will be Innina's. Ereshkigal will grudgingly give it to them. They will sprinkle the Water of Life on the corpse. They will sprinkle the Food of Life on the corpse. And Innina will arise and ascend from Aralu.''

Enki smiled strangely at her, and her heart stopped beating. "Of course,'' he said softly, "there is a price to pay for such magic. No one may leave Aralu unless they provide a substitute.''

Ninshubur closed her eyes, swallowed, and nodded. She had served Innina all her life. Now she would give the last thing there was to give.

The slender man paced back and forth. The giant warrior slouched carelessly in a chair and watched him. "The Jotun,'' Surt muttered, "do we know anything of the Jotun, faithful Serpent?''

Jormungand shook his head in negation. "Never even heard

of them before. From what Khamuas said, he doesn't know a whole lot more. Sound pretty wild to me."

Surt turned on him and snarled, "Wild? They can be as wild as they wish as long as they hate the Aesir and will help me destroy them. We need to find out more about these horsemen who dwell on the grasslands north of the Iving. Send Thiazi and a group to make contact. I'd send you to do it yourself, but I want you here, getting the army ready."

"They're ready, Surt. Or at least as ready as drilling can make them. They don't have any real enemies to fight, so I have no idea how they'll behave in actual combat, but they're thoroughly trained, I can guarantee that."

"Good," the Ellilutu of Muspellheim grunted. "Keep them sharp as a good dagger, loyal Serpent. The time draws close when we will test their edge!"

He turned and began to pace again. "There are none who dare stand up to us, none! In all of Yggdrasil our power is supreme! Our armies cover the land! The demons of the Kur cringe and obey our every command! It is time! We will ride north and smash the barbarians, crush them beneath our might!

"At long last I will be avenged!"

There were three of them, as once there had been long ago. One spoke from within its deep hood. "So you escaped Aralu?"

Innina's cowl moved slightly. Her voice was weary, hollow, and still full of remembered horror. "Yes. Thanks to your help, I escaped."

"And did Ereshkigal accept Ninshubur as your substitute?"

"That was a vile thing to do, Enki."

Enki laughed. "Surely you didn't expect me to waste one of my own servants, did you? Besides, she was happy to do it for you. The woman was utterly devoted to you."

Innina turned burning eyes on Enki. "Do not speak so lightly, Enki." She shuddered slightly. "You have no idea what it was like. I went prepared for anything. I had the seven Me in one hand, the lapis measuring line and rod in the other. I set the Shugurra crown on my head and carefully arranged the dark locks on my forehead. Around my neck I hung the small lapis lazuli beads. On my breast I placed the double strand of beads. I wrapped myself in a royal robe. My eyes were daubed with a special ointment. I wore a magical breastplate and bracelets of pure gold. I was ready for anything in the Kur or in Aralu.''

She paused and moaned softly. ''Yet when I finally came before my sister Ereshkigal, I was naked and defenseless. She fixed me with her eye of death, spoke against me the word of wrath, uttered against me the cry of guilt.'' Her voice dropped to a harsh hiss. ''And then she struck me. She turned me into a corpse, a piece of rotting meat. And she hung me from a hook on the wall!''

She stared fixedly at Enki with a glare so intense it made the Patesi of Eridu and Kish feel uncomfortable. ''No,'' she finally continued, ''do not speak so lightly. Of the three of us, only you have spent the last few years without endless suffering.''

Enki sneered. ''Because I'm the only one of the three of us smart enough to stay at home, that's why. I notice, dear Innina, that when you had a chance to leave Aralu and return to the luxury of your palace in Der, you took it. You were quite willing and eager to accept Ninshubur's offer to stay hanging on the hook in your place.''

Innina's eyes flared. ''She will not be there even as long as I was. I have promised Ereshkigal another to take her place soon.''

''An-another?'' Enki stammered.

''Yes,'' Innina hissed malevolently.

''Who?''

''Surt!'' she snarled in reply.

Enki chuckled uneasily. ''That's not as simple as you might think. Surt is very powerful. As I told Marduk, even combined, the only way we could hope to beat him would be if he were looking the other way and—''

''And that is exactly what he will soon be doing, Enki,'' Innina interrupted. ''Soon he will be looking the other way.''

''Ah,'' Enki said, leaning forward with interest, ''you know something.''

''Yes. Aralu rings with rumors. Even those on the stakes cannot help but hear them. There is talk that the Dark Empire is about to wake from its long slumber and try to rule the world once more. Surely such a thing will keep the Ellilutu occupied, perhaps long enough for us to strike when he is least expecting it.

"And there is something else too. Before I entered the realm of Nergal and Ereshkigal, I wandered the Kur looking for Dumuzi."

"Ah, did you find him?" Marduk asked. "And . . . by any chance did you see Enkidu?"

"No to both," Innina answered curtly. "I wandered all over the Kur and never found the place called Arali, the place where the holy fly told me Dumuzi was being held prisoner. Perhaps the fly lied. Perhaps it was a minion of the Black One, sent to misdirect me. I don't know.

"But I did find another prisoner. A Svartalfar named Horus. He was at the bottom of a chasm with sides so steep and slippery no creature could climb up or down them. The serpent dragon Musirkeshda had placed him there, many, many sars ago."

"And so?" Enki queried, unable to make the connections on his own.

"Horus was an enemy of the First Dark Empire. He would be one of the Second as well. I released him."

"How can one Svartalfar make any difference?" Enki asked, his voice peevish.

"This Svaltalfar was once king of his people. He fought the Sons of Muspell long before the First Dark Empire reached the height of its power. He fought Alalgar of Nunki, Enmeenlu of Badtabira, Ensibzi of Larak, Enmeendur of Sippar, the whole lot of them! And he nearly won. It was only when Musirkeshda appeared and carried him off to the Kur that his forces were finally defeated and his people forced into slavery under the Dark Empire.

"Horus hates the Dark Empire more than anything in the world. When I set him free, he pledged to rally his people and lead them against Surt."

"Hmmm," Enki mused. "Small problem there. The Svartalfar have already joined Surt's side. They're allies."

"What?" Innina said in surprise. "How is that possible?"

"Ah, well, you see Horus has been gone a long time, my lady, and the Svartalfar somehow got a new king in the meantime. Some fellow named Khamuas. And Khamuas has just allied himself with Surt. The Black One announced it in the Anunnaki the other day. It's all part of the Ellilutu's plan to invade the north and destroy some piddling tribe of barbarians he has a grudge against." He paused thoughtfully. "The

Black One seems very excited about the whole project, though for the life of me I can't imagine why. But given his interest in the whole thing, it could indeed distract him and give us an opening.''

Innina's brow was furrowed with thought. ''Then the rumors were indeed true, and perhaps releasing Horus was not wasted effort after all. An invasion of the north, eh? Like the First Dark Empire attempted in its foolish pride. All Muspellheim is not enough for the Black One. One would have thought he would have learned something when he visited the ruins of Badtabira.''

She paused and looked at the other two. ''Let us think on these matters and confer again. Surt doesn't suspect that Marduk and I are back from our little trips. His ignorance is to our advantage.''

The other two figures nodded and disappeared. Innina sat alone and smiled. ''So, I draw nearer to my revenge against Bel Nergal. He may have Dumuzi once more, though I didn't see my brother and lover in Aralu. But even if he does, he won't have him long! Webs within webs, that's what I must spin. Webs within webs. It's time to visit Utu.''

''Innina, what a pleasure,'' the Patesi of Sippar and Larsa said as the sorceress swept into the room. ''It's been a long time since last I saw you. Have you been away?''

Innina laughed. ''You know damn well where I've been! Tell me, what have you seen in the *Baru* about Surt?''

Utu laughed out loud. ''I expected more subtlety from you, my lady! A frontal assault is hardly your style. Hanging on a hook in Aralu has changed you somewhat.''

''Are you willing to tell me anything or not?''

''Well, yes, I'm willing to tell you a few things. First, Dumuzi is not in Aralu. He's in the Kur in Gnipa Cave, guarded by Garm, the hellhound Surt created. He's not comfortable but he's not dead either.''

She bowed her head in homage. ''Thank you, Utu. There are times when you are . . . I hesitate to say it, but there are times when you are kind.''

Utu smiled bleakly. ''Don't be too certain how kind I am for telling you the things you will hear, Innina. It is the *Baru* speaking, not Utu. And the Book of Foretelling knows neither kindness nor cruelty. It merely knows the many versions of the future.

"So, as to the original question. Surt will march north, carrying the flaming sword of Muspellheim against his enemies the Aesir, and their allies, the Vanir and the Alfar. His power is vast, his magic dire, his armies cover the plain. He seems to be invincible."

"Seems?"

"Ah, your time on the hook has not dulled your ear nor your wits, my lady. Yes, seems. There is a chance, a moment when those prepared can strike. A moment when all the power is turned in one direction, a moment when victory is just within grasp and the hand is extended to clutch it. Then . . ." He paused and gave her a significant look.

"Ah, yes, then," she murmured. "Thank you. We shall be ready, Utu."

The Ellilutu looked around the Anunnaki and smiled coldly, "It is agreed, then? We will send a party north to negotiate with the Jotun, and to stir up any other trouble it can. Thiazi will lead it. In the meantime we will begin to move troops north to Uruk and Der. We will establish a main supply base at Der and another at the feet of the Smoking Lands, just to the north of the Twisted Lands."

Surt paused dramatically and glared around at the group. "Within a year I want to be able to move north of the Smoking Lands and attack," he declared, his voice filled with gloating at the anticipated satisfaction of his burning desire for revenge.

There was utter silence. An looked down at the floor. Enlil and Nannar avoided anyone's eyes. Only Enki sat and looked back at Surt, a half smile playing about his lips. "How fascinating this whole thing is, Bel Black One," he finally said into the silence, his voice slightly mocking. "What a pity that noble Marduk isn't here to enjoy it. He so loves military things. And Innina. Too bad she has disappeared. The, um, exotic nature of the endeavor would appeal to her. Utu, of course, would be bored to tears by the whole thing. Nothing the Anunnaki does ever seems to interest him in the slightest."

"Yes," Surt replied dryly. "Such a pity. If that is all, I

have many things to do. I'll bid you all good-bye.'' They rose as he did and then filed out past his watchful eye.

Jormungand came from the door after they had left. Surt was sitting, chin in hand, thinking. "Enki," he murmured, "watch him for me, Serpent. He's far too confident. I don't trust him. Not even a little bit."

"Huh, not much I can do," Jormungand replied. "Use your magic, Surt."

"I am using my magic, Serpent, and that's what's worrying me."

"Try that again, Black One. It passed me by."

"I mean that I'm using my magic to spy on him, but I'm not learning anything. The man is damnably well-shielded. I've tried to suborn every one of his servants, without luck. No matter what I've tried, all I end up with is a blank. So keep your eyes sharp, Serpent. Enki is up to something, I can feel it. Perhaps you'll notice something I've failed to see."

"Something important I've failed to see," he murmured as he rose to leave the Hall of Duku.

THE DARK GATHERS

XVIII

~~~~~~~~

VILI watched as Baldur, Hod, and Vidar waged a mock battle. Vidar was the oldest of the three by a good four years, but she was always gentle and kind to the two younger ones. Baldur and Hod, now five years old, were unusually large and well developed for their age. To look at either of them, you would have guessed them to be at least seven or eight. Well, Vili thought, their mother is big and strong and so is their father, so that doesn't really seem so odd after all.

Right now it was Hod and Vidar against Baldur. Vidar was coaching Hod as to where to strike, for the child had been blind since birth. Baldur made plenty of noise so Hod would always know where he was. Hod swung his light practice sword and connected solidly with his brother's ribs.

"Be careful, you ruffians," Vili called out good-naturedly. "Don't cut Baldur up too badly!"

Hod turned and grinned at her, his pure white eyes shining with pleasure. "I got him, Vili! I got Baldur!"

"Aww, it doesn't count," Baldur said. "Hod can't hurt me. Nobody can hurt me! Ha! I have a magic spell of protection." Baldur began to make passes with his hands as if weaving a spell.

Vidar leapt forward, her sword high. "Let's just see how good your protection spell is!" she shouted. She swung her sword and missed Baldur by inches. "By Sigfod!" she gaped in feigned amazement, "he really is invulnerable! My sword won't bite on him at all!" She turned to Vili and laughed. "Look, Vili! Baldur's invulnerable!" She swung again and missed by inches, a grin splitting her features. "Baldur's

invulnerable, Baldur's invulnerable, Baldur's invulnerable,''
she chanted, swinging her sword and missing every time.

Hod took up the chant and began to swing his sword in
time with Vidar's. ''Baldur's invulnerable, Baldur's invulnerable, Baldur's invulnerable,'' he shouted. He swung so hard
that he spun around and fell down. Seeing him fall, the other
two dissolved into laughter, and he joined in, laughing even
harder then they did.

In a group they trooped over to Vili and sat down at her
feet. ''How come you never come down to Gladsheim?''
Vidar asked. ''You always stay here in Asgard.''

''Well, I just like it here better, I guess.''

''Our mother never goes to Gladsheim either,'' Hod said
solemnly to Vidar. ''And your mother never comes here.
How come?''

''Don't be silly,'' Vidar scoffed. ''My mother doesn't want
to come here. She has a big hall in Gladsheim. Why would
she want to come here? How come your mother doesn't come
down to Gladsheim, huh? That's where Voden is most of the
time.''

Baldur stiffened in anger. ''Our mother's the queen of the
Aesir. She stays in Asgard where the queen of the Aesir
belongs. Your mother stays in Gladsheim because she's the
queen of the Vanir and she doesn't belong up here.''

Vidar was about to reply when Vili stepped in. ''Well, yes,
Baldur, that's almost right. Frigida isn't really the queen of
the Aesir, though. She's just your father's Aesir wife. And
Freyja is his Vanir wife.''

''Why does he have two wives?'' Hod asked. ''Nobody
else does. Why does he?''

''Well,'' Vili said slowly, ''he's the leader of both the
Aesir and the Vanir. As chieftain of the Aesir, he must have
an Aesir wife. As king of the Vanir, he must be married to
the Vanadis of the Vanir. So that's why.''

The three children considered this for a while. Then Baldur
turned to Vidar and asked, ''How come you dress like an
Aesir boy and play boy's games? Father even gave you a
sword, a shield, and a helmet like a boy gets here in Asgard.
Is that the way the Vanir are?''

Before Vidar could respond, Vili said, ''Many of the Vanir
girls learn to fight. They have a special group of women

warriors know as the Valkyrja. Someday Vidar will probably be the leader of the Valkyrja. Would you like that, Vidar?"

Vidar nodded solemnly. "Yes. When I grow up, I'm going to be the leader of all the Valkyrja. And I'm going to protect Voden and Freyja wherever they go! I'm going to be the best warrior in Vanaheim and Asaheim!" She gave both Baldur and Hod a challenging glare, as if daring them to deny her dream. Hod just blinked his milky white eyes. Baldur looked down at the grass.

"Well, that still doesn't tell why she dresses like an Aesir boy," Baldur mumbled.

"Voden's coming," Hod said, he head tilted to one side as if he were listening.

The others looked at him with awe and respect. "How can you always tell, Hod?" Baldur asked. "He always knows, Vili."

"Perhaps he sees in a different way since he can't see through his eyes," she suggested.

Voden appeared from around the corner of a hall and waved at them. As he approached, Baldur, Hod, and Vidar ran to greet him. "Father! Father!" Baldur cried. "I'm invulnerable! Vidar and Hod can't land a blow on me! I've got a spell of protection!"

The chieftain of the Aesir smiled gently. "Ah, yes, that one begins with Thurs, like this." He drew a straight, vertical line in the air. Then halfway down its right side he drew two lines so that they formed an equilateral triangle with the base resting on the vertical line. "There's more to it, but you're still a bit young for that."

"Is he *really* invulnerable, Father?" Hod asked. Voden picked him up and stroked his head, looking deep in his milky eyes.

"No one is *really* invulnerable, Hod. Spells like that just help a little. But there's always a way around them."

Baldur pouted. "But I want to be *really* invulnerable. You know magic, Father. Isn't there any way?"

Voden thought for a moment while he placed Hod back on the ground. "Yes, there is. But I'm afraid it's already too late. If, before you were born, Frigida had gone all over the earth and made everything swear an oath not to harm you, why, then you'd be invulnerable."

"Everything?" Vidar asked. "Even wood and stones and leaves and bugs and . . . everything?"

Voden nodded. "Oh, yes, everything. If even one little thing, even a little sprig of mistletoe, failed to give its oath, the charm wouldn't be complete and Baldur wouldn't be invulnerable. It'd be a big job."

Baldur laughed gaily. "Well, Mother must have done it! Because I'm invulnerable! Watch, Father!" And Hod and Vidar, joining in with Baldur's ebullient mood, began to swing at him with their practice swords as before, missing him with every stroke and chanting "Baldur's invulnerable!" as they swung.

Gravely, Voden watched them play. Ah, he thought, if only I could make you *all* invulnerable. For there are things coming that I would give a great deal to protect you from. Surt sends scouting parties farther and farther north, and tries again and again to probe my magical defense. He's even attempted small raids into Vanaheim. Disastrous, all of them, but disturbing nonetheless. The prisoners the Vanir captured knew nothing worth telling, except that Muspellheim was massing troops and materials at Der, just the other side of the Great Wall to the south of the Twisted Lands. The intent was obvious and disturbing.

Thank Fornjot that at least the Jotun are temporarily neutralized, Voden thought. Though, he admitted, I almost wish I'd allowed Lao-Kee and the others to kill Hrodvitnir. If he should ever escape Lyngvi— He cut the thought off short. It didn't bear thinking.

And now there were stirrings to the west. Bands of Svartalfar had been sighted along the far bank of the Gopul by the Vanir foresters. They'd never journeyed that far east in the memory of anyone in Vanaheim.

He gazed at his playing children again and felt a great sadness well up in his throat. What kind of a future have we willed you? he wondered. One filled with blood and rapine and death and horror? He shuddered inwardly.

But there is hope, he reminded himself. I've seen that hope, sensed it, guided myself by it. It may not be hope for me, or even for most of the Aesir. But it is hope for the future, for another chance to do it right. We must try to keep the light alive, for if we don't, surely darkness will triumph and rule Yggdrasil forever.

He knew it was the same choice men had faced once before, a long time ago, when they fought the First Dark Empire. Then they'd met the evil face to face, and though the battle took a horrible toll, evil had been beaten down. Now it rose again, and once more had to be met and defeated. It would happen again and again, he knew. And always there would be that choice to yield or resist.

He felt a sudden hollow ache in his chest. Vili, Vidar, Baldur, Hod, how he loved them all! His single eye shone briefly with his feelings, then it died down and slipped under control. I love them so much, and yet I can't ever show it the way I'd like to. Why? What's missing in me that makes it impossible to let my love open up into the light of day? It's the same way with Freyja. I can't seem to reach beyond the walls I've built around my love. I'm like a man holding a flame in cupped hands, wanting to light a bonfire with it but afraid to open my hands and touch the flame to the wood for fear the cold winds will extinguish it.

Was there no way to trust? No way to show the love he felt, to tell them all, to gather them in his arms, hold them, whisper it to them?

A chill passed through his body, shaking him. He bowed his head in grief. I never let Borr know how much I loved him. He never let me know how much he loved me. Can't I be better than my father? Or am I doomed to repeat his failure?

Doomed. The word echoed in his mind. He shook his head to clear it, but it stayed there, reverberating endlessly. There's so much more than just my love involved here, he tried to justify to himself. But he knew it was only another way of expressing his own fear and cowardice. There was little room for soft things in his life. And he made no real effort to create more. He would fail, even as his father had. Suddenly feeling very alone, he reached out and put his arm around Vili's shoulders. He drew his sister to him with a slight hug. She looked up, surprised but pleased at this unusual display of emotion from her brother, and smiled brightly.

Hod walked over and gazed up at Voden's face with his white eyes. "Where's Lao-Kee?" he asked. "I haven't heard her. Didn't she come with you and Vidar, like she usually does?"

Voden nodded. "Yes, Hod, but she didn't stay around. She wanted to take a little scouting trip up into Jotunheim to see how things are going up there. We haven't heard much about what's been happening since Hrodvitnir disappeared."

"That's dangerous," Baldur said gravely as he joined them. "I hope she's being careful. Maybe I should give her my charm of protection."

"Maybe you should," Voden agreed. "It'd be a very nice thing to do. I'm sure she'd appreciate it. But I think she'll be all right. She's half Jotun, you know, so she understands how to deal with them. I'm sure she'll stop by to say hello to all of you when she comes back. It shouldn't take her too long." He frowned slightly. "She should return soon."

Lao-Kee knew she was in serious trouble. The four Jotun who had ambushed her almost seemed to be waiting specifically for her and her alone. But that's impossible, she thought. No one even knew I was coming. Nevertheless, they had caught her totally unaware, and now she rode in their midst, tied hand and foot.

She'd tried several times to ask them their names and clans, but they had stubbornly refused to respond to her questions. They wore no badges or insignia of any kind, which was strange in and of itself and worried Lao-Kee. Could they be Risar, determined to get revenge against the sister of their missing enemy, Hrodvitnir? If so, she was as good as dead.

They rode for several hours until, topping a rise, she spied a circle of wagons in the distance. A camp. And obviously their destination. Soon she would know.

Geirrodmir's smile was thin and cold as the bound woman was led in front of him. He simply sat and looked at her for several moments without speaking.

"So," he finally said, his voice icy, "the little traitoress returns to Jotunheim." Lao-Kee decided the wisest course was to remain silent. Geirrodmir nodded approval of her silence. "Yes, little one, wordless is best. There's really nothing for you to say, is there? You caused the death of my brother, murdered by that Aesir bastard, Tror. Don't bother to deny it. I've talked to many of my brother's men. I know all about the horse race and the duel. Very neat, I must admit. Ah, well, Hrungnir was always something of a fool."

He paused and glared at her. "And then there's the matter of Hrodvitnir's disappearance. Yes. Only one man returned, and his story was very confused. According to him, the party was jumped by Risar and everyone except him was killed and carried off. Strange, then, to see you here, no?

"We tortured him to see how well his story held up. It fell to pieces. In fact, he never even saw a Risar. Only some dim shapes he assumed were Lodfaffnir and Hodmir. It turns out that someone struck him from behind and he never saw anybody kill anybody. When he woke up the next day, he was bound and gagged. The wound he had was self-inflicted.

"We tortured him for a long time, to make completely sure we had the truth." He sighed with mild disgust. "He died poorly, like all cowards and liars.

"He didn't know much. Only that the party that joined Hrodvitnir's there by the Amsvartnir Sea consisted of you and some Aesir, two of whom sounded amazingly like Voden and Honir.

"We caught Hodmir. We tied him up and slung him on a pole and hung him between two roasting fires, just like juicy dog. He cooked nicely and made a lot of noise. But the interesting thing was that to the very end he denied ever having talked with the Aesir or having been anywhere near the Amsvartnir Sea that night."

Geirrodmir motioned to two of his men, and they moved Lao-Kee right up to him. He reached out his hand and gripped her by the throat. "Now," he said softly, his voice heavy with menace, "we're going to talk, you and I. You're going to tell me a few things, little one." His smile was vicious and heartless, and Lao-Kee couldn't repress a shudder.

"Among the Jotun," he said, "I'm known for the strength of my hands, Lao-Kee. I've strangled many men. And women. With only one hand. Once I strangled two at a time, one with each hand! An amazing feat, don't you agree? I imagine my hands are so strong because I'm a smith of sorts. Yes, that must be it." He looked at his free hand and flexed it. "Smiths always have such strong hands," he murmured, as if to himself.

"Now, I'm going to squeeze slowly, cutting off your air gradually. See, that's the way. You're beginning to turn red. Soon your eyes will bulge out and you'll start to struggle. But you're tied up, poor thing. Hopeless. Hopeless.

"Ah, I can see the fear in your eyes now. Yes, you're beginning to suffocate. There's no air coming in, and your neck hurts horribly. Things are spinning and turning red. There's a roaring in your ears. Your head feels light. You feel like you're going to pass out. Ah, but now, Geirrodmir releases the pressure and you get a little gulp of air.

"I can do this for hours, Lao-kee. All day, if necessary. Give you a little breath here and there to keep you alive. It will take a long time to die this way."

He let her go, and she sprawled on the ground, gasping in fear. For several moments she was unable to speak. Then, her voice trembling with terror, she managed to croak, "Wha . . . what do . . . you want?"

Geirrodmir smiled. His voice was friendly, almost jovial. "Ah, you take very little persuading. Somehow I expected you to be made of sterner stuff. But then, you're only half Jotun."

He leaned forward suddenly and grabbed her by the throat once more. His smile was gone, his voice harsh and demanding. "I want Tror! I want the bastard who killed my brother!"

"That . . . that's easier said than done."

Geirrodmir snarled and tightened his grip. "Killing you is easier done than said. You have your choice. Promise to bring Tror to me, or die slowly. I'll be revenged on one or the other of you. I'd prefer it to be Tror, but I'll settle for you, little one. Decide."

She nodded frantically. Geirrodmir relaxed his grip and let her fall back. She gasped and coughed for a few moments, then croaked, "I promise."

"Being among the Aesir has made you wiser, little one," Geirrodmir said with a sneer. "Now listen carefully. I'm going to move my camp to the west of Bifrosti's Ford on the north bank of the Iving, just across from the Himinborg. In two weeks' time you'll bring Tror to me, just the two of you, without his damn hammer. I don't care what lies you make up. That's your concern. You're obviously very good at it. You fooled Hrungnir and Hrodvitnir. Now fool Tror."

He stood and turned away, then turned back to smile down at her. "Oh, yes, I almost forgot. Don't try to make a fool of me, Lao-Kee. In case you didn't notice, you just gave your promise from the middle of a Trul magical drawing. The White Bear made it for me himself. And I'll cut a lock of your hair for future use, if necessary. Should you break your promise, you'll die in a way that will make strangling by me seem pleasant.''

Lao-Kee swallowed painfully and nodded. She had seen someone die as the result of a Trul curse. It had been horrible enough to watch. She shuddered to think what it must be like to die that way.

"I'll . . . keep my promise.''

Geirrodmir nodded. "I know, I know. I and my sons, Greipnir and Gjalp are looking forward to seeing you and Tror in two weeks.'' He turned to his two sons. "Kill her horse and cut off its head. Tie the head to her. Wrap her arms around it as if she were hugging it. Then take her almost to the Iving and dump her. She'll find a way to get rid of the head before she crosses the river. And the walk back to Asgard will do her good.'' With a last frigid smile, he turned and left.

"Oh, come on, Tror,'' Lao-Kee urged. "We can stay with old Grid tonight and then sneak over the Iving tomorrow early.''

Tror grumbled uncertainly. "I don't know. I don't have Mjollnir with me. I don't like the idea of going into Jotunheim without my hammer.''

"That's silly. Geirrodmir's a smith, not a warrior. And he's friendly too. He said he's dying to meet you and ask you about some of Volund's techniques. You know, Tror, you may be the last man alive in Yggdrasil who knows your father's techniques.''

"Well, when Magni gets old enough, I'm going to teach him. He's so strong for such a young boy! He'll be a great smith, just like my father,'' Tror said proudly.

Lao-Kee laughed. "You're so modest! You're a great smith yourself. That's why Geirrodmir's dying to meet you. Besides'' —she winked—"I'll bet you could trade some of Volund's secrets for good, solid gold. Geirrodmir's got plenty, and he's not stingy. I'll bet Sif would give you quite a welcome if you came home with a saddlebag full of gold, eh?''

Tror paused dubiously. "I just wish I had Mjollnir, that's all.''

"Oh, well.'' The slender Jotun shrugged, her voice slightly scoffing. "If you're afraid . . .''

Tror scowled. "I'm not afraid. On the contrary, the Jotun are afraid of me. Why, ever since my duel with Hrungnir—"

"You're right," Lao-Kee interrupted, "and that's why you'll be safe. They're afraid of you. And besides, if you show Geirrodmir those fists of yours . . ."

Tror held up both his hands. They were covered with gloves made from fine iron mail. "Aye," he grunted, balling his hands up into fists, "aye, fists of steel, these be now. One of the cleverest things I've ever crafted, these gloves. Volund himself would be proud of them. You're right. Geirrodmir will be mightily impressed with these gloves of mine. I can assure you their equal can't be found anywhere in Asaheim or Jotunheim. Why, with an iron-sheathed fist like this, I imagine I could kill Jotun as easily as Buri Axehand did."

Lao-Kee grinned. "That's it! That's the Tror I know. Not afraid of anything! Always ready for a little adventure. Let's go to Grid's. She'll take us in and feed us. And she makes the best damn ale in all of Asaheim. Come on!"

Lao-Kee fell into a drunken slumber after about eight horns of ale. Tror laughed woozily and took a deep sip of his tenth horn. "Aye, the Jotun's too little to be much of a drinker! No place for it all to go, so it goes right to her head. Not a bad sort, though. For a Jotun."

Grid scowled. "I wouldn't trust her too far were I you. She went to Jotunheim about two weeks ago, she did. And she came walking back, a very sour expression on her face. Now why is she so all-fired eager to go back, I wonder?"

"I'm thinking she doesn't like this Geirro . . . Geirum . . . whatever, very well and wants to do him a bad turn. Show him up, you know. Sounds like a fool Jotun to me."

Grid shook her gray head. "Don't underestimate Geirrodmir. He's a crafty old fox. Those of us living here on the frontier know him all too well. Go if you must, Tror, but go carefully. And go armed."

"Mjollnir's in Asgard. I left it there because we were only going for a short ride. Too heavy to carry on a short ride. Then this came up. No time to go back."

"Well, then," Grid said, "I've a staff, iron bound and near unbreakable, to lend you. Best have something."

"Aye," Tror said, stretching and yawning. "I'll take it,

Grid, and many thanks." He stretched out on the bench and was almost instantly fast asleep.

Grid stood and came over to him. She patted his red hair and smiled softly. "Aye, sleep now, Tror. And take my staff with you. My staff and Sigfod's blessings." She took a fur rug and placed it over him. For a few moments she stood and gazed down at him. She sighed. "Volund made that staff for my man many years ago, when he first came to Asaheim. You were just a little boy then. But so serious." She paused and stared silently into the past. "The Jotun killed my man. Yet he killed eight of them with that staff before they pulled him down. He was a good man.

"Then afterward, when I was all alone and grieving, your father was so kind to me. Saw I never went hungry." She paused again and looked down at Tror. "You never knew it," she said quietly, "but your father and I . . . Ah, well, that was long ago. I'm just an old lady now. An old lady with memories."

They arrived at the circle of Geirrodmir's wagons when the sun stood highest in the sky. Geirrodmir, with his sons Greipnir and Gjalp on either side of him, came out to greet them, his face curved by a broad smile. "Lao-Kee! Tror! Ah, what a pleasure! Tror, you've no idea how long I've been wanting to meet you. Your father's work has always been an inspiration to me. I've heard so much about things like the necklace Brisingamen which he made for Fiorgyn. And you've actually seen them! And probably even watched as he made them!"

"Aye," Tror nodded, relaxing a little to find Geirrodmir so cordial. "I pumped the bellows often for Volund."

"Why, then, come over behind these wagons. I've set up my forge and would like to test you there. There's much I would love to have you tell me."

Tror and Lao-Kee dismounted and Geirrodmir's two sons took their horses. The Jotun chieftain led them across the open space in the center of the circle and between two wagons to the far side. There, glowing redly, was a huge forge. All of Geirrodmir's people were gathered around, watching. Tror began to feel uncomfortable. There didn't seem to be a friendly face in the crowd.

Geirrodmir walked to the forge and suddenly spun around. His face was totally transformed. Where once there had been a smile, now there was only a snarl. Tror looked about and suddenly realized he was surrounded by Jotun. Greipnir and Gjalp had stepped behind him. He glowered down at Lao-Kee, but she carefully avoided his eyes.

"So," Geirrodmir hissed malevolently, "we meet at last, killer of my brother! Yes! Hrungnir was my brother, you bastard! And now I'll have my revenge!

"A most fitting revenge, too, against the son of Volund, the master smith of the Aesir." He drew on a pair of thick gloves and picked a pair of tongs out of the forge. They were glowing redly and held a bright red iron ball. "Your father was once captive here in Jotunheim. Bergelmir kept him on the island of Saevarstod and demanded he create wondrous things. Aye, that he did!" His face twisted into a snarl. "But like you, Volund was a killer at heart, a dangerous animal Bergelmir should have done more than just maim. Your father murdered Bergelmir's two sons, then made cups from their skulls. He raped and profaned Bergelmir's daughter and then fled south to the Aesir."

"I remember," Tror said, and spat angrily on the ground. He felt a furious rage rising within him at the mention of the treatment he and his father and sister had received at the hands of the Jotun. It all came back to him in a sudden flash, the cuffs and slapping, the harsh words and abrupt demands. His mind slid even further back to that night when the Jotun had raided his home village. In his memory he heard the screams and cries once more, especially those of his mother. His voice was shaking with the power of his emotion when he finally spoke. "Aye, I remember, Jotun! I fled with him in the boat Bergelmir's two sons had used to sneak out to our island. But before that I helped him stuff their bodies into the offal pit. And I'll stuff yours after them!"

Out of the corners of his eyes he sensed that Greipnir and Gjalp were moving forward, one on each side, in an attempt to catch him between them. He gripped Grid's staff carefully. We'll see who catches whom!

Without warning, he stepped back directly between the two of them. They had thick cudgels in their hands. Before they could strike, however, Tror stepped to the right toward Gjalp and swung the tip of his staff up from the ground, striking the man right in the crotch. Gjalp howled in agony and flopped to the ground.

Tror spun quickly and deflected Greipnir's blow with the upper end of the staff. Then he slammed downward with the lower end, smashing it into his opponent's knee from the side. The man moaned and fell to his knees. Tror spun the staff and slammed the end over the Jotun's head. His skull cracked like a ripe melon and his brains spattered out over the ground. He fell forward without a sound.

Geirrodmir roared with fury. He pulled back both arms and flung the red-hot iron ball at Tror. Tror dropped his staff and caught the ball in midair in his iron gloves. Everyone gasped in wonder as he did so. He raised his right hand, the ball in it, beginning to smoke. Then he took two quick steps forward, and threw the iron ball back at Geirrodmir with all his might.

The glowing ball caught the Jotun in the stomach. He shrieked in agony and doubled over. The ball had hit with such power, it had penetrated his stomach. Now he writhed around on the ground, the red-hot iron ball burning into his guts. He screamed and screamed, his voice losing any human qualities and becoming that of an animal in hideous pain.

For an instant everyone stood stock still, staring at the writhing Geirrodmir in horror. Then Tror gave a bellow of rage. Everyone turned to look at him. His eyes were blank and staring, and foam flecked his mouth. His face was almost as red as the glowing iron had been.

With a scream that almost matched that of Geirrodmir in its bestiality, he leapt forward, his staff swinging, and attacked the watching Jotun. The men grabbed for their swords in a panic, the women screamed, and the children began to wail. They started to run in every direction, totally unhinged by terror.

Tror waded among them, his staff a whirling death, brains and blood spattering out in showers from his path. He made no differentiation between men, women, or children. He killed everything he came near.

The screaming and howling seemed to go on forever. Then suddenly, unexpectedly, the only sound that could be heard was the dying, whimpering moaning of Geirrodmir. Tror stood, his shoulders sagging, his face, hands, and clothing covered with gore. He looked dully at the ground. At his feet lay a little child, the last Jotun he had killed. The head was split in two.

Blinking, he gazed around, as if unsure where he was.

There was death everywhere his eyes wandered. Not one creature stirred. His breath sobbed in, then out "I . . . I . . ." he tried to speak.

Lao-Kee crawled out from under two bodies and cautiously approached him. "Tror?" she whispered, her voice trembling as badly as her body. "Tror, are you . . . ?"

The red-bearded giant nodded numbly. "I'm . . . I'm . . ." His voice wouldn't work properly.

"By Gymir and Nerthus," Lao-Kee said in awe, "I've never seen anything like that. What happened?"

Tror shook his head. "Don't . . . know . . . guess it . . . guess I went berserk."

Lao-Kee nodded. "I've heard of Aesir doing that. Some kind of battle frenzy. But by all the gods, I never thought I'd see anything like that! You . . . you killed them all. Men, women, even the children. I—" She couldn't speak any more. She began to shudder and cry.

For many minutes Tror just stood there and stared stupidly at the mayhem around him. Slowly intelligence crept back into his eyes. With it came horror at what he had done. "Killed them," he murmured, "killed them all."

He turned and his glance fell on Lao-Kee. The slender Jotun was bowed over, weeping uncontrollably. Her whole body shook with the power of her tears. Tror watched for several moments in surprise. "Lao-Kee," he finally croaked out, "I . . . I killed them all. Every one of them." She nodded.

He looked over the twisted bodies one more time, then his shoulders began to heave. He retched and retched until there was nothing left in him. Then he began to cry, his sobs coming from somewhere deep within him. Somehow, indistinctly but surely, he knew that what he had done had changed the world forever. Nothing would ever be the same again. He wept not only for the Jotun he had slaughtered, but for himself and the world that had died as they had died.

Weak and suddenly exhausted, he turned and began to withdraw through the bodies. He walked like a man asleep, or like one afraid to wake up completely. Now and then he stumbled, even when the ground was clear of corpses. He reached the circle of the wagons and walked through it. Then he walked past it, out onto the grasslands of Jotunheim. In the distance he could make out the Iving and beyond it, the rising Himinborg.

Dimly, he realized that over there somewhere was safety and peace. He began to trudge in that direction, his shoulders bowed, his head down. The staff dangled from one iron-gloved fist and dragged behind.

Lao-Kee watched him go. Then she took one last look around Geirrodmir's camp. "I . . . I kept my promise," she muttered unsteadily. "I promised to bring Tror, and I did. I'm . . . Oh, sweet Nerthus! I'm not to blame!"

Her eyes streaming tears, she stumbled after Tror's slowly retreating form.

XIX

***

Jormungand shrugged. "I can't do much about the snows in the Smoking Lands, Surt. The last four or five winters have been absolutely horrendous up there. And for two summers now the snow hasn't melted enough to let large numbers of troops through the passes. Thiazi and a few parties have made it. But to try moving a whole army north, well . . ."

Surt scowled. "Perhaps some of my allies can help if the weather refuses to cooperate. Some storm demons to bring a warm wind from the south." He sighed. "A major undertaking, Serpent. One I'd rather not mount unless I absolutely must. I wish to save as much of my power as possible for the final confrontation with Voden. To drain it ahead of time . . ." He mused silently.

"Well," he began again suddenly, "we shall see, we shall see. What news does Thiazi bring in any case?"

It was Jormungand's turn to scowl. "Precious little. The Vanir guard their forests well, especially those damn women warriors, the Valkyrja. Every attempt we've made to break through to the north has failed. Thiazi himself damn near got his throat cut one night.

"I just sent him north again, with a hand-picked crew. He's going to try one more time to sneak through the forests and make contact with the Jotun. I told him to succeed this time or not to come back."

Fifty men to start with. Twenty left. Damn! Thiazi kicked a rock and sent it flying across the plain. He took several deep breaths to calm himself. Then he turned and looked back at the forest. The Valkyrja probably won't follow us out here, he thought. Or if they do, we can at least see the bitches coming.

The anger rose up in him again. Thirty good men lost! And there hadn't even been an opportunity to get even! The damned Vanir never showed their faces. They came invisibly in the night. Every morning when Thiazi's men rolled out of their sleeping sacks, two or three didn't roll. They just laid there and looked up at the forest canopy with sightless stares and slit throats. It didn't matter how many guards he put out. Somehow the Valkyrja always managed to slip by and take their nightly toll.

And the horses. They'd even killed the horses! He was down to one mount per man, with only five more for the pack train. He'd started out with more than seventy!

He heaved a sigh. At least now we're out of the forest, he reassured himself. We made it this far. The rest has to be easier. He shaded his eyes with his hand and looked northward. As far as he could see, a grassy plain rolled off to the horizon. To the right it rose swiftly to form a high plateau. Dead ahead a river ran more or less directly north. That, he estimated, must be the Geirvimul.

This time Thiazi had changed his tactics and had avoided following the Geirvimul through the forest, though it would have been the easiest way to go. On past attempts to reach the north, he'd marched along its banks, using the river to float down his supplies. But there were Vanir settlements all along its length, and Thiazi had learned the hard way that there was no way around them. So he'd decided to strike off into the forest and avoid the river, hoping to simply disappear among the trees, elude the Vanir, and emerge unscathed onto the plains.

Thiazi had clearly underestimated the Vanir yet again. It didn't seem possible to him that anyone could locate a party of fifty men and seventy-five horses in that wild and tumbled terrain. In most places the forest was so dense you couldn't see more than fifteen feet in any direction.

The limited horizons, intense greens and dark shadows of the forest, made the men from Muspellheim feel oppressed and claustrophobic. They were used to wide vistas and the stark beiges of a semidesert environment. No wonder I find it so hard to understand the Vanir and their command of the forest, Thiazi thought. We have nothing like it in Muspellheim.

They'd probably be just as lost on our stark, horizon-to-horizon plains. But here in their forests, they're totally at home. He felt sure that they were intimately acquainted with every rock, twig, and leaf. We must have stood out like mountains on a plain, he admitted.

Whatever the reasons, he reminded himself, my plan was a miserable failure. They found us quickly and never lost us. They seemed to know exactly where I was going to go next and precisely where we would camp every night. He didn't even want to think about the trip back. You were righter than you realized, Jormungand, he silently addressed his absent commander. I just might not come back this time.

Enough brooding about the past, he chided himself. It's time to act. He turned to face his men. "All right," he growled, "mount up. And keep a sharp eye out. This is Aesir country and we don't want to meet any of *those* bastards." They grumbled to each other as they swung up into their saddles. When everyone was ready, Thiazi gave a curt gesture and they started off, single file, north onto the Aesir Plain.

Lao-Kee was in a foul mood, and the yelling of the children wasn't making things any better. Tror wasn't even talking to her anymore. Tyr pretended she didn't exist. Heimdall continued with his unremitting hostility. Honir tried to avoid her. And Voden, even Voden, was cold and distant.

It's all Tror's fault, she tried to convince herself bitterly. The dumb bastard really thinks I set him up for Geirrodmir to kill. Stupid. I had it all figured out. I knew he could defeat Geirrodmir, no matter what. But Tror wouldn't accept that. Probably Sif convinced him I was trying to get him killed. Silly little bitch. Cow eyes. Always mooning at all the men, especially Voden. Bitch.

And Freyja. By the gods, how she hated that one! She and Voden were getting chummier and chummier. Pretty soon Freyja'd be sleeping with him again, she was sure. And then where would that leave one particular half-breed Jotun?

Lao-Kee cursed under her breath. Damn the noise Baldur, Hod, and the others were making! She could hardly think with all the ruckus. Always playing at war with those silly, dull children's swords. She scowled and tried to ignore them. She was partially successful, and her mind drifted back into her angry thoughts. She knew she could make Voden happier

than either Freyja or that cow Frigida could. She should
simply creep into his sleeping cupboard some night and crawl
under the covers with him. She could slide her hand down his
stomach and between his legs, stroking ever so gently, arous-
ing him, making his breath come faster and faster. Then she
could follow her hands with her tongue and her mouth and
take him into her and . . . She shuddered with ecstasy. By
Nerthus, then he'd reach for her and push her back. He'd start
to explore with his fingers and tongue, stroking and licking,
nipping here and there, and finally he'd roll on top of her and
slide—

The sword slammed into her shoulder and nearly knocked
her over with surprise. She leapt to her feet and glowered at
the children. Hod stood here, looking blankly in her direction, his hands empty. "My . . . my sword," he muttered.
"You knocked it out of my hand, Baldur. I . . . where is it?"

Lao-Kee bit her tongue. Hod. Of all of them, she liked
Hod the best. She detested Baldur. The little boy was so
beautiful, so perfect. Everyone adored him. Especially Voden.
She scowled. Voden spent more time with Baldur than he did
with her.

She walked over to Hod, her mind filled with spite. "Don't
worry about your sword. I'll teach you something better than
stupid old sword play." The children began to gather around
her, Baldur at their head.

"Teach me too," he demanded.

"No. Only Hod. The rest of you go sit down." Baldur
frowned and hesitated. "I said sit down," Lao-Kee commanded. They all sat. She turned back to Hod. From one of
her boots she took a slender dagger and handed it to him,
placing it directly in his hand and closing his fingers around
the grip. "That's a Jotun dagger," she explained. "Test the
weight and heft of it. Nice, eh? Well-balanced. Perfect for
throwing." She jerked suddenly upright and a second knife
appeared in her hand for an instant before it was gone, hissing
through the air. An instant later it was quivering in a slender
tree that stood about twenty-five paces from where the group
sat.

Baldur exclaimed softly in amazement. "Show me how to
do that, Lao-Kee, please."

"No," she snapped irritably. "Only Hod."

"But he can't see," Baldur protested.

"Doesn't matter." She made great show of taking another dagger from somewhere inside her waistband and closing her eyes, placing one hand over them to act as a blindfold. She pulled her hand back and the second knife whizzed through the air to land with a solid thunk, inches from the first. "It's about three fingers higher than the other one, right?" she asked, her eyes still covered. The children all shouted affirmation, Baldur the loudest of the lot.

Lao-Kee turned back to Hod. "Have you got the feel of the knife?" she asked. The blind boy nodded. "Good. Now let me guide your hand and show you how to throw. Like this, slowly now, for overhand. Like this, that's good, underhand. Overhand, underhand. Overhand, underhand. Right, right. Smoothly. Now a little faster. Good, good, you've got the motion.

"Now the tricky part." She frowned at the other children. "You've got to be silent for this. Absolutely silent." They nodded in awe, several putting their hands over their mouths to assure their own stillness.

"Hod, you have very acute hearing. Use it. I'm going to throw a pebble out. I want you to make the throwing gesture in the direction the sound comes from. All right. Now!"

Hod swung his arm in an overhand throw. Lao-Kee shook her head. "No. Not good enough. Listen very, very carefully. Concentrate. Try it again." She picked up another pebble and tossed it beyond the ring of children who sat staring up at Hod and her.

Hod turned more smoothly, more accurately this time, but his throw was slow. "You need to throw faster, but you had the direction right that time. This is a very good technique for you, Hod. No one would ever expect a blind man to be able to throw a knife. They'd be taken completely by surprise. If you practice hard, you'll learn to throw with great accuracy. Now this time, really throw the knife. Try to visualize in your mind how far away the pebble is as well as the direction. Now!"

Hod threw the knife. It went in the correct direction but fell far short of where the pebble struck. Lao-Kee was pleased, though, and all the children were impressed. Baldur was about to stand up and ask again to be taught, but Lao-Kee scowled at him so fiercely he sank back down looking very hurt and annoyed.

"You've got to throw harder. Here, this is my last dagger. Probably the best balanced for throwing of the lot. Get the feel of it. Nice, eh? Now I'll throw another pebble, and I want to you throw the knife really hard this time. Ready? Now!"

At the instant she threw the pebble, Baldur ran out of patience. He stood and blurted out "Please . . ." Hod heard the sound and spun, the knife swinging in a powerful arc and flying out of his hand with a hiss. It stuck Baldar in the left eye.

Baldar gave a single shriek and fell over backward, knocked off balance by the force of the blow. He hit the ground and lay still. A horrified silence held them all in its grip. Lao-Kee was frozen in position, her arm still outstretched from throwing the pebble. She gaped in disbelief at the still form of Baldur, the knife buried in his head up to the hilt, blood oozing out around the guard. "Oh, Nerthus," she said, her voice barely a whisper.

Suddenly the children leapt up and began to scream. Lao-Kee rushed to Baldur. Hod stood in confusion. "What's going on?" he pleaded. "What's happening?"

Vili and Frigida came running up, brought by one of the children. Frigida saw Baldur in Lao-Kee's arms, the knife sticking in his head, blood covering his beautiful face, his body slack and lifeless. With a wail of despair, she sank to the ground next to her son and took him from Lao-Kee. The slender Jotun stared at her, eyes confused and filled with horror. "He . . . he's dead," she muttered, her voice stunned and broken. "Dead. Baldur's dead."

They recrossed the Iving just north and east of where it was joined by the Fimbulthul. Thiazi was well-satisfied. He still had his twenty men, and now he had two mounts per man and ten horses in the baggage train. Plus an escort of fifteen Jotun who were going to accompany him to meet with Surt. I'll return after all, Jormungand, he thought. Half a year later than expected, but return all the same.

They were a day into the Aesir Plain when he began to wonder if he hadn't spoken too soon. It was the middle of the morning when the Jotun scout he had sent forward came racing back pell-mell. The man had jabbered with his fellow Jotun in their strange dialect of the common tongue. Then the one who was best able to communicate had ridden over to talk with Thiazi. "Many Aesir up ahead," the man grunted. "Draumir thinks maybe they know we're here."

Thiazi groaned inwardly. By Nergal's left testicle! "How many of them?" he asked.

The Jotun shrugged. "Maybe fifty, sixty."

By both Nergal's testicles! Thiazi cursed. He looked around, wondering what in the world to do. The landscape was rolling and fairly open here. If the Aesir came over a ridge and saw them, it was all over. Fifty or sixty of the bastards! Namtaru must already be on his way to Aralu with Thiazi's name at the top of his damned list!

As he swept the horizon with his eyes, he noticed a copse of trees in the distance back to the north and west. He made a quick decision. "We'll go there and wait until the sun goes down," he commanded, pointing to the trees. "From now on we only travel at night."

Lao-Kee let the horse pick its own way. She sat listlessly in her saddle and stared dully at the ground. It was all over now. There was nothing left. No hope. When Voden had come to Asgard for Baldur's funeral, he had clasped Vili and shared his tears with her. He had clasped Frigida and shared his tears with her. He had never even so much as looked at poor Lao-Kee.

Poor Lao-Kee, she thought bitterly. They all think I did it on purpose. They think I tricked Hod into killing his brother. They all hate me. Even Vili, my one friend, Vili. She hadn't even been willing to talk to me. I was all alone with my guilt and my sorrow.

Oh, Voden, she sobbed mentally, couldn't you have just held me for a moment? Couldn't you have just put your arms around me and let me cry as hard as the others cried? I had as much to weep about, even more. Didn't you see the tears and the grief waiting in my eyes, ready to break forth in a flood of mourning? I never shed them, never let my anguish twist my features. I stood there, dry and rigid, a mocking smile frozen on my lips because you ignored me, shunned me, hated me. Oh, Voden!

She sobbed openly now, the tears running down her face and totally blurring her vision. She rode blindly, aimlessly, not caring where she went. She didn't even see the Jotun until she was falling from her horse, already halfway into dark unconsciousness.

She opened her eyes to stare at the strangest face she had ever seen. The skin was dark, shiny black. The eyes were large, black, and beautiful. They were filled with lively intelligence and wit. The nose was broad, but not flat. The lips were full and sensual. The shape of the face was generally round. There was a full head of black hair, and a slight, pointed beard of black adorned the chin. She had never seen anyone even slightly resembling this man in her life.

"Ah." A soft voice came from the full lips which curved slightly in a half smile. "You've decided to rejoin us. I am Thiazi and you are Lao-Kee." His smile widened at their obvious surprise. "Yes, Lao-Kee. We should start out being very straightforward with each other. Let me tell you right off that I need your help. In return, I can offer you your life." He sat back.

Lao-Kee tried to raise herself on one elbow and discovered that she couldn't. She was tied hand and foot. She looked up at Thiazi, her gaze cold and accusing. He shrugged. "It was their idea," he excused himself. "They said you were too tricky to trust unbound."

She swiveled her head to take in her surroundings. About thirty men stood in a circle, looking down at her. Some ten of them were Jotun. She recognized several.

She recognized something else too. There was a rope leading from her feet to a horse. It was an old Jotun torture. Tie a victim up, attach him to a horse, and set the horse galloping. The screaming creature tied behind it, bobbing and bouncing around, scared the horse and made it run faster and wilder. It would gallop over rocks, through thickets of thorns, across streams, until the burden it dragged stopped screaming and it was exhausted. Eventually it would find its way back to some Jotun camp, and the shapeless bundle tied to it would be cut loose and allowed to decay where it lay. It wasn't a swift or a pleasant way to die.

Thiazi nodded to her as he saw she understood. "It wasn't my idea. Your fellow Jotuns thought it up. We . . . have more civilized methods, though I doubt they are any more effective.

"Of course, I've already assured them the whole thing is

totally unnecessary. I'm sure you'll be happy to help us. Am I right in my assumption?''

"What do you want, Thiazi?" she croaked, her mouth and throat suddenly dry with fear.

"Aid. We find ourselves in the midst of large numbers of Aesir. Several large groups, in fact. We need to find a way through them."

She nodded. "They're on their way back from Baldur's funeral. There were rumors of some strange people out here on the Aesir Plain. Even rumors of a Jotun incursion south of the Iving. I see both are true. On their way home I guess they decided to have a look around. I'm afraid they're very likely to find you."

"That much I have surmised myself," Thiazi said crisply. "The questions are really two. First, can we avoid them in some way none of us have thought of? Two, is there a way to gain safe-conduct through them? Have you any ideas?"

"Don't bother with her," one of the Jotun spoke up. "She's one of them. Lives with them. She won't help us. We'll have to die a warrior's death."

"I haven't come this far to die any kind of death," Thiazi said with a scowl. He turned back to Lao-Kee. "Are you one of them? Are you on their side?"

The slender Jotun paused, eyeing the horse. "I was," she said softly. "I'm not so sure anymore."

Thiazi picked up on her tone instantly. He looked at her shrewdly, a friendly grin lifting the corners of his mouth. "Betrayed your trust, eh?" She nodded. He squatted next to her, his face sympathetic. "I know that feeling." He snorted. "For years I led scouting parties across the Smoking Lands, discovering the passes, making quick runs into the forests of the Vanir. Dangerous work.

"And what was my reward? Ha! Another job, even more dangerous . . . come north and find the Jotun, talk to them about helping us crush the Aesir."

"Crush . . . the Aesir?" Lao-Kee said in surprise.

Thiazi nodded solemnly. "Yes. Surt intends to crush them like a nut between two rocks. The Jotun to the north and the legions of Muspellheim to the south."

"Crush them," Lao-Kee said musingly. She paused as ideas jostled for attention in her mind. "Will . . . will you kill all of them?"

"No," Thiazi replied. "That would be a foolish waste. We'll break their armies and then enslave the rest." He caught the flicker in her eyes. "We might even give our allies some of them as slaves. Do you have any you'd like to have?"

"Aye," she said grimly, "several." Her glance lightened and became almost soft. "One in particular, though he wouldn't be an ordinary kind of slave." Her voice was almost a sensual purr.

"You can have him," Thiazi said with a throaty chuckle. "Help us and you can avenge yourself on those who have wronged you. And I'll personally see to it you get the man you want as your slave. To do anything you desire," he added, his voice heavy with insinuation.

Lao-Kee thought for several moments, a strange smile curving her lips. Thiazi sat patiently by. Finally she nodded. "I'll help. I have an idea on how to get you past the Aesir."

She paused uncertainly for a moment and gazed at the Jotun in the circle around her. Then she made a decision and her eyes became as hard and deadly as those of a serpent. "I have another piece of information that might interest you. It's about a man on an island. Yes, it might interest you a great deal!"

Vili looked up to see the excited face of Lao-Kee. "Vili," she blurted eagerly, "I've discovered something so wonderful. . . ."

Voden's sister smiled wanly, almost surprised there was still happiness and enthusiasm left in the world since the death of Baldur. "I'm sure you have."

"Oh, Vili," the slender Jotun said, catching her friend's hands and hugging them to her chest. "Baldur is gone forever. Don't weep and mourn for as long as that. There's still beauty and joy in the world! Open your eyes! Come, I have something wondrous to show you! Come! A short ride will do you good, put some color back in your cheeks. Come!" Insistently she pulled at Vili, forcing her to rise. With a slight smile and half-hearted chuckle, Voden's sister yielded to Lao-Kee's importuning. Together they rode out of Asgard, heading east, away from the afternoon sun.

• • •

They had been spotted and Thiazi watched the Aesir coming and tried to look confident. Everyone was nervous. This damn well better work, he thought, or I'll never see the sun of Muspellheim again.

The Aesir thundered to the top of the ridge in front of them and strung themselves out along it. By Namtaru's damn list, Thiazi cursed under his breath, there must be a hundred of the shaggy bastards! He held up his hand to halt his party, then gestured to those immediately surrounding him. "Let them see her," he ordered softly. "Ride her out in front a few feet and let them see her."

Four men moved forward surrounding a fifth figure. Vili's hair was uncovered and shone golden in the morning sunlight.

For a few moments the Aesir on the ridge were silent. Then there was a great cry of outrage and they drew their swords and axes and shook them in the air in fury. Their leader rode out in front and held up his hands to calm them. When they were under control, he turned his horse and came alone down the ridge toward the group of Jotun and the men of Muspell-heim. Thiaszi rode out to meet him.

"You have Vili," the man snarled as they came within hailing distance. "Let her go, you bastard!"

Thiazi laughed. "I may well be a bastard, my hairy barbarian friend, but I'm not a fool. If any of you come any closer, even within bow range, the girl dies."

The Aesir cursed so hard Thiazi could swear the air around him grew heated. Finally, though, the man exhausted even his copious repertoire of curses and aspersions about Thiazi's parentage. He sat silent for several moments and glowered threateningly. "What in Fornjot's name do you want?"

"I want Vili to live," Thiazi said smoothly. "And she will, too, if you let us pass."

"And if I refuse?"

"Then you kill your leader's sister."

"I need time to decide," the Aesir said slyly.

"Fine," Thiazi responded. "I give you to the count of three."

"But I must talk to Voden! I must tell him—"

"You'll tell him nothing! Stand aside now or she dies! Or would you like to be the one to carry the message of Vili's death to your leader?"

For a moment the Aesir looked uncertainly from Thiazi to

Vili and back again. Then with a curse, he spun his horse and charged back up the hill. Thiazi sat quietly watching the man gesture and shout to the other men. They shouted back and argued, but in a few moments they began to sulk off in all directions. All except for one, who Thiazi saw racing off toward the west. He smiled to himself. Soon Voden would know that his sister was hostage. They would have to ride like the wind, but he felt sure they would cross the plain unscathed.

Voden paced the floor of Valholl. "How could they have gotten hold of her?"

Heimdall spoke coldly. "She was seen leaving Asgard with Lao-Kee."

Voden spun around and stared at him. "Lao-Kee? But Vili was her best friend! She loves a prank, but this——"

"Goes beyond a prank?" Heimdall finished for him. "Yes, just as taking Tror to Geirrodmir's camp did. Or as tricking Hod into killing Baldur did. I have warned you many times not to trust Hrodvitnir's half sister, Voden, but you would not listen."

"Dammit, man, we swore a blood oath!"

"Blood oath!" Tror rumbled disgustedly. "She betrayed her own brother, Voden. How much do you think a blood oath means to a woman like that?"

Voden sank onto the High Seat and buried his head in his hands. "Vili," he muttered, his voice stark with grief.

Tyr stepped forward. "We have to go after her, Voden. We have to rescue her or they'll take her with them to Muspellheim."

Voden stiffened and his head snapped up. "Of course! This is all Surt's doing! The Black One wants to use Vili against me magically! Oh, by all the gods, the man's a monster!" He jumped from the High Seat, his single eye ablaze with passion. "Tyr's right! I've got to go rescue Vili. If I don't, the consequences could be horrible."

"I'm with you!" Tyr shouted.

"I'll come too," Honir said.

They all looked at Tror and Heimdall. Tror was frowning deeply. "I think I have a different task. Yes, I think both Heimdall and I have a different task."

Heimdall nodded solemnly. "I agree. Voden, Tyr, Honir, go and try to rescue Vili.

"Tror and I will find and capture Lao-Kee."

They rode hard, harder than they had ever ridden in their lives. Even Sleipnir was almost floundered by the third day. One horse had already gone down beneath Tyr, and Honir was on his third mount. Other Aesir joined them as they went, and soon they were over two hundred strong.

When they reached the forests of the Vanir, they found a contingent of Valkyrja waiting for them. They left ten men with the horses and poured under the trees.

The majority of the Aesir were clumsy and slow in the woods, but Voden and a few others kept pace with the Valkyrja and soon were far in the lead.

As the ground began to rise, they came across fresher signs of the passage of the party from Jotunheim and Muspellheim. Voden alternately prayed to Fornjot and cursed him, demanding and pleading that they catch up with the kidnappers before they reached the safety of the passes. Although he was already almost reeling with exhaustion, he picked up their speed.

They burst out of the forest and stared wearily up the slope. There, high above them, were the black dots they pursued. Many of the men crumpled to the ground. The Valkyrja slumped against trees and rocks, gasping for breath.

Voden swayed. He lifted his arm and pointed. "There they are," he croaked. "Come on. We almost have them."

Honir moaned from where he lay. "Why do we have to catch them? Can't you just hurl some magical spell at them?"

"I could, but I don't dare," Voden replied. "I'd have to use something broad and general, especially at this distance. I'd . . . I'd be just as likely to hurt Vili as them. I'm afraid we'll have to do this the hard way."

Honir sat up and grunted with pain. "I . . . I don't think I can make the climb." But he struggled to his feet and stumbled toward Voden. Tyr rose, too, and hobbled forward. With a weary smile of gratitude, Voden acknowledged the loyalty of his friends. He turned and began climbing the slope without looking back. If he had, he would have seen the rest of the party rise, one by one, and stagger after him.

• • •

Thiazi's hands were bloody and his fingers raw as he pulled his tortured body up the last slope. This was the hardest, steepest pass, but the closest. He prayed to Nergal that the men he had posted there were still in place. If only Jormungand hasn't given us up for lost, he hoped.

The rest of his party scrambled behind. Several had given up, just in sight of salvation. The Aesir had found them and killed them as they climbed in pursuit. Thiazi looked back. Vili was right behind him, a man on either side forcing her to climb. He knew they could have traveled a lot more swiftly without her. Once the final race up the pass had begun, she was really of no use as a hostage any more. Her last value as assurance for their safe passage had been in the forests. She had kept the Valkyrja and the foresters at bay.

But now she was just an encumbrance. And yet he kept her. The men grumbled, but he was firm. She comes with us, he'd ordered. He knew they wouldn't understand why, so he didn't bother to explain. He wasn't even too sure himself. But somehow he knew, instinctively, that Vili was very important and that Surt would reward him more for her than for anything else he'd done. Vili stayed all the way to the end, and that was that. He pulled himself up another ten inches and groaned. The climb seemed to take forever.

Voden himself cut the Jotun's throat. The man had tried to defend himself, but he was too weak to put up much of a fight. Still, it had taken valuable seconds at a time when there were none to spare. The delay chaffed Voden, and he stepped over the still-twitching body to continue the climb.

He looked up. So close! Not more than a hundred yards separated him and the last of the kidnappers. He looked again and felt a chill gather around his heart. The top of the pass was only a quarter of a mile or so ahead. The climb steepened to reach it. If Thiazi and his men got there in time . . . "Faster," he grunted hoarsely. "We've got to go faster!"

Thiazi pulled himself over the top and reached back to grab Vili's wrists. He dropped her by his side and helped other men up. He was amazed to see how few had made it. Seven of his own and four of the Jotun. He looked around. In the distance he could see a body of armed men approaching on the double. He waved to them and shouted with joy. The guard! They were still there, and fully armed! In their hurry to climb, his own men had thrown away all their weapons but their knives. They couldn't hope to hold the pass against the Aesir with knives. But the guards had bows and swords and javelins!

He turned back and peered down the slope. He shook his fists and cried out. "I won, damn you all to Nergal! I won!"

Voden heard the cry and looked up. Thiazi stood, Vili by his side, armed warriors swarming around him. The newcomers had bows and were already nocking arrows to rain down on them.

Voden gestured to the others to take cover, then leapt up on a boulder where Thiazi could see him. "You've won, Thiazi. I admit you've won! So you've no use for my sister anymore. We won't pursue any farther. Set her free!"

Thiazi sneered and laughed. "Free? Why free? She has an appointment in Maqam Nifl with Surt!" He grabbed Vili by the arm and began to drag her back from the edge.

She struggled and cried out, "Voden!" She repeated the cry as she disappeared from her brother's sight, her voice filled with horror and hopelessness.

Voden screamed her name in a voice so huge it shook the very rocks of the mountain and started several small avalanches. "Vili!" he roared again and again. "Vili! Vili!"

His voice echoed back from the rocks, but that was the only response he got.

XX

LAO-KEE realized she had to find a place to hide. She knew she didn't dare return to Jotunheim. Both sides there had good reasons to wish her dead. Asaheim was clearly no place for her now either. They couldn't help but figure out who'd delivered Vili to Thiazi. Someone, probably Heimdall, would come hunting for her, intent on exacting revenge.

There was always the Western Forest, of course, but Lao-Kee was not a woodsman and knew nothing of how to survive in such a wild and primitive environment. Besides, she admitted, she wanted to be somewhere where she might catch some rumor of what was going on, of how Voden fared, of what happened to the Aesir and the Jotun. There was always a chance, she thought wistfully, that Voden—Stop fooling yourself, she chided angrily. There is no chance. Voden hates you now, just like all the others.

Could I have done anything differently? she wondered. Had there ever been any real hope? She thought of the first time she'd seen Voden. He'd come to Utgard to save his father, Borr, who'd been captured alive on the raid that had burned Asgard. Voden had hung on the tree in Nerthus's Grove in his father's place. Every day she'd crept into the grove and watched him from afar, her heart beating wildly in her breast. No other man had ever affected her that way. She wept secretly, knowing that the Aesir would die on the tree. Every night she'd broken the most scared Jotun laws and lifted up food and drink to him on a long pole. For a while he'd taken it, deliriously, unconsciously. Then he'd stopped altogether. She'd wept bitterly, sensing he was doomed.

But miraculously, Voden had survived. He'd hung for nine days and nine nights, and when the White Bear and the rest of the Trul had gone to cut down his dead body, he was waiting calmly for them by the foot of the tree.

She'd been so happy, she'd been unable to control it. She'd ridden far out on the plain and laughed and cried so that no one would see her and wonder. Then she'd done her best to convince Hrodvitnir of the value of a truce with the Aesir and the need to invite Voden to return to Utgard as a friend. When Voden had actually come, she'd nearly burst with joy.

The joy was gone now. Tears welled up in her eyes. Everything was gone now. All that was left was a bitter, aching void. And the need to find a place to hide like an animal until this blew over. If it ever did.

But where? A memory from many years ago rose in her mind. She'd been on a trading mission to the Dverg and had gotten lost. She'd turned east, knowing that if she followed the rising sun, she would soon reach the River Gopul. Then she could turn upstream and eventually return to someplace she recognized.

She'd heard the river long before she'd seen it. The air was filled with a roaring unlike anything she'd ever heard before. When she rode her horse through the last underbrush, the sight that had met her eyes had taken her breath away. The land dropped away suddenly in front of her. To the east she caught a splendid panoramic view of the forests of the Vanir. They lay spread out perhaps three hundred feet lower than the forest through which she had been traveling. At the point of the drop, which was steep and sudden, the Gopul formed a huge falls, the water tumbling down for a good two hundred feet across its entire width of perhaps one hundred yards. The air was filled with mist, and the ground trembled constantly with the thunder of the crashing water.

She'd spent a day exploring the area and had found several shallow caves in the upper face of the cliff, close to the falls. They were a bit damp, but otherwise seemed safe, comfortable, and easily defensible. She'd spent the night in one. The next morning, after a breakfast of salmon caught fresh near the base of the falls, she'd turned northward and continued her journey. The Dverg she'd traded with later told her the falls were called Franang's Falls after the Dverg who'd discovered them.

Franang's Falls would be an ideal place to hide, Lao-Kee decided. There was shelter there, and plenty of readily available food in the Gopul and in the surrounding forests. Any fool could catch it. In addition, the falls were far enough away from any habitation—Vanir, Aesir, or Dverg—that the risk of being discovered was minuscule. Yet at the same time, it would be possible to visit the Dverg for information, or perhaps even to cross the river and spy on some Vanir village.

She nodded to herself, Franang's Falls it was. Let the damn fools try to find her there!

Hrodvitnir controlled his excitement. Too many times in the past few years he'd stood here and looked off to the east, hoping to see a sail, and sometimes even believing he saw one. But it had always been the same. Nothing but the empty waters of the Amsvartnir Sea stretching off in every direction from the island of Lyngvi. No boat, no rescue.

But this time the sail had grown and grown until he'd realized it was real. When the hull of the boat had come into view, his heart had leapt into his throat and he'd felt as if he were going to burst.

Then a thought had occurred to him. Perhaps this was the Aesir, returning to do away with him completely. Or suppose the Risar had discovered where he was and were coming to rid themselves of him forever? So he'd hidden close to the shoreline in order to see who stepped from the boat when it finally ground its keel ashore.

The Jotun who'd waded onto Lyngvi were from all four of the clans. And with them was a man like no other Hrodvitnir had ever seen. A man with skin the color of night, and hair to match. The final person to step onto the island had been the White Bear himself.

Hrodvitnir stepped from behind the tree that had hidden him and stood in plain sight. He held his head high and proud and placed his fists on his hips.

It was a few moments before any of the visitors sighted him. Then the White Bear spotted the Jotun dressed all in skins, and cried out in a great voice, "Praised be Gymir! Praised be Nerthus! Our Warlord lives!" The others turned to follow his pointing arm. When they saw Hrodvitnir, they stood for a moment in awe. Then with a cheer, they rushed forward to surround him, their faces split from ear to ear with undisguised joy.

The black-skinned one stood by calmly and watched, a slight smile arching his full lips. He seemed almost as pleased as the Jotun.

Tror grumbled and shook his head. "Not a damn trace of the bitch. We know she didn't head north. Or east. She may have gone south into the forests of the Vanir. We've alerted the foresters and the Valkyrja."

"Or," Heimdall said, "more likely, she may have gone west."

"If she went into the Western Forest," Tror complained, "we've lost her for sure."

"If she went into the Western Forest," Voden replied, "she's dead for sure. She'd never survive there. At least not through the winter. Somehow, though, I think she's closer than that."

"Could you use magic to locate her?" Tyr asked.

"I've already tried," Voden answered. "I needed something personal of hers. She must have thought of that, because she left nothing behind."

"She always traveled light, just like a Jotun," Tror grumbled. "It's no surprise she didn't leave anything behind. Did the magic tell you anything?"

Voden nodded. "I couldn't do anything really powerful without something of hers, but I did get a very strong sense she isn't all that far away. A couple of days ride at the most."

Tror leaned forward in interest. "Any directions?"

The leader of the Aesir frowned. "Confusing ones. Setting sun and rising sun. Water and rock. Trees. Loud noises. Trembling ground. Cave. I couldn't make much sense of it all. No coherency."

Heimdall looked thoughtful. "Water and rock. Loud noises and trembling ground. Interesting." He paused as if considering. "Perhaps," he said, "we should consult the Dverg. They know many things. And Lao-Kee has moved among them fairly often. She is known by them, and most importantly, disliked by them."

"Ask the Dverg?" Tror snorted. "As soon ask the stones. The Dverg may not like Lao-Kee, but Fornjot knows they don't exactly love us either. I can't imagine they'd be willing to tell us which way was down."

Voden was looking at Heimdall. "You may have something there. Tror's right about the Dverg not being our friends, but they always respond to one form of reasoning."

Heimdall nodded. "Yes. Gold."

Voden smiled. "Take all you need. Go and see what you can find out. What the Dverg won't do to help us, they might do to harm Lao-Kee. For a healthy profit, of course."

"Khamuas, the Keri Heb of the Svartalfar, has pledged his support. He will strike from the east when we give the word. We will attack from the south. If you join us and pour over the Iving from the north, we'll have the Aesir surrounded. We will trap the Aesir between us and smash them." Thiazi finished and sat back, looking slowly around the circle seated in the lodge, trying to judge the effects of his speech from the looks on their faces. Damn, but they don't show a thing, he thought.

An old man to his left made a slight motion with his hand, and Hrodvitnir nodded in his direction. "Huh," the old man grunted, "I have heard many words here from the one with the black skin. He says we can crush the Aesir. All well and good. But it is not only the Aesir we must crush. There are the Vanir too. And the Alfar, who have pledged their aid to Voden.

"You say you will sweep north and strike the Aesir from the south. But you must cross the Smoking Lands to do that. And more importantly, you must pass through the forests of the Vanir. Tell me how you will do that."

Thiazi sighed. He had feared this question. Both he and Jormungand had advised Surt it would be asked. The Black One had just smiled and handed Thiazi a branch. "When the time comes," he had said, "tell them this is how we will pass through the forests. Just don't get frightened by what happens, and drop it. That won't make a very good impression."

Thiazi picked the branch up now and held it out to the circle. "Crossing the Smoking Lands is hard, but it can be done. I have done it ten times." A chorus of grunts met his claims. "As for the forests, Surt, the Ellilutu of Muspellheim, has bid me show you this. And to tell you he will bear the Bane of Forests before him when he comes."

As he completed his words, the branch he held suddenly burst into flame with a whoosh. Despite Surt's warning, Thiazi almost dropped it. The Jotun reacted with explosive shouts of wonder and fear. The branch burned fiercely. Thiazi held it up for a few moments and then tossed it into the fire in the center of the circle. He sat back silently.

Hrodvitnir nodded. "So. You will burn the Vanir out of their trees, eh? A very wise plan. Your master, this Black One, is a mighty wizard, no?" Thiazi nodded. "Hmmmm. Then he can do this thing?" Again the man from Muspellheim nodded.

The Warlord of the Jotun Horde closed his eyes. For endless minutes he sat unmoving. Thiazi did his best to contain his impatience. This council had been going on for three days! Would these damn Jotun never decide?

Hrodvitnir opened his eyes again and gazed around the circle. He met each man's eyes briefly before moving on to the next. Finally he stopped at one gray-haired old Jotun whose hawklike face was set in a permanent scowl. His lips were tightly compressed, as if holding in great pain. Hrodvitnir bowed his head slightly to the man as a mark of respect. "We have not heard from Loddfafnir, wisest of all the Risar. We would know his mind."

Loddfafnir looked around the circle slowly, his eyes as pitiless and piercing as those of a bird of prey. His voice was soft as he began to speak. "Long have we of the Risar resisted the ascension of Hrodvitnir-Fenrir to the position of Warlord of the Horde. I was one of his most bitter opponents."

His voice grew in strength. "But then he disappeared, victim of a foul Aesir plot, and I realized something. While we here in Jotunheim fought among ourselves, our enemies across the Iving were waxing strong and stronger. They murdered our women and children without compunction, and even dared strike directly against some of our strongest men, like Hrungnir and Geirrodmir and his whole camp. We had great need of a leader to pull us together or the Aesir would eventually slaughter us separately.

"So I went to Lyngvi with Thiazi and the others to bring Hrodvitnir-Fenrir back to Utgard so that he might become our Warlord. My individual feelings had to yield to the greater needs of the Jotun." There were grunts of approval at his words.

"Yet is that enough, I ask myself? If we had even a handful of years, we could be ready for anything. But do we have that long? As I look southward across the Iving, I see the Aesir and the Vanir and the Alfar banding together and becoming stronger than ever! Three people against one! For there can be no other reason for what they do than to attack and destroy the Sons of Ymir!" They shouted their agreement, angrily shaking their fists in the air.

"Could we stand against such might? Even united in one Horde? Possibly, yes. But how much Jotun blood would water the grass of the plains to defeat them? How many of our young men would lie down on the field of battle, never to rise again, never to raise the love flute to their lips and trill songs to their chosen ones?" Murmurs of concern ran around the circle, making the air tremble.

"Now Thiazi comes and tells us of his plan. It is a dangerous one. But is it any more dangerous than facing the Aesir on our own? I say ride with Thiazi and his master Surt, the Black One! I say death to the Aesir!" They roared their approval, beating their open palms on the ground.

Hrodvitnir smiled so slightly, Thiazi wasn't even sure he saw it. The Warlord nodded once to Loddfafnir and continued his circuit around the circle of men. He gazed at each one for a moment, held their eyes just long enough to read their feelings, and then moved on to the next.

When he had completed the circuit, without a word being spoken by anyone else, he nodded and fixed Thiazi with a penetrating stare. "We have decided," he said with deceptive softness. "We will join you. We will help you destroy Voden and the Aesir."

In the midst of the wild whooping that followed these words, Thiazi sat smiling broadly. At long last they would fight!

They heard the roar of the river long before they reached it. When the vista opened out in front of them, they were stunned at the beauty of it and sat for several moments, drinking it in.

"I almost wish we were here just to enjoy the view," Tror said sadly. He sighed and motioned to Kvasir. "Snoop around and see what you can find. The rest of us will dismount and wait here out of sight. And keep a sharp lookout. Lao-Kee's both clever and dangerous." Kvasir nodded and dismounted. With a quick look around, he moved swiftly and smoothly toward Franang's Falls.

Within an hour he was back, his expression serious. He walked up to Tror and Heimdall and held something out toward them. Heimdall took it from his hands. "A net," he said, "for catching salmon."

Kvasir nodded. "Aye. I found it in one of the caves on the face of the cliff. The way's steep, but it can be negotiated if one goes slowly and carefully. There were fire scars on the floor of the cave. And one pile of ashes was still warm."

Tror sighed. "It has to be her, Heimdall. Those Dverg said they thought someone was living here and that it might be her."

Heimdall was still looking down at the net. He raised his eyes to meet Tror's gaze. "What now?" he asked.

Tror mulled for a moment. "We'll split up. You stay here with Kvasir and one other. I'll go with the other two to the bottom of the falls. We'll scour the woods down there and attempt to flush her out if she's lurking somewhere. If we don't find her, we'll hide and wait until she comes back. Then we'll jump out and catch her the way she catches salmon."

"Best catch her before she gets back to her cave," Kvasir advised. "She could defend it very easily against far more than six men." He looked around uneasily. "I've seen her throw those knives of hers, and I'd not want to be hanging out there on that cliff as a target for her. It might be easier if—"

Tror scowled. "I want her alive, Kvasir. Remember that, all of you, *I want her alive*."

The only light in the cave came from a strange, cold, greenish phosphorescence on the walls. The three stood in a circle facing each other, their hoods drawn far forward.

"A rather damp and dreary meeting place," Enki complained. "I much preferred the other. I've always been more partial to mountaintops than to their roots."

"This is more secure," Innina murmured. "Surt's minions are everywhere. The air is full of them. No word spoken in any place where daylight ever reaches is safe from his ears."

"What words do you have that are so important, then?" Enki asked sarcastically.

Innina turned and gestured for Marduk to speak. "I've contacted those in the army still loyal to me," Marduk said. "They chaff under the yoke of this upstart Jormungand. He's a harsh master. Very demanding. Drills them endlessly. Beats or executes any who shirk. If we raise the standard of rebellion, they'll join us instantly."

Enki sneered. "Wonderful. What would the odds against us be, Marduk? Ten to one? A hundred to one? Don't be fooled by your grumbling friends. Jormungand is a very competent commander. Most of his men adore him and would fight to the death for him. Raise the standard of rebellion? Ha! Do so and you'll raise yourself as high as the nearest gibbet!" He directed his gaze from the grumbling Marduk to Innina. "I hope you have more to say for yourself than this fool."

Innina was silent for a moment. "More to say? Yes, I have more to say." There was a slight edge of anger to her voice. "First I will say you judge Marduk wrongly. He is not fool enough to blithely raise the cry for rebellion in the quiet of peace. Such a cry must wait for exactly the right moment, and then it will be a thunderous clarion call."

Enki scoffed. "Just the right moment? Of course! Why didn't I think of that? And when will this right moment be? In a few thousand sars, when Surt is old and feeble?"

"It will be," Innina hissed, "when he is least expecting it, when his attention is directed toward something totally absorbing. It will be when he is vulnerable. And it will be soon!"

"Soon?" Enki yawned with theatrical boredom. "How soon?"

"When the sun reaches its highest point in the northern sky, then the battle with be joined. It will be a battle such as has not been seen since the last days of the First Dark Empire."

Enki blinked and shifted uneasily. "How do you know this?"

Innina smiled slowly. "I have been to see Utu."

"Utu," Enki said with a sharp intake of breath. "He . . . you consulted the *Baru*? But . . . but Utu never lets anyone . . ." His voice trailed off in dismay as he saw her smile widen.

"Never before. But for certain . . . services . . . he was willing this time. And I say Surt will be vulnerable at the height of that battle. Even more so in the instant he wins it. If he wins.

"I have readied my allies in anticipation of that instant. Marduk has rallied his friends. We expect you to do the same with the demons you control.

"Then, fully armed and ready, we will wait for the moment, the exact moment, to strike!"

Something seemed out of place. Lao-Kee stopped and looked around carefully. Dusk was beginning to fall, and she was returning after a day of checking her rabbit traps in the forest. She carried four fat bucks, two slung over each shoulder. They would make a stew that would warm her and fill her for two or three days.

After peering into the gathering gloom for several minutes without sensing anything else, she shrugged and began to walk toward the base of the falls again. She kept her eyes moving, searching the forest for any sign of movement, especially since the roar of the falls would have made it impossible to hear an army approaching.

She reached the base of the cliff and settled her load before she began the climb to her cave. Then she saw it. A footprint in the wet soil. A big footprint, easily as big as . . .

With a yelp of recognition she began to scramble up the cliff. She cast a quick glance over her shoulder, already knowing who she would see. Tror was racing from the forest, his hands reaching out to grab her. Two other men sped in his wake.

She climbed for all she was worth, throwing caution to the winds. Tror was right behind her. If only I can get to my cave, she thought, I can hold them off.

Being smaller and lighter, she was better able to scramble up the steep slope. She decided on a desperate strategy, hoping to lose at least one of her attackers. She moved closer to the falls, where the footing was sodden, more treacherous, and more likely to give way under the weight of someone larger than herself. She prayed fervently to Nerthus that the slippery, crumbly rocks would hold her and dump the others into the swirling waters.

Higher and higher she climbed. She glanced back over her shoulder and saw that Tror was still hot on her trail. In shock, she realized that he had actually gained a little!

Suddenly afraid, she lunged for a handhold and missed. At the same instant, Tror made a huge effort and surged up to grab her by the ankle. She was unbalanced and scrambled wildly to gain a purchase on the face of the cliff. Pieces of rotten rocks came off in her hands and she felt herself beginning to fall.

Tror realized what was happening and tried to get a firmer grip on her ankle. His hands were wet and covered with the claylike soil that was part of the cliff face.

Lao-Kee screamed, "Nerthus! Help me!" and fell. Tror tried to hold on with all his might, but the pull and wrench was too much for his grip, and Lao-Kee slipped from between his fingers. He almost lost his own footing making a last wild attempt to grab her as she tumbled past. He watched in horror as she hit the water of the falls and disappeared.

For long moments he clung to the face of the cliff, trying to see where the raging water had swept her. It was difficult to tell, because the mist from the falls kept getting into his eyes and blinding him.

Voden, Tyr, Honir, Frey, Freyja, Hild, Rota, and Yngvi stood around the table and ran their eyes over the map that lay on its top. "There and there," the head of the Valkyrja said, pointing, "are the best places to hold them. The area is known as Mirkwood. They already have control of the heads of both passes. But Yngvi's men know of a track that goes around here and comes out in their rear. I'll keep them occupied while he and the foresters will take them from behind. It's tricky, but it might work."

"We can't take too many men over the track, Voden," Yngvi explained. "It's much too steep and narrow for an army. But if a good number of us suddenly appear in their rear, we may stun them enough to break their lines and force their retreat."

Voden looked at him with a stern glance. "It's dangerous, Yngvi. If they don't break . . ." He paused. "How many men will you need? And who?"

"I'll take fifty of my best foresters. And Rota will be leading a picked group of about fifty Valkyrja."

"Harbard will lead the rest of the foresters to support you against the Jotun," Yngvi continued. "We're putting all the lads that fought with the Aesir during the truce period in that group. They know the Jotun and have experience fighting them.'' Finishing his part of the report, he nodded to Frey, who was Voden's minister to the Alfar.

''The Alfar,'' Frey said, ''will fight with Hild's forces. I'll lead them. We fight best in the forest, Voden. I fear we wouldn't be much use against the Jotun.''

Voden nodded. ''From the way the Jotun are massing, we expect them to try crossing the Iving in two places. The biggest assault will be at Bifrosti's Ford, as usual. But we think they're also going to attempt a breakthrough to the east of Fimbulthul. I'll be here at the ford. Tyr and Tror, when he gets back, will lead the group to the east of the Fimbulthul.''

He looked around the group. Every countenance was serious. ''Are there any questions?''

''Aye,'' Tyr said slowly, ''what of the Svartalfar? We've been hearing rumors Khamuas has allied himself with Surt and will strike from the west.''

Voden nodded and smiled slightly, as if amused. ''Ah, yes. The attack from the west. Someone came in last night who can tell us more of the doings of the Svartalfar.'' Voden turned toward the door to his private quarters. ''Anhur,'' he called out, ''come enlighten us.''

The Svartalfar came out from behind the door, a grin on his face, enjoying the stir his sudden and unexpected appearance had caused. ''Enlighten you, indeed!'' he crowed. ''Horus is back!'' The exclamations from the group almost drowned out his next words. ''And all of Svartalfheim is in an uproar.

''Ah, if only the old Yellow Robe were still here,'' he complained, ''how he would love to talk to Horus! The rightful Keri Heb of the Svartalfar has almost as much to say as Kao-Shir did, though it makes a good bit better sense than that old man's stuff and nonsense!''

Tyr and all the rest of them looked puzzled but relieved. ''Exactly what's going on?'' the one-handed Aesir asked.

''The followers of Khamuas are on the defensive already! They've retreated into Ro-Setau after a rather bad mauling outside the walls of the city.''

''Will you be able to send us any help to fight the Jotun or the men from Muspellheim?'' Yngvi asked hopefully.

''Ummmm,'' Anhur stalled, ''well, uh, I guess not, really. Uh, Khamuas is on the defensive, to be sure. But, ummm, in all honesty, we have everything we can do to keep him bottled up in Ro-Setau." His face became grave. "We . . . we're fighting a very bitter war, my friends. Very bitter, for it's brother against brother." He paused and looked down at the floor. "Truly," he said softly, "many Ba will be seeking Aalu."

He looked up again and tried to speak several times before he was able. "I fear . . . perhaps . . . ah, but this . . . this may be the end of the Svartalfar." His gaze became suddenly fierce and proud, and he glared defiantly around him. "But if we destroy ourselves in destroying the evil of Khamuas, then so be it! His vileness has stained Yggdrasil for too long as it is!"

Voden bowed his head so no one could see the troubled expression in his eye. "Aye," he whispered, "so be it."

Jormungand stood in front of Surt, his armor splendid. "We're ready, Black One."

Surt rubbed his hands with evident glee. "Good, good! And I have prepared my allies as well. Zu is eager to spread death and destruction northward. And the Bane of Forests is ready to hand. Yes! Borr's people are about to feel the wrath of Surt!"

Jormungand sighed. "Look, Surt, can't we think this over again? I mean, why go all the way up into that Igigi-forsaken country just to slaughter a bunch of hairy barbarians? And not to mention get quite a few of our own men slaughtered while we're at it. Why not stay here at home and enjoy being the Ellilutu? Why not—"

The Black One swelled with rage. "Enough!" he screamed, "I won't hear any more of this . . . this . . . ."

"Damn it, Surt, it doesn't make any sense! I can understand your being angry at Borr." He reached up and touched the place where the Aesir's ax had sliced off his ear. "I'd have liked to settle my score with him too. But he's dead now. What's the point anymore?"

"The point is that I cursed the Aesir and all his people," Surt replied, his voice rising rapidly toward the hysterical. "The point is that as I lay dying on the Vigrid I had to call on Nergal! The point is that—"

"The point," Jormungand interrupted harshly, "is that you're crazy! You're so damn obsessed with your revenge that you're missing things that are right under your nose!"

Surt forced calm on himself. "Under my nose? What do you mean, faithful Serpent?"

Jormungand gave his master a sour glance. "Now it's 'faithful Serpent' again, eh?" he muttered. "All right," he continued in a normal tone, "I'll tell you what I mean. Marduk's back, Surt, did you know that? And so is Innina. And that bastard Marduk has been trying to suborn the old officers from his army. They're up to something, and we're turning our backs on them to march up north and kill shaggy barbarians!"

The slender wizard stood thoughtfully for several moments. "Marduk and Innina, eh? And no doubt Enki as well."

As he seemed about to say something, a strange thing happened. His expression changed from thoughtfulness to suspicion and he glared suddenly at Jormungang. "So," he hissed angrily, "you are trying to trick me, are you?"

The giant black warrior was nonplussed. "Trick . . . what are you babbling about?"

"This nonsense about Marduk and Innina!" Surt shouted. "You're trying to divert my attention from the Aesir and my revenge! Damn Marduk and Innina to Aralu! I don't care if they've returned. I don't care if ten like them have returned! My power is absolute, utter, complete! They can do nothing to stop me! No one can!" His voice dropped from a shriek to a mutter. "No one can stop me, no one. No one."

Jormungand stood watching Surt for several moments. The slender wizard was so wrapped up in thoughts of his revenge that he had clearly forgotten Jormungand was there. With a sigh and a shrug, the giant warrior turned and left the room.

Tror tenderly laid the body on the table. "She . . . she slipped. I tried to grab her. By Fornjot, I tried! I almost went in myself. I . . ." His voice failed him and he stopped, gazing silently down at Lao-Kee's still form.

"She drowned in the falls," Heimdall said matter-of-factly. "We found her floating face down about two miles below the falls in a backwater of the river. She never had a chance."

"Never had a chance," Voden echoed gently, his voice cracking slightly. "No, she never had a chance."

THREE COCKS
CROWING

XXI

~~~~~~

THE view from the head of the pass was magnificent. To left and right the jumbled, volcanic chaos of the mountains stretched off as far as the eye could see, stark black and gray on stark black and gray. To the north, though, everything was a dense, vibrant green, beginning to turn red and golden at the first touch of fall. In the far distance, just beyond the edge of perception, was a sense of vast, open plains rolling off endlessly toward the diamondlike glare of the Icerealm.

Neither of them had ever seen anything like it. The huge one sat his horse in easy wonder, his eyes bright with excitement. The slender one's eyes were shining as well, but the light that glowed from them had a hellish gleam and seemed to smoke with dark desire.

Jormungand sighed. "Fantastic. I never realized how . . . how *brown* Muspellheim is. All this green is so . . . so alive. I wonder if our land was like this before the fall of the First Dark Empire?" He looked at Surt out of the corner of his eyes. "Do you really have to use the Bane of Forests, Surt? I mean, to destroy all this . . ." He swept an arm at the horizon.

The slender wizard shrugged. "Trees, bushes, animals, nothing important. The important thing is that our enemies will use the forest to hide in, to attack from. It is a weapon in their hands. We must destroy that weapon."

The giant warrior sighed. "I know, I know, but still . . . so much beauty . . ."

Surt scowled. "It will grow back," he said, his voice harsh.

"Like it did in Muspellheim?" Jormungand replied quietly. "Some things may never come back, Surt. Once they're gone, they're gone for good."

"Then other things will replace them," the Black One snarled. "The strong, the worthy survive. Nergal take the rest!" He jerked his horse's head around. "Come, Serpent, we waste time."

Jormungand took one last look and nodded sadly. "Aye, we waste time. Yet still," he murmured to himself, "it is beautiful." He turned his horse until he was facing his trumpeter, a small man dressed in the rust-red uniform of the elite corps. "Sound advance, Vidofnur. And crow loudly, my little cock, for you must wake the Lord of Hosts and all the demons of the Kur!"

Hrodvitnir-Fenrir, Warlord of the Jotun Horde, sat on his horse, the fur on his wolf-pelt cape stirring restlessly in the predawn breeze that swept across the grasslands. Loddfafnir was on his right, the White Bear on his left. Just the other side of Loddfafnir, the strange black man from Muspellheim, Thiazi, sat glancing looking around at the silent Jotun host.

Hrodvitnir and Loddfafnir gazed southward, across the dark ribbon of the Iving. The White Bear looked east, awaiting the first glint of the eye of Gymir. Around them men's eyes were almost equally divided between the two directions. The only sounds were the occasional snort of a horse and the creaking of leather.

"Gymir comes," the white bear said softly without turning his head. "Ready yourselves."

Loddfafnir shot a quick glance at Hrodvitnir. "Will it work?"

The Warlord of the Jotun Horde shrugged. "The mass of them, led by Voden, guards Bifrosti's Ford. Across from them are many fires, indicating many warriors. Last night, if their guards crept across to scout, they saw all those warriors seated or sleeping around their fires. This morning as they look north through the rainbow that the mist and the rising sun will create over the ford, they'll see masses of warriors. They have no reason to shift troops to the east."

Loddfafnir chuckled. "Ha! Dummies around the fire, dummies mounted on horseback! A strong contingent of real men, plenty to keep Voden and his troops busy holding the ford.

But the real warriors, the main force here! It is a good plan, Hrodvitnir!'' He paused. ''May I ask a favor?''

Hrodvitnir smiled slightly and nodded. Loddfafnir bowed his head briefly in response, then raised his eyes to the Warlord's and said, ''My youngest son, the child of my old age, Fjalar, over there in the red cape, fights for his first time. I would ask that he be allowed the honor of blowing the Lur-horn to sound the advance.''

The Warlord of the Horde glanced at the White Bear. The leader of the Trul nodded almost imperceptibly. Hrodvitnir considered. It would be good to cement his relations with the Risar as thoroughly as possible. Giving Fjalar this honor would help bind Loddfafnir to him more firmly than ever. ''Call your youngest son, my friend,'' he said with a smile, ''and we shall see if his lungs are strong enough to blow down a world. He shall be our cock to greet the morn as Gymnir's Eye breaks free of the night and sends us south to victory!''

Voden sat his horse, his spear Gungnir gripped tightly in his right hand, and stared through the mists of Bifrosti's Ford to the dark shapes that lined the opposite shore of the Iving. Something didn't feel right. He shook his head, as if to shake off some worry that clung to his hood.

He turned to his right. Harbard sat there uncomfortably, unused to riding a horse. Voden grinned slightly. The forester never felt at home in the wide-open spaces of Asaheim. He preferred closer horizons and trees around him. He was a good man, though. One of the ones Voden knew he could count on.

The leader of the Aesir glanced to his left, toward the Himinborg. Heimdall was up there, ready to signal them as soon as he saw the Jotun begin to move. Today, Voden thought, we'll stop them on the very banks of the river. Usually we let them cross and then attack. Not this time. We'll hit them hard while they're still in the water. He ground his teeth in anger. The fewer of them that even set foot in Asaheim, the better! Let their blood pollute the river rather than the land of the Aesir!

He wondered how Tror and Tyr were doing off on the other side of the Fimbulthul. By the number of Jotun camp fires the last two nights, and by the number of dim shapes mounted and ready to attack on the other side of the Iving, he estimated that the group that faced his two friends was smaller than originally anticipated. Well, he thought, when they finish with them, they have instructions to join us here. It would be good to have a flank attack sometime this afternoon. We've broken them that way before.

He looked north again. I wonder which of those blobs is Hrodvitnir? Voden felt a strange thrill as he thought of the Jotun Warlord. We're destined to fight, he realized, and only one of us will survive the combat. I wonder who?

Gullinkambi rode up next to him, his golden helm gleaming softly in the predawn light. The man was a bit of a cockscomb, and especially loved gold ornaments. It didn't really matter, though, for he was one of the strongest fighters among the Einherjar. He carried his war trumpet with him. Stopping next to Voden's horse, he bowed his head. "I'm ready to sound the charge, Voden."

Voden smiled slightly. "Wait until you hear Heimdall's signal. When he sees the Jotun move, he'll give a blast on his Gjallarhorn. He's way up in the Himinborg, but we'll still be able to hear it."

"I'll blow for all I'm worth when I hear the Gjallarhorn, then!" Gullinkambi said with a wide grin. "I'll blow so hard the rising sun will think I'm a giant cock calling out a greeting! I'll blow so hard that Fornjot's ice hall will quake and Sigfod himself will sit bolt upright, wakened from his slumber! He'll leap into his armor and race to be here with us!"

Voden laughed. "We can use him! We need every good sword hand we can get to work the wolf's feast!"

"No worry, there. There'll be plenty for the wolves to feed on come nightfall," Harbard growled. "Just pray that Audhumla wills that we won't be invited to the feast ourselves!"

Voden laughed, but a sudden chill swept up his spine. Damn, he thought again, something doesn't seem right.

At the moment the sounds of a distant horn came drifting down to them from the tops of the Himinborg. Voden turned to Gullinkambi and nodded curtly. "Blow the attack!"

It was beginning. And ending.

The Valkyrja was dirty, torn, wounded, and exhausted. She slumped, tried to stand erect while she delivered her report, then slumped again. "We . . . we met them at the edge of the forest, before they were expecting us. Their whole first line went down under a shower of spears. Then we closed in, hand to hand. They aren't very good at that. We decimated them." She coughed. "Lost a few of our own too." She paused to accept a canteen of water from Frey. "Ah, good." Her voice grew stronger. "Then their second line hit us. Too much. We fought as hard as we could, but had to drop back. They fight damn well in the open. Form a shield wall and advance behind it. They have short swords and jab out from behind the shield with them. Archers stand behind the line and fill the air with arrows."

She paused, her eyes haunted, coughed a few more times, took a long sip of water, and then continued. "We made them pay for every foot, but slowly they forced us back into the forest. We broke and fled before them." She grinned at Yngvi. "As you said they would, they charged after us. Your foresters took them on the flanks and we turned around at the same time." She laughed but was cut off as it changed to a cough. A little bit of blood trickled out of the corner of her mouth. She sagged again, and another Valkyrja stepped next to her to help support her. She nodded her thanks.

"We smashed them," she said with quiet satisfaction. Then her eyes became clouded. "By that time there wasn't much left of my original command, so I folded my survivors into other units."

"That was the point at which their main body arrived. By the Vettir! They swarm like insects! They poured toward us, the whole slope black with them! It shook us to see so many, but we held firm against their first shock." Her face became sad, "But there were so many of them.

"We . . . we held and then faltered. And then began to pull back, hoping to draw them deeper into the forest, deep enough so that the trees could swallow their entire army and Yngvi and his men could creep around behind and attack."

She paused, and her face became frightened and desolate. "Then . . . it happened. The . . . the *things*"—she shuddered—"came out of nowhere. They . . . they were horrible! And they . . . everything they touched burst into flame!" Her voice rose, an edge of hysteria creeping in and replacing her attempt at military crispness and calm. "The whole forest is on fire! It's . . . it's sweeping this way! We'll all be burned to death!''

Hild turned to look at Yngvi and Frey, her face drawn and pale. "They've fired the forest! Dear Audhumla, the forest! How could anyone . . ." Her voice ran down, choked off by horror.

The leader of the foresters frowned. He was pale himself. To fire the forest was the most sacrilegious act imaginable. Wanton destruction of the Vettir! He shook himself. Can't let horror overcome me, he silently commanded. Must keep control, think, act. He looked at the Valkyrja. "The fire is sweeping this way?"

The woman warrior nodded miserably. "Yes. We . . . we fled before it. We . . . we could hear the Vettir screaming . . . we . . . it was horrible!"

"What are we going to do?" Hild said, gazing at Yngvi with stunned and helpless eyes.

Yngvi tried to think. His mind and body felt numb, paralyzed. The forest was on fire! He felt a hand on his arm and turned his head to meet Frey's eyes. The man's face was grim, but something gleamed in his eyes that suddenly gave Yngvi hope. "You have an idea?" he croaked.

Frey nodded. "A terrible idea. If the forest burns, it's because the gods will it. If the Vettir are destroyed in the fire, it's because the gods will it. But if we're destroyed with the forest, it's because we're fools.''

"But what can we do? We can't stop the fire! It's too huge," the Valkyrja wailed. "Some of us tried. They . . . they burned to death." She hid her face in her hands. "Horrible. Horrible.''

Frey's face was determined. He turned to Yngvi and Hild. "I, too, love and revere the forest, as one born to the Vanir. But I've been with the Aesir so long that I'm both more and less than a Vanir. I was educated among the Aesir and have lived in Alfheim. I . . . I see things differently now. So I . . ." He paused and drew himself up to his full height. His face took on the look of a king about to give a command that could not be denied. "Warn the villages to the north and west as far as the Svol. Tell them to get out, every last one of them, and head to the other side of the Svol or into the Aesir Plain.

"And then," Frey continued, his voice stern, "we'll set our own fires!"

They all gasped in renewed horror. But Frey remained firm, his eyes holding them all under his control. "We'll start our own fires, then move into the burnt area to wait for the invaders. Their fires will die when they reach the area we've already burnt. We won't be able to save the forest, but we will save our army. *And we will stop theirs*!"

Voden knew what was wrong. He'd ranged through the battle, riding back and forth across the line, searching, searching for the wolf's-head helmet and shaggy cloak of Hrodvitnir. If I can engage the Warlord of the Jotun Horde, if I can kill him, it will break their fury, weaken their bravery, he'd thought. Perhaps we can throw them back more quickly that way and save many Aesir lives.

But wherever he'd gone, wherever he'd looked through the rising dust of the battle, he'd failed to catch sight of Hrodvitnir. Which could only mean one thing. Hrodvitnir was not here. And if he was not here, that meant this was not the main thrust of the Jotun.

A deep chill gripped his heart. He called several of his Einherjar to him. Harbard heard the call and came too. They crowded around, eager to do his bidding. Honir was among them, frowning, his sword bloody, his shield in tatters.

Voden looked into his friend's eyes. Honir looked back into his single eye. "There aren't enough of them," Voden said quietly. Honir nodded his agreement. "The main body must be facing Tror and Tyr. We've got to send reinforcements!" He gestured to Harbard. "You and the Vanir stay here. Keep a third of the Aesir with you. Hold the ford at all costs. If it falls, retreat to Asgard and fight from the walls."

"Where are you going?" Harbard asked, already guessing.

"I ride to help Tror. The Einherjar come with me. The main body, with Hrodvitnir at its head, is attacking on the other side of the Fimbulthul!"

Tror and Tyr stood side by side. It was late afternoon and the fighting had been going on all day. Tror was spattered from head to foot with mashed brains and clotted blood. Some of the blood was his own, oozing from more than a dozen wounds. Tyr, as he could see from the corners of his eyes, looked the same.

Mjollnir hummed in a great arc, shattering anything that came within reach. Mouths opened in agony, eyes bulged in pain. But Tror could hear nothing above the endless, undifferentiated roar of the battle. It sounded like a single monster, howling with a thousand voices, each out of tune with and grating against the next.

He no longer knew who he fought, who he killed, how many, how long. There was nothing to know. There was only swinging Mjollnir back and forth, smashing, crushing, destroying. If a shattered face was swept away, a new one took its place instantly, and he shattered that one too.

Pain had fled a long time ago. He was beyond it now, in a realm where everything was dulled. The throb was there, just below the surface. It might come back at any moment. If it did, he knew it would overwhelm him and fell him like a lightning-struck tree.

He was dimly amazed he was still standing. A good dozen arrows hung from his body. He had pulled out a half dozen more. The only reason he didn't have twenty, fifty, a hundred more in him, was because the Jotun had simply run out.

Bodies were strewn everywhere. Here and there one of them moved, waved a hand in the air, sat up and gaped blearily around. Most were still, and would be that way for all eternity.

Where, he wondered wearily, is the glory of battle, the thrill of combat? Here there is nothing but the grinding strain of swinging Mjollnir back and forth, back and forth.

We still stand, Voden, he thought. Nine-tenths dead, but we still stand and deny them their crossing. So many of them, so many. Too many to kill all of them. Too many.

He heard a sudden swelling roar and knew what it meant. The line on the right had finally buckled. The Jotun were through. Now they would surround the left flank and attack from all sides. He smiled grimly, exhaustedly. It was only a matter of time now. Only a matter of time until he could put Mjollnir down. Until he could lie down himself. Will I see you, Father, in Fornjot's icy hall? Are you his smith, Volund?

They slammed into the Jotun just as they had closed their circle around the few remaining Aesir. Voden saw Hrodvitnir in the distance and tried to make his way toward the wolf's-head helmet. He roared with frustration and anger, striking about him wildly with Gungnir, stabbing and slashing the Jotun in his path.

The Jotun reeled back, and Hrodvitnir was borne away from him in the press. Voden changed his direction and pushed toward Tror and Tyr, who stood side by side, finishing the few Jotun who remained in their front.

"Thought you'd never figure it out," Tror grunted as Voden vaulted from his horse and ran to grab his friend by the shoulders. "Had to do all the work ourselves while you dallied around at the ford."

Voden laughed with relief. "Still alive, old red-beard! And Tyr too! By Sigfod, your one hand is better than most men's two!"

"Aye," Tyr grinned weakly, "though it's a very tired hand right now, I'll tell you."

Voden ran an appraising eye over the two men's bodies. "How much of that blood is yours?" he asked, only half jesting.

"Enough," Tror answered slowly. "If it were much more, we'd be—"

A roar interrupted him, and Voden spun around to see what had happened. Honir came riding through the press. "Voden, Voden!" he cried. "Hrodvitnir's around the right! He's heading south!"

Voden stood and blinked for a second in dismay. South? Why would the Jotun retreat south? Jotunheim was north, back across the Iving. There was nothing to the south but the Aesir Plain and—By Fornjot! he suddenly realized, nothing but the plain, and at its other end, the Vanir facing Surt's forces! If Hrodvitnir struck from behind . . . or if he joined forces with the men from Muspellheim . . . !

The leader of the Aesir had long ago realized he had the best position strategically. He held interior lines and could shift his men around to protect them more readily. Surt and his allies were on the outside, broken up into separate units that couldn't combine to exert maximum force because the enemy lay between them. But if Hrodvitnir was successful in breaking through and joining with Surt in the south, they could easily crush the Vanir and then turn, united, against the Aesir.

He looked around him and saw that Tror, Tyr, and Honir all had the same realization. "We've got to stop him," Tror breathed.

Tyr laughed bitterly. "How? At best we can follow him, dog his footsteps. We don't have out full forces here. We'd need those left at the ford to be able to offer a pitched battle and have any real hopes of beating him. By Sigfod, Tror, you saw how many Jotun he brought with him! They still outnumber us, even with the men Voden brought."

"Somebody's got to warn Hild and Yngvi," Honir offered. "If the Jotun catch them . . ." He let the words hang in the air.

Voden nodded. "Go Honir. Take Sleipnir. He's tired from the ride from the ford, but he's still the fastest thing on four legs. Ride, my friend, as swiftly as you run. Tell Ynjgvi . . ." He paused, trying to think. What should he tell Yngvi to do? Ah! "Tell Yngvi to let the Jotun through. Then try to push the whole lot back to the passes. They'll be exhausted from the ride, and we'll be on their heels the whole way, pressing them. If he can push them back up into the Smoking Lands . . ." An idea was half formed in his mind. "Yes, tell him that. And tell him when he's done it, to meet us at the Geirvimul. That'll have to do for now. Ride, Honir! Ride for all you're worth!"

Honir turned and ran to Sleipnir, vaulted into the saddle, spurred the beast, and plunged south through the press of men and animals. Men leapt frantically to get out of his way.

Voden watched him go, then turned to face the others. "Gather the men. Tend to the wounded. Everyone eat. We'll send to the ford and tell Harbard to bring his forces to meet us in Gladsheim. From there we march as swiftly as possible southeast toward where the Geirvimul comes out of the forests of the Vanir. And then, unless I very much miss my guess, we head south, perhaps even across the Smoking Lands."

Jormungand was covered with ashes from head to foot. He cursed under his breath. *I almost wish that damn wizard would unleash his pets now and give us some rest!* He shuddered suddenly at the thought of Zu and the others screaming through the air. *I take it back,* he chided himself. *Bad as it may be, this is better.*

The damned Vanir hadn't been destroyed in the fire. In fact, the sneaking bastards had set fires of their own! Then they'd hid in the ashes, waiting for us to arrive. Caught us flat-footed, a total surprise. In a broad valley where there shouldn't have been even an insect alive, the hillsides had suddenly exploded with foresters and Valkyrja!

The battle had been furious. At first Jormungand's men had been hurled back and had nearly panicked. But he'd ridden through them, urging them on, even leading two counter-charges. They'd rallied and held their ground.

Now, under the furious assaults of the Vanir, they were moving back, foot by foot. The danger was a flanking movement, an attempt to turn his line and get behind him. If there were warriors in one pile of ashes, why not in every pile?

By the rotten tits of Ereshkigal, he groaned, this battle never seems to end! Two days now! It had all seemed so damn simple when he and Surt had planned it back in Maqam Nifl. He raised his eyes and looked south. On a hill in the distance he could see a dark cloud. In the center of it he knew Surt lurked, protected by his most valued demons. He wondered what the Black One would do if the Vanir pushed them back that far.

The roar of battle increased suddenly off to the east. His heart rose into his throat. By Neti's ass! he cursed. There *were* more of those damn Vanir in the ashes! He began to run in that direction. Can't let them flank us!

The soldier was old to be of such a low rank. And right now he looked much the worse for wear. He bowed low before the three cowled figures that stood, dark shadows in the last gray of twilight. Soon it would be night.

The age/rank discrepancy was easy to explain. He'd been a commander in Marduk's army. Jormungand had demoted him to a mere trooper. The man had slowly been working his way back up through the ranks. He was bitter, but determined.

His disheveled condition was also understandable. He had been in the lines and like all those whose loyalty was suspect, he'd been right where the fighting had been the heaviest.

He looked up from his bow. "Bel Marduk," he said in a rough voice, "I come to report." Marduk nodded for him to continue. "The battle goes closely. The fire tactic didn't work, and that fool Jormungand walked right into an ambush. We held our own and were even beginning to advance when they launched a flanking attack against our right. Jormungand himself lead the counterattack, and I must admit,'' he said grudgingly, ''that without him we wouldn't have been able to beat them back, We're withdrawing now to consolidate our lines. Tomorrow we will launch another attack.''

Marduk nodded and looked significantly at the other two hooded forms. ''Perhaps it is time?'' he asked.

A woman's voice came from one of the hoods. ''What about Thiazi? Has any word been received of how the attack of the Jotun goes? How do the Aesir fare?''

The corporal looked grim. ''A Jotun rode into camp just before I came here. His horse was half dead and he wasn't in much better condition himself. Rumor has it that Thiazi and the Jotun broke through the Aesir line but failed to destroy them. Apparently Voden realized what was happening and rode to support his men. Now the Jotun are riding south to join Jormungand. They hope to crush the Vanir between them.''

''And no doubt the Aesir will be hot on their heels, hoping to crush the Jotun between themselves and the Vanir,'' Enki said, his voice heavy with sarcasm. ''It sounds to me, dear Innina, as if this battle is going its own way, a way no one had foreseen.''

Innina nodded. Marduk looked at the two of them and spoke. ''Should we act now? Surt is surely confused and—''

Enki laughed shortly. ''Surt hasn't even lifted his little finger, noble Bel. He lurks with his demons in a protective cloud and waits. The hellhound Garm is at his feet. He is as powerful as ever. To strike now would be suicidal. Don't you agree, my dear?''

''I do. Jormungand and the army are far from beaten. Winded, perhaps. But Surt is still as powerful as ever. We must wait and see what develops. I want Surt extended, exhausted, overconfident, and then we will strike, both with physical and with magical force. It's still too early. We must emulate the spider and sit quietly in our web. The time to act will come, Ah, yes, it will come.''

The corporal gasped with wonder and fear as the three shrouded figures faded from his sight without a sound. In a moment he stood alone in the first full darkness of night.

• • •

Both Freyja and Vidar were defiant and determined. Voden was exasperated. "But it's war!" he declared for the third time. "Battle! We don't know what will happen. The Jotun could break through, and Fornjot only knows what Surt has up his sleeve. The man's a wizard and he could loose almost any kind of demon. He's sure to—"

Freyja shook her head stubbornly. "All the more reason for us to be there. Vidar is old enough to fight. You've trained her yourself and have said many times that she's as good as any of the young men."

"Yes," Vidar interrupted, "and you were only thirteen when you killed your first Jotun, Father, so . . ."

Voden frowned, his eye haunted with sudden memory. "Killed my first, aye. I'd not have you experience that, Vidar, not just yet. Besides, who knows what—"

"But there's an even stronger reason," Freyja interrupted, "and that's precisely because Surt *is* a mighty wizard. You have the Galdar-power to help fight his magic. But you'll also be quite busy serving up the raven's joy. Can you both protect against Surt's magic and fight? And even if you can, is the Galdar-power enough against Surt?"

Her voice became reasonable and persuasive. "I'm strong in the Seidar-magic, Voden, something Surt has probably never come across. While you fight, I could help protect you and our men with my power."

A look of uncertainty crossed Voden's face. He looked at Freyja, then at Vidar. "Vidar," he said gently, "please go see if my horse is ready." Vidar looked startled, then glanced at her mother. Freyja nodded, and the girl grudgingly turned and left Valholl.

When she was gone, Voden and Freyja stood looking deeply into each other's eyes. Voden seemed about to speak and then hesitated. Finally he cleared his throat. His voice was husky when it came from his mouth. "Why is it so hard to say this? I . . . I don't want you to come because you might be killed. And I . . . I don't want you to be killed."

Freyja smiled slightly, sadly. "So much is hard to say between us. I don't want you to be killed, either, Voden. But if you are, I want to be there with you. I want . . . I want to hold you for the last time. I—" Her voice broke and she looked down at the floor of the hall.

Voden stared at her, his throat working, words pushing their way up out of his heart. He saw the tears in her eyes and realized there were tears in his own. He stepped forward and put his arms gently around her. Her arms wrapped around him in turn.

"Freyja," he murmured, his voice cracking slightly, "I . . . I don't have the words anymore. I haven't used them for so long that I'm not even too sure what they are any longer. But . . . I've missed you for—"

She raised a finger and touched his lips. "A flood of words aren't necessary. Three will do nicely."

He laughed, deep in his throat, suddenly happy. "Aye, three will do. I love you." He paused, then hugged her fiercely. "How empty they sound!"

Freyja looked up at him, the tears running freely down her face. "Words are always empty. Only action can fill them." She lifted her lips to be kissed.

He lowered his head and met her. It was a long and gentle kiss, one filled with longing. It meant more than all the words in the world. When it was over, he looked into her eyes and smiled warmly. "What I fool I've been!"

She laughed. "And I, too! We've hidden from each other for so long, hidden from the pain of the past, that we've lost our future and damned our present. We could have been so much more to each other than we have been."

A wave of bitterness surged through Voden's eyes. "So much lost! And why? Because of something the Nornir wrote before I was born? All my life I've been hounded by this fate, driven from one thing to the next, from one pain to another. And all my struggles against it have brought it on me just as surely as if I'd simply sat back and let it all happen!"

Freyja touched her finger to his lips again. "A world is ending and a new one is being born. There's much suffering in that, and much joy."

"Joy?" he replied angrily. "Where is the joy? I see the pain, Fornjot knows I feel it in every fiber of my being. But I still can't see the joy." He suddenly buried his head against her neck and shoulder. "Oh, damn, damn, damn, why can't I see the joy? Then all the pain might be worth it!"

She could feel the slight shaking of his body and knew he was crying silently. She stroked his back and held him close.

"Does the caterpillar know the joy of the butterfly?" she murmured into his ear. "Does dusk know the joy of dawn?"

"I'm not a damn caterpillar," he mumbled, his voice muffled, "I'm a man. And when I die—"

"You will die like a man," she finished for him.

"But why?" he protested again. "I want to know why!"

Freyja pulled her head back and looked him straight in the eye. "I don't know the answer. But I do know this much. Your death isn't something outside you, something that comes on you from a distance. It's with you from the day you're born. It's yours and only yours. It forms and shapes your life, whether you're conscious of it or not. It is, Voden my love, the very thing that makes you ask why, the very thing that makes you demand an answer before you die."

He returned her gaze, then dropped his eye. A laugh that was half sob burst from him. "Everytime I think I've found an answer, I discover I've just uncovered a deeper riddle. My mother, Jalk, Kao-Shir, all those who've tried to help me understand have spoken in words that hide as much as they reveal. And all my own questions have only shown me that the answers always lie just beyond my grasp." He sighed deeply. "Always just beyond. Seemingly just close enough that if only I reach a little further, try a littler harder . . . But the result's always the same, I reach, I try . . . and I fail again."

Freyja was silent a moment. "Perhaps that's all there is."

"What? Failure?"

"No. Trying. Maybe . . . maybe questioning is more important then either what's asked or what's answered."

"Perhaps," Voden responded thoughtfully. He shook his head as if trying to shed his somber mood. "I still haven't answered your question, have I?"

She smiled slightly. "No."

Voden returned her smile and hugged her to him again. "I . . . I've waited so long, I've nothing left to offer you but the opportunity to share my fate with me."

Freyja looked up at him. "That's all I've ever asked," she said gently, her eyes luminous with tears.

The Vanir and the Alfar let the Jotun pass unopposed. And then, when they had crossed into Jormungand's lines and were milling around in confusion, when the men from Muspellheim were trying to bring order out of the sudden chaos, they attacked.

They pushed the men from Muspellheim and their Jotun allies back yard by yard. The Aesir arrived and joined in the attack. Jormungand brought his mixed command under control and movement in either direction came to a halt.

Then the foresters under Yngvi suddenly appeared behind them at the same moment the united Aesir, Vanir, and Alfar launched a massive assault. The confusion among the men from Muspellheim was total, and Jormungand had no choice but to retreat as rapidly and with as much order as possible.

In the process, Jormungand annihilated Yngvi and his entire command. Voden found his friend's body surrounded by dead Jotun and many black warriors. Rota lay by his side. The wounds they bore were all on the fronts of their bodies.

Sick at heart, Voden watched the invaders retreating up through the pass over the Smoking Lands. Tror and Tyr stood by his right side, Freyja and her brother on his left. Honir was off with Hild, trying to get a fix on the casualties.

Tror sighed hugely. "Well, that's that. We won." His voice was weary and his broad shoulders slumped with exhaustion. "And not a moment too soon, if you ask me. I've grown sick of this warrior nonsense." He raised Mjollnir and looked at his hammer. It was covered with blood and gore. "I'll clean Mjolllnir now. And never use it again to strike anything but hot iron. Aye. There's far more glory in that than in war."

Voden looked sadly at his friend and shook his head. "I'm sorry, Tror, but I fear that is not that. We've won this battle, but not the war. The time hasn't come yet to strike iron instead of skulls."

Frey nodded as he leaned wearily against the seven-point stag's antler he used as a weapon. "Precisely. Do you intend what I think?"

Voden shrugged. "I don't see any alternative. We have to end this. We'll pull ourselves together and follow them." He looked at Tror's surprised face and smiled grimly. "We must finish it, Tror. There's no other way."

They took the pass and poured over the Smoking Lands. The men from Muspellheim and their Jotun allies retreated before them, moving southward as swiftly as they could. They kept good order in their march. They weren't a defeated army, merely one looking for a new place to turn and fight.

Surt rode at their head, Garm ranging before him. His face was calm and the slight hint of a smile touched his lips. Yes, he thought, yes, this is best. We will go the the Vigrid and they will follow. There we will meet. There is a special spot, one Jormungand will remember well, one where two ravines flank the road the caravans take, we will turn and meet the son of Borr. And there I will loose all the power of the Kur against my enemies. He looked around. Things were beginning to look familiar. It wouldn't be long now, he estimated. Not long at all.

The roar as the two armies met shook the ground. Voden led his forces, Gungnir in his hand, his single eye blazing with battle lust, his gaze sweeping the opposing host, looking for the wolf's-head helmet of Hrodvitnir-Fenrir. Tror had long ago decided that the giant black warrior who led the men from Muspellheim was his personal quarry. Frey kept his eyes on the dark place just behind the lines where he knew Surt hid. He and Tyr were determined to break through and confront the Ellilutu.

Warrior hacked at warrior in a vast turmoil. Mouths opened in screams of victory and despair. Arms, legs, heads, hands, flew in all directions, spewing blood from their stumps. The ground became slippery and finally muddy with spilled guts and blood. And the deafening roar went on and on until it deadened the mind and numbed the soul.

For several hours the two lines stood face to face, neither one advancing nor retreating. Like two mad giants locked in a deadly embrace, they stood and traded blows. From his refuge Surt watched, his expression becoming grimmer and grimmer. They are my equal at war, he realized gloomily. Can they match my power in magic?

He began to dismantle his protective shield so he could call his demons and throw them into the fray. It's almost time to act, he decided. Almost time to show them my true power. He summoned Garm and set the hellhound in front of him to guard against any chance physical attack. Then he began to call his minions.

•   •   •

Tror found his man and screamed his challenge at him. Jormungand saw the red-bearded giant wading through the battle toward him, his hammer sweeping shattered bodies out of its way to create a path. With a laugh of sheer joy, he shook his sword at Tror and started in his direction.

They met, and a space was instantly cleared around them. Tror swung Mjollnir in a roaring arc that met and shattered Jormungand's shield with one blow. In disgust, the Serpent threw the shield aside and gripped his huge sword with two hands. He slashed at Tror and his blade met the hammer in midair. The two weapons clanged like ringing thunder, and sparks showered out from them like bolts of lightning. Each man met the other's glance and both smiled broadly, realizing they had met a truly worthy opponent.

Jormungand thrust and slashed, whirling his sword in a blur of motion. His blade hummed death, and blood flew from it in all directions. He wounded Tror again and again, but the red-bearded giant seemed to be impervious to the pain. His hammer smashed Jormungand's left arm into a pulp.

They fought with a fury that neither had ever felt before. They were borne on a wave of exhilaration that made pain recede and the world narrow down to nothing but the other man. They were like lovers who had eyes only for each other.

Jormungand's sword snuck past Tror's guard and opened his side so deeply his intestines were bulging through the slash. Sure of his victory, the giant black warrior raised his sword on high and stepped in for the kill.

He had underestimated his foe's battle frenzy. The wound was clearly fatal, but Tror didn't even feel it. As Jormungand raised his sword, Tror roared with fury and swept Mjollnir up from the ground. The hammer slammed into Jormungand's groin and lifted the black giant off his feet. His face twisted in agony and surprise as he fell backward, his sword falling from nerveless fingers. With a cry of victory, Tror stepped in and brought his hammer down on his opponent's head. Jormungand's brains splattered all over Tror, and the Serpent crashed to the ground lifeless.

Tror roared out his victory, took nine steps back and, tripping over his own intestines, stumbled to his knees. He gazed at Mjollnir. The haft was still in his grip, but the head of the hammer was resting on the ground. Tror tried to lift it, but found he no longer had the strength. He nodded to his weapon and murmured, "Smithing was better." For a moment longer he swayed on his knees as if trying to rise. Then he pitched suddenly forward. He was dead before his face hit the ground.

Jormungand's death galvanized Surt. He dropped the protective shield completely and began to chant and make arcane gestures of summoning in the air.

Before he could complete even one calling, however, two men charged him. Garm leapt at the throat of one, a man with only one hand. The two went down in a tumble, the dog trying to grab the man by the throat, the man frantically stabbing the hellhound with his sword.

The second man threw himself at Surt. The Black One barely had time to draw his sword and block the attack. He was surprised to see that the weapon the man was wielding was a stag's antler with seven points. The unorthodox weapon was covered with blood, indicating that it was effective and that the man knew how to use it. They circled each other, trading testing blows, each trying to feel the other out. "Who are you, feeble mortal, who dares to attack Surt, the Black One, Ellilutu of Muspellheim and the mightiest wizard in all of Yggdrasil?" Surt demanded.

His opponent smiled and replied. "I'm Frey, brother of Freyja, now of the Alfar. You fight well for a wizard."

Surt grinned wolfishly. "Before I pledged myself to Nergal, I was a raider here on this very plain. Many were the desperate battles I engaged in. Many the men I killed. Soon," he sneered, "I shall send your name with Namtaru down to Aralu. And your spirit will follow on his heels. I dedicate you to Nergal, Lord of Hosts, King of Aralu!"

There was a terrific growl from Garm, and the two opponents looked to see what had happened. They saw the monster grip Tyr by the neck with his gaping jaws and rip upward, tearing the Aesir's throat out with one motion. At the same instant, Tyr's sword jabbed deep into the dog's side and found its heart. They died together in a welter of blood.

Surt recovered faster than Frey. He knocked aside the antler and struck Frey a blow that slashed his side deeply and sent the Vanir reeling. Frey blocked the next blow, then felt himself weaken rapidly as the blood poured from his wound in a bright cascade. The gleam of triumph in his eyes, Surt struck again and again, and finally split Frey's skull in two. The brother of the Vanadis crumpled and lay dead at the Black One's feet.

Honir fought valiantly, covering Voden's left side. He bore many wounds, and the blood from one on his forehead kept getting in his eyes. That was why he didn't see the blow coming. The sword hit him in the face and stretched him out on the ground. He moaned once and then darkness overwhelmed him.

With dismay, Voden saw him fall. They're all dying, he thought grimly. One by one, they go. But each takes ten with him. There is yet hope.

Suddenly he saw what he'd been looking for. Hrodvitnir's wolf's-head helmet! With a cry that rose above the tumult of the battle, he surged in the Warlord's direction, eager to do battle with his enemy.

Hrodvitnir saw him coming and a lupine grin spread across his features. The two of them met in a flurry of blows. Voden jabbed and slashed with his spear Gungnir, made from Kao-Shir's staff. The Jotun parried with his curved sword and tried to get close enough to land a blow.

For many minutes they circled, exchanging blows, inflicting wounds. Yet neither seemed able to gain the advantage over the other. The battle surged around them, and men screamed in open-mouthed agony as they died brutal deaths.

Then Voden slipped on some foulness on the bloodsoaked ground. His right foot shot out from under him and he went to one knee. He tried to pull Gungnir up in time to block the overhand blow that Hrodvitnir had aimed at his head, but was a split second too slow. Though he was able to deflect the blade so it missed his head, the edge struck his neck where it joined his shoulder. Slowly Voden, leader of the Aesir, fell forward to his hands and knees.

As Hrodvitnir raised his sword again to finish his kill, a short, slight figure darted forward and swung a blade with all her might, aiming at the Jotun's rib cage. The edge hit and sank deep, slicing Hrodvitnir's heart in two. Blood showered from his chest in a torrent. With a look of surprise, the Warlord's jaw dropped and he fell, dead before he reached the ground. Vidar, her sword dripping with gore, threw herself beside Voden and wept wildly.

In an instant, Freyja was at Voden's other side. She called his name, and he turned his head to look at her. "Dark," he muttered, trying to sit up, "so dark. Can't see. Can't . . ." Blood gushed from his mouth and he pitched forward.

He felt Geri on his right and Freki on his left. "Get up, little brother," Geri growled. "This is no time to be lying about sleeping."

Voden sat up, and Hugin and Munin landed on his shoulders. Freki nudged him again, and he stood. The huge gray wolf grinned, his tongue lolling out the side of his mouth. "That's better. Come, we can't keep Raesvelg waiting."

"Raesvelg?" Voden mumbled. "What is the Engulfer of Corpses doing here?"

Geri howled a laugh. "Look about you, brother! Have you ever seen so many corpses in your life?"

Voden glanced about. The battle was spread out around him, the dead and dying piled deep in every direction. He looked more closely and saw his own body, face down, with Vidar and Freyja weeping next to it. "Ah," he said softly. "So this is the third time I meet my Fylgjur." The two wolves nodded solemnly, and the ravens croaked their agreement.

The group stepped forward and began to soar, leaving the blood and stench of the battlefield behind them. They passed through the clouds and soon, in the distance, Voden spied the towering branches of Yggdrasil.

They landed near the top. Above them, his eyes closed, Raesvelg sat, his wings folded tightly around his body. The giant eagle opened one eye and glared at Voden. "Sing the Power Song I gave you!"

Voden stood upright and threw his head back. With all his strength he sang.

> *"In days gone by I once was Ygg*
> *Ere Voden they did name me.*
>
> *And I was Har and Jafanhar*
> *And also hailed to Thridi.*

Bileyg I'll be and Vafudar
Till falls the mighty Ash Tree.

Then I'll be Ygg as once I was
Ere Voden they did name me."

Raesvelg nodded sagely, both eyes open now. "Well has he served his purpose. As Vafudar he wandered until he became Bileyg. Then the Bones of Audna made him Thridi. And among the Jotun he earned the names of both Jafanhar and Har.

"Now, on the plain of the Vigrid, truly he has become Ygg, the Terrible One, the destroyer of worlds, the Rider of Yggdrasil." Raesvelg paused and cocked his head to one side as if listening to a voice. "Yes, Master," he finally said.

The giant eagle bent his gaze down to Voden once more. "It time to enter a nest high on the Tree, little one. There you will be born again. And there you will be readied for your next test. Perhaps you will end a world again. Perhaps you will help it be born."

Voden spoke one word. "Why?"

Raesvelg closed his eyes again. He opened one and stared at Voden. "All your life you have been asking that question. And still you find yourself no closer to an answer. Perhaps, small one, it is not for man to know. Perhaps, the only thing man is capable of is asking the question. Perhaps only Vilmeid knows. And perhaps even He must wonder forever. Farewell." With a roar of wings and a rushing of air like a hurricane, Raesvelg took off and disappeared into the sky.

Geri and Freki looked up at Voden. "Come, little brother," Geri said with a throaty rumble. "We will take you to your rest. You have earned it."

Freyja looked down at Voden's body. She felt suddenly empty. He's gone, she thought. All that's left is dross. Soon it will rot, and then weather away until all trace is gone.

Her mind wailed, utterly alone in a desolate waste. Gone, she wept, gone for all eternity. Then dark dread brushed the edge of her awareness. She raised her eyes to where the Black One stood, his hands outstretched like claws, demanding, summoning. She saw the roiling clouds on the southern horizon and felt the chill of the horror they brought. There's no

she told herself. I must save that until
ter. Now I must cease mourning and act.
y ounce of power she had, she threw her

Muspellheim was unprepared for the as-
backward and seared his mind. For several
azed and reeling, unable to concentrate. He
feet and looked to the south. They were
 regain control!
 him and he spun away from it, knocked off
Panic rose in his throat. I've got to get
 chittered. My demons come and I must be
em to my will!
to his feet and turned to face his assailant. A
he sneered. Then he was thrown backward
 struck for yet a third time. The Black One
 feet in a flash this time. She's weakening, he
 done her worst and I'm still alive!
ed his hands out and hurled fire at Freyja. It
 she fell back, writhing in pain. Surt pressed his
rowing everything he could at the Vanadis. She
 shielding as best she could, trying to buy time.
rd from Muspellheim was too powerful for her.
 his advantage relentlessly, pouring power at her.
 there was nothing to attack. Surt almost fell
 surprise at the unexpected disappearance of resis-
woman's body was still there, lying twisted on the
 . . . Somehow her spirit, her essence,
 . . . alized. What-

"Does the caterpillar know the joy of the butterfly?" she
murmured into his ear. "Does dusk know the joy of dawn?"

"I'm not a damn caterpillar," he mumbled, his voice
muffled, "I'm a man. And when I die—"

"You will die like a man," she finished for him.

"But why?" he protested again. "I want to know why!"

Freyja pulled her head back and looked him straight in the
eye. "I don't know the answer. But I do know this much.
Your death isn't something outside you, something that comes
on you from a distance. It's with you from the day you're
born. It's yours and only yours. It forms and shapes your life,
whether you're conscious of it or not. It is, Voden my love,
the very thing that makes you ask why, the very thing that
makes you demand an answer before you die."

He returned her gaze, then dropped his eye. A laugh that
was half sob burst from him. "Everytime I think I've found
an answer, I discover I've just uncovered a deeper riddle. My
mother, Jalk, Kao-Shir, all those who've tried to help me
understand have spoken in words that hide as much as they
reveal. And all my own questions have only shown me that
the answers always lie just beyond my grasp." He sighed
deeply. "Always just beyond. Seemingly just close enough
that if only I reach a little further, try a littler harder . . . But
the result's always the same, I reach, I try . . . and I fail
again."

Freyja was silent a moment. "Perhaps that's all there is."

"What? Failure?"

"No. Trying. Maybe . . . maybe questioning is more important then either what's asked or what's answered."

"Perhaps," Voden responded thoughtfully. He shook his
head as if trying to shed his somber mood. "I still haven't
answered your question, have I?"

She smiled slightly. "No."

Voden returned her smile and hugged her to him again. "I
. . . I've waited so long, I've nothing left to offer you but the
opportunity to share my fate with me."

Freyja looked up at him. "That's all I've ever asked," she
said gently, her eyes luminous with tears.

The Vanir and the Alfar let the Jotun pass unopposed. And
then, when they had crossed into Jormungand's lines and were
milling around in confusion, when the men from Muspellheim

He almost had them under control when the new attack hit him. It knocked him over and over as though he were a leaf in the wind. Yet the wind was hot and searing and scorched his very soul. He felt himself falling, battered and ripped by the demons that had come to his call.

Then the ultimate horror rose before him, the black, snickering emptiness that he knew was Nergal come to claim him for Aralu. He screamed in anguish.

The moment Innina had been waiting for so long had arrived at last. Bel Nergal had left the security of seven-walled Aralu to personally come and claim Surt. With a wild laugh of joy she attacked her ancient enemy, throwing every bit of power she had into one, all-out assault. Even as she did it, she knew it would destroy her. But she didn't care. For she also knew it would destroy Nergal.

The world erupted in flaming chaos. Men ran screaming in every direction, but there was no escape. Demons bellowed and raved, savaging each other and any living thing that came within range of their claws or teeth. The ground heaved, throwing up vast billows of dust. With a rending, tearing sound, cracks gaped wide in the earth like hungry mouths and swallowed the living and the dead alike. The Smoking Lands awoke and spewed molten rock and great clouds of sulfurous smoke into the air. The skies darkened as if it were night, and the sun disappeared.

Then a great roaring filled the air, and a towering wall of water swept from the west and the Sea of Mists. It inundated the land and sank it beneath the boiling sea.

Aesir died. Vanir died. Jotun died. Alfar died. The men of Muspellheim died.

The world died.

---

to retreat as rapidly … In the process, Jormungand annihilated … e command. Voden found his friend's body surrounded by …ad Jotun and many black warriors. Rota lay by his side. he wounds they bore were all on the fronts of their bodies.

sick at heart, Voden watched the invaders retreating up through he pass over the Smoking Lands. Tror and Tyr stood by his right side, Freyja and her brother on his left. Honir was off with Hild, trying to get a fix on the casualties.

Tror sighed hugely. "Well, that's that. We won." His voice was weary and his broad shoulders slumped with exhaustion. "And not a moment too soon, if you ask me. I've grown sick of this warrior nonsense." He raised Mjollnir and looked at his hammer. It was covered with blood and gore. "I'll clean Mjollnir now. And never use it again to strike anything but hot iron. Aye. There's far more glory in that than in war."

Voden looked sadly at his friend and shook his head. "I'm sorry, Tror, but I fear that is not that. We've won this battle, but not the war. The time hasn't come yet to strike iron instead of skulls."

Frey nodded as he leaned wearily against the seven-point stag's antler he used as a weapon. "Precisely. Do you intend what I think?"

Voden shrugged. "I don't see any alternative. We have to end this. We'll pull ourselves together and follow them." He looked at Tror's surprised face and smiled grimly. "We must finish it, Tror. There's no other way."

They took the pass and poured over the Smoking Lands. The men from Muspellheim and their Jotun allies retreated before

HEIMDALL

XXII

HONIR woke to pain and darkness. He felt a hand on his shoulder. "Who . . . ?" he mumbled, unable to make his lips work properly.

"Heimdall," came the reply. "Do not try to stand yet. Give yourself a few moments."

"Is . . . is it night, Heimdall?" Honir asked, his voice a weak croak. "I can't see anything. It's so dark."

"Here, take this." Honir felt a water skin pressed into his hands. He suddenly realized how dry his throat and mouth were, and drank greedily, spilling water over his chin in his haste.

"No, Honir," Heimdall said gently when the Aesir had finished drinking, "it is not night, although the sky is dark with threatening clouds. But even if the sun were shining brightly, you would not see it, my friend. Your wound . . ." He paused, his throat suddenly too full of bile for the words to pass.

Honir reached up a tentative hand and touched his face. His fingers met wreckage. The nose was smashed to one side. Above it was a slash and two holes where once his eyes had been. He gasped and lowered his hand.

"I have done what I can," Heimdall said softly. "There will be no infection, and the wound will heal. But . . . I fear you will never see again.

"At least not this world. But you will see the world that is to come, Honir. You lose the sight of the present and gain a glimpse of the future."

"A blind seer?" Honir laughed bitterly. Then his face grew melancholy. "Never to see the grass ripple under the wind again?" he said wistfully.

He turned his face upward and gazed with sightless eyes at

Heimdall. "Is the new world as beautiful as the old, Heimdall? At least tell me that."

"Aye." Heimdall replied. "It is. As beautiful."

"Ah. And is it as good a place? Or did evil survive?"

"Evil always survives," Heimdall answered. "But the great evil that threatened to take over and rule the whole world, that has been destroyed."

"Forever?"

Heimdall paused. His voice was heavy with musing when he finally replied. "No, not forever. Evil will always be with us, Honir, even great evil. It will come again and again. And every time it returns, we will have to fight it once more."

"Then the fight, all the death and destruction, was all in vain? Good will never triumph?"

Heimdall's voice was weary. "Good will never triumph. But the battle against evil was not in vain, Honir. For though good may never totally vanquish evil, it always has the chance to defeat it and keep it from triumphing."

"So we fought and died for nothing but the chance to fight and die again." Honir paused. "It . . . it seems a heavy price for such a scant return," he said, his tone edged with bitterness.

Heimdall gave him no time to brood. He pulled at his sleeve. "Come," he commanded, "rise up. There are a few others still alive. Help me find them."

Honir rose and stumbled after him.

Vidar had survived, but had lost all memory of who and what she had been. Heimdall gave her a new name, Lifthrasir. A young Vanir warrior her own age was also found alive. Heimdall named him Lif. He and Honir took them and all the other survivors they could find to Hodmimir's Wood. There they cared for them until they were able to care for themselves.

Wherever the ancient blind man wandered, the children gathered around his feet and listened in rapt wonder to his tales of the glories that awaited them in the future. And the white-haired man who was always at his side, leading him through the world, told them endless stories of the past.

When the blind man finally died, they raised a great mound over his body and mourned him for many days. When the mourning was over, the white-haired man, who was neither young nor old, disappeared into the Western Forest.

GLOSSARY OF NAMES AND PLACES

Adalbeahya—The Ten Grandmothers. The ten Medicine Bundles of the Jotun. Important religious items.

Alterjinga—spirit world of the Trul.

Andvari—Dverg. Owner of gold hoard stolen by Lao-Kee.

Atra-Hasis—Exceedingly Wise. Title of Utnapishtim.

Aurvandil—Groa's missing husband.

Ba—Svartalfar concept similar to soul. It leaves the body after it has rotted and seeks the paradise of Aalu.

Bab-Apsi—magical opening to the part of the spiritual world inhabited by the demons.

Baldur—Aesir, son of Voden and Frigida. Killed by his blind twin brother, Hod.

Baru—the Book of Foretelling, owned by Utu.

Billing—Aesir, father of Sif.

Bilskirnir—Tror's hall in Gladsheim.

Dumuzi—Brother and lover of Innina.

Dur-An-Ki—magical opening to the part of the spiritual world inhabited by the gods.

Eljudnir—hall of Erlik Kahn and Glitnis Gna in Niflheim.

Enki—Patesi of Eridu and Kish. He owns two books of magic, the *Nimeqi* and the *Shipti*. His consort is Damkina. He lives in a castle called Eengurra, built on a rock just off the western coast of Muspellheim by the city of Eridu.

Enkidu—close friend and general of Marduk's armies.

Erlik Kahn—ruler, with Glitnis Gna, of Niflheim.

Fafnir—son of Hreidmir.

Falar—Dverg, brother of Galar, murderer of Kao-Shir.

Fenrir—Jotun of the Risar clan. Fights Hrodvitnir. Hrodvitnir takes his name.

Franang's Falls—falls on the River Gopul where Lao-Kee hides.

Frigida—Aesir wife of Voden. Mother of Baldur and Hod.

Galar—Dverg, brother of Falar. Murderer of Kao-Shir.

Galdar-power—type of magical power granted by Vilmeid. Usually practiced by men.

Garm—hellhound created by Surt.

Geirrodmir—Jotun, brother of Hrungnir. Killed by Tror.

Gjallarhorn—Heimdall's horn, which he blows to signal the fall of a world.

Gjalp—Jotun, son of Geirrodmir. Killed by Tror.

Gladsheim—capital city built by Voden where the rivers Gunnthro and Svol meet. Site of Valholl.

Glitnis Gna—ruler, with Erlik Kahn, of Niflheim.

Gnipa Cave—cave at the edge of the Kur where Surt creates Garm and holds Dumuzi captive.

Greipnir—Jotun, son of Geirrodmir. Killed by Tror.

Grjotunagardar—site of the duel between Tror and Hrungnir.

Groa—witchwoman of the Aesir. She has one eye, claiming to have given the other to Mimir as the price for drinking from her well.

Gullfaxi—horse owned by Hrungnir.

Gymirling—Alfar, father of Iduun and Beli.

Heimdall—ancient being. Comes from the west and is doomed to see nine worlds fall. Friend of Voden's.

Hnoss—Vanir, daughter of Freyja and Od. Name changed to Vidar by Voden when he rescues her from Niflheim.

Hod—blind son of Voden and Frigida. Kills his twin brother, Baldur.

Hodmir—Jotun, important member of the Risar clan.

Holmganga—Aesir institution of dueling.

Horus—son of Anqet and Osiris. King of the Svartalfar after defeating his uncle, Sutekh. Defeated by the Sons of Muspell and carried off by the dragon Musirkeshda.

Hrodvitnir—Jotun, nephew of Bergelmir, half brother of Lao-Kee. Becomes Warlord of the Jotun Horde.

Hreidmir—Jotun, Risar clan, father of Ottar, Fafnir, and Reginir.

Hrungnir—Jotun, Risar clan, brother of Geirrodmir, owner of Gullfaxi. Fights a duel with Tror and loses.

Huluppu tree—tree where Enlil hid the Tupsimati.

Idun—Alfar, daughter of Gymirling.

Innina—consort of the Patesi An. A powerful sorceress. Sister of Dumuzi.

Ivaldi, Sons of—Dverg. Creators of Sif's golden hair.

K'ado Lodge—special lodge built by the Jotun for the dance to Gymir.

Lao-Kee—Jotun, half sister of Hrodvitnir.

Loddfafnir—Jotun, important member of the Risar clan.

Lyngvi—island in the Amsvartnir Sea where Hrodvitnir is marooned.

Magni—Aesir, son of Tror and Sif.

Marduk—Patesi of Muspell. Originally the general of Enlil's armies.

Me Muti—Waters of Death which Marduk must cross to reach Utnapishtim.

Mjodvitnir—Mead Wolf. Jotun clan name given to Voden.

Moon Calf—name given to the giant man of clay built by the Jotun at the site of the duel between Tror and Hrungnir.

Nergal—King of Aralu, Lord of the Dead. Also Lord of Hosts, the god of war.

Ninshubur—Muspellheim, loyal servant of Innina.

Ottar—Jotun, son of Hreidmir. Killed by Lao-Kee.

Reginir—Jotun, son of Hreidmir.

Seidar-magic—type of magical power granted by Svarthofdi. Usually practiced by women.

Shaman—magician/healer of the Jotun. Members of the Trul clan.

Sibu Issahir Amelu—plant which can restore lost youth.

Sif—Aesir, wife of Tror. Known for her beautiful hair.

Sinmora—Muspellheim, consort of Surt.

Sleipnir—horse, given to Voden by Lao-Kee.

Sygyrd—Jotun, kills Fafnir and then Reginir.

Thialfi—Aesir, young man of Tror's household who accompanies him on his duel with Hrungnir.

Thiazi—Muspellheim, soldier who leads expeditions across the Smoking Lands and makes contact with the Jotun.

Thrymir—Jotun, has Tror's hammer, Mjollnir. Killed by Tror.

Ull—Aesir, Sif's son by her first husband. Adopted by Tror.

Upuatu—Opener of the Way. According to Svartalfar legend, a being who will come to open the way so that all the Svartalfar, living and dead, may join together to form a mighty nation once again.

Urshanabi—Muspellheim, boatman who accompanies Marduk across the Me Muti.

Utu—Patesi of Sippar and Larsa. Worshipper of the Igigi, the original gods of Muspellheim. Owner of the *Baru*.

Valholl—name of the hall Voden builds in Gladsheim.

Vegtam—name Voden takes in his first trip to Niflheim.

Vidar—name Voden gives to Hnoss, Freyja's daughter, after he rescues her from Niflheim.

Vidblain—chief place of the Alfar in Alfheim.

Vili—Voden's younger sister.

Vingolf—Freyja's hall in Gladsheim.

MICHAEL MOORCOCK

THE CLASSIC ELRIC SAGA

___ 0-425-09957-1	ELRIC OF MELNIBONE, BOOK I	$2.95
___ 0-425-10329-3	THE SAILOR ON THE SEAS OF FATE, BOOK II	$2.95
___ 0-425-10407-9	THE WEIRD OF THE WHITE WOLF, BOOK III	$2.95
___ 0-441-86039-7	THE VANISHING TOWER, BOOK IV	$2.95
___ 0-441-04885-4	THE BANE OF THE BLACK SWORD, BOOK V	$2.95
___ 0-425-10249-1	STORMBRINGER, BOOK VI	$2.95

THE CHRONICLES OF CASTLE BRASS

___ 0-425-07514-1	COUNT BRASS	$2.75
___ 0-425-09042-6	THE CHAMPION OF GARATHORM	$2.95
___ 0-441-69712-7	THE QUEST FOR TANELORN	$2.95

THE BOOKS OF CORUM

___ 0-425-10333-1	THE SWORDS TRILOGY	$3.95
___ 0-441-10483-5	THE CHRONICLES OF CORUM	$3.95
___ 0-441-45131-4	THE KNIGHT OF THE SWORDS (Book 1)	$2.95
___ 0-425-10130-4	THE QUEEN OF THE SWORDS (Book 2)	$2.95
___ 0-425-09201-1	THE KING OF THE SWORDS (Book 3)	$2.95
___ 0-425-09359-X	THE BULL AND THE SPEAR (Book 4)	$2.95
___ 0-425-09052-3	THE OAK AND THE RAM (Book 5)	$2.95
___ 0-425-09391-3	THE SWORD AND THE STALLION	$2.95

THE DANCERS AT THE END OF TIME

___ 0-441-13660-5	AN ALIEN HEAT (Book 1)	$2.95
___ 0-441-13661-3	THE HOLLOW LANDS (Book 2)	$2.95
___ 0-441-13662-1	THE END OF ALL SONGS (Book 3)	$3.50

Tales of THE ETERNAL CHAMPION

___ 0-441-16610-5	THE DRAGON IN THE SWORD	$3.50
___ 0-425-09562-2	THE ETERNAL CHAMPION	$2.95
___ 0-425-10146-0	THE SILVER WARRIORS	$2.95

And look for Moorcock's new hardcover, THE CITY IN THE AUTUMN STARS,
on sale at bookstores everywhere!